Primitives

OF KAR

DENNIS K. HAUSKER

BookSide Press
877-741-8091
www.booksidepress.com
orders@booksidepress.com

DEDICATION

Again, I dedicate this story to my wife, Bunny. We're approaching 54 years of marriage and she still lets me live, so I must be doing something right. My favorite genre has always been epic fantasy, so the bulk of my prior books are that. Enjoy the story, and buckle your seatbelt. It's a bumpy ride.

CONTENTS

CHAPTER ONE
Tragedy

A heavy fog lay close to the ground on this terrible night. The hunting party crept along the trail peering intently for any signs to follow. Along with the other Vikar scouting parties, they'd been searching most of the night without success.

Toma, the tribal chief, crouched low to the ground trying to pick up some sign of the invaders. Being so late at night, combined with the thick fog, it made it virtually impossible to discover if the enemy had passed this way. Wagwa, the only tribal elder in this war party, touched Toma's shoulder.

"My chief, we must return to camp. This is hopeless continuing the search under these impossible conditions."

"Wagwa, there are members of our people held captive and at terrible risk out there somewhere. They're depending on us to find them." Toma spoke in frustration.

"That won't happen tonight. We must sleep and eat to be strong for this pursuit. It falls on our stolen girls to find their own strength to endure this test until we can find them."

"I know, Wagwa, I know. We'll return to camp but I'm filled with such rage, I doubt I can sleep."

Signaling the scouts, they started the trek back to their camp. Wagwa walked beside Toma.

Wagwa spoke. "It strikes me they picked the perfect time to raid us. With this being the time of changing seasons, the warriors were away from camp hunting to build up our stores of meat for the coming winter.

1

Nearly all of the women and children are at the winter camp preparing it for our migration. The only ones left in the summer camp were a few old men and women, and some girls left behind to tend our stores of meat and vegetables."

"I've thought that same thing. It's difficult to imagine any neighboring tribes attacking us like this. They know they couldn't hide from our wrath. I think this enemy is an outside force, and yet they would need to be close enough to study our routines."

"I worry our women and children are in danger at the other camp, if they haven't already been attacked."

"That's also a danger, but that camp is a long journey from here. Plus, there are warriors with them to make a defense."

Arriving back at the summer camp, others of the hunting parties were straggling in, also with no success in finding the enemy trail.

The bodies of the dead were lying lined neatly in a row. Seeing them, friends and relatives, stoked their rage again. Toma stood looking down on the deceased, men and their mates he respected, men who'd helped raise and mentor him along with their wives. Grandparents and elders were highly revered among the Vikar.

Wagwa stood by silently staring at the fallen. Toma said reflectively, "I know they fought for their lives as there was a serious battle before they were slain. See all the damage done to the huts during that fight."

Wagwa replied. "At their ages, they shouldn't have been forced to face this cowardly attack. The enemy clearly has no honor slaughtering and torturing old people. Gnawing on our people and eating them, no one does that. They carried away their own dead, whoever they are."

He turned to face Toma. "We must put this out of our minds to sleep now to be ready for tomorrow. As you say, we have those girls to rescue. One other thing, my chief. I've lived over sixty-five snows. Never have I seen anything such as this. We must call a 'seeing.' With what council elders remain who were out in other hunting parties, we must prepare the sacred hut for the ceremony...tomorrow."

"Yes, we will do it."

Toma went sadly to his hut to sleep. It was difficult to block out the desecration of the dead, or thoughts of their girls and what they were going through.

It seemed no time had passed when he awoke with a start. The sun was already on the horizon.

All of the scouts had returned so the surviving elders gathered at the sacred hut. Wagwa led them inside to speak the rites, both for the dead, but also for guidance from the ancestors about a path forward. Outside, the warriors assembled around their chief.

"I'm sending five of you to the winter camp. Our families must not return here. The boys there must supplement you and the other warriors already there. Defend the camp with your lives if this enemy tries to strike there. Do you accept this charge?"

The warriors whooped, quickly gathered their things and raced out of the camp at a sprint to mount their horses.

Already, cold gusts were sweeping through the area. It sounded like a great wave rushing through the trees of the nearby forest. The full fury of winter was only several weeks away.

It was an all-day wait for the elders to complete their ceremonies. In the meantime, the warriors dressed the hunting kills to extract the meat for the journey to the winter camp. Normally the women would have returned for that chore, but that couldn't happen now. If they'd left the winter camp, Toma banked on his five warriors getting there fast enough and turning them around before they became vulnerable on the move.

At the fringe of the group, a silent figure regarded the chief. Korban reflected darkly on the events of the night. These were his people, a savage lot, fierce and courageous, born and bred for battle. They'd made him one of their own even though he wasn't the child of Vikar's parents. Fully embracing him into the tribe as a child, they'd taught him all of the skills a Vikar warrior needed to conquer the elements of a hostile world. He knew nothing of his parentage. His birth and beginnings were unknown and his survival miraculous. Found as a babe in the wilderness, a Vikar hunting party stumbled unto him lying at the feet of a giant Korban

3

Lynx, the deadliest predator on the planet. For unknown reasons, it was watching over him protectively. The cat eyed them balefully, but allowed them to slowly approach. Once they didn't attack and were near enough, the mighty cat turned and padded away leaving the baby to the Vikar tribe to raise and protect. They named him after the mighty cat and held him in awe thereafter.

He was somewhat larger than the other boys in his youth and seemingly clumsy in his growth into manhood then. With his strange history, silent countenance, and his seeming awkwardness, it led to him being teased in his youth by his companions. Consequently, he spent much of his time alone. The Vikar people had black hair, but Korban's hair was brown.

Korban was raised by a grisly old warrior named Shosa. Although a tough man, he developed an attachment for this strange youngster and taught him everything. The son he never had as they had two grown daughters, Shosa had all the pride in this pseudo-son he would have for his own child. The first lesson Shosa taught was inner strength in the face of his comrade's taunts. Korban developed a stoic manner to ignore his youthful acquaintances and their pranks. Shosa's wife, Menga, tempered his hard lessons with her love and Korban grew in his foster family's care and eventually blossomed.

Now, at the age of nineteen snows, he already had broad shoulders and was noticeably larger than any Vikar man, and the Vikar were not a small people.

After the elders finally emerged from the sacred hut, Toma walked over to Wagwa.

"What have you found? We're ready to move."

Wagwa stared off at the forest for a moment. "I wish I could tell you we found clear answers and a clear path. However, much of what we glean and decide is interpretation and speculation. I'm sorry. I know you want more."

All the warriors stood by listening intently.

Looking at the chief, he continued, "You must make the plan, Toma."

"If that's all we have to go on, I'd separate the warriors and send half with the supplies to the winter camp, and keep the others to resume searching for a trail to find these enemies."

"That is what I would have recommended. In any circumstances, we need these vital supplies taken there. Afterwards, those warriors can return to rejoin us in the hunt, but it could go in any direction and could cover great distances."

"I wouldn't choose to divide our forces, but we have two serious missions to complete."

"It shall be done, my chief."

"Also, our council of elders is normally seven men. With only five remaining survivors including you, could that have hampered your divinations?"

"I suppose that is possible. I didn't see anything different in there, but who can say. It did seem weaker than usual so our connection to the beyond with the ancestors could be compromised. Also, it did seem more taxing. Some were left in a trance for a while afterwards."

"I feel anxious about this, more than just having our missing daughters in danger."

"We've lived in a known environment. Our lives reflect our confidence in knowing what is around us and our ability to deal with anything we face. With something happening we can't explain or understand, it brings up old stories and vague legends about strange lands outside our boundaries, evil doings and demons living there. Because we have no contact outside of our mountains, it doesn't mean there aren't unknown hazards stalking us. At this point, we have no solution to the unanswerable, and that must change."

"We only have our weapons and our physical strength. If there is more in this world beyond us, what can we do?"

"I have no answer for that. I can only say our tribe depends on us to lead them. We must meet any challenge from any enemy and beat them in the process."

"If this is beyond us, I say we won't go quietly." He spoke fiercely.

The warriors roared in response.

During the exchange, Korban stood back with his brooding stare saying nothing. Something struck him about the unusual surprise attack and the lack of any signs to follow the raiders. Resting his hand on the hilt of his sword, he pondered the dilemma, but he had nothing as far as ideas to add for the group discussion. His mind continued looking at the problem from all directions.

Wagwa continued speaking to Toma. "Because our neighbors tend to fear us, we feel safe. People from outside our lands wouldn't have that same fear."

"This is true, but as you said, now is the time to take action."

Reluctantly splitting his forces, Toma sent the surviving elders away with the group going to the winter camp with the meat and other supplies. Hurrying them on their way, Toma split the remaining forces into equal groups, ten in all.

"Your task is to find the trail of these enemy people. If you find a trail, or discover their camp, do not attack. Call the rest of us to join you. This is not a battle to lose."

The squads filtered away going in nearly every direction.

Wagwa was the only elder Toma allowed to stay with the search forces. He kept him close by to personally protect him. In truth, he worried about the unknown. Having Wagwa's wisdom and experience was all that he had to counter it.

Also, in the chief's group was Korban. It was reassuring for Toma to have his skill, size, and strength for the challenge.

Toma called him over as they walked.

"I know you prefer to keep your own company, but on this hunt, you must be actively involved with the others. I ask that you walk near to me and aid us in protecting Wagwa."

"Yes, my chief."

"You don't seem to realize it, but you have some rare skills. There may be things ahead that I need for you personally to handle that perhaps no one else among us could do."

"I...eh..."

"Korban, you're no longer a boy. It's time you act as the man you are. Don't tell me your doubts. I don't care to hear them. You're capable of so much more than you think. Will you do that?"

"I will, my chief."

"We're all fearful and have our personal doubts. We can't let them hobble us."

"You feel fear, my chief?"

Wagma chuckled along with Toma.

Wagwa spoke. "Everyone feels fear. That isn't important. Overcoming the fear is the real test. You may not realize all of your comrades would rather be you. They know you're the best of us all. They are the ones feeling inadequate."

Korban was stunned, unable to reply, so he returned to the task at hand.

Searching the path, it helped to be in daylight. However, there were still no signs they could find to guide them.

Toma spread them out to be sure nothing was missed, however, only in pairs as he wanted nobody alone against whatever was out there. There were still dangers from predator animals in addition to this new enemy.

As the sun reached overhead, they didn't stop to eat. Instead, they ate dried meat and drank water on the move. The afternoon was more of the same, disappointment at finding no clues.

Korban continued walking silently beside Wagwa who talked to Toma. He scoured the ground for any signs.

Wagma uttered, "We're known as the best trackers there are, but we can find nothing? How can that be?"

Toma answered tentatively, "If they went a different way, perhaps that explains it? It may be another of our scouts will find a trace of them."

"Meanwhile, our daughters are still in their vile hands. I can't get those worries out of my mind. If they have some strange power to conceal themselves from us..."

"I don't believe that. What do you say, Korban?"

"I try not to think in that way. I approach every matter deliberately to find a way to succeed. It's what I've always done."

"How can we succeed here?" Toma asked.

"I think we need to keep foraging about. If we're going the right way, we'll find something eventually. Nobody is perfect, including this enemy. Also, I don't only check for signs. I pay attention to other things."

"What other things?"

"Like the animals. If there are men creeping about, the animals will react. If everything suddenly goes silent in the forest, there is a reason. That's when I pounce."

"It sounds simple, and yet it's true, we can overlook the obvious. I like how you think."

"Thank you, my chief."

Continuing into dusk before they halted, the group gathered for the night. Consummate hunters, they were well versed in the life of the forest. Being outside during predator hunting times was a peril, but they didn't fear it. Those normal sounds of the forest were all about, which meant their enemies were not.

Korban took a late shift guarding the camp. He pulled an arrow from his quiver so he could make a quick shot, if need be. Climbing up into the bole of a tree, he watched all about. In the distance he heard the squeal of an unfortunate prey unable to escape a predator. That chase was not close to the camp. He stayed awake until the sun arose over the horizon before he climbed down to rejoin the camp. There was a smell of moisture in the air along with a chilly gust of wind, like a reminder winter in the mountains was often brutal.

The warriors ate and resumed their search. Clouds started to fill the sky as the wind increased. The sound of the wind in the trees escalated. In the distance in the clouds, lightning flashed and then thunder rumbled. As the weather front approached, Korban felt a strange prickly sensation. Looking up at the storm he felt foreboding.

The rumbles increased in volume as lightning crackled ominously.

"I think we are going to get wet," Korban muttered.

Everybody chuckled. However, a little later when the heavy storm broke loose, nobody was laughing. An absolute deluge, it was impossible to continue the search so they climbed a small hill to wait out the drencher.

Surprisingly, a doe scrambled up the hill with her fawn to escape a predatory cat. In a surprise, the animals didn't hesitate to come into the midst of the troop. When the cat started to give chase toward them, the warriors dissuaded it. Mama deer and her baby had stayed alive by taking a calculated risk. Once the cat slunk away, mother and baby lay down, still in their midst, to fall asleep. It was a remarkable occurrence like she could sense they were safe amongst the warriors. Some of them actually fed the two forest denizens and covered them with blankets against the driving rain. The fawn lay her head on Korban's lap to fall sleep. He gently stroked her head and neck.

The ferocious storm did not relent and kept flooding the forest for most of the night.

When the rain finally ceased in the morning, the camp arose. The two deer weren't in a hurry to leave. The fawn eyed Korban who finally gave her a little snack. When the troop went down the hillock back onto the path, the two deer walked with them. It was just after dawn, so predators were out in force. They were alert looking all about and kept within the protection of the warrior column for a time until she seemed to sense when they were out of immediate danger. She looked at the warriors before gracefully bounding into the forest along with her baby.

Toma looked at Wagwa who shrugged.

"Toma, I can't explain it. Perhaps the Great Spirit touched them. I hope they don't try to approach other hunters."

Korban answered. "I think they will return to normal caution. I don't know why I feel this way, but I feel certain of that. These seem to be strange times in many ways."

Looking about, they were at a loss. If there was a faint trail for them to find, it seemed certain the storm had washed it all away. It was a very discouraging moment.

Everybody looked at Toma. He grimaced.

"I have no answers. If anybody has ideas, say them now."

Wagwa shook his head and then everybody looked at Korban.

"I have no magic ideas. If we go back to the summer camp, what does that do? Nobody is there. Our instructions were if anybody finds a clue they signal and we go there. As foolish as it might seem, I would trudge ahead to see what we find. We need to see if there is anything ahead for us to find of value. Our girls are still captives."

No one objected, so they walked forward staring at the soaked ground. Toma walked quietly beside Wagwa.

Wagwa turned. "I know what you're thinking, my chief. You have no fault here so don't think those distressing thoughts."

Toma grumbled.

Korban was aware of them talking, but not paying attention. There was something niggling in his mind, but he couldn't corral it. Whatever it was, it was elusive, like their mysterious raiders.

Rounding a bend in the path, they smelled a cook fire.

"We have a place to go now," Toma commented. "This is good. Do you see what I was saying? You have ideas we need, Korban. Perhaps you're finally understanding what I said.

After a brief walk, they came to a crude hut, alone in a tiny glade.

Walking up to it, the door opened as they arrived. They were shocked at who stepped out.

A spindly ancient man smiled. "Do you remember me? I am Volta, the eldest member of our tribe."

"Volta, how is it you're here, living alone amongst the predators? When you disappeared, we could find no trail or trace of you back then."

"It was something I had to do. I knew this day was coming and now it is here."

"We don't understand. We're here because our camp was attacked while the warriors were gone. They slaughtered some elderly folks and stole the girls we'd left behind to tend the meat and supplies. We're out here now trying to find our girls, but we've found nothing. What tribe would attack us?"

He sat down on a large log. In a quivering voice that grew stronger as he spoke, Volta began his tale.

"You know me, I'm the oldest living Vikar. I've seen more snows and more hunts than I can remember. I've seen all of the mountains of Krole from the Valley of Fire to the Peak of the Moon, I know the five tribes and have been among them all. I know the Dracker murderers and their dark ways, I know the Stakar and their animals, the Alkar the largest tribe, the traders, the builders, the keepers of knowledge and of food. I know the Kominkar, the makers of weapons. Yes, I've seen all of the tribes. I saw the gathering of a hundred snows when all the tribes met at the plateau of Heaven. I say this to you now, no tribe of Kar has struck our village.

Toma looked bewildered. Wagwa looked worried.

Volta continued. "Our old ones were killed and mutilated; young girls were taken, while the animals were left untouched in their pens? No mountain tribe mutilates, it's not our way. This was not a raid for booty, or glory. This is a much different enemy. We cannot speak their name because we don't know them. For us, it's not a time for raids. War is at our doors, but like nothing else in our history. It will test all of the tribes of Kar. None of the tribes can stand alone against this trial. Only by cooperating can we hope to deal with this deadly threat."

"Volta, you know there has never been unity amongst the tribes. It would be mortal peril to stray onto any of their lands."

"And yet, it will take casting aside old grievances and prejudices to survive because the threat is that serious and total annihilation really can happen to us. Courage can take many forms and not just in battles. Sometimes the greatest courage is required to step courageously into danger to heal wounds on the lands of our adversaries. There is no easy answer here. You must realize and accept what is inevitable."

"Are you saying we must abandon our search and leave our girls in the hands of this heinous enemy?"

"Toma, you must understand, they captured our girls to lure you into ill-conceived actions in places of their choosing. They're a deadly and dangerous foe but we're not helpless. The Vikar peoples are known to have the greatest warriors in the mountains and perhaps the greatest anywhere. This enemy will know that. If they can destroy us, there is nearly no way for the remaining tribes to survive. Are you hearing me? This is not a negotiation. I'm telling you what the real truth is. Harming our girls serves no purpose for them right now. Don't get me wrong. They would have no qualms about doing their worst and I'm sure they have foul plans for those unfortunate girls in the future. In the short term, we must rise up to become our best and we must bring the other tribes along with us."

"What is it I must do first? With as selfish as we all are, how can it be done?"

"First, gather all of your people together. You cannot separate them any longer. "Secondly, your winter haven will need to be fortified and that will require the help of other tribes. Making contact with the other tribes can't be avoided regardless of the risk. Also, know that there are many other peoples in this world other than the five mountain tribes. We're seen in the lowlands as barbarians. You can't take offense in dealing with others. We are barbarians."

"This is a heavy mantle you've put upon us. I'll do what I can, but I worry I'm not up to the task."

"There is a reason you're a chief. You're not alone. Look at Korban who is already a great warrior. He will achieve much in his life. He's trustworthy to handle any task."

"Do you plan to remain living in isolation here?"

"No, I can now return to the people. The reason for staying alone has been accomplished."

"This is good as you can return to the sacred council. Two of our council members were killed, so we still need to add another new member in addition to you."

"I've already packed what I need for the journey, so we can leave now to go to the winter camp."

"I regret abandoning our girls."

"There is nothing you can do about that at this moment. If you were able to find them where they're being held, they would slaughter you. A raiding party is too paltry an attempt. Their army is vast, numerous like the stars in the sky."

Shortly, the scouts changed direction, turning to travel toward the winter camp. Considering his advanced age, Volta was surprisingly spry. The rapid pace Toma set didn't seem to bother him. Of course, the younger men carried his personal items.

Almost like the enemy was controlling the elements, it started to rain again and as the temperature dropped, it turned to a snowfall. The footing started to be treacherous which slowed their progress.

Hunting at dusk, they felled a deer for meat to complete the trek. Briefly, Korban thought about the mother and baby deer they'd saved and protected, if they were still alive.

During the entire search, they'd never left Vikar claimed territory. When they stopped each night, they lit fires to cook the food. Toma and Wagwa had asked Volta beforehand if it was safe to do so.

"I don't believe the enemy force stayed here. Their coming in force will happen when the war starts."

The poor weather persisted for a week making the march unpleasant. However, these skilled warriors handled the adversity seamlessly.

"What of the other searchers?" Korban asked.

"They won't leave our borders, so they'd return to the summer camp to gather and then they'd start for the winter camp when I'm not there. I'm not worried for them."

"It's just me pondering, but I worry about all possibilities. I can't stop my thinking."

"You shouldn't stop thinking. We need to be ready for anything. Unexpected events can happen at any time. As you heard from Volta, trust yourself and continue to do what you think is prudent. I'm grateful to have you working with me. I can miss important things too."

Although the trek remained a slog, eventually they approached the winter camp. They were greeted with surprise. The villagers were particularly happy to find Volta still among the living and safely returned to the tribe. He was universally treated with great deference.

Toma's wife, Loti embraced him firmly.

"We rejoice at your return, husband."

With Shosa still away in another of the hunting parties, Menga, his wife and Korban's adoptive mother, made a bee line for him.

"Hello, mother."

"Hello, son. It's good to have you home again. We women never feel safe while the men are all away."

"That won't be a problem now. Volta has announced we'll no longer be separated. You'll have the men close at hand to complain about."

She laughed. "We don't complain, we point out areas for improvement."

"Of course you do," he replied, snickering.

"Quiet with that. Are you hungry? I have a full pot of stew simmering."

"I could eat."

They both laughed and went to her hut. On the way, they were stopped by Timian, one of the sub-chiefs, and the most revered of the sub-chiefs.

"Korban, I want for you to join my scouting party as we survey the edge of the escarpment. We want to see what is happening below in the lowland realm of Tranta."

"Of course, Timian. Mother has promised me a serving of her stew. I can come to you after I eat."

"That's good. We need to keep fed and ready for whatever comes our way.

After multiple helpings of his meal and chatting with his mother, Korban went out to find Timian. It was a scouting party of twenty men.

"Men, we've been given the charge to watch the northern border areas with the Kominkar, and also the escarpment east along the ocean as well as south overlooking Tranta. Obviously with that large area, we will be traveling for long periods of time. I picked most of you for both your skills and also not having wives and children. You're freer to concentrate on our task without thinking about people back home. Do you have any questions?"

"Do we fight?" An older man asked.

"We defend at this point. The leaders need information. Having Volta back has given us a greater understanding of current happenings. Attacking for no good reason other than pride isn't why we're out here."

"So, if a Kominkar war party challenges us…"

"We simply ride away."

"Is that honorable, sub-chief?"

"This isn't the time for boasts and displays. Those days are over. As Volta has said, we must join the five tribes together. War is coming."

The man shrugged.

Timian scowled. "Hear me, you will not violate my orders as you would be punished."

The troop responded with a shout.

Timian walked over to Korban.

"In your case, it means you must be a part of us instead of an onlooker. I really need you to accept and understand who you are."

"I'm being forced to see a new way. I won't be a problem."

"That's good to hear."

CHAPTER TWO
New ways

Korban had packed extra arrows in his quiver before he went to meet Timian. Rather than start along the northern border, Timian decided to start with the southern leg of the trip.

It took a week of rapid travel riding steadily to reach the far edge of the escarpment overlooking the lowland nation of Tranta. Starting on the western most point of their trek near the border with the Stakar tribe, they turned back to travel eastward surveying the open lands below. For mountain born and bred nomadic folk, seeing the distant grasslands, farms, villages, towns and cities, it was a strange sight. What movement they could see below looked like ants moving about. Farther away, they could see in the distance, the outline of the huge Lake Hilan, a blue splash of color in an otherwise green landscape.

It was their first clear day in a while, with not a cloud in the azure sky. Although a clear day, it didn't mean a warm day, not at this time of year, and up here at this elevated point. The warriors wore heavier clothes colored to blend into the forest background.

The first day of the survey was uneventful as was the night. However, on the second day of riding after noon, Korban noticed a uniformed troop below riding toward the escarpment. Riding steadily closer, they rode up a sizeable hill covering nearly half the distance of the escarpment when were suddenly attacked from ambush. There were possibly twenty soldiers plus five civilians in the column. The ambushers greatly outnumbered the armed troops and they were too close with the sudden attack hindering the soldier defensive response. Korban stopped, staring downward causing the others of his comrades to stop and watch the attack below. It was a disaster from the start.

The soldiers wore royal blue uniforms, while the strange looking squat attackers wore dark brown garb.

At this point the fight was close enough they could hear the shouts and the clash of weapons. The soldiers fought valiantly, but it was a hopeless situation from the start and they started to fall quickly. Korban could hear screams and realized there were women caught in the middle of the battle, the five civilians. As the battle became desperate as soldiers fell and the defense faltered, their officer tried to lead the women to escape away from death and defeat, but surrounded, the savage attackers swarmed overwhelming and slaughtering him. They were then free to pull down the unprotected women from their mounts.

What happened next appalled the Vikars. The enemy beheaded soldiers and began to eat the bodies raw. The women were not spared from this horror. Only one of the women escaped this dire fate only because a group of the savages took her up to the top of the bluff, holding her down as they ripped off her clothing.

Korban was incensed. Taking a very long rope while his mates held on firmly, he quickly climbed down the rope near to where the heinous enemy assault was happening.

They were not as tall as the dead Tranta soldiers, dark haired and dark skinned, squat, stumpy creatures with large mouths and gnashing teeth.

Being occupied with the woman, they didn't see Korban creeping over to attack, sword in hand. Korban noticed one of them was bigger and appeared to be the leader. While smaller ones held the woman down, the big one looked about to dishonor her. Korban was incensed and struck quickly, ending the man and his vile plan. The others seemed to lose focus at that point.

By the time he'd finished off the five holding her down, others of the Vikar scouts had climbed down to join him. The ensuing battle with these noisome foes, still trying to feed on slain Trantans, occurred rapidly. Although outnumbered, it wasn't a fair fight as the highly skilled

Vikar warriors showed no mercy in wiping out this enemy scourge of seemingly lower intelligence beings.

Korban knelt down to the shivering young woman. She eyed him fearfully, trying to cover her nakedness with her hands. He quickly retrieved what remained of her dress. Though ripped up, it was sufficient to cover her, mostly.

Korban noted her long blond hair and blue eyes, not genetic traits they saw in the mountains. Nor did they see such delicate and angelic facial features and the stunning physical beauty she possessed.

"Are you injured?" he asked.

She gave no reply and continued to stare at him.

"Come, we'll help you."

She didn't move.

"Do you understand what I'm saying?"

Again, she gave no reply.

The other Vikar warriors joined him, grabbing the woman and easily lifting her up. Putting the rope around her waist she moaned in fear. She tried weakly to fight them, but that didn't work. Hoisting her up the cliff face, the rest of the troop climbed the ropes and soon they were riding away, heading for the winter camp. The woman never made a sound and once tried to jump off the horse, but Vikar scouts were there to stop her from falling to the ground. When they stopped that night, at first, she refused to eat, but Korban tasted a mouthful of the stew to prove she wasn't being poisoned.

When they lay down to sleep, they tied her wrists to a Vikar warrior on each side of her which they did again the next night. The following day after swift riding, they arrived back at the winter camp. The blond woman looked terrified.

When Toli came out along with Menga, they took the young woman into the chief's hut. The woman seemed surprised at Toli and Menga's gentle treatment of her.

Korban had the same protective feeling about this woman he had about the deer and her baby. He tried to stay away but his curiosity was too strong. Failing to conquer his feelings, he went to the chief's hut anyway. Poking his head inside, the woman was eating more stew. Looking up, she scowled at Korban.

He stepped inside. "All is well, mother?"

"She had a great terror, but I think she understands we won't harm her."

"Good. I found it difficult when she didn't understand my words. We saved her life."

She turned her head and spoke in perfect Vikar. "I understood you, and thank you for saving me."

"Why didn't you...well, no matter. I'm sorry we couldn't save your comrades. The attack was already nearly over. At least we saved you."

"May I ask you what you plan to do with me? My father wouldn't take kindly to ransom demands."

"What? Why would you say that?"

"Why would I not? You're mountain barbarians. Isn't that what you do?"

"You think we act without honor? We saw your peril and chose to save you. Judge us by our actions, not some concocted prejudice of yours." He was angered and his terse tone reflected it.

She turned her head fully to eye him thoughtfully.

"I'll judge you by my treatment, as you request. I have no other choice. You have me at your mercy. These women tell me your name is Korban."

"Yes. What's your name?"

"I will keep that to myself for the time being. I have my reasons."

He felt frustrated, but arguing with her at that point would not have been a good choice. Feeling disrespected, granted it was by his own determining, it seemed to be his new future as Volta had indicated humbling themselves was necessary. Regardless, it irked him. Scowling at her to her smirk, he exited the hut. He hadn't failed to notice again her great beauty; the most beautiful woman Korban had ever seen. The fact she smirked, it showed him she was aware of his male reactions to that beauty. That further put him in a foul mood.

As he walked away Timian approached him.

"That was incredibly courageous on your part. You saved a life and gave us a view of our enemy. They're disgusting and savage, but they're not invincible."

He noted Korban was uncharacteristically upset.

"Wait, Korban, are you vexed? You seem provoked."

"That woman, she confounds, and insults me."

Timian eyed him thoughtfully. "I see. A woman can perplex as easily as changing a cloak. They are complex creatures beyond our understanding."

"She is delicate, not like our women."

Timian eyed him mirthfully. "Yes, she is very delicate, pretty like a sweet flower."

Korban scowled at him. "Do you mock me, sub-chief?"

"Of course not. All of us have faced where you are now. Women are our treasures, but sometimes it seems like a curse."

"Well, I care not for her. I will think no more about her, ever!"

He stormed off as Timian chuckled.

His mother had come out of the hut in time to observe the conversation. Timian smiled at her. "I think you have a son with strong feelings for a girl for the first time."

"I have no doubt. I think I'll make twice the stew for dinner tonight. He eats more when he gets upset."

"Perhaps you should make a great deal more stew."

Again, they laughed.

Korban went from his stressful moment out to practice his war skills alone in the woods. He hacked and slashed, leaped, pivoted, and swung the sword from every possible angle. When he finally stopped, his skills hadn't really changed and his sour mood remained.

Grumbling, he ambled back into the camp going to his parent's hut. He could smell the stew long before he went in the entrance. Shosa had arrived in the meantime.

"Greetings, father."

"Hello, Korban. Your mother said you miraculously rescued a young woman by climbing down the escarpment to battle an enemy force. This is a good thing."

"She is..."

"Grateful?" Shosa laughed heartily.

Korban frowned. "Mother, did you really need to tell him about...her?"

"He's your father. Of course he wants to know about events in your life."

"That event happens to be something I prefer to forget. Father, did you talk with Volta? He gave us much to ponder, and much to worry about."

"I did talk to him and to Toma and Wagwa. What a surprise to find him. It's a great boon for the tribe, although his charges are daunting. Trying to woo all the other tribes together, I doubt it can be done, but..."

"I think I may go hunting to add to our winter supplies. I worry we can't store enough food for what we may face."

"There are others who would like to join you. I am one of them. Once all the remaining scouts return, we must face Volta's tasks. When he chooses warriors to do that, I'd like to be elsewhere too."

"I don't fear to do my duty for the tribe."

"But it seems you fear that young woman, eh?" Shosa laughed heartily. Korban scowled.

"Have some stew," said his mother, quickly. She handed him a steeping bowl of the steaming food.

Still scowling at his father's amused face, he wolfed it down and then had another, and then another.

Toma appeared at their doorway. "Can all of you come with me? Volta awaits us."

They followed him to the large hut where Volta now lived. Going inside, Korban nearly turned around. 'She' was standing there, talking to Volta. Toli was eyeing Korban mirthfully as he strongly reacted. Also, there were all five of the sub-chief's present.

Menga went over to stand with the women.

"Greeting's men, thank you for coming. I must tell you we can afford no delays. We must start our contacts with the other tribes, but in light of what happened to the princess, I believe we must expand farther outward and bring in the lowland nations into an alliance too."

The jarring idea crashed around in Korban's head. *Leave the mountains? Why?*

"The Princess has given me insights into our opponents. The force you defeated are called the Brogs. They live in caves under the surface. It is said they are like a plague waiting to well up out of the ground to consume all life. The fate of the Vikar tribe and all the other tribes must now also consider the welfare of the other peoples."

He paused and looked around the room.

He noted Korban's steady dour glance at the Princess to find her smiling at him. It unnerved him as he tried to stifle a reaction. Volta made a mental note.

"Princess Lanai, would you like to address our leaders?"

"Thank you, Sir." Her voice was dainty and melodic. Korban noted her poise, this moment wasn't too big for her. When she continued to speak, people hung on all of her words.

"Again, I want to thank mighty Korban for saving me. That attack and the slaughter of my people shocked me to the depths of soul. However, I was saved and that is behind us now. I propose I be escorted back to my home to meet my father, the King, in the palace. Perhaps Korban would be kind enough to lead that protecting force? I wish for my father to meet my savior and to forge the needed bonds of cooperation going forward. Believe me, Tranta will be your easiest stop in searching for allies. We're advanced over our neighbors. There are things we can teach, and can help you in building your own defenses against this enemy scourge."

She turned her head and stared directly at Korban. Her smile pierced him into reacting, which he couldn't stop. His blood rushed to his head and his face reddened. There was no escape.

She saw his dilemma and pressed her advantage, cajoling him sweetly. "I would feel very safe in your care. Would you consent to protect me and bring me safely to my home?"

"I...how could I deny such a request? Volta, is there something else you need me to do instead?"

"No Korban. She's the highest priority now. Forging these alliances must be accomplished rapidly."

"Then I will do it...for the tribe."

"Good, and thank you, Korban. The princess can explain their ways and proper conduct in their palace. I'm sure none of you will shame the Vikar people. Korban, you must impress upon their King all that we know and the deadly threat we face. We can only go forward united with them and all other people's everywhere."

"It will be done."

"Meanwhile, the others of you must make those difficult forays to visit the other tribes. You know already, at the very least they will try to embarrass and shame you and look to provoke an incident. You cannot take the bait. Stay calm no matter what you face. All of our lives depend on it."

After the meeting, Princess Lanai, hurried over to corral Korban before he could escape. That was his plan, but too many people blocked his way for a quick exit. Hence, she snared him.

"I apologize for before, but you must understand, I didn't know you or what I was facing. What strangers might do; I didn't know."

"I understand."

"Before we leave to make the long journey, perhaps we can spend a little time together. I feel we need to know each other much better to establish and feel full trust. I'm not like your Vikar women, and you're not like Trantan men. I like the fact you don't have royalty and therefore don't pamper me. In my life, it's a refreshing change."

Korban noted her change in tone, and in her approach. "We act friendly to others; princess, will that provoke your father?"

"I'll speak with him and explain all that he needs to know."

"How did you learn our tongue?"

"In the past, a Vikar family came down from your mountains to settle among us. He and his wife taught us your language and about your ways. He did make you sound more ferocious and savage than you are."

I can act savage if you wish."

She laughed.

"I want to explain to you so you understand, princess, I'm confident in my skills, but for others in my tribe, they see me as too young for responsibility. I'm surprised they gave me this task. Will it be an issue for your people?"

"You won't have a worry there. You're much bigger than most Trantan soldiers so I don't think they'll try to intimidate you, especially after you saved the life of their crown princess."

"Then, I suppose you can come with me to my parent's hut, if that is your wish. We can share some time there until you go back for your sleep."

She walked with him, but much closer than he expected. He'd never really pursued girls.

Letting her go first into the hut, Shosa and Menga smiled.

"Welcome princess," Menga said, rising up to embrace her. She hugged her warmly.

Lanai smiled; however, she maintained her regal bearing. "Thank you. I appreciate having this time with you and your son. I understand how serious is this mission. I really do want for your forces to trust me."

"That's not a problem, princess," Korban replied. "We are very good at focusing on our tasks. We will not fail you."

"I have no doubt."

"Can we offer you food?" Menga asked her. She sounded almost apologetic. "We must seem very crude for your refined tastes."

"Yes, I'll eat with you. I find great charm in your camp and in your close ways. Your entire tribe are like a giant family. In my lands, people aren't so close, regretfully. Courtesans vie for the attention of the King. It can be contrary and a tiring situation."

Korban commented. "As his daughter, it must mean they vie for your attention also. Are you betrothed?"

"I am not at this point, although my father has discussed marriages advantageous to the crown."

"What does that mean?"

"Alliances, trading pacts, these are what's important to him. Marrying me off to royalty or important people from competing realms, the Manta, the Strella, the Lamali, or the Greka, for example, or even from other royal Trantan families. He's even considered sending a delegation to the Belshik plateau to assess the situation, though we know nothing about the people living there."

"Are you in agreement with this?"

"I don't have a choice. The King decides such things. It is very fortunate I wasn't raped by those creatures. I was rescued just at the right time to spare me that outrage. Purity is a requirement for a royal princess. Losing it is held against women, regardless of how it happened."

Korban and his parents scowled at the patently unfair situation she described.

Menga asked. "What does your mother say?"

"The queen died during childbirth. I've mostly been cared for by her sister, my aunt. She's loving and very good to me. Her husband is a key advisor to my father and her children are like my brothers and sisters."

"This is fortunate. Every child needs parental love, and losing your mother early could have harmed you for life."

Shosa added. "It's not so different from Korban. We took him in from a strange beginning as our son and he has prospered. I knew he would be a man of significance. We don't know anything about his birth parents, but to have a Korban Lynx guarding him as a baby was unexplainable."

"Truly?" Lanai looked at Korban with astonishment.

Korban returned her glance but said nothing. He still struggled to contain escalating feelings for this stunning young woman. As he stared agog, she realized again his romantic fascination. In her life, she saw it often.

"When do you feel we should leave, Korban?"

Though her manner and tone evoked, it broke his inert mood bringing him back to the task at hand. Batting her eyes was like a punch to his face, more proof she was well aware of his fascination with her. He took a moment to fight off his emotions before continuing.

"I realize your father wants you returned at the earliest possible time. I would still like to help out here preparing the camp for winter. Perhaps if you allow me a few days of hunting, or maybe a week, depending on what we can accomplish in the forest."

"It's not up to me. At home, I live in a gilded cage. The only reason I was out when you found me was a lark, just to get away. We had no idea these creatures were lurking about or I would still have been cooped up in the castle. No Trantan citizen would have dared to touch me as the King's daughter. I'm not in a great hurry to rush back home. Tasting freedom living with your tribe pleases me greatly."

Korban looked at his mother.

"Korban, having her stay with us is not a problem. I'd say your idea to keep it to a short time before you leave is wise. The logical route for you to take her home would be going west for a brief circuit through Stakar lands down to the lowlands and then entering Tranta. That route will take some time."

"That is my thought too. I would hope to avoid trouble with the Stakar. I wonder if that Trantan King will be irked by what he may feel is an inordinate delay."

Shosa asked. "What do you say, princess. What sort of man is the King? What is his temperament?"

"He is a person striving to be in full control. His rule benefits the nation, but he brooks very little, and certainly no dissent. He is a strong ruler."

"How this applies to our warriors taking you into his realm is what concerns all of us. We need peace, but if the King chooses to take offense, it would not be good for either side."

"I'll speak to him on your behalf. Beyond that, I can guarantee nothing. Women do not have standing in any lowland nation. We're in the custody of male relatives until we marry. I'm merely his daughter, an asset to use as a piece in his grand plans and strategies."

"If he can't be brought to understand the threat facing all peoples, I agree with Volta that none of us will survive. We both wonder if there is more involved than just these dull cave dweller creatures. Perhaps another race, or races in the background directing the attacks?"

"That is very concerning. However, as a female, I can only speak out as I'm allowed to at home."

Korban looked at his father. They both wore thoughtful expressions.

She continued. "I want to say also, as I have been here with you, I've seen a much different people than I expected. We're taught the mountain barbarians are crude, uncultured, simpletons who kill indiscriminately. You're given no credit for any higher thinking skills. If we can get past the King and his counselor's initial disdain and prejudice, then we would have a chance to achieve our goals. I say our goals, because I'm now committed to your cause. Do you understand what I'm saying? They've been content to live in ignorance of the barbarian tribes. It's one of our critical tasks, changing their minds and their perceptions."

Shosa replied. "Korban, you can see how difficult this mission will be. You won't be able to approach this King in strength. They won't respect you and perhaps will act in ways which will inflame our angry feelings. Do you still wish to do this difficult task? Can you endure the scorn, the ridicule, and perhaps the abuse?"

"I...would not like it, but I feel it must be endured. I will not see us all perish."

"You inspire me." The princess spoke warmly, smiling broadly.

"I don't minimize our danger. It's easy to speak bravely here safe in our homes, but in your palace, I have no doubt it will be a severe test. I hope I can measure up to that challenge."

The princess continued to smile at him.

"Let's cease these heavy words and eat," Menga said. "We're all clear on what the dangers will be. Now we will talk pleasantly to know each other better, as the princess has requested."

Korban took a large helping of stew. Lanai a far more modest amount. She ate daintily as Korban wolfed down his meal.

Korban looked at her looking at him with her smirk. "What?"

"I'm not around large strapping hungry men gulping down their fill. It amuses me how much you enjoy the food, and how much you eat." She chuckled.

"I'm glad I amuse you so much." He eyed her dourly.

"I mean no disrespect." She grinned broadly, taken with the moment.

"Right."

Both women chuckled.

Korban asked. "As your ways are much different, I need for you to school those of us from the scouts on this journey. We need no inadvertent mistakes to offend your people."

"I agree. Let me start by saying a royal princess would never have close contact such as we have here. That is a matter I won't discuss with the King. I will only tell him the Vikar acted appropriately in all things. As far as me sleeping in Toma's hut, that couldn't happen in Tranta. All Vikar have been respectful to me and about me, but the normal close contact of your lives could never be explained away in Tranta. Again, I won't go into any details when I talk to my father. I must tell you an embarrassing thing. He will have his nurses examine me to assure I'm still a virgin. It's mortifying for me, but it will go a long way in helping our cause verifying I wasn't touched in that way."

"Will you mislead him about the attack on your person and the state you were in when we found you, how the enemy had unclothed you? I think he needs to know that truth. One cannot lessen the nature of the caveman threat just for personal embarrassment. Let him focus his rage on the correct enemy."

"I'll consider it."

"If he chooses to wrongly blame us because we saw you in that condition, it will be a sign to us of his true character and what we're dealing with. Do you understand?"

"Yes, I do understand. It's a risk, but I know why you would take it."

Menga decided to chip in. "Princess Lanai, the Vikar people have standards of behavior too. Our girls and young women aren't loose about intimacies. Our boys and men are taught to be respectful about that with severe penalties if any are weak. Perhaps your people might think us thoughtless and uncontrolled about our passions, but that is based on nothing other than their concocted prejudice. This Vikar family you say came down to live among you must have explained all of this."

"He probably did, but it was a long time ago. I'm amazed his teachings carried on to today."

She turned her head to Korban. "So, what are your plans?"

"As I said, I'll help with stocking up the camp with food, but probably we'll leave within a few days."

"I'll plan accordingly. Perhaps I'll join the women in the meantime to learn their skills since princesses learn no survival skills at all. Also, I notice women here handle weapons. Will you teach me to defend myself? Being helpless in the hands of those brutes terrified me and I never want that to happen again."

"I have no objection. We can cover a level of training while we travel, but understand part of it would normally be building up your strength. That task can't be accomplished in the limited time we have."

"I would still like to get what training I can, while I can."

"So be it."

Lanai arose as the hour was getting late.

"I'll leave you now, but please find me tomorrow to join the women, Menga."

"I will, princess."

The men arose and nodded to her.

"Good night, princess," said Shosa.

"Princess," said Korban.

"Gentlemen."

After she walked out, Menga stepped close to Korban. "She likes you, my son."

"I'm a simple warrior, not a mate for royalty. Besides, I doubt she can make proper stew."

Both his parents laughed heartily.

"Indeed," said his father, smiling wryly. "As men, we must eat."

The following several days passed quickly and the time to begin the trek arrived. Getting up with the sun, Korban gathered his twenty warriors and the provisions they would need. The princess had been provided forest garb in the meantime and even was given weapons, a sword, a knife, a bow and a quiver of arrows. Tying up her hair in a long ponytail, she was still incredibly fetching, but she looked like a different person, and she no longer acted reserved and aloof.

During the first day of travel, it was a big adjustment for a woman not hardened to long days traveling on the trail. She suffered in silence, but Korban had a pretty good idea about her issues.

"Princess, we'll try a blanket on your saddle while you adjust to riding, and here is a salve for your saddle sores."

"Thank you, Korban. I know I'm pathetic to you, but I'll do my best."

She didn't back down that evening from her desire for martial training. Although predictably weak, Korban was surprised how rapidly she picked on the fundamental moves and techniques he taught her. An inner fire drove her to try to impress him. Once she even surprised him with a sudden swipe which caused him to parry quickly. The warriors laughed and chided Korban at the challenge, like she had bested him.

After the bouts, she looked haggard.

"You're sore, but after a week, you'll feel stronger and do better. This was a good first day, princess."

"Oh, thank you, Korban." She spoke in sincere gratefulness. "It was very difficult."

Hanging on between the long daily rides, and then the evening bouts, her face was usually a grim mask of determination. Each night she put her bedding directly beside Korban, quickly falling asleep from exhaustion. As with the fights, when she practiced with the bow, her strength was inadequate, although each night she improved noticeably.

She quickly learned Korban's lessons, perfecting her archery form and concentration before the shot. Vikar strengthening work was grueling, but she was willing to pay that price.

During that time, the group traveled along the edge of the escarpment so they could look down on Tranta, their ultimate destination. Kordan didn't hurry the pace; he was entertained in Lanai's training and with what he felt was her remarkable progress. Her determination strongly evoked him.

By the time the first week passed, what Korban had told her had come true. The debilitating aches eased, her strength increased, and for the first time, she had rudimentary skills with her weapons well on her way toward passable. She even started to learn forest lore.

"By the time we arrive in Tranta, I'll be able to forage on my own and defend myself, don't you agree?"

Korban gave her a smirk. "I assume you're jesting with me. You've made good progress, but being competent and independent, that would be a long way down the road."

"I'm much better than I was when you found me."

"That is true, but it's a giant leap from there to say you're competent now. We can't get ahead of ourselves."

"I know you doubt me, but I will do this difficult thing, Korban. You'll see."

"Yes, I'll see."

"Mock me if you must, but I will not be deterred."

"That will be a great day, princess."

That evening, she was fierce in her attacks and did the best in battling Korban for the entire period of their training. He mostly parried her strikes, but threw in some offensive moves to acquaint her with that side of fighting, defending oneself. It got her attention. Afterwards, he drilled her completely in defensive moves and once again, she did better than he anticipated.

Lanai demanded to keep fighting much later than usual. Hence, it was later that they could finally eat before climbing into their bedding to sleep the night. As always, Lanai had no problems falling asleep rapidly into a deep sleep.

The following night, the princess surprised Korban.

"I would like to take a turn guarding the camp tonight."

"Why?"

"It's something I want to experience, being part of this team, pulling my weight."

"We have two people at a time, one on each side of the camp. You have no training about hazards to guard against. If a predator came close, the guard must take action."

"I don't want to put us in jeopardy, but perhaps if I can join the two on duty to experience this?"

"So, losing sleep is appealing to you?"

She chuckled. "Of course not, but I want to do this. Will you allow me?"

"Lanai, it isn't a matter of me allowing. This isn't like your people where women are invisible. You can make your own choices among us."

"Then I choose guard duty."

Korban shook his head. "Okay, I'll put you on first watch. It goes for half the night."

"I understand."

Immediately, she took out her sword to practice her strokes.

Korban smirked as he walked over to the two early sentries.

"The princess wants to join you this evening for your shift of duty."

"What? Why?" they both spoke in unison.

"All I can say is, safeguard her, but don't lose sight of protecting the camp."

"What if she talks?"

"You have the chance to teach her about silence."

They all chuckled.

After the meal, she proudly headed for the two guards.

"Thank you for accepting me. I won't be a bother."

They nodded, smiling wryly. The other scouts smirked at them.

Sitting down, she stayed to chat with them until the camp bedded down. Following the guards later, one of them took her to one side to find a good vantage point. It gave him his first chance to school her about the silence necessary and the attention they needed to safeguard the troop. He did whisper to explain some things during the night which he spotted that she would need to know. Once a cat crept toward the camp, but soon turned away and left without forcing them to act.

Lanai had pulled an arrow for her bow, just in case.

Finishing the shift without issues, she felt proud. The guards patted her back as she went to her bedding beside a sleeping Korban. Morning came early, but she was happy nonetheless.

"Was it all that you hoped for?" Korban asked with a smirk.

"Actually, it was very enlightening. It gives me far more respect for what you do and for the lore I'm learning. It was worth the time I spent. The guards were nice men. They could have shown me great disdain."

"We wouldn't do that. We're not a people to humble and dishonor friends."

"Tranta can learn much from you, Korban. I hope we can get past the issues and misunderstandings that are inevitable and get to a better place quickly."

"That's my hope also. That is why we've come."

CHAPTER THREE
Civilization

After crossing out of Vikar territory into Stakar lands, they moved efficiently. Only after they'd descended from the mountains down into the foothills did they see a Stakar patrol emerge behind them. It was fortuitous that they'd shadowed Korban's force and chose not to take action. Korban, as leader, and his Stakar counterpart nodded in acknowledgment of avoiding a needless fight.

Crossing into the lowland nation of Strella as they turned east, again they saw a patrol riding behind them. This time it was Strellan soldiers in their red uniforms. As it was clear the Vikar warriors were going to quickly cross into Tranta, again a patrol left them in peace.

"We're lucky twice," Korban commented.

Lanai looked at him. "Do your various forces normally fight when they meet each other?"

"I wouldn't say usually, but it isn't rare when there are difficulties. It helps us the Vikar reputation for being the best of warriors often dissuades some possible skirmishes. You picked good companions for your little vacation ride."

Lanai smacked him on the arm. "Vacation ride? Among other things, sir, I'm learning you're a smug man."

"I'm not smug. We're confident, and that is based on our deeds, crown princess."

"Apparently." Her sharp tone irked him. It seemed to happen often.

They stopped that evening to camp on the border just inside Strella.

Lanai continued her training and had even recently started sparring with others of the troop. The princess had become incredibly popular among them. Her appealing looks and vibrant nature predictably stirred the romantic ideas of the young men.

However, the following morning, it was time to reenter her homeland. For her, it was an anxious moment. There were so many things that could go wrong.

"How long will it be before we can arrive at the city of the King?"

"Probably a week, or two at the most, I think. If we encounter royal forces, I will speak to them. I apologize in advance for any unfortunate misunderstandings, or incidents."

"We'll try not to be barbarians," said Korban. The troop laughed.

Within an hour, they came upon their first Trantan settlement. It was a small town.

The princess rode at the lead beside Korban. The locals were shocked on many levels. Not the least of which was having 'barbarians at their gates.'

Korban gave instructions to his forces before they entered the town. "Make no moves toward your weapons. Leave them to stare at us, but don't stare at them. We just want to pass through, peacefully."

That got them about halfway through the small berg before the local sheriff and some deputies came out to face them.

"Princess Lanai?" the sheriff asked in shock. "We were told you and your soldiers were killed. What has happened? Why are you riding with barbarians? Where are your clothes?"

"Sheriff, obviously I wasn't killed. Here I am. These are members of the noble Vikar tribe of mountain peoples. They saved my life and are escorting me to the palace to rejoin my father. Please clear the way as we have a long distance yet to travel and are pressed for time."

"I...eh...is it safe to..."

"Move sheriff, they've treated me with respect for all of this time. We have no time for any needless delays."

The sheriff reluctantly stepped aside. Lanai spurred her horse to gallop away along with the warriors. Thereafter, they chose to go around rather than through settlements. It worked for a week as they were able to find small groves of trees to make camps for the nights away from prying eyes. Lanai fought particularly fiercely those evenings. Her skills continued improving along with her strength. Korban taught her new moves and was amazed how she could incorporate higher fighting skills so rapidly.

The next day, they got an early start, but settlements got bigger as they moved toward the capital which made it more difficult to avoid notice.

A second night unencumbered by issues seemed a miracle, and it was. More fierce fighting practice didn't fully assuage her worries about what they would face.

However, on the third day as they approached a town, before they could veer off, a large royal patrol thundered out of the settlement straight toward them.

"Here we go, stay calm, men," Korban muttered.

They simply ambled forward, unable to avoid the meeting. His warriors followed their instructions and maintained non-threatening poses.

"They have pretty uniforms," he muttered to Lanai.

She looked worried.

When they came close, the Trantan captain eyed the Vikar band grimly. "So, it's true, you're still alive, your majesty."

"I am, thanks to my new friends from the Vikar peoples. They saved my life and protected me until we could make this journey home."

The captain eyed Korban balefully. "Princess, may I ask what happened to your clothing? I see you have weapons. What have they done to you?"

They've done nothing. What you see are my choices. After the terror of nearly being slaughtered by those vile creatures, I will no longer tolerate being helpless."

"Royal forces defend you at all times."

Like the royal forces who died in the ambush? I'm sure you came upon their half-eaten corpses. My hand maidens were not spared that horror either.

"This is a matter for the King. You can only ride with royal armed forces. These others must release you into our custody." He still stared at Korban, challenge in his eyes.

The entire Vikar force felt provoked, but they stoically obeyed the dictate to remain passive and calm.

When she didn't move, the captain rode over.

"Are you under some restraint, princess?"

"They do not restrain. There is no need. I choose to ride under their protection."

"That is not a choice you can make, now ride with me into the Royal patrol. They can go away."

"Captain, in addition to bringing me home, the Vikar require a visit with the King. It is vital."

"How can anything of the barbarians be vital to Tranta?"

She eyed him grimly before speaking. "I will introduce them to the King, my father. If you wish to ride with us, that's your choice. May I remind you; it isn't for you to dictate to the King's daughter, and sole heir to the throne, what I will do. If you wish to test us, I must say, I don't like your chances. I doubt you've seen the Vikar warriors in action in a fight. I have when they saved my life wiping out four times their numbers."

Korban and the troop felt sudden pride at Lanai's boast. At that point, they would have charged behind her into any battle without a qualm. The captain noted the subtle shift in them, a quick shift from passive to readiness for battle. The sudden steely looks in their eyes, it was unnerving as the large Vikar warriors were legends as fighters everywhere.

"You're trying to put me in a difficult situation. My charge, now that we've found you, is your safety and returning you to your father. These barbarians may ride with us, if that is your command, and only to go to the capital. We will surround them. Understand princess, we will tolerate no hostilities, and certainly no improper behavior. How the King will see this sorry incident, we shall see."

"They didn't come here to make war, captain. If you or your troops try to provoke them, believe me when I say there will be many fewer royal troops to ride about harassing innocent people. Your need to provoke potential allies will not go unnoticed when I speak to my father." She glared at the captain.

The captain was livid, but deployed his forces nonetheless without further posturing. They rode through the town and continued riding until they arrived at a Trantan fort just before dark. Leading them inside the military enclosure, with their prodding, the princess grudgingly went inside a building to sleep. The Vikar warriors were kept in the open yard, surrounded. They were given no quarters protected from the elements.

The Vikar troop ran a cold camp that night nibbling on dried meat and drinking a little water. A rainstorm made for an unpleasant sleep time. At dawn, Kordan gathered them to talk softly.

"We knew what to expect. These annoyances are meant to provoke us into action. We won't allow it. This mission is too important. Stay passive and we will do what we must to get through it. They shame themselves with their poor actions."

When the princess came out much later, she'd been forced to change into fancy feminine clothing befitting her high station. Her forest garb she carried to Korban, folded up neatly.

"It wasn't my choice, but fighting them over this issue wasn't worth it. Here are my weapons, but keep them close at hand. I'm not done, no matter what the stuffed shirts think."

Korban bowed to her.

They left the fort far later than Korban would have liked. The soldiers refused to let the princess ride with the Vikar scouts. The ride toward the capital was slower too.

Muttering, he whispered to himself, "you must not take the bait."

It was the theme for the day as the beefed-up Tranta patrol taunted the Vikar warriors for a response. By the time the day ended, the Vikar scouts were a grim-faced lot, on edge like a lit fuse.

On this night, they approached a large city. Stopping at an inn, the officers took the princess inside. The glut of Trantan troops led the greatly outnumbered Vikar band behind the building and surrounded them there. Again, it wasn't a pleasant night.

One other night sleeping outside in a second larger city was the last time, as the next day they approached the capital, the city of the King. It was not a small city so it took some time before they could reach the palace.

Word of the reappearance of the princess had long since preceded them. A veritable army of Trantan troops awaited them, arrayed in overlapping ranks along the entire route, to the protected palace. Grim angry faces abounded.

The princess was well ahead of them in the procession and she was quickly whisked away out of sight. The Vikar warriors waited patiently but as hours passed by, they realized quickly there would be no prompt audience with the King.

One of his men muttered to Korban, "We would not treat our worst enemies this rudely. We've done nothing wrong, yet we're treated such?"

"Be strong. Insults may not be the worst things they'll try to do."

"And they call us barbarians?"

"Patience, my friends. They're just words. They mean nothing."

To no one's surprise, they didn't see the princess that day, or for a week, as they languished in the courtyard in front of the palace. Korban ordered they tap into food and water supplies sparingly. It was impossible to know how long they would be here, immobilized.

Korban's short-term worry was even as they were feeding sparingly off their supplies, the Trantans showed no inclination to ever provide food, or shelter. With the possibility they were trying to starve them into departing, or worse, it was also going into winter here. Weather everywhere could vary radically at this time of year.

At long last, a column of the palace guard filed out of the palace and flanked the small Vikar troop. Their officer motioned for them to enter the palace. Once inside, they saw reinforced rows of wary soldiers lining the walls the entire length of the long hallway, weapons at the ready. Torches flamed from sconces mounted on the wall providing flickering light, but also smoke in the foggy air.

Korban followed the officer along with his command behind him unsure what to expect.

When they approached the throne room, teams of muscular men operated pivots to open the massive heavy doors. The great chamber was full of ranks of troops with weapons drawn. Ahead they could see the thrones. The queen's throne was empty. The King sat glowering as they entered the royal chamber.

The officer led them toward the throne, but stopped them short.

"Kneel before his royal majesty, Meron, King of Tranta."

Korban was feeling put upon and belligerent, however after waiting for a time, enough to irk their hosts, he went to a knee. The other Vikar followed his example.

That barely mollified the King who was already in a foul mood.

"You are the one called Korban?"

"I am, Korban of the Vikar tribe."

Motioning to the side, Lanai was brought in by royal soldiers. The King motioned for her to stand to his left.

"These are the men you praise?"

"Yes." Her voice was barely above a whisper.

How weakly she replied to the King cued Korban something was amiss.

"You there, come closer." He pointed at Korban. Purposefully, Korban stayed kneeling for a time before he slowly arose. Walking slowly and deliberately, he glided toward the throne like he was stalking prey. His angry eyes spoke volumes that the Vikar were at the end of their tolerance.

The king returned an acid glare.

My daughter tells me you discovered her. Is this true?"

"Yes."

"Her escort was ambushed and wiped out? Only she survived because you killed a force that could wipe out an entire column of the royal soldiers?"

Korban made no reply.

"Do you deny this? It's apparent you came there as she ended up in your mountains, detained in your camp." He snapped at Korban tersely.

Korban said nothing. His patience was at an end.

"Did you think a royal princess of Tranta would fetch a large ransom to line your pockets?"

The surrounding Trantan soldiers clearly saw Korban was highly provoked and poised dangerously, who could spring to the attack at any moment. They inched closer though he remained stationary.

"She tells me that these alleged cave dwellers who supposedly killed my soldiers, took her aside to take away her maidenhead. That she was unclothed when you say you interceded. You saw my daughter's nakedness?" He spoke in an enraged hiss.

"Yes, King, I did see her. She was laid out by their rough hands. Removing her clothing was their doing, not mine. What are you trying to say to me?"

"She is high born, the heir to my throne, not a person to be seen in that way by barbarians."

"So, I should have turned my back and left her to perish, to be used shamefully and then eaten as their food? What sort of father are you? Vikar children are cherished by their parents and by the whole tribe. Where is your honor?"

The assembled Tranta host roared in anger and started forward.

The King seethed, he stood and held up his hand until his soldiers stopped and the room quieted.

"I do care about my daughter, as if you can judge me. I'm going to find out the truth in the midst of your fantastical tale. Were the attackers really your Vikar brethren." The entire Vikar troop leaped to their feet, moving quickly and seamlessly into forming a defensive ring around Korban. As the royal soldiers started to attack, Lanai acted.

Suddenly Lanai shouted. "Stop!"

The room stood poised for a battle, but all eyes, and ears, were focused on her.

"Father, you are my King, but I tell you now in front of your people, you shame us. There is nothing fantastical in what I told you. The truth is the truth. I was treated with more respect and decency than I could

41

ever have hoped for, both in the rescue saving my life and later staying as a guest in their camp. There was nothing I could find fault with. In private here, I acceded to your indecent demand that I be checked by your nurses. They certify I was not deflowered. You call them barbarians, but who is acting the barbarian here and now. They came here for no other reason than the need for all peoples, barbarians and low landers, to ally together to face this dire threat. Do you show such courage as these heroic men in the face of your unseemly taunts and insults?"

She walked down the stairs to stand with the Vikar warriors, as the Trantan peoples watched, gasping in horror.

For a very tense time, everybody waited for the King's response, anticipating the worst.

Every Vikar warrior was fearless, like a coiled spring ready to the attack, weapons at the ready facing every direction.

"I am not happy, Lanai. I think no member of the royal family in history has acted so brazenly and then to side with these barbarians? It's outrageous. Return her to her room under guard. Escort our 'guests' to the dungeon while I ponder this matter. They're clearly too dangerous to be left wandering about freely."

The mass of soldiers edged slowly toward the Vikar. In response, Korban pulled Lanai into their defensive circle.

Korban spoke in a deadly hiss. "If you wish to imprison your own daughter, come and get her, if you can. We'll be waiting for you. This is as good a day to die as any. Just remember, you already have a war you can't win against a pitiless foe. Your dead soldiers should tell you that, but if you want to also fight us, you'll also have a war with all the Vikar peoples, and the other four tribes of Kar as well. We don't lose wars. You'll be a nation of dead bodies. It's not too late to use reason. No blows have been struck and none have died...yet."

It was a chilling threat. Everybody paused and looked up at the King. The Vikar squad had drawn their weapons and deployed into a defensive array, with death in their eyes.

For the first time, the King looked daunted.

After a time, Lanai stepped out of the circle and walked up to her father.

She spoke gently. "Cool your anger, father, because it is wrongly placed. These men deserve to be honored, not ridiculed. They came here in peace and stood down to our bad behaviors. They wish to be our allies. It's not difficult to admit the truth in this case, Tranta is wrong in how we acted."

She embraced him which surprised the King. His angry looks evaporated.

After returning her hug, he spoke. "My daughter has taught her father a great lesson. I must be a worthy King for my people. I can't make these kinds of mistakes. My troops, you may return to your barracks. Our Vikar visitors are to be treated as guests and accorded appropriate respect. I will accept your account of the incident, Lanai. As my daughter has said, she was proven to be unharmed. Thank you for your intervention to save her life, Korban. The Trantan nation owes you a great debt and we agree to an alliance."

The Vikar warriors were as stunned as everyone else at the abrupt turnaround. They sheathed their weapons.

The King added. "We'll have a banquet tonight to celebrate the beginning of a new way for both our peoples. I hope you can put aside these unfortunate difficulties."

"We can, King. We weren't sent here to make war. We don't have royalty in the Vikar world so there was no palace for your daughter living among us anyway." The King actually chuckled at the jest.

Later, after the Vikar warriors had experienced the royal bathes, had been clipped and trimmed by servants, and dressed up in Trantan clothing, they looked at each other in amusement. In every case, Trantan clothing was too small on the large Vikar bodies.

One of largest of them spouted, "I would be a great nobleman. I look splendid."

The entire troop laughed.

At the banquet hall, Lanai sat between her father and Korban. Leaning to see around her, he struck up a conversation nearly immediately with the King.

"King, we received a great boon in finding Volta living alone in the woods. He's our oldest and wisest tribal member who mysteriously disappeared without a trace some time ago. He's a great visionary. We thought him dead. He asked that Tranta send your craftsmen to help us build our winter camp into a fortress. We have no experience with fortifications. We move about a great deal."

"We can do that."

Although the King was amicable, his generals and advisors were far less so. Though they would whisper or speak their counsel in low tones to the King, they would not speak to any of the Vikar men. Korban did not fail to notice, nor did his comrades. That didn't stop the Vikar from eating amply from the delicious feast. Seeing the glut of food on the tables struck the tribal members badly. Often accustomed to sparse meals, this banquet struck them as being a wasteful exercise.

Lanai had no problem speaking with her Vikar friends a great deal which added to the ire of the King's staff of advisors. It struck them on many levels, not the least of which was a subservient place for women in Trantan society. They did not like their crown princess flaunting Trantan norms and breaking Trantan rules. The King was not unaware his beloved daughter was basking in the moment.

The next potential issue arose when Lanai announced she intended to continue her martial training with the Vikar. That evoked an angry response from all of the military folk at the banquet.

Loudly berating her, and their Vikar guests, in response the princess arose ominously. "Silence you louts! You weren't the ones in my party slaughtered and cannibalized by an enemy you too easily dismiss. Your arrogance seems to me to be based on absolutely nothing at all. A small band of Vikar warriors wiped out that entire force of those cannibals when your invincible soldiers were easily killed and eaten, as they then laid unclean hands on me. It is the Vikar people who spared me shameful acts and my own death. I grieve with our families for the death of their loved ones, but if you don't change your thinking, this war is lost before it starts. I will no longer be helpless to defend myself. If you think I cannot fight, or it should be unseemly for women to do so, come to the training yards. We'll be happy to school you in reality."

Livid, and red-faced, the Field Marshall of all Royal Forces arose.

"If this is the benefit of dealing with barbarians, this insolence we see, I think it is you who needs to change your thinking. Our traditions and standards are long standing and..."

"Long overdue for the trash heap of history. I repeat, come to the training pits. Bring your own ceremonial sword and test your skill against me, if you dare."

The room was aghast at the colossal affront. Korban worried the most of all. Lanai had come a long way in her competence but she had far to go. Her skills were coming along, but her strengthening was still in fairly early stages.

Meanwhile, Lanai stood her ground. Whether she could withstand a fight with the Field Marshall of all Tranta, he didn't know. Granted, he was well past his prime, portly from too many banquets, but he wouldn't have risen to a key leadership role for no reason. Korban felt fear for her. However, the gauntlet had already been thrown down.

The King watched the scene without interceding. Seemingly, he wouldn't stand in the way of the fight. That surprised Korban, and added to his worries. If Lanai was any bit worried, she didn't show it. She continued to glare at her opponent.

The festive air, what little there had been, was gone from the feast replaced by deathly silence. The schism remained between the princess and her progressive views, and the male military's reactionary position defending the male dominant views of the provincial old ways.

The King made a wave of his hand and everybody arose and left the room. Lanai ignored and resisted her father's guard's orders swatting away their hands and followed the Vikar warriors away to their sleeping area.

Korban had to speak. "Princess, have you thought about this challenge? You could have benefitted from much more training and practice."

"I know that, Korban. I'm not stupid. This bloated man hasn't had a serious fight in...forever. I think I can win, even in my infant stage of martial skills."

"I would say this, if you're determined to go through with this, you must fight defensively. Remember my lessons. The longer the fight goes on, the better your chances as I think he will tire."

"I want my forest clothes back, and my weapons you're guarding for me."

"Of course, your highness."

She eyed him. "Are you taking sport with me?"

"No, I'm making a point to remember who you are to these people. Winning a bout against their primary military leader after you tried to shame him about that ambush, make this fight calculated and smart. Both sides need to win. If you prevail, don't taunt and lord over this man. Go humbly and celebrate both of your efforts. They think that somehow, we've turned you into a Vikar and therefore a traitor to your people."

"That's not right. I'm trying to open the eyes of our women that this system is wrong and shouldn't be allowed to continue."

"You and I know that, but your men feel threatened. They will fight back. This will never be an easy step for your society, if it can even come to pass."

"I will try. From my fights with you and the other Vikar men, fights go a lot of different ways. Usually, it isn't a matter of my controlling it. Usually, I was reacting and defending myself."

"It will be the same here. Don't let him dictate the fight. Mix both your defensive prowess which is decent, with sufficient offensive moves. Remember your goal is to wear him out. That's the first best plan. You're much younger so your vitality is a great boon. He will come to understand that and will get cagier. That is the critical time to be very careful."

"I understand."

"I'll be with you, Lanai."

"Thank you. It means a great deal to me. I won't let you down."

When they arrived at the barracks, taking out her forest clothes, the princess shocked the royal guards by changing clothes right there in front of everyone. Further, again she ignored her guard's orders to return to her royal suite and bedded down among the Vikar warriors to sleep the night. Those guards wisely did not challenge her with the provoked Vikar standing nearby.

The following morning, she countermanded royal protocol and had breakfast brought to the barracks.

It was fairly early in the morning when they went to the training arena. Royal soldiers packed the stands already. The King and his retinue of courtesans and advisers filed in to take seats in the royal box.

Lanai went out first from the tunnels under the stands leading the column of Vikar warriors marching behind her. In spite of her being crown princess, there was rampant boos and derisive calls from the people in the stands. Some shouts were unseemly.

Ignoring the bedlam, she went toward the royal booth, drew her sword and saluted the royal party. Her father looked down at her without betraying any emotions. However, the others sitting with him had no restraint in showing great scorn and revile. Some even voiced some very disrespectful taunts. She ignored them with completing her obligatory obeisance to the King.

Returning to the Vikar troop, she waited.

The Field Marshall was in no hurry to exit the tunnels. When he finally emerged, he was dressed in the combat uniform of the Trantan army. Korban noticed the tight fit over his ample mid rife. Great cheers and a round of applause accompanied his march to salute the King. Whatever he said to the royal booth, she could not hear, but it brought another great cheer from the soldiers.

Lanai turned back to Korban walking over to him. He saw the fear of the moment in her eyes.

"Relax, Lanai, you can do this. Calm your worries. He is afraid too, I guarantee it. Keep your mind free and concentrate on the strategy we discussed. If you can fight against Vikar warriors and live, there is no other opponent you need to fear."

The Vikar troop gave her a martial shout and knelt down to her.

Taking a deep breath, closing her eyes to calm her nerves and attain battle focus, she turned to watch him approach her.

The Vikar scouts moved backwards out of the fighting area. Every one of them was provoked, itching to jump to her defense in case she had serious trouble, as if she was in mortal peril from her own people.

The Tranton's head military officer, the national leader of their military, suddenly ran at her and made a savage swing to end the bout in one fell swoop. She was ready, darting quickly aside and parrying the blow deflecting it rather than taking the brunt of the strike. She made a quick counter swipe directed at his ribs that startled him at the speed of the movement. He barely avoided the blow. After that, there were no further wild swings. He'd learned in one stroke she couldn't be taken for granted.

The bout became a cautious fight, each probing and searching for weaknesses.

As she battled, Lanai came to understand what Korban had said. She'd been tutored by the finest fighters in the world. Her Trantan opponent showed her nothing of a surprise. Adjusting for his male size and his strategy to overwhelm and try to beat her down, she continued making surprise quick jabs and swipes to keep him wary and off balance. As the fight went on, she noted the sweat beads developing on his forehead and his increased breathing. Gradually, she started more offensive attacks causing him to expend more energy trying to evade her rapid sword strokes and thrusts.

The battle was still going on for over an hour, far beyond the quick victory the soldiers anticipated, when her opponent decided he could not go on like this as his strength was ebbing.

He attacked like suddenly she was an enemy to be crushed and slaughtered. His swings were suddenly feral. The crowd was shocked gasping audibly at the deadly turn. Lanai was frightened, but would not concede. She'd come too far with this. In response, she launched a savage and swift series of lightning counter strokes she'd just learned from Korban. The bout was transformed, in doubt about the outcome and with both opponents in danger of serious injury, or even death.

Korban was on the verge of racing in to end the suddenly dangerous fight. However, he saw her gain the edge as the Trantan general was forced totally onto the defensive, and her strikes were coming closer to doing real damage. Before such blows could happen, suddenly she ceased and took a step back.

The Field Marshalls head drooped, panting for breath. He was covered in sweat rolling down his face.

She walked over to him, very close and then gave him a firm hug. Whispering to him for a time, eventually he walked with her over to the royal booth. They gave salutes with their swords.

"Father, we agree we've gone on far enough. I hope you can accept both our efforts on behalf of the Trantan nation and Trantan peoples." The soldiers quickly reversed their aversion for their own crown princess and cheered loudly, shouting her name. It was obvious to everybody she could have won and allowing him to retain some dignity was surprisingly magnanimous, from their male perspective.

The King arose holding up his hand as the crowd was silenced.

"Let this be the end of the matter and the end of enmity. Tranta will enter this new world my daughter proposes. We will send our craftsmen to the Vikar camp to help build their citadel. In return, I would hope the impressive skills of the Vikar fighters can be shared with us to improve our own martial skills in our armed forces."

Korban and the Vikar patrol gave a martial shout. The day that had started out with great foreboding and danger had miraculously resolved with both sides intact.

Crown Princess Lanai had proven herself to her father and to her nation, but in her mind, she mostly felt she'd validated herself to Korban as a *protege*. He moved her greatly.

Korban held back while the princess stayed with mending fences with the Field Marshall of all the Trantan leadership.

She spoke sincerely, "I wish we had been able to avoid this scene. I had no wish to embarrass, harm, or shame you. In spite of what you seemed to think, I'm still a loyal subject of Tranta. I just felt we needed a new path for women."

"I didn't handle it well, princess. I apologize to you for that. Your fighting skills are impressive in such a short time in their hands. You surprised me. I knew I was too old and fat, but I thought I needed to defend Tranta honor."

"Your honor was never a part of it, but I saw no way to negotiate it. I think the soldiers needed to see what the Vikar people can do teaching us with their training. They truly are a force without peer."

"What do you propose next? Do we flood our ranks with women?"

"Of course not. I was personally driven to accomplish this formidable task for my reasons. There are other women who could do the same, but that's not most women. Teaching them to defend themselves is a good goal though."

"Okay, we can look at your new ideas and make plans accordingly. I hope you will hold no enmity toward me going forward."

"No, I respect you a great deal, sir. Many would have been ruled by their disdain of women."

"Perhaps we can have another banquet but with a much better mood. Our Vikar friends seem to like to eat."

Lanai laughed. "That they do."

It was a different air as the crowd filtered away. The excitement of the fight had receded, but so too had the tension. No longer did the Vikar visitors seem a savage threat in their midst and an ongoing hazard to the 'modernized' Trantan people.

With the script flipped, suddenly the Vikar visitors were celebrities, deluged by the curious. Many Trantan soldiers inquired if they could get training.

Korban was bewildered initially, but decided to delay offering training sessions in the short term.

He talked with the Field Marshall who was now anxious to be friendly.

"I hope you can understand, our mission in addition to bringing back your princess, was to gain an alliance. With your King agreeing to send the craftsmen we need to build one of your fortresses, I feel we need to return to our home. I'm sure you'll be provided with Vikar warriors to aid in sharing Vikar battle skills. Whether that will be us, or others, I can't say."

"I understand. I must tell you how you handled our bad treatment with such composure amazes me. If I had been in your home and received such treatment, I doubt I could have endured it without a serious fight."

"We had a vital mission and we could not afford to fail. Do you see?"

"It would be beyond me to endure the scorn."

"So, let us prepare for this banquet. We are a hungry lot."

They laughed.

Later, the banquet was a full production and on a much larger scale. Courtesans, civilian dignitaries, and Trantan royalty joined the military for the occasion. It was an impressive sight for the handful of Vikar warriors in attendance. The princess sat, once again, beside her father and Korban. She glanced at the glut of Trantan nobles, and their lame sons. What could have been her future now disgusted her.

Korban attempted his best behavior, although what constituted best behavior for the Trantans, the Vikars weren't fully sure.

Liberal drinks relaxed and then loosened up the crowd. After a time when the lengthy meal was eaten. Trantan folk came over to talk to 'real live barbarians.' Some maidens looked for something more than talk.

The princess walked around like it was her duty to protect the warriors from untoward lures.

She told Korban, "I know your single men are free to ponder potential wives at your home, but these offers aren't at the proper times, places or people for your bonding. These females look for a thrill, a night of pleasure. They're not intent on marriage."

"Truly? Thank you for telling us. We don't approach such intimate things casually."

"I know that. I'd say we should all have a fairly early exit tonight to avoid any difficulties."

"As you wish, princess. We trust your counsel."

CHAPTER FOUR
A strong-willed princess

Korban chose to gather provisions for the trek back to the Vikar winter camp without delay. The weather continued to erode as the icy blasts became more frequent rolling off the high ground. Climbing the mountains back up the escarpment concerned him, especially with the large Trantan contingent of craftsmen, soldiers, and assorted curious nobles and their families tagging along. The amount of food necessary to feed this mob was daunting. The train of pack animals would be as long as all of the riders combined.

As the time to depart approached, Korban was curious they hadn't seen Lanai in a week.

Going to the palace to inquire where she was, he was advised at the palace doorway she'd been in conference with the King. They took him to the closed throne room doors, but didn't admit him. He could hear them shouting at each other inside the chamber.

"What is this about?" He asked the pretty young servant girl waiting patiently.

"I'm here in case she calls for me to come inside the throne room. The King requires her to stay here and meet with suitor candidates he's selected for her marriage. As you can hear, that does not meet with her approval. She's railed at him all week long and we wonder that the King hasn't subdued her."

Korban smiled. "I think the King saw her perform in the arena and understood things will change in Tranta. She is no longer a vassal to be moved about on his chess board. And yes, we know about chess in our Vikar camp."

The young maiden snickered.

"What does she want from him, ma'am?"

"She's demands to go with you."

"Me?"

"Yes, she says she wants to oversee the work of the Trantan craftsman at your village, but we think it's just a ploy. She wishes to be with you."

"Be with me? What does that mean?"

"You're unmarried and she is of an age to take a mate."

"How could that be a thought in her head? I'm a Vikar. There is no palace in our camp to house her, and I would not live here."

"That doesn't matter to her. She sees a chance for a different kind of life, and freedom by following you. The King is very upset about this."

"I see, and I can hear. Can you tell her, we of the Vikar desire to wish her well before we depart? If she can see us, we would appreciate it. If she can't, we understand and still wish her well."

"I'll get a message to her, my lord."

It dawned on him after he walked away. He muttered, "Lord? I'm not a lord. These Trantan folk are strange people."

Returning to the barracks, he related the story to his men. They used it as an opportunity to needle him. 'Korban the splendiferous, the royal lord of lords.' He eyed them wryly, but secretly he was amused.

The Trantan contingent were not rapid in their task of assembling adequate supplies and packing for the trip. This gave the princess and her father more time to argue and shout, which they did with gusto. Korban and the Vikar warriors stayed away from those explosive deliberations.

Days later when, finally, the pack animals were loaded, Lanai made an appearance at the Vikar barracks. She was accompanied by an entire host of palace guards.

"Greetings my dear friends. I'm sure you're aware of my disagreements with the King. He permits me to see you now only to say our goodbyes. This is not my wish, but he's intent on paring me up with some weak son of a Trantan royal person, "for the good of the realm?" I beg to differ. I will not marry some fop. That matter is not closed."

Korban spoke. "I'm sorry you find yourself in a situation that you find to be disagreeable."

She eyed him directly with the merest of a smile. "Yes, so it would seem. I'm thwarted in determining what's best for me. We'll see how that plays out." Her tiny smile widened slightly.

He nearly laughed out, realizing her mind was at work on some plan.

"We've enjoyed knowing you, your majesty, and we wish you the best for your future. Your spouse-to-be has no idea what he's getting into."

Lanai laughed. "That is so true. Safe journey to you all."

All of the Vikar men came over to speak to her. Over time, she'd grown immeasurably in their esteem. Her accomplishments in rapidly learning weapons tactics and skills far surpassed any woman they'd ever known, not to mention her shocking victory over the Trantan Field Marshall. They too recognized she had ideas percolating in her head. Her continuing rigorous martial practicing had increased her strength and reshaped her body into a consummate physical specimen. She turned heads wherever she went.

"Thank you for coming to see us off, princess. Perhaps we'll see you again sometime."

"Perhaps you will." She smirked, but quickly blanked her expression to turn back to the guards with a scowl. The Vikar warriors watched her walk away, elegant in everything she did.

The King had come out also. His grim-faced daughter walked past him without acknowledging or even looking at him. He walked up to Korban.

"As you can see, my daughter is displeased. It's a difficult life wearing the crown and being forced to make tough choices. I want her to be happy, but I must consider the welfare of the people first."

"It's not for the Vikar people to judge you, or make your decisions, but I will say, I don't know why your choice can't serve your people and make your daughter happy too. We will leave now as the weather won't wait and we have a difficult climb back up into the mountains."

Riding away later, Korban thought about Lanai, but soon turned his concentration to the upcoming trek. The Trantan soldiers and craftsmen were moderately competent, but the nobles and their families were burdensome right from the start, complaining often, demanding too many rests and breaks, and eating the food too rapidly without concern for eating up the considerable supplies before getting to the Vikar camp. Their children were spoiled imps, annoying the Vikar warriors terribly. With only Vikar children as a gauge, they had no experience with unruly child behaviors. When one impish son tried to order a Vikar warrior like a servant, it nearly led to a serious incident.

Once they got to the border and the nobles saw the mountains looming, Korban hoped they would turn tail and go back. However, surprisingly they stayed with the column and crossed into Strella, but the level of their grumbling increased as the terrain became more difficult.

It was several days into the climb approaching the border of Stakar when they got a surprise in camp. The princess Lanai rode in accompanied by five of her hand maidens. Korban wasn't surprised, nor were the other Vikar scouts. Interestingly, one of the young maidens was the same girl Korban had talked to outside the palace door when Lanai argued with her father.

Lanai leapt off her horse smiling broadly. "Gentlemen, it's good to see you. Our adventures continue."

"Princess," Korban replied, smirking.

The Trantan officer in charge attempted to approach the princess, but she angrily waved him away.

"I'm here, so leave it at that, captain. I and my maidens will be staying in the company of our Vikar friends. My maidens have secretly been working and training with me. They will now have the full benefit of the expert Vikar martial tutoring that I have enjoyed."

She turned back to Korban, "Let me introduce my ladies, Lucia, Wella, Mandia, Shana, and Lila. You met Lila who brought your message to me in my suites."

"Hello ladies, welcome to our camp. I do remember Lila, but I never got her name then. I'm Korban."

Lila replied. "We all know who you are, Korban."

The princess pressed him. "Do you agree to add them to our training sessions?"

"If that is your wish, your highness. I'm sure you told them it will not be easy."

"I did. They're eager to change their lives, as I did. The days of Trantan women cowering at the whim of some man are going to end."

The Vikar warriors all smiled ruefully.

"Indeed," Korban muttered. "I think maybe they already have."

Turning his head to the maidens, he said, "Your princess has lived among us, but she's a special person, driven in her goals, and relentless. If you think you can match that determination, we will aid you in your efforts. It falls upon you to do the hard work."

Lila replied, "We're ready, my lord."

The Vikar warriors chuckled.

"Lila, you do know I'm not a lord. The Vikar do not have royalty."

"You're royalty to us, my lord."

They heard cries of outrage from the nobles who were eavesdropping nearby. Korban walked over to them.

Grim faced, Korban spoke tersely. "This is a matter which does not concern you. Your princess has made her choices, as well as her associates. You're in the Vikar camp now, so you hold no sway here. You will hold your tongues, or you can leave right now to return to your own land. If these young ladies choose to better themselves, we see it as a good thing. Any questions?" Towering over them with his great stature, his icy facial expression silenced any response from the spineless nobles.

In spite of his warning, the nobles and their families continued to be an irritant, and their complaining actually escalated further. Having the escort of fifty Trantan soldiers seemed to give them a misplaced belief they had no consequences. However, those soldiers knew their numbers would not have prevailed against the twenty Vikar warriors. They couldn't even be certain their crown princess would side with them in a fight.

In their Trantan minds, it was the greatest of scandals the crown princess, and her young maidens, slept in the midst of the Vikar warriors, and not among the Trantan soldiers.

Korban ignored their ire concentrating on the most difficult leg of the journey, ascending into the mountains now snow covered and treacherous. No soldiers from Strella appeared, but when they crossed into Stakar territory, a column did approach.

Korban tried to act calm, but his troop was ready.

The Stakar leader rode close.

"I understand we are now allying; all of the tribes are to be as one. We saw you passing down the mountains earlier. It would seem your quest was successful as you still have your heads on your shoulders. The Vikar warriors chuckled.

"What is all of this? Who are these people you're dragging along?"

"We made a pact with Tranta. They agreed to lend craftsman to help us fortify our winter camp for the coming war."

"What war?"

"Tranta was attacked by vile creatures that live in the ground. They kill all in their path, and cannibalize the slain."

"We had not heard that. It is dire news. I understand more now about this strange banding together of the tribes."

"You'll need to turn to your martial skills in the future. I know you live to care for the animals, but tribal purposes are going to change for all the tribes. By the way, this is Lanai, the crown princess of the Tranta."

"It is my pleasure to meet you, princess. You're very lovely."

"Thank you. As Korban can explain, my focus is in perfecting my military skills. I would have a new way of living for all women."

"I see." He smirked at her, and then at Korban."

"Let me tell you, captain, what she says can't be taken lightly. She's fought men successfully already."

"That is remarkable. If you're agreeable, we'll ride with you up to the border into your realm."

"That would be appreciated. One can never have too many friends at hand in uncertain times."

"Perhaps we can see some of this female prowess you've mentored."

"I'll leave that decision to the Princess."

Lanai had been listening and watching the exchange, but turned her head away at the 'frank' perusal by the Stakar's warriors. When they snickered and muttered amongst each other, she reacted turning to face toward their captain.

"Perhaps you and your people should keep your eyes in your heads. This is unseemly treatment of a woman."

"We apologize," he replied, with no real contrition.

Korban recognized her rising indignation, and her simmering ire. He spoke to head off another of her explosions. "We need to be moving. There is too much to be done with too little time. The enemy can attack at anytime and anywhere."

The combined forces rode away climbing out of the Strella foothills going into the mountains of Stakar. Getting some separation from the Stakar forces, Lanai's foul mood gradually cooled. They were ahead in the lead with the Vikar vanguard guiding them toward the border with Vikar lands.

She rode beside Korban.

Turning his head, he asked. "Are you back under control?"

She glowered at Korban.

"I mean no offense. I must monitor any situation in my camp. Your battle readiness is among them."

"I can assure you, I'm more than ready to do battle. I can show you that when we stop if those Stakar buffoons need tutoring."

Korban chuckled. "I don't think that will be necessary, your majesty."

"You don't understand the life of a woman. We're taught from childhood that men are the superiors and we should defer to them. Why? Where did that come from? We should have been seen as more than just baby makers all along."

"I have no argument with you."

"I don't want an argument with you either. I'm just explaining the frustration of all women. Is that too daunting an idea for you to hear?"

"No, ma'am."

"Perhaps we should spar tonight."

"Do you feel I need to further hone my fighting skills?"

She glared. "We are definitely going to spar, Mr. man."

"As you wish, Miss woman."

"I will join my maidens now." She turned her horse to fall back to where they were riding.

Korban glanced back. One of his warriors muttered. "You have great skills with women. We are learning much."

Korban glowered. "Do not push me." His men chuckled.

The climb up the mountains was much slower than the descent had been for a variety of reasons, not the least of which was the annoying gaggle of royals. They amused the Stakar who only had to deal with them for a brief time.

Each night, the martial training and sparring sessions became the focus and main camp entertainment.

Lanai was showered with cheers and applause when she presented for any bouts. It annoyed and secretly pleased her both at the same time. Doing her utmost to appear the dangerous fighter, Korban battled her in a way not to humble her and expose her weaknesses. Those flaws, in her case, were receding as her strength continued to improve and her practices taught her a great deal. The maidens were still in fledgling stages so they posed no threat of being competent in any way. At this stage, they were mere pretty things performing for an adoring male audience.

Lanai made a point of keeping them segregated in the camp to avoid the attentions of the men. Many had ideas which the princess would not permit. Regardless, the maidens were agog. After a lifetime of subservience, to now have attention and celebrity as companions of the princess, it was a life they could only have dreamed of. In spite of their humble start, even in their cases, they all started to strengthen and improve. By the time they reached the border to go into Vikar lands, their steady progress was noticeable.

The Stakar captain engaged Korban and Lanai just before they left Stakar lands.

"This was good to spend peaceful time with you. It makes me wonder why the tribes had such rivalry and enmity all these years. I'm glad we're allied now."

"Thank you, captain. I feel the same. Stay safe and be on your guard at all times. Our new enemy slinks about very skillfully. They can turn up anywhere, so keep your camps alert and well-guarded."

"I hope we see you again." He smiled at Lanai.

She nodded to him, but acted aloof, and regal, turning her head away.

After they rode into Vikar lands, Korban spoke to her. "I think one of your skills is in making men feel pathetic and unworthy."

"I don't ask for their attention. If they learn to leave me be, I'm a happy person."

"Who could take exception to that?"

Lanai scowled at him. "You're a lout too. All women can see how confounding you are."

"Apparently."

She increased the pace of her horse to ride ahead to join the lead scout who was startled when she came up beside him, but he smiled.

"Princess, I must pay close attention to the trail and what is around us. If you want to talk, you should return to the main party."

"I have no need to talk. I'll watch your actions and learn about scouting."

"So be it."

"I want to learn all aspects of life as a Vikar."

"Yes, ma'am. You're well on your way."

She stayed riding with him through the stop at noon, and then resumed riding with him until the evening stop. He led the troop over to just within the tree line of a small grove of trees. Korban directed setting up camp. He always placed the nobles at the farthest point away from the Vikar troops that he could. They were always guarded in the night by Trantan soldiers.

On that particular evening, the lead scout shared something with Lanai that on this day, "Korban has now reached twenty snows in age."

Later, when Lanai congratulated him, he was at first confused.

"What?"

"This is the day of your birth, they tell me."

"I guess it is."

"Do you not celebrate your birthdays in Vikar lands?"

"My mother does some special things, but I've never been one to pay much attention to such things."

"In Tranta, we have grand celebrations of our major life events. I think we have a much better way than Vikar indifference."

Korban pondered whether to rise to the bait. He opted not and merely shrugged.

"Thank you for your royal enlightenment, princess. I will keep it in mind for the future."

Before she could tie into him, the nightly animal sounds around them abruptly ceased. Instantly the Vikar were alert and started to deploy. The confused Trantan troops saw the Vikar reactions but were slower to respond while the Trantan nobles responded not at all, standing agape like dull-witted sheep.

With the edge of the escarpment behind them, they arrayed facing toward the woods. Lanai donned her weapons, gathering her armed maidens around her.

In addition to the Trantan troops, the Trantan craftsmen armed themselves too.

Suddenly howling dark shapes raced toward them at surprising speed. Instantly, Vikar bows peppered them with arrows, and that included

Lanai firing well aimed shafts that found their marks. The attack into the teeth of Vikar skill and fury did not go well. However, they heard screams of terror to their side from where the nobles were camped.

Lanai leapt up along with her maidens and ran down the line to support the royal troops who had their hands full fighting the feral enemy charge. The princess started dropping enemy attackers with her arrows. Her maidens occasionally hit some targets with pure luck, but every little bit helped. Lanai whooped, drew her sword and raced into the midst of the royal troops. It startled them, but it also stiffened their backbones in the fight.

"Defend the princess," they shouted and hacked ferociously at their surging adversaries.

For Lanai, it was cathartic being able to exercise revenge. She fought doggedly but this was a serious threat and her opponents were equally driven. When they started to focus on her, she went into a defensive mode of fighting in order to survive. Each time she could slay an enemy, it seemed three jumped in to take its place. Her situation became gradually more precarious as she was pushed backwards. A determined enemy bowled into her legs as she fell to the ground imperiled with this creature on top of her. It snarled and snapped trying to bite her neck. Suddenly it was knocked off bodily by Korban's savage blow.

The Vikar warriors had wiped out the attackers against them and they rushed to rescue the other parts of the camp. The desperate Trantan soldiers were rescued and the remaining enemy attackers were quickly killed off.

Lanai stared at Korban wide-eyed. She expected him to berate her, but instead he lifted her to her feet. She embraced him tightly.

"Again, you saved my life. I know it was foolish for me to run here, but I couldn't let my people be slaughtered by these things."

"I understand why you did it. It was brave, but never forget, you can't allow them to kill you. You're the hereditary line to your throne. Your father would chase me to the ends of the world for revenge if you were lost."

"I'm sorry. I'll use better sense in the future."

"And I'll also use better sense. As much as your nobles annoy us, I shouldn't have put them so far away from our protection."

"We suffered some losses, both in Trantan soldiers and some civilians that the enemy could get to, and kill. It's horrible, their gnawing on people. We must find a way to wipe them off the face of the planet."

"Yes. I hope the nobles have gotten the message we need to get to the winter camp. We can't dawdle along any longer to suit their moods."

That night it was difficult for anybody to fall asleep. The sentries were doubled and kept closer to camp. In the morning, mostly everybody was poorly rested but they were up at dawn nonetheless and into the saddles riding at a faster pace to cover more ground. The incessant drone of the nobles complaining had ceased, and even their children acted much better. It was reassuring to hear the normal sounds of animals around them as they traveled.

The Vikar warriors never took chances and stayed especially vigilant the entire day and that night. The Trantan troops picked up on the necessarily increased caution and did the same. Trantans dying horribly before their eyes had gotten their attention. When the Vikar troops led Lanai and the maidens through their training sessions, on this night all of the Trantan troops joined in.

When they finally approached the Vikar winter camp after a lengthy journey, it was a different assemblage than had left Tranta. The Trantan troops were remarkably transformed into much better versions, the Trantan nobles had learned humility and restraint. They also learned to be thankful to the barbarian Vikar warriors for their lives. Lanai was far more accomplished as a fighter and her ladies had improved much.

The winter camp was greatly increased, not only with drawing in Vikar settlers but there were large groups visiting from Kominkar and Alkar. Work had started in making a huge outer perimeter for a proposed the new city. When Korban's group rode into camp, they had a quick meal and then the Trantan craftsmen jumped in to join the construction work.

The first thing they started to do was to start drilling deep into the ground. They had equipment, knowledge and skills in how to do this. Their head craftsman explained.

"If you housed a large city-type population and were cut off and besieged, it would be critical to have a dependable reliable source of fresh water. You can't be in a position to allow your enemy to starve you out. Once the wells are dug, there are other measures we must take regarding food stores."

Volta had come over and listened.

"This is very good. The Vikar people are grateful for your help."

"You're Volta? We've been told great things about you."

"I'm well past my time. Death and passing on to the next life are nipping at my heels. Look to Korban for a Vikar man of the future. He will have the remarkable life you seek, and he can save us all."

Lanai hugged Volta. "It's good to see you again. I'm glad all is well here in the camp."

"Thank you, princess. My worry is with time. I don't know what we can get done before time runs out. I fear there is more than just these cavemen for us to contend with."

The Trantan foreman replied. "We're going to join the work, but please come to us whenever you like, if you have questions, observations, or suggestions. Tranta is happy to be of help."

"Much of what you do is beyond my experiences, but as a curious spectator you'll see me often. Thank you, princess, and you, sir."

Timian had been standing nearby and walked over to Korban. He glanced at the princess and nodded to her. She smiled warmly.

"Hello, sub chief. As you can see, we've returned unharmed."

"I took a risk sending Korban out to lead the scouts with this task, but I wasn't worried. He's grown into leadership and there is no limit to what he can do. They tell me you had a scare while camped in Vikar lands, Korban."

"Yes, their attack was sudden and dangerous. There were a few royal soldiers lost, and some among their nobles."

"The nobles were foolish to come. They can't defend themselves and therefore are a burden on those who must. Their spoiled lives didn't prepare them for such a trek. It is fortunate for them that their losses were not worse."

"I agree, sub chief."

"What's this with the princess and her maidens fighting? What are you planning?"

"It was her wish to be able to defend herself, and she wishes for women to have better lives, ones of significance."

Volta spoke, "Princess, there could be no more significant life than what you will live."

"What, what does that mean?"

"It isn't something for me to explain. With time, you will see."

Lanai spotted Toli and Menga approaching. She hurried over into their hugs.

"I love you like mothers, or aunts of mine."

They chuckled.

"Let me gather my maidens and we can have some pleasant woman time together.

All the women went off to Toma's hut.

Volta and Timian looked at Korban watching her walk away. Timian spoke, "That princess is a wildcat. I wonder if there is any man who can tame her? I think not."

"I doubt it," Korban answered. "She will be more than a measure for any man or woman ever born. I agree with Volta she will have a significant life, and not just for Tranta, but for the whole world. I'm happy to have met her."

In the background, the Trantan craftsmen were already setting up equipment to begin digging the deep wells. Others of them went to join the construction of the perimeter walls of the developing settlement. Korban, Timian, and Volta followed them to listen.

The lead craftsman stood to explain to the workers, "These walls we will build must withstand the assaults of wars and sieges. There will be three layers needed, an exterior of thick wood beams soaked in fire retardant, an inside coarse of stones to add strength and durability, and then another layer of the thick wood on the inside the wall. On top will be a flat file for warriors to stand on and fire down into the enemy. The entrance gates will be wood, but heavy, thick, and reinforced like the protective walls. There also, we must construct them to withstand sieges. As you can see, we'll dig the wells deep to underground water sources so ample clean water will always be available, and we will build huge storage buildings for food stores. As I said, on top of the wall we build walkways for troops to stand and fire over the wall into the enemy soldiers. It's standard construction practice for fixed fortifications. Once the structures protecting the city are completed, we'll move on to build war devices to mount on the structure increasing our lethal force. We'll start with properly anchoring the walls digging deep with our foundations. We can't have this wall teetering under blows from enemy ballista, or ramming devices. Also, since the attackers live in the ground, we'll create deep defensive structures to keep them from being able to dig under the walls and emerge inside the compound."

He paused and looked at the faces of the Alkar and Kominkar workers, as well as the Vikar workers. There were no disagreements or comments.

"Good, let's get to work. We have much to do."

Korban turned to Volta. "It's easy to see the wisdom of your ideas and suggestions. What the Trantans bring to the mountain tribes is fortuitous. How did you know?"

"It isn't some great thinking of mine. As I sleep in my later years, my dreams stay with me. If I'm somehow getting thoughts from others, I can't say, but this is what guided me. I knew which day you would find me, Korban. This is how I was packed and ready to leave when you arrived at my door."

"I hope our enemy leaves us time to finish all of this work."

"I think there will be a great war and I believe we'll be ready for it. I have nothing other than my feelings about that."

67

"How did tribal workers know where to place the walls, and how large to make it?"

"I gave them my vision about it and none disagreed. It seems to work for our Trantan friends, so I feel I didn't misguide our efforts."

Korban and Timian chuckled. Timian noted, "Volta, there are none in our camps beyond you. Your help is a blessing."

Korban asked, "I haven't forgotten our lost girls. Do you foresee our finding them?"

"I didn't get any direction about that, but I won't rest until we right that wrong."

"It evokes me greatly."

Timian uttered, "It evokes the entire Vikar tribe."

They left the workers to their tasks and went to the chief's hut. Toma was there inside listening and laughing with the females in their chattering. Lanai's sometimes haughty manner had transmitted into her maidens. Their boasts and bragging tickled Toma, and then also Korban, Timian and Volta when they arrived.

Volta asked them slyly, "What have we wrought?"

Lanai heard him and turned her head. "You've wrought a new day. Women will finally make their mark."

Her maidens cheered, along with Toli and Menga. The men could only shake their heads.

That evening after an ample supper, Lanai gathered her maidens, joined by a number of Vikar women, to practice fighting. For the Vikar women, although they hadn't been formally trained, they were well versed in forest lore, rustic living, and skills with weapons seem to come naturally to them.

It was a lively session. The men were much amused. Women were loud in their efforts, whooping and crying out to the amusement of the male onlookers.

Meanwhile, work on the fortifications went well. Digging the wells moved along nicely until they reached a point of needing to dig through buried stone substrata, part of the natural formation of the mountains. It required craftsmen to descend into the shaft to physically hammer through the impediment, but also to remove chipped debris out of blocking the shaft. That slowed the progress of the work substantially. Additionally, being at that mountain altitude, the distance downward they needed to drill was considerable. The work on building the walls went much better. By the time the drill teams succeeded in reaching underground water tables, the walls were nearly built. Installing pipes to pump the clear clean water to the surface introduced a luxury the mountain tribes had never had. In addition to having water easily available, they were getting water which wasn't polluted with contaminants and diseases like river and lake water could have.

It had been a difficult effort to accomplish, and it took far more time than they'd hoped, but at last, they had a functional fortress city in the mountains.

With building the storage buildings for meat, grain, fruits and vegetables, and then also to store weapons, the site was increasingly more formidable. The Kominkar weapons masters started a steady stream of caravans of their highly crafted weapons. They intended to properly arm all of the tribes, and then potentially soldiers of the nations of the lowlands. A new troop arrived from Tranta including many more craftsmen. Those craftsmen started the construction of permanent winches to ferry people and materials up the cliffs saving on the long difficult circuitous ride Korban had taken. A permanent garrison of Trantan troops took up residence in a barracks in the expanded Vikar city.

By this time, each of the tribes were routinely interchanging visiting warriors with the other tribes in all the lands. The Vikar winter camp, now a large city, was named Warkine and became the power center and the central focal point for all the mountain tribes. Warriors from all five tribes now lived there. Soon members of all five tribes had sent contingent delegations to reside in the Trantan royal city, Tarium. The Kar tribes created their first ever embassies.

Universally, the mysterious Drackar were the most talked about, and feared. Dressed all in black when they came into Warkine, with wraps over their faces, their long column of warriors moved stealthily, even in daylight they looked all about, gauging levels of potential threats. Agile as cats, they exuded competence, and danger. Their profession as consummate assassins evoked a great deal of whispering and speculation. Seldom had anybody ever seen one in person and lived to talk about it. They'd been employed by leaders of the tribes for centuries, but only with feeling like they'd soiled themselves in doing so, indelibly staining their spirits.

Korban wasn't sure what to expect, nor anybody else.

The newly functional main gates opened to admit the long dark column riding into the large courtyard.

Toma came to stand beside the other tribal leaders, Eska of the Kominkar, Recka the Alkar chief, and Dorn, chief of the Stakar.

The Drackar contingent stopped. There were no visible signals anywhere, but they were coordinated in perfect sync. Two at the head of the column dismounted and approached the other tribal chiefs. Unwrapping his facial covering, for the first time the assembled saw a Drackar face, and their chief. He was heavily tattooed with jet black hair, muscular, and very confident in his mien.

Korban's glance strayed to Lanai to see her reaction. This confident man was handsome and she smiled at him. That irked Korban.

The Drackar chief walked up to Toma.

"I am Skarn, chief of the Drackar tribe. You are Toma, chief of the Vikar. You're known and respected by our tribe. Your warriors are well respected for their formidable fighting prowess. Moving down the line, he greeted the other chiefs by name.

"I'd like to introduce a comrade."

The other figure who'd come forward unwrapped and to their surprise, it was a woman.

"This is my fellow chief, Lena. In our tribe we have a male and a female chief, equal in all things."

She was also tattooed and also very attractive. Neither of those Drackar chiefs were old, by far the youngest of the assembled chiefs of the other tribes.

Toma spoke, "Thank you for coming. You're welcome here. Since you already know the other chiefs, I'd like to introduce one other distinguished guest. He nodded and Lanai walked forward. "This is Lanai, crown princess of Tranta."

Skarn smiled warmly at her and she returned a warm smile.

"It is my honor and pleasure to meet you, princess. We've heard about your harrowing journey, and your efforts to pursue martial skills."

"Thank you, chieftain. We know of you in Tranta."

She glanced at Lena who then spoke. "I was very anxious to meet you. You make an impressive appearance physically and in your regal manner. You're very lovely, princess."

Lanai eyed her thoughtfully. "Lena, you're very lovely too, but you know that. Why do I feel I don't have your respect?"

"Whatever gives you that idea?" Feinting false outrage, she didn't hide her smirk.

CHAPTER FIVE
Issues of Alliances

Korban was slightly confused as he observed the meeting, although fascinated by the dynamics of the actions of these two remarkable women. They were in a class of their own. Their reactions hinted to him at some form of rivalry, but Korban couldn't grasp it. With few prior close interactions to guide him, females were mystifying, and to an extent had always been.

Lanai spoke, with a piercing look. "Glib words and superficial actions don't fool me, madam chieftain. If we're now truly allies, I think you must consider new ways in how you act toward others. Don't you agree?"

"Well, first, I'm not married, so I'm not a madam, but I can't disagree with you. We do need to change our ways."

Lena laughed and glanced at her smirking fellow Drackar chieftain. "I like this very much, Skarn. We seldom get opportunities for such entertaining exchanges. Our usual encounters are of a much different nature."

"Yes, she is a delightful package, but she does make a good point. We're here to forge bonds of friendship. Can you be her friend?"

Lena laughed. "Of course. I think she wishes to school me about her idea of friendship."

Lanai's look hardened. "I'd be happy to teach you friendship, or anything else."

Lena laughed heartily. "I so look forward to that, your eminence. Is that the correct term to address you?" Her flippant tone irked Lanai.

Korban nearly rushed over. Lanai looked on the verge of drawing down on Lena. The possibility daunted Lena in no way at all.

Toma stepped in. "With introductions out of the way, can we invite you into my hut to share a meal. We have much to talk about, and time is not our ally.

"Of course," Lena replied. Grinning broadly, she winked at a glowering Lanai.

Servants guided the large contingent of waiting Drackar warriors to a barracks set aside for them while their chiefs were led away along with the other chiefs.

Korban was not a chief, so he didn't enter the hut. However, as the leaders started to walk away, Lena made a beeline for him. Lanai glared at both of them.

"You are Korban. We know of you. You have my great respect." She had a sparkling glint in her eyes, eyeing him appreciatively.

"Thank you, madam chieftain, or Miss. That means a great deal to me. Your renown goes without saying. I know nothing of your ways, but I suspect your training would be the envy of any peoples anywhere."

She smiled warmly. "You would be correct. We feel we're unmatched in our preparations and our high standards. You would have made a good assassin."

"Ugh...thank you?"

She laughed heartily. "I hope to spend time with you during our stay in your city. You're an intriguing man."

"I'm sure that can be arranged."

Even how she walked away as she left to join the other chieftains was compelling on a number of levels. A sensuous feminine manner combined with agile grace and lethal skills.

Timian sidled over. "Are you now in love with a second beautiful woman? Remember this one can easily slit your throat."

"No, I'm not in love with her, and yes, I'm well aware of her lethal skills."

"She is very impressive. I'm being forced to view women in a different way, at peril of my own life."

Both of them chuckled.

"It's about time, sub chief."

Meanwhile, Lanai noticed Lena staring her, and also following near to her. Later, when the maidens gathered for the nightly session, there were women from all the tribes gathered also, as well as Vikar warriors there to give the lessons. It irked the princess and made her feel self-conscious having so many Drackar eyeballs staring at her every move.

With the initial salvos, Lanai was a bit distracted, while also trying to see Lena's reactions. Her Vikar warrior trainer recognized it and made a feint and then an aggressive strike causing her to fall back to the parry the heavy blow. In spite of chuckles from Lena and her female assassins, Lanai focused quickly, gathering her wits to fight as if this was a real battle. The Vikar warrior was surprised at the sudden shift, but was well able to handle real battles. The contest drew the notice of the entire camp as Lanai refused to relent. Although she'd managed to quiet the mirth among the Drackar spectators, she was aware of the attention. Concentrating so intently on the fight, everything else faded out of her view as her battle focus took over.

At long last, her opponent stepped back. "Have you managed to sooth your anger yet?"

She smiled meekly. "Yes, I'm sorry. I'm sure I annoyed you."

"Actually, it was a great fight. I was honored to be part of it. Your skills have advanced remarkably, princess."

"Thank you."

She looked around for Korban, but first she was greeted by Lena.

"Was that performance intended for me? It was a nice entertainment. Thank you."

Putting aside her emotions with some difficulty, Lanai replied. "Your people don't spar and exercise to keep fit and hone a sharp edge?"

"We do. Honestly, I questioned the stories that came to us about your growing skills and prowess. Now I understand. Fighting a Vikar warrior evenly for such a long time is a commendable accomplishment. I applaud you for that."

"Thank you. I'm trying to bring a new day for all women. I was a princess in a gilded cage at home and it chafed me every single day in that condition. Meeting Korban gave me the chance to change my life. I think I'm moving in a good direction."

"You inspire me as I hear your aspirations. Women of the Drackar have always been on an equal footing with our men, but you're right. Every woman everywhere needs to break the chains men put upon them."

Lanai listened to Lena say the right things, but it was difficult to dismiss her niggling feelings, like something was amiss. Understanding what the assassins do as their work was chilling. She smiled at this formidable woman with the wonder if she could someday suddenly become an adversary, a deadly one. In her mind she pondered, *what if she...Can a person come to love taking lives?*

All of the Drackar people had a predatory look in their eyes that frightened, and that included their women.

Lanai could think of no ready reason to dismiss Lena, so when she followed Lanai into Toma's hut for the evening meal Lanai felt unnerved.

Toma and Toli acted pleasant. Skarn was already there. Rather than sit beside him, Lena chose to sit close beside Lanai. Touching her, eyeing her often, like they were sisters, or long-lost dear friends, Lanai was disconcerted. With Lena suddenly giving Lanai a hug, she was at a loss at how to cope with such unexpected familiar behaviors from this deadly woman.

Toli had cooked a large serving of her delicious stew. Receiving servings from Toli gave Lanai a brief respite as they ate the stew. Finishing their first helpings, Lena grinned at Lanai and patted her knee.

"Ah, this is nice, yes?" Lena commented. "We of the Drackar don't get enough of these pleasant social occasions outside of our tribe."

Skarn agreed. "I must say, I'm happy to have this great alliance of all the tribes."

Toma asked. "Don't you worry it will affect your business?"

Lena and Skarn laughed. Skarn replied. "Business, that is an interesting way of putting it."

Toma replied. "I hope you don't take offense as none was intended. For us, your profession is difficult to..."

"There is no offense taken. You have in your minds a view of us and our ways. The assassin work stemmed from the demand for such actions. We have always been kept very busy. Petty rivalries can often develop into feral actions. If you blame us for that, we think you're wrong."

"I hadn't thought of it that way."

"Perhaps we can speak of more pleasant topics," Toli suggested.

"Yes, of course."

Lena turned her head and smiled at Lanai. The princess still found it chilling, like someone stepping on her grave. This new found fascination about the princess for Lena was inexplicable for Lanai. She glanced at Lena with a weak half-smile.

"Our ways are different than yours, princess. Perhaps I can guide you to a better understanding? We're just another Kar tribe, no different than any other." When she talked to Lanai, Lena faced her fully, and tended to lean toward her. Touchy-feely acts from the queen of the assassins were not what Lanai expected. If this was usual behavior among the Drackar for friendship and relationships, Lanai couldn't decide. She tried not to visibly cringe.

After a moment to collect herself, Lanai eyed her skeptically. "Just another tribe? Really? However, certainly one cannot have too much knowledge. I'll grant you that."

Lena grinned. "Good, thank you, princess. I'm interested in hearing about your world and your life. We can both learn, wouldn't you say?"

"Yes?" Her stilted tepid reply tickled Lena who chuckled and patted Lanai on the knee, again. This time she rested it there before finally taking it away.

"This is so entertaining."

"I'm happy you're so entertained."

Skarn laughed too.

Lena turned to Skarn. "Can you see what I said. Is it not true this is a good new course for the Drackar people? Our past doesn't need to be our future."

"It is as you said. I had my doubts the other tribes would ever accept us. I think it will take some time to work past prejudices and concerns. This is a good start. Sitting in the hut of the Vikar chief for a meal would have been impossible not so long ago."

Toma reflected, "I agree that it will take some time to become comfortable in new ways, but it's worth the effort. Our new enemies won't care about our pasts, any of us."

"The Drackar fear no one, but this coming war worries us. It's part of why we agreed to an alliance."

"I believe we can blend our ways to get to better understandings among all the tribes."

"Yes, I look forward to it." Lena replied. "What do you say, princess? The Drackar have much to share with you that will benefit and enrich you."

"Eh...okay."

Toma continued. "Volta fears there is another force, or forces in the background. It's difficult to plan without knowing all of the truths."

"Volta is known and respected by all of the tribes. If he is worried, we are all worried. What word do you have from your people about extending the alliance to the other lowland peoples, Princess Lanai?"

"I'm sorry that I've heard nothing yet. I must tell you, I didn't really leave the palace with the permission of my father, the King."

Lena laughed. "I like you the more that I hear. You're our kind of woman."

Lanai shrugged her shoulders and continued, "As far as the lowland countries, we have contact and some ties with the Mantu and Strella. Some others of our traders have gone through the Crystal Pass into Lamali. They tend to be a solitary people and focus on a fleet to sail into the Ocean of Marm. Off their coast is the island of Iscali, but I know nothing of them there. To the south, we haven't really tried to have contact with peoples living on the Belshik Plateau, nor have we contacted the mysterious Greka peoples in the southern forest. We hear of the Isle of Doom below our continent though we know nothing about it, and to the south is another continent, but none have been there. I could ask our Vikar friends about the area north of the Alkar territory."

Toma answered. "It's an unexplored region. The climate is so severe, we doubt people could sustain living there. Beyond that we know nothing. The few brave warriors who tried to search that realm did not get far and were forced to turn back. Freezing to death is not much of an incentive to forge ahead. What of the Ocean of Tarsial off the coast of Tranta?"

"We do have fishing fleets and a small navy, but our focus has always been inland. There has never been an enemy approach from the sea. If there are hostile navy's out there, we don't know of them."

Lena asked, "What of the Mantu? They're your neighbors directly to your south."

"Mantu is a vast country with a vast population. They could have gobbled up Tranta long ago if they were of an aggressive warlike persuasion. Fortunately, we were no threat so they leave us be. Mantu is mostly grasslands and the Mantu pride themselves on their horse culture. Their herds of horses are too numerous to count. Horses, and their care, are like a religion to them. Their mounted forces are unmatched. If these Brogs wish to war with the Mantu, I think there will be many less Brogs running about. They would be good allies to have. Also, I forgot to mention south of our continent to the west of the Isle of Doom, is the Cornean Sea. There is a chain of islands there, but again, we know nothing. If these enemies come from the unknown areas, I can't say. Does this help you?"

"It does," Toma answered. "We must broaden our horizons beyond our mountains and just the Kar tribes and consider other possibilities."

Skarn mentioned. "Those southernmost realms are a very great distance away. I don't think any Kar tribesmen have traveled there."

Toma replied. "I believe you're right. I think mountains continue down much of the western coast, but none of our tribes ever moved there. If there is a hazard keeping us away from that area, we don't know of it."

Lanai explained. "The climate is much warmer there. Perhaps that didn't suit your ancestors who favored colder climes."

"That's true. We still favor the cooler weather."

Toli asked, "Did everybody get enough to eat?"

"Yes," they all said. Skarn arose. "We'll return to our people now. Thank you for the good food and the talk." Lena didn't immediately stand. Lanai glanced at her. Lena turned her head, grinning. She always seemed to show a mischievous smirk. It was difficult for Lanai to interpret her continued fascination.

"I will see you again, princess." She smiled even more broadly.

"I don't doubt that." She eyed Lena ruefully.

Lanai didn't get up until the Drackar pair left the hut.

"I find our new friends off-putting."

Toma and Toli chuckled. "They are a different sort." He replied.

"I feel the need for some exercise. I'm going to find my maidens."

Later, when she squared off for some relaxed sparring, they were surprised when Lena appeared along with some of her female assassins.

"Perhaps we can join you, princess?"

"We didn't intend anything rigorous tonight. Just some light exercise."

"That would be fine for us. After that full meal, we can use some gentle work."

Lena didn't wait for an answer. She shed her cloak, as did her women. They were scantily clad and for the first time, Lanai saw the tattoos weren't only on their faces. They covered all of their bodies.

She walked up to close Lanai. "Have we managed to capture your interest? These body markings all have significance. If you look closely, you'll notice they are different on each one of us. Perhaps you can say, we ascribe something of a religious, or a mystic connotation for our tribe reflected on our bodies. What do you say?"

Lanai took a quick glance at her supple, curvaceous, and very fit body, rapidly averting her eyes. Lena displayed her body readily and unabashedly.

"They're...different." Lanai muttered.

The Drackar women laughed.

"We're not shy about showing our stories, princess. We're proud of how we look. I can set you up with our artist if you'd like some of the body markings of your own."

"That won't be necessary. You're all very fit and attractive women, but these markings are not my taste. I mean no offense."

"None taken."

Moving ahead, like she was in charge, Lena paired her women with Lanai's maidens.

The initial action was relaxed, but gradually, the Drackar ladies ratcheted up the speed and intensity. Before long, Lanai was in a testing battle with Lena. Lena was strong and very good, but Lanai was determined not to buckle under the attack. Her maidens who were far less trained fell away rapidly in their bouts. They weren't at a stage to fight at this high level, yet.

When Lanai was the last one standing, Lena honed in with dizzying strokes that Lanai could barely deflect. After what seemed like days to Lanai, Lena stepped back.

"You have exceeded my expectations. It's obvious to me you're new to fighting, but your prowess in so short a time amazes us. I thank you for the match. I think we can teach you some helpful things in many areas, if you're agreeable."

"We're always willing to learn new things. Thank you for the offer."

"Think about my other offer. You'd look good with body markings." She grinned, eyeing Lanai's entire body.

"I'll pass on that offer." She smiled ruefully, shaking her head, crossing her arms protectively from their avid scrutiny. That made the Drackar women chuckle.

Lanai's maidens gathered around her happily, like she'd won a great battle.

Lila chirped, "my princess, who've done Tranta proud. I'm sorry we were so weak."

"You're not weak, Lila. You'll get to where I am, but we both know I have a long way to go. She was true in saying I have much to learn. Perhaps our new Drackar friends can provide us valuable guidance and training. Obviously, we'll continue our main tutoring with the Vikar masters."

Mandia asked, "Do you think these Drackar folks intend to teach us to be assassins?"

Lanai snickered. "I don't believe so. That's funny, Mandia."

Meanwhile, Korban came to Toma with a request. "My chief, I'd like your permission to take a force of the brethren back to the area of the summer camp. I want to carefully search the area for any subtle clues we may have missed before. Our girls have been in the hands of these Brogs far too long. If they've been killed, we need to know that, and if there are hidden pockets of Brog, they need to be rooted out and destroyed."

"Yes, Korban. Take as many warriors as you wish."

When he went to gather a force of the men he trusted as the best, Skarn wandered over.

"What is this you're about?"

"We want to find our captured girls. We're returning to our summer camp to begin a deep search."

"Would you permit I and members of my tribe to help you. We are very detailed in everything we do. Perhaps you'd find us a boon in your search."

Korban pondered a moment. "If that is your wish, we welcome your help. It's something of a far journey."

"That isn't a problem. My people can get restless sitting around. Normally we're very busy."

"We'll leave immediately."

"I'll gather my best warriors. Thank you, Korban."

Korban was surprised that nearly all of the male Drackars joined the expedition. The force Korban led out of the gates numbered over a thousand fighters.

Skarn rode beside Korban to talk during the journey. They traveled at a steady pace.

"Korban, I'm curious about this Trantan princess. She is as appealing a woman as I've ever seen, and yet she craves to be a consummate fighter.

81

With her life of pampering in her palace, it's strange to me. Why do you think she's doing it?"

"Well, she says she hated her life of semi-imprisonment and wants a new way for all women. I have no reason to doubt her. She's the most determined person I've ever met, male or female."

"There's much talk in your camp she's taken a liking to you. That she followed you here against the wishes of her father and her King. Is there a budding relationship I should know about?"

"There is no romantic connection, Skarn. Does that matter?"

"If she's looking outside her people for a mate, perhaps I should express my interest to her."

Korban eyed him dourly.

Skarn laughed. "So, there is a bond in your heart. I suspected as much. When she fought Lena, I saw you twitch and twist on every blow. You were highly invested in her efforts."

"I only wanted my training to be adequate to the test."

Skarn laughed again. "Your explanation is partially true. I believe the full truth goes far beyond just caring for a pupil."

"Skarn if you want to present yourself to the princess as a suitor, that is your choice. She can decide if she's interested in a life of assassinations. I'm sure Trantan people would love to have an assassin sit on their throne."

"You wound me, Korban. I haven't besmirched Vikar ferocity or intentions."

Korban glanced at him. "Is this your plan, to annoy me during this entire long ride to the summer camp?"

Skarn laughed again. "No, but I warn you the Drackar people are very curious. We seek out the truth in all things. You will see our dogged ways will help in the search for your stolen girls."

"I would hope so. Perhaps your seeking about the princess can wait for other days?"

"Fair enough. Now...you're young to have a command of Vikar warriors. I admit you're very strong, but how..."

"Perhaps I did something right?"

Skarn was fully entertained. "Yes, perhaps you did do something right."

"I'm going to ride ahead to join the vanguard. I want to discuss what's ahead and my instructions about possible perils. I trust you can find others here to question in the meantime."

Korban didn't wait. He spurred his horse leaving Skarn behind.

Skarn had managed to put the thought of Lanai back into his head. She was never easy to dismiss. He scowled and tried to do just that, without success. The image of her stunning face and lively eyes plagued him still.

Once he reached the lead scout, the best in the Vikar tribe, Marka, he eased back to match his pace.

"Korban? Is there something wrong?"

Marka was somewhat older than Korban, and among the most respected of the entire large Vikar tribe. He'd earned his esteem over many years of hunts and skirmishes. Marka had an uncanny sense for danger. Any column with him leading the way virtually never had mishaps. His full beard lent a grisly appearance making him look particularly fierce.

"There is nothing wrong, Marka. That Drackar chief was pestering me about the princess. I needed some distance to escape his irksome questions."

Marka smiled, but it was always difficult to tell with his mouth buried in the thick beard.

"You know there is much talk about you and her. You shouldn't let this disturb you. Tongues will wag whether you like it, or not. Don't waste your time thinking about that. We have a serious mission here to find our precious girls. That is what to think about."

"Of course, you're right. Thank you, Marka."

"It may be these Drackar warrior's help will be vital. Let the silliness wait until we return to camp. Then you can claim your bride."

Marka laughed heartily, as did the other scouts in the vanguard.

"Why did I think to find clear heads here among my brothers, instead of more wagging tongues and silly taunts?"

"We're not taunting, Korban. You know that. We're amused this rare prize has set her eyes on you. Who can say where this will go?"

"I certainly can't. Coming back to the mission. You're probably already doing it, but I want to look for signs of this enemy along the way too. We can't say where they came from or where they went. My thoughts are if you see anything unusual, we should investigate. Do you agree?"

"Yes, I had some of those same thoughts. I'm going to have my scouts' fan farther out on both sides of our trek to look for signs."

"Don't let anybody get out of sight. If somebody stumbles onto any Brogs, we want ample men nearby for that fight."

"I'll do it. With the cold season, it's easy to see farther into the trees which helps us."

It was a prophetic adjustment in their approach. Korban was still talking to Marka when a Vikar scout called out to them. He was partially up a rise. The troop thundered over to the hill.

There was a large area of fresh soil. Marka jumped off his horse along with Korban, kneeling down at the edge.

Marka spoke, "These are creatures that live in the ground, this could be a place they dug into, do you agree?"

"I do, Marka. We brought Trantan digging tools with us."

In the meantime, the balance of the force arrived. Instantly, Skarn was all business, examining the site carefully.

"I think this may be what you're looking for. Our opinion was the mountains would have been too tall for them to dig up through, not even considering the impediment of the mountain bedrock. I think they came over the ground and picked places to dig as their camps. This site may or may not have Brog down there but I think this is their work."

Korban spoke. "There's only one way to find out."

The digging was fairly easy in the loose soil and they made rapid progress. The Brogs digging had been on an angle. Within an hour they broke through into the makeshift Brog underground site. It was empty, but at least now the troop had an idea what to look for. They didn't bother refilling the opening.

Over the next week, they discovered more Brog excavations, but they found no Brogs, or Vikar prisoners.

Skarn was a much different riding companion as they honed in on the excavations. "Korban, how far is it to your summer camp?"

"I would guess only a few days at most."

"It's difficult to know if these digging sites were a single Brog force, or whether separate groups."

"This is why I brought such a large force. I wanted to be ready for anything. I will say, having your numbers with us is reassuring."

"It's a rare treat for us to share missions with our Kar brethren. The tribes should never have been allowed to become isolated and fearful of each other."

"Hopefully we've moved into a new day. It's too bad it took this serious threat to bring us together."

"Yes, it is."

One of the scouts called out. They went to join him. Here was the largest excavation they found, by far. The dirt was very fresh.

"Perhaps," Skarn muttered.

The entire command surrounded the site digging fiercely. Unlike the other sites, they broke through nearly immediately. Startled Brogs yelped as Vikar and Drackar warriors flooded into the underground camp scything them down.

It was not a small gathering. Other Brogs streamed out from within like a plague of locust, but they met savage deaths from Kar swords and bows. The fight went on for nearly an hour before they honed in on the head of the Brog force. He was a thick necked, taller being, strong and dangerous. Korban worked his way to the front of the battle to challenge the being. He snarled and roared, battle-frenzy in its eyes. Korban had no less hatred and started the deadly fight battling his enemy with all his might. The Brog attacked aggressively, but Korban countered every move following quickly with countermoves that gradually put the Brog on the defensive. Meanwhile the other Brog fighters were being exterminated. Because there were so many, it took time. The Brog attackers never surrendered.

The Brog leader seemed tireless maintaining a deadly level of fighting the whole time. Korban would not relent. The thought of Lanai was in his head, not disappointing her, remembering her ultimate determination and perseverance. Noting before his biggest swings, the Brog slightly dropped his shoulder, Korban waited and struck ducking and swinging under the swipe of the Brog. His eyes bulged as Korban's sword plunged into his chest. Dropping to his knees as Korban pulled out the sword from the killing blow, the Brog spoke in perfect Vikar.

"I protected your young ones."

He fell over. At that moment they heard squeals from the back of the cave. The warriors found the girls huddling there. Bringing them out, they were caked in mud and soil, but alive. Once it dawned on them that they were actually rescued, they cried out and hugged their Vikar and Drackar saviors.

Korban led the command out of the excavation into the sunshine and clear air. The girls were taken to a nearby stream to be able to wash off the caked-on dirt and mud and then to get some food and water.

Afterwards, Korban sat down with them to talk. They sat close together; many were hugging each other. "Is anybody hurt, did they hurt you?"

The bravest of the girls spoke for them all. "It was very scary, but they didn't harm us. We talked together, but being always in the dark was terrible. I wondered if we'd ever see the sun again. They did feed us, but it wasn't good Vikar food. I'm not sure what it was, but we ate it in order to live. That chief talked with us every night. I'm not sure why he tried to act kindly. It could have been so much worse. That day they came to our camp, it was horrible. What they did to the elders, it will never leave our minds. For that part, I'm glad you killed them all." She paused a moment before continuing. "Will the people forgive us?" She eyed him sadly.

Korban was moved by her plea and her worries.

"You have no wrong in this. You're girls. It's a miracle we'll celebrate that you're still alive."

"Truly?"

"Truly. Your families have missed you terribly and feared the worst. It took great courage for you all to persevere. It will be a joyous event to bring you home back into their loving arms. We're living at the winter camp. You'll find much has changed. The tribes have banded together and we've had help building defenses at our camp."

"I can't wait to see my family" The girl started to weep which caused the other girls to weep. Korban and the other warriors gave the girls hugs, further proof to them they really were rescued and safe.

Packing up the troop they started the ride for home. Each of the girls got a seat on a horse in front with a Vikar warrior. Korban took the brave spokesperson of the girls onto his horse into his arms. It wasn't hard to imagine if he had a daughter, having someone to love and cherish.

Each day they traveled; the girls got happier. At night they sat close with their guardian warriors, as if they'd been adopted by big brothers. Being outside in the fresh air was like a tonic for their spirits. Even with the cold weather, it wasn't a problem as the warriors wrapped them in their cloaks hugging them as they rode during the day and then at night they were wrapped in warm blankets in camp.

There was no further sighting of Brogs and in time they approached the now formidable walls of the Vikar city. There were now sharpened spikes sticking out of the top of the wall on an angle to make it nearly impossible to scale the walls.

Korban's passenger asked meekly. "What is this place? Do we live here?"

He gave her a hug. "Yes, we've fortified the winter camp. The Brog may plan on warring with all the Kar tribes. You'll see there are people here from the other four tribes, just as you saw Drackar warriors riding with us to find and save you."

"So, my family is here?"

"Yes, darling, you'll see them in a moment."

Riding up to the open gate, the column rode inside to the cheers and celebration of all the people. With the people crowding around, crying out the girls were finally reunited with families and able to go to new homes safe in the city.

Predictably, there was a great fest that evening as everybody celebrated the miraculous rescue and safe return of the girls.

The princess sought out Korban, even with Skarn standing with him and Lena joining Skarn, she stepped close to Korban.

"Returning in triumph, I see. Congratulations. You're building quite a following among your people, and that includes from the other tribes."

Korban struggled against his strong urges to keep from grabbing her up in his arms. "Thank you, your highness. We did what we could."

"You did much more than that. I wanted to tell you also, I heard from the Trantan palace. Although my father isn't happy that I left without his permission, he has moved on. Also, he's very impressed with what we're doing building this great city. It seems he's decided to defer punishment and to allow me to live. This plan of his to marry me off to some stuffed shirt is on the back burner, at least for the moment."

"This is what you wanted, to choose your own path."

"Yes, it is. His marital plans are never going to happen, even if I must live alone."

"That doesn't sound like much of a life, princess."

"That from a solitary man seemingly content to stick his head in the sand."

"What? What does that mean?"

"I'm sure if you think hard, you can figure it out."

He glanced at Lena when she chuckled.

"What?"

Lena asked, "Are you typical of every Vikar warrior?"

"Perhaps, what is it you mean?"

"Do you really expect us to believe you don't understand what the princess is telling you? I didn't take you to be a blockhead."

"Perhaps you should explain it to me." He scowled at her.

She laughed and started to speak.

"No Lena, leave it be." Lanai interrupted.

Korban glanced at Skarn would was also highly amused.

"Did you want to add anything, Skarn?"

"I doubt I could add anything you care to hear."

"I agree."

Korban turned his head as he felt a tap to his shoulder. The young girl he'd saved and had ridden with him, the vocal girl, eyed him shyly.

"May I speak to you?"

"Yes, what is it?"

"I'm Kiya. My parents wanted me to express their deep thanks for saving us."

"That isn't necessary."

"I wanted to know if you'll allow me to learn to fight from the princess and these other women. I know I'm not full grown, but I badly want to learn to fight. Being helpless is not acceptable. I learned that lesson very well sitting in that dark hole."

"It's not for me to say what you can do. If your parents want this, you should speak directly to the princess. She's standing right here."

"I didn't know if we were allowed to speak to her."

Lanai laughed. She knelt down, smiling warmly. "Kiya, there are no rules forbidding our contact. You're more than welcome to join us, and any of your friends."

"That would be so wonderful. Can I go to tell them?"

"Yes, you can. I look forward to seeing you all." She looked at Lena. "Is this acceptable to you? I assume you'll be there helping us with the teaching."

"I'm happy you'd include us. Of course we're interested, our children are our treasure and we start to teach them at an early age."

"I assume you don't mean teaching our girls assassinating."

Lena snickered. "No, princess, I agree that would not be appropriate."

CHAPTER SIX
The road untraveled

When Lanai gathered her maidens and the large number of Vikar women looking to add martial skills to their abilities, the number of girls who appeared were far more than just the rescued girls. They were nearly all of the girls in the city.

To singularly teach such a vast throng wasn't realistic, so Lanai delegated her maidens, Drackar women, and the most skilled members of her early recruits to take segments of the throng for training in manageable groups. The children greatly benefitted by inclusion in the structured women's group and the quest for competence began. Having women involved helped organize and direct the girls in constructive ways.

The first day was predictably chaotic, but everybody persevered through the day battling doggedly. In spite of swords frequently knocked out of untrained hands, the new recruits stayed focused. Still, there was a sense of play among the younger ones, chuckling and joking. With more time, and stern women correcting child distractions, that would change.

It left many men making their own meals at lunch time and feeding the little children. Meanwhile, Korban led his warrior brethren out into the countryside to hunt for enough food to provide for the huge number of mouths they needed to feed.

During this time, inter-tribal travel became routine as old animosities faded away. That the Drackar could go about peacefully to the other tribes was a remarkable success. Their primary occupation dissipated substantially to the point of disappearing. Seeing them assume normal duties went a long way toward appeasing fears of them. However, other tribe members didn't really rush in to find Drackar husbands, or brides. That was a slower moving process.

The Kominkar especially were overwhelmed with demands for high caliber weaponry, the finest of blades, spears, battle axes, maces, and other implements of war. Arming the women called for considerable new armaments. Crafting weapons girls could use was another adjustment for Kominkar craftsmen. Of course, when the girls got to take that step into training, the boys were not far behind, forming their own teams of young fighters in training. Vikar warriors were forced to make efficient use of their time between training the masses and still managing to hunt for sufficient food. Kominkar miners worked overtime in mountain mines continuously providing the ore and raw materials for the weapons their craftsmen were making.

Korban rarely went to the training sessions. He did make cameo appearances as a warrior of incredible renown from time to time, but the time-consuming tedious sessions, he left to others.

A month into this new world, he started to get restless. Going to Toma's hut, it happened Timian was also there talking with Skarn.

"Am I interrupting, gentlemen?"

"Come in, Korban," Toma replied. "You know you're always welcome here. How is Shosa, that old grizzly bear? I hear that he grumbles when Menga isn't home to feed him when going away, she 'idles' with the other women, to use his words."

"He's still old and grizzly, and yes, he grouses a great deal. My chief, I wonder if all this time we're taking is wise. I don't say it's bad to train our people, I'm thinking we also need to act about the enemy threat. That nest of Brogs were living right under our noses. How many more could be out there in the area, and whatever else is there in the way of threats?"

"Did you have something in mind?"

"I would like to lead another expeditionary force farther afield. Perhaps to hit some 'out of the way' places."

"What spots?" asked Skarn.

"If I go west through Alkar territory, and then into Drackar lands to eventually hit the coast of the ocean, I can turn south to see if this is a route the enemy is using to place their forces within our midst here in our mountains."

"That would mean possibly crossing very high mountains. It is where the Peak of the Moon and the Plateau of Heaven are located. The climate is always difficult, nearly as bad as in the unexplored region to the north. Going south from there you must cross the Valley of Fire which is dangerous in a different way. Peaks there can erupt and spew hot lava at any time. It's a difficult trek to cross. If you got through, you would eventually enter the Lamali lands. They don't court visitors and strangers are not welcome. As far as reaching the Lamali's coast to try to sail to Iscali Island, that is a huge question in itself."

"Have you been to these places, Skarn?"

"I have traveled some, but with our tasks, we seldom have enough time for exploring. I won't say this trek can't be done, but it's very risky, and if the benefit of reaching those lands make it worth it, I doubt it."

"That is a dour view, but I'm not dissuaded. I believe I can find hearty Vikar lads willing to serve the needs of the people."

The men chuckled.

Skarn replied. "Don't so easily dismiss what I'm saying, my friend."

"I'm not, but life is hazardous by nature. We must battle the elements constantly. I'm willing to feel that meeting the Lamali will be worth it. Perhaps part of your problem with them, Skarn, is your pleasing personality and reputation of killing everybody in sight?"

"Ah, another swipe at the Drackar, Korban. Someday I hope you'll come to peace with us. We're Kar tribe members too. If we were to completely stop our work, do you think the demand from the other tribes would cease? I think not. You don't know how often we're requested."

"I was just trying to add to your perspective, Skarn."

"I have sufficient perspective, Korban."

"Perhaps the Lamali don't like tattoos?" Everybody laughed but Skarn.

"Ah yes, enjoy your moment among friends, Korban. I guarantee there will be no mirthful moments in the places you're choosing to go. It will be a battle against the elements merely to survive inhospitable environments. I can't go myself as chief of the Drackar, but I can offer good people to join you. There are a few here that have been to those difficult regions, so they can aid you on such a quest."

"I welcome the help."

"With you gone, I'll present my romantic charms to the princess. If you make it back, I may already be wed to her."

"A Drakar King for Tranta? What a prospect. I'm sure Lanai will jump at the chance. Toma, what do you say about my ideas?"

"I understand your reasons for the journey, Korban. I also hear Skarn's warning. Can I afford to commit key warriors and an esteemed member of the tribe to the risk, and for a large time span? I need to think about this, and talk to the council."

"I'll await your decision."

"If I were younger, I'd want to go."

"You'd be welcome, my chief."

"Those wild days are over for me."

"I'll return to the hunt for food in the meantime. By the way, a Kominkar master craftsman presented me with a newly made sword. He said it's the finest he's ever made and that I deserved to have the best weapon. It even has some jewels in the hilt. I was honored, and I must say I think he's right. The balance, the new type of metal he used, the razor edge that stays sharp and isn't affected by the impacts of fights, I feel a better warrior now, though I doubt I deserve it."

"That's excellent, Korban, and never doubt yourself."

"I asked him to make such a weapon for Lanai. She needs it to fend off the clumsy advances of the Skarn's of the world."

Skarn eyed him ruefully as Korban snickered.

"Well, I'll be going. If you can talk to your people in the meantime, Skarn, I'd appreciate it. If I get permission from Toma, I'll leave nearly immediately."

"I will, my friend. Good hunting."

Korban left the hut, headed for his men to gather a hunting party, and then they mounted their horses and rode off as the huge gathering of trainees went through their exercises. It was a cold crisp day, cold enough that their breath billowed out visibly in little puffs from the men and the horses. Although the sun was up, in the mountains it didn't warm the air. The warriors were dressed in furred coats to stay warm. Freshly fallen snow from the night before wasn't yet deep enough to impede their ride. With the trees bared, they could see greater distances. However, animals weren't clearly abundant to see. The higher amount of hunting parties made them wary in addition to culling their numbers a bit.

Korban was forced to travel farther afield seeking his prey. They turned north going into Kominkar lands. They met a Kominkar hunting party and both joined together to cover more ground. Eventually finding herds of deer, they took only what they thought was the minimum necessary. These herds needed to replenish their losses too.

Camping at dusk, Korban showed off his new sword to the Kominkar warriors. They were agog. Easily recognizing the work of their greatest master, the fact he'd selected Korban to receive it lent great credence to him as a man of great significance in the eyes of these Kominkar tribesmen.

"This is truly an exceptional piece. We know your name in Kominkar. It's an honor to meet you."

"I don't think it's an honor for you. I'm just a man like any other."

"What you have already accomplished is remarkable. At your age, to have enough of a full life, filled with the remarkable, it dazzles us."

"I hope that's true. Now let's share a meal, my friends. There is always too much yet to do."

They were several days ride away as they started for home the next morning. A hungry pack of wolves shadowed their ride, but didn't come close enough to attack.

"They probably smell blood and the meat from our kills," Korban muttered. The nearby warriors nodded at the rhetorical statement.

When they finally arrived and went through the city gates, the women were still busily perfecting martial skills. The exercises looked better organized and the women, and girls, looked a bit more practiced. Lanai was on a platform overseeing the routines. She glanced briefly at Korban and his party. The meat was off loaded into the hands of older women who weren't pursuing any war skills. The men helped them lifting the heavy carcasses and then helped them dress the kills to extract the meat.

Korban helped with the work. When he came out afterwards, Lanai was walking by.

"Korban the butcher? Is this your new occupation? You have blood everywhere on you."

"I haven't been able to clean up, yet. I'm just helping out, ma'am."

"I heard about your proposal to travel to distant places. Since you didn't invite me, am I not welcome?"

"This will not be an easy mission, and we have no idea what we'll find. I didn't exclude you. I thought you were busy with training the women."

"I don't personally do much now. They can carry on without me."

"If your father was angered you defied him before, what would he say now about taking such a serious risk like this, crown princess of Tranta?"

"He has his opinions, and I have mine."

Korban smiled. "You have a rebellious and contrary nature, my lady."

"What nature do you have, esteemed warrior? I can say you do as you please. Why am I not accorded that same right?"

"I honor the dictates of my chief, Lanai. That's the difference."

Her eyes narrowed and he expected a tirade. However, she changed to a calculating look. "You're right. I've found great interest in talking to Menga and Toli about your youth. I think you're not one to call me rebellious."

"Are you going to draw down on me?"

She laughed. "I should, you great pompous oaf. Korban the mighty, terror of the world."

"I think I'll go to find Toma, to see if they've made a decision."

"I'll walk with you. By the way, did I tell you Toli and Menga have taught me to make your Vikar stew? Now you know I can cook."

"You did not tell me. It's good to know you won't starve."

Lanai turned her head to scowl to him. "Why are you always so dense?"

"What do you mean?"

Can you not comprehend anything? I...eh, well...just forget it, Korban." She grimaced.

"You're the strangest princess I've ever met."

"I'm the only princess you've ever met."

Going into the hut of Toma, they walked into the aroma of stew cooking over a fire.

"Welcome," Toma said. "Your timing is perfect. Toli made plenty of food."

"I wasn't intending to intrude on your meal. I wondered if you've made a decision on my mission?"

"We talked a great deal. There are many aspects to consider. You already know the great risks."

"So, what did you decide?"

"Not everyone agreed, but enough did to allow your venture. I'd say you should take sufficient numbers to ward off any attack, but not enough that you appear to be invaders. Also, the more warriors you have, the more supplies you'll need, and the more time needed hunting along the way."

"I've thought about that. Skarn offered Drackar warriors to join us. I was thinking perhaps we include a contingent from every tribe. "

Lanai piped in. "I'd like to include some Trantan soldiers too. My father would want to be a part of this mission."

Toma replied. "The council felt around a thousand members, more or less, should be the most we send."

"I agree. Have the other chiefs been informed?"

"Yes, they've picked who they feel are the best candidates. I think you'll find the greater number are younger men."

"There are no women included in your plans?" Lanai questioned. "Why?"

"Lanai, this will call for the keenest of skills which means experienced people. Your women are progressing nicely, but such an onus as this is beyond them at this point. They need more time."

She got a calculating look.

"No, princess," said Korban.

"I said nothing."

"I know you think to try your tricks and would ride into our camp later."

"That's a good idea. Thank you for suggesting it."

They glowered at each other.

"Let's eat," said Toli, to break the impasse. She'd already started ladling bowls with the stew.

Korban ate more than his usual ample helpings. Walking home stuffed, he thought about Lanai the entire time. Having her on the trip was both alluring and annoying at the same time. Her presence in his life was blotting out the person he'd been before her rescue. He pondered that reality, *Is that a good thing?*

It took a week before arrangements were completed. There were a hundred warriors each from the Alkar, Kominkar, and Stakar, two hundred from the Drackar, and the other five hundred were Vikar, along with the token force of Trantan soldiers. Also, to his surprise, Korban was named as another sub chief of the Vikar tribe. He was the youngest warrior ever to be accorded such rank and esteem.

He looked around for a reaction from Lanai, but she was nowhere to be seen. Skarn came over with Lena.

"She and her maidens left the city. I don't know if they intend to return to their royal palace in Tranta. No one knows."

Korban looked at Skarn. "I'm sorry, it appears your romantic plans to marry a princess have been cancelled as well as your plans for taking the throne of Tranta. Princesses are fickle creatures."

He smiled wryly. "Safe journey to you, my friend. My people can guide you most of the way. Be very careful out there. All of these other people we're looking to enlist as allies may not be interested. They can be a threat too."

"I will, and thank you. If the princess returns, tie her down so that she doesn't come traipsing after us."

Lena laughed, patting Korban on his broad shoulder. Smiling, she added. "Be cautious out there." She gave him a firm hug.

At long last, a great crowd gathered to watch and cheer the departure of the small army of their finest. Some Drackar warriors joined Korban's Vikar scouts in the vanguard riding steadily toward the west.

Korban rode at the head of the main column. They placed the train of pack animals in the center of the formation with Vikar contingents at the front and the rear of the procession. With a week of travel, Korban began to think perhaps the princess had gone home. It took another week to reach the far border of the Alkar. An Alkar patrol rode up to them looking alarmed.

"What has happened. Is there something we need to know? We've seen or heard nothing unusual."

Kordan explained. "We're traveling all the way west to the ocean and then turning south to go down the coast to make contact with the Lamali and then to possibly sail to Iscali island."

"That is a very difficult journey. Can it be done going that way? The Valley of Fire is said to be deadly with lava. Even the air is hazardous to breathe."

"We're going to test ourselves against it."

"We have a small fort nearby. I see you have Alkar warriors among you. Perhaps you'd like to stop there for the night?"

"Thank you."

Korban called forward the Alkar troops to join the vanguard patrol in leading them to the Alkar fort.

When they were welcomed inside the walls, Korban and his leaders were taken to the commander's office. Walking in, they were all shocked and dumbfounded. There sat Lanai, along with her maidens. She smiled mischievously.

"It took you long enough to get here, Korban. We've been here for days."

She laughed at the look on his face, as did her maidens.

He was at a loss at what to say. Starting an argument or trying a dressing down of a royal princess would not be a good choice, so he said nothing.

Lanai's smug look irked him, but he was a sub chief now and carried the onus of a far greater responsibility. Acting punitive would seem small and served no good purpose at this point. She was already here.

The garrison troops at the fort were cordial, but as with every place they went, the Drackar were off-putting for those who'd never met them. They always had plenty of space to themselves.

The commander housed the women in his quarters while he bunked in the barracks with the men.

In the morning, Lanai was ebullient, another of her gambits, another win in her pocket. When Korban ignored her, she brought her breakfast over to sit down and eat with him.

"So, are you going to glower at me the whole time we're on the move?"

"I know you feel the need to gloat, but I see no need for me to participate in that. The trek from Tranta is nothing compared to what we'll face on this journey. The dangers are real, your eminence."

"For your information, we can take care of ourselves, and I can survive your sour moods. I'll do just fine."

"Good for you. Now please allow me to eat my breakfast in peace. We have a long hard ride ahead today. We'll be ascending into higher altitudes. The Peak of the Moon is the highest point in the continent."

"That is a sight I look forward to seeing."

"We'll see how much you enjoy the frigid weather."

"We're prepared. Lena explained things and helped us to prepare."

"Did she now." His irritation came out in his tone.

Lila came over and sat on the other side of Korban. "Hello Korban, they said you were promoted to sub chief. Congratulations. We all knew you were destined for great things. This doesn't surprise us. I can think of no better situation for this trek than to be safe in your hands. We all thank you for...being you."

It struck them funny. Korban couldn't help but laugh.

"Lila, you're a rare young lady. I hope we'll have reasons to laugh with what's ahead. There could be some very unpleasant experiences, and there is a chance we could suffer losses. I hope Lena told you the whole truth."

My lord, we know the dangers, but we've decided to live lives of significance. What women can match such a feat as what we'll face?"

"None."

"This is a good thing, my lord."

"Lila, I'm not a lord."

"Yes, my lord."

The thought of the petite little Lila coming to harm punished his mind. She was the daintiest and slightest of the women, one of those women who looked younger than she was. She grinned warmly at him.

He eyed her reflectively, with a sigh.

"Well, gather yourselves, ladies. It's time to hit the trail."

When the column pulled out of the fort, the Alkar warriors had joined the vanguard, at least for the leg traveling though Alkar lands. Although it was far less distance to reach the Drackar border, it was slow going with constantly climbing higher and with the heavier accumulations of snow to fight through. They were able to stop at Alkar settlements each night so the women stayed at the town inns in the comfort of beds and baths. The inns couldn't accommodate a force of over a thousand so the men camped outside.

When they reached the border of Drackar lands, the Alkar warriors fell back to their assigned place in the column. Here it was an even steeper climb and there were fewer small settlements. They tended to stay in much larger Drackar communities. Still, the women could have a few comforts and defer the full weight of the trek for the moment.

As the weather continued to deteriorate, the women broke out the heavily furred coats Lena's people had provided. The travel was draining on everybody. When they stopped to rest and have a quick bite, people huddled together for warmth. Some days the wind was very strong testing the limits of their clothes to protect them. On those days, they brought the horses all within the circle to shield them too. Riding covers were put on the horses to protect from stinging cold gusts. Reaching the base of the Plateau of Heaven, the women had their last stay in an inn. When the riders started the ascent upwards in the morning to reach the plateau, it was brutal. The trail was slick and treacherous, the horses had to labor up the steep trail, and the single file riders worried about slips and falls. It was very stressful which took a mental toll.

To climb the trail here was made more difficult as one couldn't stop once they started and it was a sizeable distance to climb to the top.

Only the hardiest of individuals ever climbed up to the plateau, and never a thousand-man plus column.

By the time the first riders went over the top and onto the plateau, it was well into dusk. It took time for all of the riders and pack horses to ascend to the flat areas atop the plateau. They immediately set up camp as a blizzard whipped across the mountain plateau from a weather front coming in off the ocean to the west.

Again, the horses were gathered huddled together, centered in the camp configuration with horse blankets and covers to protect them. The troops slept abutting each other, and even the horses pressed against each other for warmth. Lanai took this occasion to lay close beside Korban along with her maidens. Lila was on his other side pressing firmly against him for warmth. With extra blankets, everybody tried to sleep, but it was still difficult. Any exposed skin faced freezing conditions.

The storm lasted most of the night. They awoke in the morning to a gray sky, plenty of fallen snow accumulated, and cold limbs.

Trying to light fires to cook breakfast was difficult. It took a time of striking sparks before they could manage to ignite a little kindling enough to get the fires going. Plenty of hot drink and food eased the discomfort in their bellies, but did nothing to warm their bodies. They left the covers on the horses during the daily rides with the severe weather and temperatures. Climbing back into the saddles, they set out again. Korban noted the sense of adventure was gone from the women's faces. Riding forward, they all looked north to see the great sight. The Peak of the Moon loomed, looking like just a short ride away as it towered over the surroundings. A Drackar warrior was riding near Lanai and Korban. He heard her ask, "can we ride over to see it since it's so close? I'll never get here again."

He piped in. "Princess, the mountain only looks to be close. It would take weeks of hard riding to approach it."

"Enjoy the sight from here, Lanai. It's the closest we can get." Korban added.

As they rode along, they felt the ground rumble and shake.

Lila commented, "I smell something burning."

The Drackar warrior answered her. "That is the Valley of Fire, ladies. You'll continue to smell it long before we get there. We should start to cover our faces as there can be deadly fumes floating about."

More stops for overnights on the plateau were equally unpleasant. Lanai came to understand the vital importance of protecting and saving your horse. Here it was a key lifeline to survive the harsh elements and to traverse the plateau. In this forbidding clime, her easy luxurious days in the Trantan palace seemed only a dream.

The column doggedly plodded on. It felt like they would never reach the far side, but one day at dusk they neared the ocean and could finally turn southward. The scent of salt in the air coming off the ocean was strong.

The descent off the plateau was scarier than the ascent. There had been a rough trail to follow coming up. Here there was only a steeper drop off with no discernible path to follow.

The Drackar guide commented. "It may be nobody comes this far to be able to climb down this side. We'll ride along the rim in both directions to see if there is a place for us to try our descent."

They set up camp while scouts went along the edges. The prospect of the descent was daunting to see. If they could find a place, whether they could manage to go the entire way in a single day, was a real question. They couldn't sleep on the side walls of the plateau. That worried Korban and also worried Lanai. For the first time, he saw fear in her eyes.

Night passed with them still perched on the plateau rim. The farther most scout traveling east was the last to return.

"There is little to give us hope, but I found a place for us to try. What I saw were chances to angle back and forth rather than risk going straight down in these icy conditions."

"We must do something," Korban patted the man. "Thank you for your courage."

It was a ride for the command to get to that spot and with the elapsed travel time, they spent another night on the plateau rim. Rising with the sun for the maximum time for the descent, the Drackar guide was the courageous first man onto the 'trail.' The entire troop watched him nervously. Korban wondered what the women were thinking. The man cautiously moved ahead, turning back and forth as the cliff formation dictated. Korban waved the column ahead to start the descent.

He turned to Lanai. "I know you're afraid. We all are. I'm going to go first and I want you and your maidens to follow me. Don't look down and don't think about anything. Just concentrate on the trail, picking our way ahead. You can see it can be done. Look how far he's been able to go. Take a deep breath and relax."

Korban tried to act calm for her, but he was equally terrified. This was unlike any danger he'd ever faced. In his own mind, he had serious doubts.

Inching his way downward, he wanted to check Lanai, but he didn't dare turn his head. The drop to the bottom was dizzying. When he got to the point of a switchback, he could glance at her riding behind him. All the women were ashen faced, gripping the saddle horns and the reins tightly. Continuing to ride cautiously, they'd carefully negotiated the dangerous descent of turns successfully, at least thus far. By now, the lead rider had a considerable distance lead between them. It was slow going for the bulk of the command, especially with leading the pack animals by the tether.

There could be no rest time, food, or drink all day. It was a mental grind as well as a physical test. Keeping steady, resisting the temptation to rush forward, it was supremely difficult. Nobody could help anybody else. Each person had to dig deep to find the personal strength to survive this nightmare scene.

Their winding strategy was working, but it was such a lengthy arduous process, Korban wondered if they could all sustain for long enough. Korban's eyes bulged as ahead he saw there was a gap in the trail. The horses would be required to jump to reach the next part of the trail. When his horse jumped, the landing was frightening with the slippery conditions. He didn't feel relieved because now the women each had to make that testing leap. He didn't dare turn around, but when nobody fell, he felt slightly better.

The only benefit they got was as they went lower, the winds whipping across the plateau were shielded down here along the cliff face. Korban had no idea how much time had passed. Although it seemed like an eternity, the remaining distance seemed too far to make it in the remaining light.

He was tempted to look up at the entire column, but that would be foolish. Down lower, the lead man was widening the gap and seemed to be moving a little faster.

With time as they got lower, Korban saw the small ledges they were riding on were getting wider. It allowed him to increase the pace slightly.

What else he noticed was noticeably warm gusts coming up at them. They were nearing the valley of fire. The warmth did manage to eliminate ice and snow on the path, which still required total concentration.

More hours passed as they rode lower. Ahead, Korban saw the lead man greatly increase his pace and then reach the floor as they were plodding downward toward the valley. The Drackar warrior looked up and signaled his success. It was encouraging, but the column still had some distance to go. It was starting to darken in the sky as dusk was at hand.

The ledges continued to widen, so Korban increased the pace. He watched the path closely, not wanting an error now with the end in sight.

Finally, they were getting to a point of sensing they could make it.

When Korban made the final loop to ride onto the floor, and safety, he looked up for Lanai. She had just finished negotiating the incredible ordeal, and then her maidens completed the task too. It was an unbelievable feat, but nobody felt like celebrating.

It took more time for the remainder of the large command to reach the floor. Making camp right away, it was a quiet night as the exhausted people whispered thankfulness it was over with no losses.

Surprising to Korban, many came to him as if he personally had delivered them to safety.

Lanai showed no further haughtiness, or voiced taunts for him. Instead, she talked privately to him before they slept.

"I want you to know I was terrified. I didn't think we could make it. You were right to warn us beforehand, but we're here now still alive. We will follow you wherever you lead us, sub chief."

"You were no less frightened than anybody else. If I'd known what we would be required to do, I might have stayed back home. I'll admit to you, I'm a fool."

"You're no fool, sir. I doubt anybody else could have led us through that gauntlet."

"Well, let us sleep. I doubt our next test in the valley of fire will be easier."

The command was so exhausted mentally and physically after the harrowing ride down the cliff face, they were slow to rise the next morning. Lanai chose to place her bedding close beside Korban who didn't object. When she did that, Lila bedded close on his other side again. As she got into her covers, she smiled at Korban affectionately.

"Good night, my lord. I feel safe with you here beside me."

In the presence of these astounding beautiful women, Korban was constantly being forced to face parts of his life he'd always ignored. The thought of taking a wife was stubborn when he tried to dismiss it, and increasingly more so with each day of shared experiences.

In spite of the momentary distraction, he still fell asleep rapidly. The sentry shifts that night were half the usual time. Having a sentry fall asleep couldn't be allowed.

In spite of the nearby valley of fire, a hungry predator, a cat, crept toward the sleeping warriors. It was an unlikely place to find any predator this close to the valley and with the sparse cover. The sentries spotted it just as it readied to leap toward a potential victim. Rushing together toward the danger, they brandished spears and swords. The cat sprinted away instead of fighting. There was no easy meat to be had in this camp.

Morning came with a cloudy sky, cloudy from ash. The rumbles they'd felt had been a small nearby eruption.

The trek toward the valley took the balance of the morning. When they reached the rim overlooking the volcanic depression, the sight was daunting. It seemed all of the walls and the basin of the valley was aglow. Heat radiated out of the valley and the roiling fumes in swirling eddies of air currents were toxic.

Korban saw no path to cross the valley.

The same skillful Drackar guide who'd led them down the mountain cliff spoke.

"I say we turn and head toward the ocean. If there is a way to continue, our best chance would lie there."

"I have no better idea. Please lead us. We trust your judgment."

Riding along the rim of the volcanic valley, it was far from pleasant. Still dressed in their heavy clothing, it was tempting to shed layers, but wisely they did not. They covered their faces against the fumes, but trying to protect their horses breathing was far more difficult. The horses weren't particularly cooperative.

Nonetheless, they made their way westward for a day until they reached the shoreline. Lava was flowing out of the valley seaward. The ocean water hissed and bubbled when the lava hit it.

They pondered the problem for a time. The Drackar guide gave his further suggestion.

"It may be our only choice is to ride into the ocean to go out beyond the lava flow. The lava doesn't make it very far when it hits the water.

"Yes, I understand. If we tried to wait out the end of the lava flowing, it could take a very long time to stop, and then to cool."

"We will need to have a warrior also lead each pack animal to be sure they don't go off and be lost, in addition to their own animal. I think the horses will need to swim for part of the way."

"We may need to get off the horses and swim also. That would mean taking time to dry out on the other side. As we go farther south away from the valley, the weather will turn cold again."

"That's true, my lord."

Korban smiled ruefully. More people were addressing him as lord these days.

"Let's get to it. I want to be on the other side of this lava stream as soon as possible."

Gathering his command, he explained the plan and what they needed to do.

No one objected, but after descending a wide path down to sea level when they actually entered the water, the coldness was punishing. The horses whinnied and bucked a bit as they went deeper into the water to reach a point where they could turn to go around the deadly lava hazard. With many warriors saddled with the difficult task of trying to lead their own horse plus also lead a pack horse, that difficult task got more difficult when they got to a point where they had to start swimming yanking two horses simultaneously. Korban made a point of being close to the petite Lila in case she got into trouble controlling her horse.

The lead Drackar warrior finally turned to cross over the path of the lava. It was a wide area he needed to traverse. Swimming through bubbles rising from below, he swam determinedly. The horse neighed, but followed his rider who yanked it along by the rein.

When he reached a point to turn back toward the coast, Korban started the rest of the warriors swimming to make the crossing. All of the women had trouble with their horses, so nearby Vikar warriors aided them. Korban was faced with choosing between Lanai or Lila. One of his men saw the dilemma and moved quickly to help Lila. When Korban reached back for Lanai, she eyed him gratefully.

Crossing over the bubbling lava bed under the ocean water was frightening. The water was hot and that added to the horses being spooked. It seemed like an eternity to get out of the danger area before they could turn back toward the shore. When they finally walked ashore, dripping wet, they set about making numerous large fires to dry wet clothing and to gather about for warmth from the heat of the bonfires. The women had to don blankets while they stripped off all of their wet clothes until they dried. They said little, well aware of the attention of an army of young naked males. In a blanket, Korban brought hot beverages for them to drink.

"Thank you," Lanai said softly, looking away.

"We've made it, princess. I hope the worst is behind us."

"That is my wish too." Also clad in only the blanket, she still wouldn't look at him. Everyone was caught in that same state. For the women, realizing decorum here wasn't important, especially in this difficult circumstance, it was still a needless issue for them. Reputations really weren't at risk, though with the women feeling vulnerable, they seemed to be unable to cope well.

CHAPTER SEVEN
The Lamali

Eventually clothing dried, fires died out, and everybody could dress warmly to resume the trek. Confidence returned to the faces of the women. Continuing southward, they decided to ride along the beach rather than try to climb back into the mountains. It meant much faster and somewhat warmer travel without the wind from the mountains punishing them. Air currents coming off the ocean pushed those weather fronts inland.

As they rode along, Lanai called over to Korban. She was looking and pointing out at the ocean. Korban looked to see a distant ship sailing southward.

"Do you think it's a Lamali ship?"

"Perhaps, they are a coastal nation."

"We have ships in Tranta, but I've never been on one. I've wondered what it's like to sail on the ocean."

"Perhaps the Lamali can explain it to you."

"I hope they don't attack us before we can explain that we come in peace."

"I won't approach them in force. We'll send representatives to clear the way, hopefully."

"I worry that they're closed to contact from outsiders. If they act first with violence, it would be a bad development."

"That's a probability, but it's part of what we must overcome. They're in danger too. The Brog won't care about their prejudices. Getting their ear at first contact is my goal. I was told they're somewhat reclusive."

"In Tranta, that is our view of them too. We never had much of a reason to go there being that we were self-sufficient. Attempts by our traders to establish agreements never really happened. The only contacts we kept was with the Mantu who tended to ride over our borders often, though they didn't come to war with us."

They camped that night at the base of the mountains. The cliff walls were steep, so there appeared to be no threat of an attack from up top. With the ocean behind them, Korban didn't foresee a threat there either.

What he did see was, as the women spent ongoing time living with the troops, they became like magnets drawing flocks of avid young men over to chat, share meals, and generally to bask in female presence and companionship. The maidens had no problem with it other than being overwhelmed by the large disparity in numbers of males to females. Trying to talk to such huge numbers of men crowding around them, it was daunting. Even the 'untouchable' princess garnered a very large following. Korban had no problem understanding the minds of his men, and their dreams. What the women thought, he could only guess.

Lanai resumed her aloof demeaner. She was polite, but gave none of the adoring males any encouragement that she was the least bit interested. No one in the camp failed to know she favored Korban. In his case, she continued their dance around the obvious, waiting for him to act.

It took a week of stops on the beach before they reached the border of the Lamali lands which was easy to know as the mountains stopped abruptly and the land flattened out. Korban stopped the column moving them back against the cliff face. He chose to send five warriors to attempt first contact, an Alkar, a Kominkar, a Drackar, a Stakar, and a Vikar. Those five volunteer men were determined to do the job, but Korban saw on their faces they were worried. He was concerned also.

Korban watched as they rode into Lamali territory. They didn't get far before they were interdicted by a large Lamali force. It was a tense moment as he pondered sending a protective reinforcing force. The Kar tribesmen did well in trying to talk to the Lamali captain. When the bellicose Lamali's demanded to disarm the five, Korban worried there would be a fight.

Surrendering their weapons, his representatives looked back at him before they were led away with hands tied. Another large Lamali force came toward the border blocking their way into the country.

Korban knew he could defeat that force, but starting a bloody war wasn't why they were there. However, it didn't relieve him of self-doubt. *Did I just make a terrible mistake?*

After waiting for a day, Korban mounted his horse and rode across the border to meet the Lamali captain. When it was too late for him to stop her, Lanai galloped up to join him.

The Lamali leader reacted predictably at first, like Korban was single handedly invading all of Lamali, however when Lanai came into view, their approach changed radically. They allowed Korban into their midst while eyeing Lanai the whole time.

The captain spoke. Why are you on Lamali land? We saw your five fools who thought to trick us, like there was no force of invaders behind them."

"There is no trick, captain. We've come here like we're going to every nation on the continent looking for unity to face the threat from the Brog. They're popping up everywhere. Nobody is safe from their depredations."

"This large force you have with you, this is supposed to show us you have peaceful intentions?"

"We aren't here to make war with you. If we were, you and I wouldn't be talking. I don't know how you feel about the mountain tribes, but you can see all five Kar tribes now have a treaty and I sent only five men, one from each tribe to meet you."

"I'm aware of who stands at our border. Do you think we're afraid to face barbarians?"

"Your courage has nothing to do with it. I'm sure you know the fighting reputation of the Vikar. Brog came into our mountains, attacked a camp and killed, and then stole some of our girls. We finally found them hiding in a hole they dug. We rescued the girls and killed them all."

The captain paused and looked at Lanai. "Who are you, maiden? You seem an unlikely rider in this force of barbarians. Are you a captive, a concubine perhaps?"

She laughed. "I would never be anybody's concubine. My name is Lanai and I'm the crown princess of Tranta."

"That is difficult to believe, although tales of your great beauty are known to us. You certainly have that beauty, but being at risk here away from your palace riding with barbarians? It doesn't seem the truth."

"Is there a reason you hesitate to talk to us? We pose no danger to you, or yours. My choices are really none of your business." The officer smiled at her.

"I will admit, we've had an appearance of these Brog creatures. We didn't have a name for them, but Lamali people were lost, killed in a hideous way and partially eaten."

Korban spoke. "Then you understand why we're here. Can you stop this posturing and allow us to address your leaders?"

"My charge is to protect our borders. Whether I can decide to bring you to our leaders, I don't know that."

"Well, you need to make a decision. You have five of my men."

"Can I ask, how did you come to be here?"

Lanai answered. "It was about the most impossible journey we could have chosen. Traveling across Vikar, we went through Stakar, and then Drackar ascending to travel the Plateau of Heaven. We came down a sheer icy cliff wall all day long to then go across the valley of fire. We were forced into the ocean to swim around the lava flow. I didn't think we would make it any number of times."

"That is remarkable. None of the Lamali would ever attempt such a trek. I'm amazed a woman could make such a journey."

"Actually, it's women. I have my maidens with me."

He stared at Lanai before speaking again. "As you have asked of me, I'll make a decision. Bring your force here to camp in the open. I'll send word to our officials. Are you agreeable to waiting until I get directions?"

"As long as it doesn't involve a long period of time. In any case, I'd like my men returned immediately. They've done nothing wrong."

"I'll explain this to my leaders."

Korban rode back to the command. "Come forth, children. The Lamali have invited us to camp on their territory, under their scrutiny."

When the full force emerged sporting five hundred Vikar warriors, the finest fighters known, two hundred of the feared Drackar, as well as the Alkar, Kominkar, and the Stakar warriors emerged, and some Trantan soldiers, the Lamali noticeably eased back in fear.

It was anomalous to have the stunning royal princess among them along with her beautiful maidens. The allied force made a strong impression for a number of reasons.

Setting up camp, the allies made no threatening moves, set about a friendly camp, and even invited some of the Lamali to join them to visit.

Days passed and each day as the foreign force remained passive; they were seen in better terms. Curious Lamali villagers from nearby appeared to see the sight of the famous mountain barbarians. When some brave parents let little children wander up to Lanai and her maidens, it was like a barrier came down. She knelt down and fawned over the children which was a perfect tonic warming the hearts of their proud parents. Those parents then approached, acting with deference. One mother told her, "We have never met a royal person."

"I'm just a woman, like any other. I envy you for being a mother. It's my goal to have my own children someday."

She glanced at Korban.

"My children are my life. It frightened us about these creatures coming up out of the ground."

"That's why we're here forging alliances where we fight together to eradicate this terrible threat."

"I would agree to your help, but I can't speak for all the Lamali people."

"Your child is a delight." Lanai gave her little daughter a hug before she returned to her mother. Lanai walked over to Korban.

"What a delight to have such precious little children, don't you agree?"

"It's very good to see parents and their children, I agree."

"She was very endearing. I could gobble her up."

"She was very cute, Lanai."

Her facial expression soured as he avoided her hint, again.

After an awkward moment as he continued to be placid, she turned in a huff and walked back to her maidens.

Korban refused to ponder the emotional tangle she posed at that moment, moving instead to talk to the Lamali captain.

"I grow impatient waiting on your superiors. The Brog are not idle during this wasted time."

The captain frowned.

"Are you agreeable to taking me to meet them and recover my men. If they won't hear my words, sitting here serves no purpose, we'll move on to meet with the Mantu."

"I...eh...perhaps I can take you, I would suggest the princess come with you. It would be far less threatening."

"Do they think a single Vikar can conquer their whole nation? What kind of leaders do you have?"

"You don't understand. We have political leaders as you do, but we also have a priesthood that makes rulings in matters concerning the people. My guess is it's there the delay has happened."

"Then we need to leave immediately to resolve this foolishness."

"Korban, I respect you a great deal, as well us all of our forces do, but understand you can't approach this like this is Vikar land. Those priests hold great sway in Lamali. They have a connection with the religion of Iscali island. It's said in the distant past, the Iscali religion came to us as a gift."

"It doesn't sound like a gift to me. Regardless, we need to go."

Although Korban didn't advise her about going, the captain sent his men to explain the plan to Lanai. She was more than happy to join Korban for a ride to the Lamali seat of power.

"Ah, we meet again, sub chief. I'm sorry to spoil your plan to ride alone to see their leaders. Their captain saw the wisdom of including me for the proper impression I make. In our camp, only you seem unable to see my merits."

Korban eyed her ruefully to her smirk.

Riding away, Lanai rode in the middle between Korban and the captain. There were ten Lamali warriors behind them. They had to spend a night in the field. Stopping in a village, Lanai was welcomed like a celebrity. There were no inns, so she stayed with a host family. The wife beamed at the perceived honor of being picked as the host. Lanai loved the fact that she had small children. It gave her another opportunity to needle Korban. He responded stoically and acted politely to the family and their children.

It took most of the next day to reach the major Lamali settlement. Entering the gates, for the first time they saw the robed priests. They eyed Korban darkly, so he rested his hand on his sword hilt and smiled grimly at them. They glowered, but wisely didn't test him.

Riding to a large building, servants took their horses while the captain led them inside. It was fairly dark with very little light allowed to come in the few windows. Torches were burning mounted in sconces in the hallways giving inadequate flickering light. When they got to the large doors, large guards were waiting on each side of the doorway.

"The throne room," Lanai muttered.

The captain spoke to the guard who went inside. They came back and opened the doors.

The captain led them in to the chief and his wife. They were pleasant enough looking, but on both sides of the thrones there were more of the robed priests. There was no welcome in their expressions.

Korban was instantly on guard, but he remembered what the captain had said about treating this situation differently.

The princess took the lead.

"Thank you for allowing us to visit you here in your city. I'm crown princess Lanai of Tranta. This is Korban, esteemed sub-chief of the Vikar. We've come to..."

A priest stepped forward, holding up a hand.

"We know why you're here. You've come uninvited to bring your dubious claims of peril along with an armed force of barbarians camped at our border. We heard your five men speak. You were told we would give an answer, yet you come here now without permission?"

"If we've offended you, or broke one of your rules, we apologize. It wasn't our intention. However, time is not on our side. Your enemy, the Brog, are not idle. You've already seen them appear up out of the ground. Do you think that was a once-only event? I can tell you, it's not. They are vicious soulless creatures. I was nearly killed and eaten by Brog attackers back in Tranta when Korban saw my peril and saved me. This is a threat which requires the unity of all the Kar tribes and all the other nations."

"Princess, we regret they held your life in their hands, but how that is the problem of the Lamali, I don't see."

Korban interrupted. "Priest, I don't know what game you play, but you will bring my men to me now. If you have these poor people in your thrall, that is not the concern of the Vikar, or the other Kar tribes. We came here in peace for an alliance to both our benefits, but if you stand in the way of protecting the Lamali peoples, we will leave you to your dire fate.

"You think you can march in here and dictate to..."

In a flash, Korban's sword was out. Some palace guards tried to attack but he knocked swords out of their hands and knocked them out with his fists.

"Do you wish to fight me, priest!" He growled ominously.

The captain was at a loss, though he agreed with Korban. The chief suddenly stood.

"Enough."

"I have not given my ruling," the priest complained.

The chief eyed him grimly. "This Vikar sub chief has spoken well. The threat to the Lamali people is the important issue. If those mighty peoples offer us their help and protection, I will listen. Do not forget who is the chief here."

The priest glowered at Korban and his own chief. He made a signal and the priests filed out. Before he left, he turned.

"Vikar, know that this is not ended. Do not think we cower in fear of you, or that we have no means to deal with you."

"Come to me whenever or wherever you like. I'll be waiting."

When he left the throne room, the chief and his wife came down to speak.

"I realize our ways are much different than yours. I must consider the priests as a part of my duties. You don't understand what that means but his threat to you was real. Don't dismiss them lightly."

"Can they truly accept the fatal presence of the Brogs in your lands? Your dead will mount until your nation is no more. Do they think the Brog won't kill priests?"

"It is difficult to explain to you. I'll put it this way, I shouldn't have allowed them to retain your brave warriors. I'll have them brought forth immediately."

"Thank you, chief."

His wife came to Lanai. "You're a princess, heir to the Trantan throne?"

"I am."

"This is an auspicious day. I wonder how your father allows you to be away putting yourself in peril?"

"He didn't allow me."

The wife looked puzzled and then she laughed. "I like you."

"You wear a sword?" asked her husband.

"I can even use it. Do you think those priests will take action against us? We aren't here to trample on your ways, but this is not a matter to leave to foolish schemes. Either you're our allies, or..."

"I understand. I would love to join you, but I need to deal with the priesthood. In answer to your question, the priests are not warriors, but they have men to do their bidding, fighters in their stead. They are very good. I'm not saying they're better than Kar barbarian warriors, but no potential opponent can be taken for granted.

The door opened and the five captives came in, newly rearmed and itching for a fight.

They smiled at seeing Lanai. She smiled warmly at them.

Korban went to his men. "Your time of basking and lazing in comfort in Lamali hands is over. We'll return to camp now. The chief has matters here to resolve and then they'll decide if they're our friends and allies, or not." The men chuckled.

Lanai piped in. "Can I ask you about Iscali Island. Going there was another of our plans."

"I can't say I'd suggest going there. The travel between us is somewhat limited. We do trade there somewhat, and the priests make frequent pilgrimages to Iscali regarding their religion. It's a secretive place. If you hope to make them allies, that would be a tall task. You saw the priests had no fear to threaten you. If you go there, you're in the center of their power. What they do is kept hidden, though there have always been rumors of dark rites and unwholesome practices. You especially, princess. I fear they would see you as a great prize, an easy plum for the plucking."

"This sword I wear is not ceremonial."

"On their island, I would fear for you. It is your choice what you do but use great caution in that decision."

Korban replied. "Thank you for that information. Is it safe for us to spend the night here? I don't fear the priests, but if they send attackers in the night, we can promise you a bloodbath. We're light sleepers."

"Men after my own heart. I can place ample guards around you for the night. I would like to spend time getting to know you. Also, I'd like to discuss you're plans."

"Then we will stay."

"Please follow the captain who will take you to rooms and will gather guards to protect you through the whole night. Refresh yourselves and we will see you later."

"Thank you, chief."

There was a main bedroom with a large bed and some smaller rooms. Lanai looked at it, and then smirked at Korban.

"The bed is yours, princess. I and the men will sleep elsewhere. If you have need of us, just call out. We won't be far."

"Need?"

"Perhaps a frightening dream that distresses you?"

She shook her head dourly as the men snickered. "Thank you, but I can manage all by myself. You can leave now, sub chief."

Her maidens who'd come separately along with some troops following after Korban and the princess began their journey, came into the large room to stay there too. They eyed Korban warmly as they walked by. Lila grinned broadly at him. The remaining allied forces arrived right afterwards.

The morning brought a new development. Sitting down to share the morning meal, the priests suddenly showed up to join them. The head priest spoke immediately.

"I'm told you have a desire to go to Iscali island? Is that correct?" He smiled, like a spider sitting on his web.

"That is true," Korban answered. The priest continued to eye Lanai intently.

"I feel that is a good thing. The princess would benefit from meeting the High Priestess of our religion. She is wise and well trained in many things."

Lanai answered. "I'm willing to meet with anyone. You know why we've come, but is there something else you feel needs to be covered, but only there?"

"I think she can uniquely explain our positions much better than I. We got off to a regrettable start. I wish to make amends."

Korban felt queasy. Stepping into traps wasn't a choice he ever willingly made.

"I have no objection. What do you say, Korban?"

"When you say we should travel to your island, are you talking about my entire force, or something lesser?"

"If you go there in force, it would make a wrong impression. Wouldn't you think a token number of guards would suffice? Perhaps five, or so?"

Korban's expression turned dark. He glanced at the Lamali chief and his wife. They were stone-faced.

"I think a 'token' force going into an unknown environment would be a poor choice. Whatever waits us on that island, we need to make prudent decisions. I will not put the crown princess of the Trantan nation at risk."

The priest got a calculating look. "Perhaps you're right. You come from the outside world, so you don't know Iscali island is a holy place. Ten men might be better. Does that suit you?"

With his ire growing, Korban paused to quell the anger and head off an outburst.

"Thank you for trying to understand, priest, but ten is not a fitting protection for the crown princess of Tranta. I will consider this and discuss it with my people. We'll talk further...later?"

"Of course."

Lanai slyly reached over and patted him on the knee.

After that, they ate the meal talking pleasantly. The Lamali's present were particularly interested in the retelling of the tale of incredible journey from Vikar and the daunting hurdles they needed to overcome along the way.

The chief's wife spoke in awe. "The idea of riding all day down a huge sheer cliff face chills my blood. I'm terrified of heights."

Lanai replied. "It was terrifying, the scariest thing I've ever done. I didn't think we could do it, but there was no other choice. How the horses could stay on those narrow footholds, and for all day, I'm still amazed."

"Stories will be told about you in many camps, both of you princess, and you Korban. You do the impossible. I'm glad we've had a chance to know you."

The priests whispered among each other and said nothing to anybody else. Their facial expressions were predatory. Korban noted it all.

When the meal was finished, the head priest arose. "We look forward to your decision about a blessed Iscali visit. Send word and I will come. Again, I consul you, the high priestess a marvel well worth your time."

Korban nodded. Lanai said nothing, looking away from the priest's inappropriate stare.

Afterwards, Korban asked the chief, "Can you and your wife join us to talk to my leaders about this?"

"We can, Korban. Thank you for trusting us."

A little later, they gathered in the chief's main room.

Korban explained, "The lead priest suddenly inviting us to travel to Iscali Island? We don't trust him. Of course, he suggested we go in small numbers to make us vulnerable. Whatever he is planning, I don't want to allow. He said Lanai should meet their high priestess? It has the feel of a trap. What do you think, chief?"

"You should be cautious in any dealings with them. None of the Lamali citizenry ever seek to travel there. In the distant past our sailors sought trade and commerce, but increasingly it changed into a darker place, foreboding, and dangerous. I don't know what rites they practice, but judging by how the priests here act and what they want us to do, you definitely should use the highest caution. I can't really say going there will accomplish anything for your cause."

"I suspected as much. Do you think they see it as a chance to snare the princess for ransom, or some other foul purpose?"

"I can't say. We only hear tales of this priestess through the mouths of the priests, so who can say what is the truth."

"What do you say, Lanai? I think there is risk greater than we need to take. We'd depend on them in their boats to get us there, they would have every advantage on their home island if it came to a fight. This priest here all but salivated about you, so I expect there would be something dire waiting there."

"I've been safely through many travails in my time traveling with you, so I trust you implicitly. In this case, I get the same creepy feelings from his frank stares. It goes through my mind to pull my sword on him."

Everybody laughed.

One Vikar man shouted, "that's a fight I'd love to see."

Lanai smiled, but continued. "It's true, I don't like him. He doesn't strike me as a holy man, nor do his priests. Going into a potential trap, I feel as Korban does. I tend to lean toward the opinion of a Lamali chief over the mouthing's of that priest. You, as chief, live here, which is meeting enough for me. I have no need to meet this priestess."

Korban asked, "Chief, if we deny the wishes of your priests, will it cause a problem for you?"

"It's difficult to say. Lately they seem to be getting more active and threatening. I think we of the Lamali would have been making difficult choices soon anyway. The fear of the priests has faded over the ages. Recently, we've had some unfortunate incidents between priests and our villagers and warriors. Their welcome here is wearing thin."

"If we've added to your difficulties, I apologize."

"We rejoice at your presence, Korban. For my part, I say we have an alliance."

Later, the head priest was invited to join the meeting.

"We've considered your invitation to visit your island and have decided against it. There are too many unknowns to take the risk. Your idea to send the princess without appropriate protections is not acceptable. If you choose to represent our position and purposes to your priestess, we'd be grateful. If you take the other path and besmirch us, that would not be wise. It appears to us we should travel on to meet the Mantu next, without delay."

For a moment, Korban saw rage in his eyes before he changed to a calculating expression.

"As you wish. I regret we couldn't convince you to experience the treasures of Iscali island as well as the sublime pleasure of an audience with our high priestess, Lavia. She is a goddess come down to bless the world."

"As I said, we'll be departing soon for Mantu. Our decision is made."

They stared grimly at each other before the priest finally left.

"That went well," Korban muttered. He didn't mean it as a joke, but everybody in the room laughed heartily.

"Chief, with your permission, we'll stock up on supplies, and leave in a day or two at most. I'm sorry to leave this issue of the priests in your lap."

"It couldn't be helped. I've delayed too long in dealing with this matter. It's our problem to solve."

When they went to bed that evening, they had no idea the priests would act. In their sleep, Lanai, Lila, and the other maidens suddenly felt strong hands grab them and push cloths over their faces with a chemical to render them unconscious. They were unceremoniously and disrespectfully hauled away by the priests and their soldiers, never awaking until much later when they were helpless in the control of the priestess on the island.

Getting up in the morning, Korban discovered Lanai's room was empty. She and her maidens were missing. Korban was in a rage. The Lamali chief sent warriors, and Korban's troops joined in searching everywhere for signs, but with all the priests missing it was clear what happened and where they went. The chief started organizing all the boats and ships they could find to transport the ally's fighters as well as considerable Lamali warriors to sail to Iscali island, which took time to get sufficient numbers and gather enough boats into the harbor.

Already, the priests had too many days of a head start. Normally a day's trip at sea, unfortunately a huge storm blew in from the ocean making it impossible to sail. The ocean was wild with vast waves crashing on the beach. It took nearly a week before the weather cleared enough and the naval armada could set sail.

Korban was rocked with the same helpless feeling as when the Vikar girls had been taken as captives. Having the princess in the hands of the Iscali was beyond unacceptable. Anger and frustration roiled in his gut.

They sailed straight toward the island main seaport. That wasn't where the Priestess Lavia resided. Her temple was far inland. The weather was still difficult, slowing their travel time.

When they neared the port, they could see Iscali fighters scrambling to mount a defense. There were huge numbers of priestly robes present too, and they were also armed.

Livid, Korban was itching for a fight.

Launching showers of arrows from the coast, the allies noted the poor aim of their opponents as few found their mark of hitting any of the ships, mostly falling short. Nobody suffered injuries.

The Lamali fleet of ships, an armada, continued approaching the sizeable settlement. As priests yelled to whip up a frenzy, their warriors joined in the cacophony. It failed to frighten the allies, all of whom were seasoned experienced fighters.

The courage of the enemy ebbed when an answering barrage of arrows were launched from the fleet like a wave of death descending from the sky. With their men dropping all around from allied accuracy, they faded back to get out of range.

Korban was first to storm ashore followed closely by his screaming troops when they landed. The Lamali warriors joined in the rush to chase down the rapidly retreating enemy forces.

Those enemy fighters chose a delaying action to slow the allied progress. Any actual fights were mismatches. Korban was frustrated there were limited horses allowed on the island, so the trek had to be made on foot. Only some priests were allowed to ride.

The center of the island rose into hillocks and mini mountains. Somewhere in the far distance, the princess and her maidens were being held captive.

The allies pressed their opponents giving them no chance to make stands or to rest. An army of inexperienced poorly trained troops was no threat and as time and miles passed, their numbers diminished. Many merely running away rather than facing sure death on barbarian swords.

Korban pressed ahead into the night, but eventually they had to stop. The priests conducted a noisy ritual to taunt the allies. Among the things they picked to say was the loud taunt, "it's too late."

"What does that mean?" Korban looked at the Lamali chief.

The chief had no answer. He had a look of concern on his face.

"If they have harmed her, we'll wipe out every one of them. Priests will be a problem for you no longer."

"Come, we must get some sleep to be able to press on tomorrow. It can't be helped." It seemed Korban no more than shut his eyes before they were up with the sun.

Moving forward at a steady trot, the priests had already moved back, but closing the gap was easy. The priests no longer taunted them and had to concentrate on breathing, running trying to stay ahead of Korban's highly motivated force. The barbarians chanted ominously as they ran, terrifying all in their path, *death is coming for you.*

Although the distant hills seemed closer, they were still forced to spend another night. Trotting for another day, the hills seemed very close, but there were no buildings in sight. If the temple was at hand, they couldn't see it. The next morning, the steady climb was more than the priests ahead could endure. Already spent, they started to fall away to the side and filter away. There was a road going over a high hill they were following. At the top of the hill, what remained of the priests turned to make their stand.

The allied forced charged immediately. It was a ridiculously easy fight. Rather than taking time to slaughter the pitiful enemy, they charged over the hill blasting through them and trampling over the priests toward a building in the distance. No defensive force emerged from the building. Whether it was some sort of ploy, Korban couldn't be sure, or even if this was the temple of the priestess. It was ornate like a temple would be, but showing no response was puzzling. Korban was first to reach the entrance. Racing inside, it was empty. The troops searched the rooms finding no sign of their women, or anyone else.

Some of the Vikar warriors dragged a captured and battered priest in the door tossing him to Korban's feet.

He was frightened, but silent.

"I have no patience for this, or for you. Where is the princess?"

He scowled in silence causing Korban to lift him bodily by his throat. Giving him a savage smack to the face, Korban dropped him on the stone floor.

"Speak!"

He was bleeding from the face, dazed.

Korban reared back to blast him again. The priest nodded and pointed to an ornate wall. They moved over to examine it closely. On the surface, it appeared connected and a single construction. However, as a Vikar warrior felt under a ledge, he hit a lever which opened the wall to a stairway. There was a sickly odor in the stale air rolling out from below and they could hear drums and chants.

Rushing down the stairs they found an entire large level built below ground. The odor was stronger as they raced toward the sounds. Finally, they reached large doors. Those doors were locked. The allies had no heavy objects to batter at them.

Here, they could clearly hear the chants, and the drone of a lone female voice, seemingly that of the priestess, Lavia, leading some Iscali rite. She stopped her chants periodically for a time. The audience cheered loudly for whatever was occurring in those interludes, before the drums and chants started again. There were six interludes in total. For the last, the longest interlude, they heard the loudest chants and cheers.

Korban stared at this last impediment, struggling for a solution to get inside. The women were right there, just out of reach, subject who knows what. This greatly irked Korban, prodding his underlying frustration into life. The force of that emotion punished him terribly, but he had no answers.

Feeling helpless, he slapped his hand against the barrier, raging in anger. It further stoked his self-doubts and his feelings of inadequacy, failing in safe-guarding the princess and her ladies. Whatever they were experiencing worried him greatly. He felt at fault and it was punishing.

CHAPTER EIGHT
Troubles

Briefly, they tried bashing at the solid doors, but that was going to accomplish nothing.

The Lamali chief had no answer either. Their wait locked outside was surprisingly short.

Hearing the bolts being pulled back and the bars removed, the thick doors were opened with a whoosh of unpleasant air full of acrid smoke and other strange scents. There were no guards waiting to attack, only more of the avid wild-eyed robed priests filling the room as the allies rushed inside. They were full of fervor and frenzy from the priestess proceedings, but wisely they didn't attack the allied forces entering the room.

The priestess cried out. "Korban, welcome, please come in and join us. Here are your lovely ladies. We've spent such a wonderful time together. I think they can give you a different view of the Iscali peoples than you seem to have. We are your friends." Her sickly-sweet smile irked him greatly. Containing his anger and a deadly response was difficult. Lanai and her maidens were lying prone on their backs in a stupor, fastened down on beds, arrayed around the priestess indelicately, helpless for all to see.

Korban entered the chamber warily, looking all about for hidden threats, and still eyeing the mob of rabid priests. There were none of Lavia's soldier's present. Still, the allied warriors were provoked and approached Lavia fiercely, weapons at the ready. She eyed them dismissively, as if she was in no danger.

"Yes, come to me. You are welcome in the holy temple, my friends."

Korban didn't reply to her. He cautiously climbed the steps onto the stage and went straight to Lanai. All of the women looked frazzled, disheveled and deep in the stupor. They appeared to him to have been heavily drugged, from what he could tell from an initial glance. Not in their own clothes, they were wearing only short shear white robes.

"Lanai?" he whispered, moving close. She did not respond or even move. Her imposed stupor was palpable. Her maidens were in the same unawares and sorry state. The scent was strong of whatever they administered. Other scents were there also he couldn't quite identify.

Korban turned to Lavia; his expression grim. She leered at him, eyeing his powerful physique impolitely and showing no fear. Her hand was resting on Lanai, like a gesture of ownership.

"What have you done to the princess and her maidens?" He took a step toward Lavia who acted undaunted and fearless.

"We have shared of our religion and we taught them about our beliefs and practices. It was their wish to participate in this ceremony. They're now consecrated in our religion, a part of our family. It is an avenue open to you and your brave comrades. Also, I've heard of your desire to add the Iscali to your collection of allies. As leader here, I want to explain we're happy to join with you. We have much to offer." Taking her hand off Lanai, she walked evocatively up very close to Korban.

He nearly smacked her, but resisted, turning his face back toward Lanai. The strange scents around her, neither pleasant or unpleasant, but strong, were not lessening. Smelling it gave him a light-headed feeling. Her closed eyelids moved like she was locked in her dreams. Her fingers wiggled in whatever she felt in that dream and he could hear her soft moans, her fists sometimes clenching, and she grimaced frequently. She whispered breathily, but Korban couldn't make out the words.

After watching for a moment, Korban nodded and warriors came up to release the women from the loops holding them tied down on the beds. Lifting her in his arms, Korban carried Lanai's limp supine body out of the temple chamber and continued all the way up the stairs to go outside into the fresh air. Even smelling the fumes had affected the troops. The priestess led her flock outside following Korban. She continued smiling and acting harmless. Korban didn't buy it, quite the opposite. The priestess Lavia was on tenuous ground, though she didn't act that way.

Lavia did manage to approach the Lamali chief and have a terse chat. The chief was not intimidated. With the small army of highly skilled barbarians, and his own army, he was bolstered to challenge her. Especially after easily routing her forces, he was provoked by her threats. Grimacing and glaring, and putting a hand to his sword hilt, he said something and she backed away.

As Korban sat down on the ground cradling Lanai's head, he noticed the head priest from Lamali capital, the kidnapper, edging close smiling wickedly.

"Did I not tell you great wonders awaited the princess? She is now among the consecrated after being one with the priestess, worthier now, and I saw it all. I told you, barbarian. We are the greater. She is ours now." Allied warriors heard him and edged close, murder in their eyes. He backed away, but the smirk remained.

Picking up the women, they carried them away from the nearby temple, making a camp and posting double sentries.

Undaunted by her peril, the priestess walked alone into their camp and sat down, uninvited and unwanted, beside Korban to share in their meal.

Korban glared. "Do you think we are children easily fooled, or that we can take no action against you, priestess?"

"Why do I get this hostility? I understand my priest used poor judgment spiriting the princess away in the night, but you must admit, you would not have given permission for her to visit me. You said that to him."

"She lies in this stupor and I'm supposed to believe this is a good thing? Clearly, you've never had dealings with the Vikar. There are consequences to actions. You are not immune."

"It's true I have not dealt with any Vikars, but I'm happy to have the chance now. The women have not been harmed. Think of them as having the best dreams possible. They will awaken refreshed and thankful for the wonderful experiences. I remember my first ceremony with great fondness. Believe me when I say, they were anxious to taste the fruits of Iscali bliss. Taste them they did with great gusto, of their own volition. It was new and wondrous to them, what we shared. They were taken to new heights. There was nothing painful or harmful. When they awaken, they can tell you themselves."

Nearby, Lanai moved slightly and let out a soft moan. Suddenly, she grimaced, gasped in her dream, and then her fists clenched and body went rigid arching her back, before she groaned loudly, muscles quivering.

Korban eyed her grimly before turning his face to Lavia.

"Thank you for your visit, priestess. We can take care of our women from here."

Lavia ignored the threat in his voice. "Oh, Korban, I so want to stay and learn about you. From what I was told, you have already accomplished unbelievable feats. That fascinates me. May we be friends?"

"Lavia, I would say to you, tread lightly. You're earned the wrath of all the five Kar tribes. That is not a good thing."

"Give me an opportunity to change that misconception. I have already talked sternly to my priest who erred in his judgment. I had no hand in what he did."

"I doubt that, but regardless, you should wait for the sun to rise. If our ladies rise also, I'll see what they have to say."

"As you wish. I'll see you in the morning. I look forward to it, my dear man."

She got up, but went over to Lanai who'd relaxed out of the spasm. She whispered something in her ear and kissed her forehead. Lanai's eyelids fluttered and her hands flexed grasping at Lavia. Lavia patted her knee, turned and smiled at Korban. Lanai muttered something Korban could not hear. It made Lavia smile broadly and exclaim audibly.

"See, she is still rapt in her wonderful dreams. This is good. I gave her the best experience we have to offer. She is doing very well with it. She is a very good pupil and a fast study. I'm very pleased. Even after so many ceremonies, I admit this was a delight for me also."

Smiling, eyeing Lanai again, and then walking over to Korban, touching him on the shoulder, she whispered something in her language with her eyes closed. With that, Lavia walked out of camp, impervious to the glares of the troops. Her smirk seemed like a permanent expression on her face.

Korban watched her leave. Her jet-black long hair was affixed in a ponytail all the way below her waist. She was physically attractive, but there was no lure for Korban. She wasn't a woman who would ever interest him. Dismissing her instantly, he focused on the princess.

That night as the women gradually started to come out of the trances, in their restless sleep they started making more sounds, moans and groans. Seemingly it was a difficult task trying to awaken as all of them moaned and groaned louder and there was considerable writhing and grimacing.

When the camp awoke in the morning the women opened their eyes, but were dull-eyed and listless. It took food, strong coffee, and time for them to start to respond. That response was tepid and they were still listless.

Korban sat down beside Lanai.

"Princess, I'm sorry you were taken. Can you tell me what happened? Did they harm you? That Iscali potion had a strong effect on you all."

"Korban, I…eh…my mind is a fog. My head hurts, very much. How long were we gone?"

"By the time we could sail to this island and trek across the island to rout her forces, it was nearly two weeks. It took us more time to fight our way up here past her sham army."

"I feel weak, I feel sad, and I feel strangely embarrassed, but I don't know why. I don't know what this illness is that assails me and my ladies."

"Does any memory help guide you about this?"

Lila and the maidens had come over to sit down. All of them looked similarly distressed and daunted as they looked at Lanai. None of them seemed to retain their normal selves. The only word Korban thought of was damaged.

"It's so foggy. I can't remember much."

"Yes, foggy," the ladies agreed in a mumble, but something in their expressions piqued Korban's attention. He tried to question them.

However, at that moment, Lavia strolled into camp and came straight over to Lanai, sitting down beside her.

"Ah, my beautiful flowers. You brighten my day with your great beauty."

All of the women looked down. It struck Korban, like they felt shame in her presence.

"Do you see what I said, Korban. They were not harmed. On the contrary, they experienced true wonders they will cherish and remember for life. I've shown them new ways to live a life, better ways."

Korban eyed her skeptically.

She ignored his dour glance. "Eat some food, ladies. You will feel much better."

She smiled again at Korban, striking a sensual pose to draw his attention. He glowered in response.

"Lavia, I can speak for all of my troops. On these 'wonders' you offer the men, we'll pass. I suspect many of us would like to offer you some of our wonders of a different sort."

She laughed loudly.

"I'll pass also, thank you."

Sitting between Lanai and Lila, her attention was still on Korban. Her posture became even less ladylike as she eyed him impolitely.

"See, ladies. The food and drink are a perfect tonic. I know your dreams and fantasies are hard to give up, but you are with your friends now in the daylight. You've lost nothing by awakening from your dreams as the wonders will stay with you."

Placing an arm around each of them, both Lanai and Lila shuddered slightly, but they made no move to deflect her embrace and actually leaned toward her resting their heads on her shoulders. In her embraces, their postures became far less ladylike too. Korban was annoyed he could be evoked by the sights. Turning his face aside, he tried to ignore what Lavia was orchestrating.

She was like a gnat impossible to swat away, ever too close and annoyingly persistent.

When she made no move to leave, and the women started to talk to her, like she suddenly mattered to them, it was Korban who left eventually to see to 'camp matters.' The priests and retainers of Lavia they'd routed had been wandering into the area. He posted guards to watch them, but they were as spineless as ever. The only priest to approach was the same head priest from Lamali who'd stolen the women. He knelt down to talk to Lavia and then to Lanai. Lanai replied to him, which surprised Korban. Lanai and Lila remained on 'display' along with Lavia, which the classless kneeling priest stared at hungrily. It was behavior neither woman would ever have done, or tolerated from a gaping indecent man.

When he saw Korban walking over, ominous like the angel of death, he got up and left quickly, although he still smirked.

"All is well here, ladies?" he asked tersely, staring at the retreating priest.

"Yes," they replied weakly in unison. Still, they didn't resume ladylike poses.

Smiling at him, Lavia stood and all the women stood with her.

"Korban, we're going into the temple to pray together and to commune. They've come to enjoy the spirit of peace we have here. We'll be back later."

He pondered sending guards, but got no sense the women resisted or felt threatened.

He was busy in camp when they emerged much later. They went meekly back to camp, not engaging anyone of the allies in conversation. All of them acted subdued and diminished, huddling and whispering in a tight group staying apart from the warriors. However, the high priestess was spirited and talkative strolling all about freely in the middle of the barbarian warrior camp like a long-lost friend. The angry looks failed to deter her.

Later, Korban saw her coming. He couldn't get away before she corralled him. His grim stare didn't bother her.

"What a time this is for me, walking in the presence of greatness. Your name will be remembered forever, sub chief."

"What do you want, Lavia?"

"Only to savor this time with you."

"Where are our ladies?"

"I'm not sure, after meditations, they went into your camp, somewhere? If they had tasks to do for you, they never said."

"Do you have no tasks to do, running your temple? Accosting some other innocent victims, perhaps?"

She snickered. "We have things well in hand here on the island. I am able to give ample time to be with you."

"What a joy."

She laughed. "I'm drawn to you. I can't say that's ever been true before for me with a man."

"There are many things I could say to that."

She laughed again, inching close to press against him. "I've never been so entertained by a man. You're a rare treat for me."

Taking a step back, he replied. "Indeed. Well, I won't hold you up, Lavia. You can return to your potions. We should depart for the coast as soon as possible. There is still a great distance to travel in our ongoing mission to the world."

"I'll go find your ladies for you. By the way, you know you can include us in your future missions."

"Thank you, but from what we saw of your military forces in action, they would be of no help to us. We have standards for our fighting forces. Feel free to stay here on your island. I don't know if the Brogs can cross the ocean to get here, so you should be free from that risk of annihilation at their hands."

"If you chose to set up a garrison on Iscali, we would feel so much safer. They would benefit from our religion, as your ladies did."

"We'll all be moving on back to the continent. Your religion can stay here with you, priestess."

"I'm sorry you feel that way. Perhaps on your next visit, we can some have in depth meetings? I'm always available to you."

"I doubt I'll have need to return here."

"As you wish."

Brushing against him provocatively, she left, finally. Turning back to the matters at hand, he sent word to prepare for their departure. Hours later, Lanai and her maidens hadn't returned, so Korban sent men to search for them.

Another hour later, the patrol returned with the moody women who were acting sullen and contrary. The warriors looked to be angry and happy to leave the women for Korban to deal with.

Korban looked at Lanai who wouldn't look him in the eyes. She seemed a radically different person, and getting worse by the day. Her bold brash personality muted to the point she was all but unrecognizable. Lila, his other 'litmus test,' was similarly ill-disposed. Her sweet appearance was gone.

"What is it, Lanai? We don't understand this change. Did the priestess and her followers do something dire, because this state we see in you is alarming to us."

Lanai looked up with hostility. "You would not understand. The priestess did nothing dire. We have a new view and understanding of things. What she brought to us is a marvel, a revelation. Your people tearing us away from her teachings and her embrace strikes us badly. There is so much more she can still share with us. What she's already given is...wonderful."

Korban stared at her at a loss for words. He had no answers. Lanai continued to glare.

"Ask any of my maidens. They are similarly in awe of the experiences. I was woefully naïve, but that's no longer the case. I've seen what else is possible in life, and frankly it's very compelling."

"Are you saying you choose to stay here rather than continue the journey?"

That question struck her. For a moment, she looked confused and uncertain.

Turning, Korban walked over to Lila. Pulling up her chin and looking deep into her eyes for a time, finally she blinked, like two realities were warring for her attention.

"Korban?" she whispered.

"I'm here, Lila. If you need my help, just ask."

"I...eh...it's confusing. I serve the princess, but the priestess is very persuasive. Our time with her was as the princess said, an eye-opening marvel. She opened a new world to us."

"We're going to return to the trek, as we must. Do you wish to stay with us, or would you prefer staying here for more of the Priestess marvels?"

She frowned, blinking her eyes. "It's a crushing choice you force on us. You don't understand what it's like, how strong is the lure."

"Perhaps I do understand, Lila. I've seen a few occasions where people became addicted. Whether there is some drug involved, or some other thing to crave, the result seems to be the same. The victims did not have a good ending. If the crown princess has been altered irrevocably, should I allow her to revel in it, to sink to the depths and be lost? Her father would kill me for such a crime, and he would be right to do so."

Lila's eyes focused. "Korban, she whispered. I feel strangely."

She collapsed in his arms.

Lanai cried out, "Lila! What have you done to her, Korban?"

Korban ignored her, picking up the dainty little woman like she was weightless and carrying her to the healers in his command tent.

Lanai railed at him, the healers, and anybody else within shouting distance. Her remaining maidens watched Lila with worry. It wasn't long before Lavia appeared.

"What has happened, sub chief Korban? Is this how you care for your flock?"

Korban was riled, turning with an acid stare, "Lavia, whatever you have done to our women, it's over now. We will leave your island never to return. Do not try to interfere. I only trust our healers to deal with their current distress."

"I did nothing, you fool. They wish to be with me. It's obvious I'm far better a person to properly care for them, for their true needs."

Rising ominously and turning directly facing Lavia, simmering with rage, he shouted. "Quiet! Leave my presence and leave my camp while you still can."

Lanai glared at Korban and for a time, standing close beside Lavia. He expected her to follow Lavia away. They whispered to each other and hugged.

Lila seemed to be lapsed back into a trance, moaning and struggling with troubling dreams.

The healers stared grimly at Lavia. She finally turned and left, pulling out of Lanai's clinging grasp. Lanai took a step after her.

The kidnapper priest who'd been the main irritant from back in Lamali, suddenly appeared in front of Korban. He smirked insolently.

"How do you feel now about the power of our religion, barbarian? We are greater than you backwards, ignorant peasants. We'll still be standing long after your kind is dead and buried."

It was the wrong time for senseless taunts. Korban suddenly reacted, grabbing the priest, lifting him bodily off the ground and smashing him with a mighty blow. He fell to the ground unconscious and bleeding from the face.

Korban turned to Lanai, enraged. "Make your choice, crown princess. Lila will be traveling with us. If you and your other maidens prefer the delights of Lavia's temple, leave now. I have no more patience for this. If you're staying with us, go now and pack as we are leaving."

Lanai paused confronting him with a scowl and a hand on her sword hilt, but her remaining maidens didn't. Recognizing Korban's battle face, they quickly hurried away to obey his terse order. At last, the princess turned and went to join them, but she glared at Korban the entire way.

"I see you clearly now, barbarian. I will not forget this."

He glared back at her. "I see you too, princess. The Vikar peoples have long memories."

Their tenuous relationship took a severe downturn, neither felt forgiving.

Presently, the column pulled away marching rapidly back toward the coast. The Lamali chief walked beside Korban.

"This is a sad turn. I'm sorry I didn't know the true depth of the danger of meeting this priestess. She is sly, acting as someone seeming to be reasonable and friendly, but what I see now in your beautiful women folk is appalling."

"It does not fall on you. They were as unknown to you us they were to us. I hold no fault on you. Whether the ladies can recover, we will see."

"The princess is much changed. She seems as much an enemy now as our Brog adversaries."

"I will lead my people away into Mantu territory, as I have planned. It falls on the princess to sort out her issues. Since we'll be traveling in Mantu and going somewhat toward Tranta, I'll point out she has the option to go back to her father in the Trantan palace."

"That would be unfortunate. She had genuine feelings for you, and I believe you had strong feelings for her. I want to believe time can heal this needless rift."

"That is in her hands. I will act as I am, a sub chief of the Vikar. There are too many important needs ahead of any worries about her royal intransigence."

"I urge you not to rest all blame on her. I feel as you that the priestess used some sort of drug to capture and sway the ladies. If there was some other lure used also, how could we know? Perhaps the healers can also rescue the princess from this scourge?"

Korban shrugged his shoulders.

"It's out of my hands. Whatever happens, I'll deal with it."

Camping for the night, Lila remained in a stasis of sorts. Meanwhile, Lanai and her remaining maidens bedded apart from the men. That choice did not pass the notice of the warriors who increasingly felt more hostility toward the women for their mystifying and contrary behaviors, seemingly getting noticeably worse by the day.

The next day, Lanai acted oblivious to the dark developments swirling around her, but her maidens recognized the genuine threat among warrior companions who'd been their dear friends and protectors. The next night, Lanai bedded them even farther apart from the men. The effect of Lavia's touch and influence dominated the women.

Angry, the warriors did not provide sentry coverage of the women for that night. It was a rare departure from Kar preparedness for all contingencies. Had Lavia sent trailing forces, it would have been easy to reclaim the women.

That didn't happen and when Korban learned about the warrior 'revenge act' he fumed shouting at the warriors.

"Regardless of any feelings we now have about them, they're still under our protection. Is that clear? I will tolerate no more incidents like this. When we get to Mantu, if the princess chooses to return to Tranta, she can do that. I'm not going to make an enemy of the Trantan King regarding his daughter through our poor actions. She can explain her views and desires directly in person there. Perhaps she will finally marry one of those royal dolts her father prefers. If she has another path in mind, I care not." Inwardly, he seethed, struggling to tamp down his rage.

When they reached the island port, Korban didn't hesitate in immediately boarding the ships of the fleet to sail back to Lamali lands and the mainland. Fortunately, this time, they didn't have a huge storm to sail through.

Later, it felt good to be back on their mounts to ride again, once back on land. The more normal things they did on the move, ignoring the women, and the farther they got away from Iscali and the priestess, the more they saw positive changes in the women, some small progress in female behaviors. The maidens improved more so than the princess. She seemed stubborn in a desire to foster the animosity and contrary behaviors. The maidens started to vary away from her moodiness, talking with the warriors, going more frequently to check on Lila. Lila came out of her stupor and improved well. Staying apart from the other women, she approached normalcy more rapidly. Korban could finally talk normally to her and see the re-emergence of her sweet disposition.

One afternoon, he spent considerable time talking with her.

"If you're agreeable, Lila, can I ask you about your time with the priestess? I don't want to pry, but the severe changes we saw alarmed us."

"I will speak about it, but I must say, I'm not fully clear. There were times where I think I was unconscious or possibly...unable to control things? I'm not sure."

"Did she use drugs, potions, or some other thing on you?"

"I have no memory of actively ingesting anything, but as I said, I may not have been aware. If they gave something to us, I can't say. The affect was...powerful, as you saw. The affect here in camp, how you started treating us like enemies, that frightened me."

"Lila, after all we've been through together, it wasn't what we expected from you. I regret, we made it seem like that with our dismal choices, like you were consciously making those dark decisions, without considering you were stolen away and taken into their custody and control. For that I apologize."

"There is no reason to apologize. I understand completely."

"About the princess? She seems an enemy now."

"I don't know why she acts more resistant. I do know the priestess concentrated far more time on her than on us. She was fascinated with Lanai? Is that the right way to say it?"

"If this new person Lavia created is a permanent change, I'm of a mind to dispatch her back to her father. With what could still be ahead, we can't have such a disruption in the camp."

"When I'm able, I'll rejoin the ladies, and I'll actively try to help her return to who she was. With the progress I'm making, if I can recover, I believe she can also."

"I would appreciate the help. The Vikar people don't make friendships lightly. Casting her aside would be a difficult choice we don't want to make. Is there anything else you remember you feel I should know?"

Lila pondered; a strange look crossed her face. "There is nothing else I should say. None of us are perfect, we all have flaws, make mistakes, and we all have personal inner demons to fight now."

"That, I understand, Lila. Everybody has inner battles. We are with you in any way we can help. Just remember, you're cherished." She smiled warmly.

Soon afterwards, within a few days, the command left the Lamali main camp.

The chief spoke to Korban. "You already have a formidable force, but I'd like to donate Lamali warriors to join you? I think when you encounter Mantu patrols, it will help to have Lamali warriors with you as we have commerce and friendships there."

"That would be appreciated. We don't need more strife if it can be avoided."

"Be careful, as I know you will. I wish I could join you, but as chief I can't leave to go on any adventures."

Korban placed the Lamali warriors in the vanguard as first contact with any Mantu they met.

Lila, left the care of the healers acting totally normal and rejoined her sisters, the servants of the royal princess.

Lanai actually smiled when Lila came to her, and their warm hug was the first hopeful sign perhaps the princess could come around. The maidens continued doing far better than their princess in recovering.

Korban made no attempt to approach or converse with her. Placing the women well back in the column, he left it to the Alkar tribe members to protect them both on the trail and at night.

The princess warmed slightly to the hesitant male contact, but mostly it was her maidens trying to dispel the warrior anger and to resume civility. Lanai remained reclusive to an extent and drew the maidens along with her, especially when sleeping at night. The maidens went along with her in having more privacy at night, deferring to her desires.

Leaving Lamali lands meant traversing the Crystal Pass. It wasn't dangerous like earlier legs of the journey but it wasn't a rapid transit. Tall mountains on both sides were reminiscent of the prior sheer cliff faces and it brought back chilling memories. That helped as the women shared in reliving their terrors while sitting and talking with the Alkar warriors in the evenings. It was a thread they both understood and went far in healing the rift.

Lanai actually came to sit down and listen though she said nothing. Lila sat beside her talking constantly. It caused Lanai to smile and eventually she gave her friend a hug.

Korban saw none of it as he was purposely camped far from there at the head of the column. Thoughts of the princess no longer dominated his mind as they had before. Her rebellion evoked a corresponding reaction in him.

What the princess started to do was use her sword for practice with her maidens. Recovering their fighting edge seemed a good sign. When Korban was informed, he merely shrugged. Completing the journey to get into Mantu lands was his focus.

They stopped for a night on the border with the Crystal Pass at their backs. Ahead were relatively flat lands with tall grasses abundant. With Mantu being the largest nation, they knew the journey there would be long. However, there were no natural formations to slow them.

Traveling the first day into Mantu country, they turned slightly north toward the great body of water, Lake Hilan. It wasn't an ocean, but an imposing sight nonetheless. Far out in the lake, they could see fishing boats that looked like little specks.

Camping that night near the shore, they had their first contact with the Mantu people.

A large war party of Mantu riders roared in, whooping and shouting, waving weapons, though they didn't strike. Per his directions, Korban's forces stood by alertly, but only watching.

The Lamali members went out to speak with them. After that, the histrionics quickly dissipated, and their captain came to meet Korban who stood patiently waiting, betraying nothing.

The Mantu leader was dressed in buckskins dyed to match the browns and greens of the grasslands. He was confident and calculating looking around the camp at the numbers and the diverse forces, the array of how they were stationed, and the equally confident manner of the Kar tribesmen.

"You have no fear of the Mantu?"

"Should I? We come in peace, as I'm sure you already know. Do you have fear of barbarians?"

The captain grinned. "Are there any tribes you don't have here?"

"No."

"They tell me you're looking to gain allies?"

"You also know that. I'm sure you've had attacks from the Brogs."

"Yes, that is true. What we don't understand is why you think we need you? We have more horsemen than you can count. We can defend our grasslands."

"That may, or may not be true. Volta has advised us it's possible there is another force or forces behind this sudden emergence of Brog attacks. Perhaps you could handle Brog aggressions, but whatever might be behind them could require all of us. We trust his predications implicitly. He has not been wrong."

"Your argument is compelling. Having all of these other peoples in your sway speaks to that. The Mantu don't bow to any others. If you think to put the Vikar over us..."

"You know that's not true."

"Are you not the leader here? You are Vikar."

"I am Vikar, but we've worked together, bled and fought together over a long perilous journey and have had no problems. Why would it be different for the Mantu?"

"Would you serve a Mantu leader in such a quest?"

"What group the leader is from isn't important. Competence is the important factor. Ask any here if that has been an issue?"

The captain smiled. "Is that stew I smell?"

"It is, please join us."

The number of Mantu horsemen was much larger than they thought, numbering over a hundred. Once they sat down together, Korban saw the princess for the first time since leaving Lamali.

"Captain, I would like to introduce, Lanai, crown princess of Tranta."

"What, truly; is she here?"

Lanai strolled over; her regal bearing returned. Though she didn't look at, or acknowledge Korban, she acted politely to the Mantu captain.

"You probably don't remember me, princess, but I met you long ago. Your father rode to our great council and brought you along. We were both much younger."

"I do remember riding to that council, though I meet so many people I can't remember them all. I apologize for not recognizing you."

"Think nothing of it. I'd heard tales about you arming yourself and gaining great war skills. As I see you, I tend to believe the stories. They also say you crossed over the Plateau of Heaven, descended down a sheer icy cliff face, and crossed the Valley of Fire? It sounds impossible."

"That is true. I say this a lot, I look back and wonder how we did it. So much could have gone wrong."

"Thankfully it didn't and you're here to grace us with your presence."

"You're too kind, captain. I'm just a woman like every other."

"We both know, you have no peer."

Lanai actually smiled broadly before she fought it off.

"If Tranta is in this alliance, who are the Mantu to deny it. We're happy to escort you across the grasslands. I warn you, it's a great distance. No matter which way you go, it is far."

Korban spoke, "We're at a point of a crossroads perhaps. If we continue with our original mission, we would turn southward to seek out the Greka in their forests and eventually ascend the escarpment to enter the Belshik Plateau to meet the people living there."

"What is your crossroad?"

"If the princess wishes to return to her country and to her father, this would be the closet point for her to make that turn. We leave it to her about that choice. She's been a great companion through all of our travails. The choice of her future is hers completely."

"Princess, the Mantu are happy to deliver you safely back to Tranta if that is your wish. Otherwise, we can safeguard you through the long journey south and southeast.

She looked at Korban for the first time. He couldn't read her expression, what it meant.

"I and my maidens have committed to this vast undertaking. I think we will see it through to the end."

It was the last thing Korban expected and he made no attempt to hide his joy. Lanai smiled at his first welcoming reaction toward her.

Korban took a chance and walked over close. "Perhaps we will realign camp deployments since we're now in safe grounds with the Mantu to watch over us."

He worried she would reject him in front of the entire assemblage.

"If you feel that is prudent, we will go where you direct us, sub chief."

Turning her head, she nodded to the Mantu captain. "It's been my pleasure to meet you."

She walked away back to her maidens, but by this time, they'd come to the edge of the circle.

Lila beamed looking at Korban. He couldn't help but smile back.

"You have these beautiful women, women of significance in your camp, women who can fight? What magic do you have?

Korban shook his head. "I have no magic; I was just a man in the right place at the right time. I hold no sway over them, believe me. They do as they please."

"I won't share that with our women. It could destroy Mantu society if they suddenly rise up against us."

"They are difference makers. Whether that will ultimately be a great good, or the end of all men, we shall see."

All of the men laughed heartily.

"I think I need more of your stew."

"Eat your fill, my friend."

When they redeployed the women bringing them back to the original configuration, they were back in Korban's immediate sphere. Lila walked up to him.

"My lord, did I not tell you to give it some time. The princess has come far in the recovery of her wits, wouldn't you say?"

"It is a pleasant surprise."

"When you took the risk with her before all the people, I could see on your face you feared the worst. I had an idea it was the best choice you could have made. There was a risk she might still harbor her grudge, but there was a better chance she wanted to put this all behind us. I'm glad you had the courage, but I expected it. You've been a great leader through all of our hardships."

"I don't want to push it. I'll leave it to you if you wish to place your bedding by me again."

"I'll make subtle hints, or maybe not so subtle hints to come back to your side. If she wants to sleep apart, she'll be sleeping alone."

Korban smiled ruefully.

CHAPTER NINE
Grasslands

With the nagging worry about the women and the long-lasting effect of Lavia's pervasive touch seemingly resolved, the troops assumed they were headed for a much easier road. The Mantu guides took them initially eastward to one of their populated centers. It was different than settlements in the other countries they'd traveled thus far.

The abundance of horses was a remarkable sight as the group traveled farther through Mantu lands. Stories about the Mantu culture didn't do justice to the reality of seeing it. Those horses were so attuned to that Mantu culture, there was no need to build corrals or to tie up the horses. They came and went as they pleased. However, the horses were never far from the care of their handlers. The symbiotic relationship of animal and human was like the Mantu and the horses were blended as a family. The Mantu needed no saddles. They rode bareback, or on riding blankets. Young Mantu learned by riding on ponies.

Mantu settlements were circular, both with individual huts, and with the entire settlement. They didn't set out sentries as they were in no danger on Mantu land. Although there were predators roaming the country, they wouldn't approach any settlements and they wouldn't attack the vast herds of the horses under Mantu scrutiny and protection.

Having Brogs welling up out of the ground had been the first real threat to Mantu society ever. That alone was the reason they were willing to talk about an alliance with outsiders.

Korban hadn't realized the issue with Lanai had been such a background stress both for him and all in his command. He personally didn't realize how much until she followed Lila over and placed her bedding near him, warming his heart.

While Lila spoke to him, at length, initially Lanai merely paid attention. She didn't yet stick her toe in the water of resuming normalcy with him.

However, she was well aware of his frequent glances her way. That evening she was slightly exaggerated in fussing over her bedding, checking the folds, and then checking again, before she finally climbed under the covers. She glanced at him at last as he was staring, before she smiled and rolled onto her side, facing the other way.

Mantu escorts bedded beside the allied camp, taking custody of the allies' horses for expert care in pampering of their mounts. Being in the midst of so many other horses invigorated those ally's horses. They cantered, neighed, and showed behaviors from being colts so long ago.

The troops enjoyed the 'show' a great deal, as well as marveling at the Mantu expertise in caring for any horse.

Being invited into the Mantu settlement was another first for both sides.

The head man of the village came out leading a large file of warriors. Korban wasn't sure if it meant trouble, but then the chief smiled and nodded to him.

"You are this Korban I hear about?"

"I am."

"My name is Nemar, the chieftain of this Kraal. Will you come with us? No strangers have ever been brought into a Kraal before."

"We would be honored, chief."

Korban noticed him staring at Lanai. "I'm sorry, chief. This is Lanai, crown princess of Tranta."

The chief gave her a nod, and a broad smile.

Lanai replied. "I'm happy to meet you, Chief Nemar, and I appreciate your gracious invitation into your homes."

She boldly walked over and took his arm. The chief literally beamed.

Korban made note of her skillful use of her feminine charms to advance their cause.

Marching into the large community, the way was choked with curious villagers and their families. A visit from outsiders was unheard of.

Lanai stooped often to touch little ones, chat with the moms and generally made a great and endearing impression.

Even within the village, free roaming horses were everywhere. The horses were comfortable walking close among the villagers.

Meanwhile, the chief talked continuously to Lanai. She smiled demurely. Korban walked farther behind with his officers watching Lanai take control of the moment.

In the center of the community, a fire roared with a great vat of cooking food. Nearby, horses were unfazed by the fire and munched contentedly nearby on hay and grasses. It was only there that Korban first saw the older children and the youth of the tribe.

Nemar waited for Korban to reach he and Lanai.

"Our young ones are our treasure, as much as we worship our horses. We never take chances by putting them in jeopardy. It has always been this way."

"It's a good plan. With the Vikar tribe, the warrior way is taught at a very early age, but we don't put them at risk if they're unready."

"There are many legends about Vikar prowess and ferocity. We've had no contact, so there was no way to judge fact from fiction. The village would love for you to tell us the tale of this epic journey you've just taken, after we eat, of course."

The assembled all laughed.

Lanai sat beside Korban for the meal. She had started speaking with him again.

"I didn't realize stew is the main dish of so many peoples."

"It serves up well and meets the needs as easily as any other meal you could choose. With meat and vegetables combined, I don't feel there is a better meal."

"In the palace, the King's chef and his staff make a wide variety of foods and desserts. I like your stew, but I wouldn't mind variety in what I eat these days."

Korban smirked. "Fine royal delicacies would be perfect for barbarian eaters."

"You're in no position to judge. Once you've feasted at length at the royal table to enjoy true variety, we can talk further about it. At least I've had a variety of food fare to have an opinion." He merely grinned at her.

Later, Korban stood along with Lanai. It was dusk so the throng was obscured from view.

"Korban spoke loudly at a near shout to be heard by all in telling their tale. With Lanai's dainty voice, he was surprised when she could speak loudly too."

Detailing not only the trek, but going back to the rescue, the Mantu were rapt with the unfolding events of their lives. As they highlighted the various harrowing dangers, the crowd oohed and aahed loudly. The mental image of the all-day ride down the sheer face of an icy cliff brought cries of fear and of awe. Equally astonishing to the throng was Lanai and her maidens training and developing martial skills.

When they finished the saga, the Mantu begged for a martial display, so Korban and Lanai squared off for a demonstration which escalated to a daunting fight as neither liked to lose.

It was like a fight to the death of gladiators in an arena, the Mantu were so taken. Korban quickly heard the sway of the cheers moving in Lanai's direction. She loved it, whooping, twisting and twirling in the battle to the delight of the throng. Korban let the contest go on stretching into a long period, before making a lightning strike. Lanai barely parried the attack and launched a strong thrust of her own. The fight was getting close to having injuring blows. Korban knew the princess would not relent, so at a point, he suddenly stepped back, gave her a salute with a sword flourish, a bow, and then he stood, waiting.

It took her a little time to quell her fighting blood. She returned the gesture of respect to him, and the crowd roared and clapped wildly.

The chief, Nemar, walked out beaming.

He spoke to Lanai. "Never have the Mantu peoples been blessed by such a masterful display. Your skills and strength are remarkable. For a woman to fight evenly with a Vikar master is...I don't have a word for it."

"Thank you, my chief." She flipped seamlessly into a feminine mode, doing a royal curtsy, and offering her hand for his kiss.

She did notice the scowling face of the chief's wife. It tickled her immensely. The chief continued to lavish praise on her, ignoring Korban who also chuckled seeing the ire of the chief's wife.

The dynamics of bonded spouses were the same everywhere. He pondered with a smirk. *I think there may be a storm brewing tonight in the chief's hut.*

When Nemar finally realized his display was too much, fawning all over Lanai like a schoolboy, he turned sheepishly toward his wife. Grim-faced, she was not looking on fondly at his embarrassing public display.

He walked away leaving Lanai to Korban. His wife turned on her heel and marched away leaving him to trail behind her.

Lanai laughed softly. "Men are so lame, don't you think, Korban."

"Crown Princess, what could I say to that? That was a fine match, by the way. I'm glad you retain your fighting edge."

"I think I could have beaten you tonight."

He didn't reply.

"You think you were just toying with me?"

"No, I don't think that. We've told you that your level of skills is very good now. You know I don't fight as a game."

Fortunately, she let it drop at that, but only after a pause to ponder it, and then a thoughtful glance at him.

Another of the Mantu villagers, a matronly woman, led them to a single hut for the night. Going inside, the idea of the unmarried crown princess of Tranta staying alone in a hut with a man which would have caused a war from Tranta, the Mantu treated it as no issue. Although she was no longer actively trying evoke a romantic response from him, the spark was still there in both of them.

It was some time before they fell asleep. As always with Korban, he replayed any fight in his mind, critiquing his moves and defenses.

She had an active mind for a time as well, but not about the fight. The legacy of Lavia was deep seated and stubborn. The allure of the temple persisted to plague her as her heart thumped and her breathing escalated. Although she had made great progress with this imposed onus from the Iscali Island, it could flare up at any time strongly provoking her emotions. This night was such a time.

Korban awoke the next morning refreshed and feeling optimistic the women had turned the corner against their malaise. Lanai awoke poorly rested with her demons haunting her still. She was able to avoid treating Korban badly with disdain only with an effort.

She smiled politely to the ongoing awed treatment from the Mantu villagers. Gradually with ample strong coffee she improved, but for her it had the hollow ring of a façade masking a distressing truth.

Dainty and petite, Lila continued to do the best of the women in her recovery. Her engaging personality warmed anybody she met. Lanai gained some help in her battle, by proxy, from basking in Lila's lively orbit.

In spite of the pleas of their hosts to stay longer, Korban ordered the command onto the horses and started the journey again. A huge contingent of Mantu warriors led them turning southward and then angling southwesterly.

On this occasion, Lanai rode beside Korban, but she wasn't talkative. Her mind was distracted. Lila noted this and instantly realized the cause. Riding up to her side, chatting amicably, she warmed Lanai's mood and eventually, she did engage, but only talking softly with her favorite maiden.

The flat plains and grasslands were like an endless ocean of grass stretching out for as far as the eye could see. Horses in great herds ambled over and paced the procession for a time before breaking off to return to the fold of their own groups. They had no fear of the Mantu or these strangers riding with them.

Each night when they camped, the Mantu warriors stayed nearby, although they mingled with the wild herds with their skillful care.

The configuration of the camp was back to the normal alignment. The women stayed near to Korban to sleep. What Korban noticed was their continuing the somewhat muted responses, furtive glances among each other about the secrets they chose not to reveal, and continuing troubles with their sleep from these powerful dreams.

With that backdrop, but still having easy riding, they got a reminder of the reason they were on this trek.

In the deepest of night, the ground suddenly erupted as the Brog welled up to attack.

These were the finest fighters of the Kar tribes. Rising quickly in response to the danger right in their midst, they fought the vicious enemy as savagely as their Brog opponents.

It was not a small enemy force and they would not relent. There were terrible casualties among the command, their Mantu escorts, and even some horses as the voracious Brog swarm cannibalized whatever they could get their hands on. The darkness didn't help the allies in locating and eliminating the foe.

The women were forced to defend themselves as the Brog attackers drew no distinction between the sexes. Lanai's incredible beauty was not a protection from hideous death. The Brog saw her merely as food.

The fight went on for much of the night. Korban was torn between trying to direct his forces in the battle and keeping close to the women. At one point, a group of Brog surrounded and grabbed little Lila.

Korban attacked them scything down numerous Brog, but they rallied to keep him from reaching her. Overwhelmed, pulled down and pinned to the ground, Lila screamed in fear.

As he battled, other Kar warriors joined him to keep the Brog from dragging Lila down into their hole. They surrounded the growing knot of the enemy fighters and hacked at them determinedly. There was never any doubt who would win this fight, but the issue was could they destroy the enemy before they harmed or killed Lila.

Lanai and the other maidens were fighting in a tight group as a single unit, but they were hard pressed as well to avoid the same fate.

As the battle for Lila reached a tipping point, the Brog realized they couldn't spirit her away and their approach changed. Yanking away her clothes to expose her flesh, they moved in to devour this precious petite woman while she was still alive.

The warriors literally leaped onto the Brog to throttle and kill them. Keeping them from biting Lila was in question for too long a time. Korban leaped over their diminishing line of enemies who were fighting to get teeth into her. He slaughtered the closest potential Brog feeders with lightning strikes. When he killed a large Brog, seemingly the leader, the Brog assault lost steam and the Kar warriors quickly finished off the remaining enemy attackers.

Lila was terrified, grabbing Korban in a tight embrace. She was bleeding from a number of injuries. Lanai made her way into the clump of warriors standing protectively looking around for further threats.

"Korban, I will take her to the healers."

Lila continued to cling to Korban until Lanai peeled her away.

They quickly put her clothes back on and led her away as Lila cried.

Taking stock after the fight, it was the worst battle of the entire mission thus far.

The Mantu contingent were as irate at the attacks on the horses as the attack on the humans.

Korban took stock of the toll blaming himself in spite of having no legitimate fault for the losses.

The Lamali contingent was angry but also shocked. Riding with the legendary Kar contingents hadn't granted them immunity from harm. It was a sobering dose of reality to shatter an illusion of invincibility. Korban made a point of seeking them out.

"I'm sorry, my friends. This was always an attack I thought would happen."

The Lamali captain had survived. "We will do our duty for our people, but I think we must change our ways. We weren't cautious enough. These vile creatures can come up out of the ground anywhere."

"That is true. From now on, I'll have double the sentries at night. I was complacent and a poor leader."

"That is not true, my lord. None could have known they were waiting there in the ground at that spot right under us with this ambush."

By that time, the sun was on the horizon. It was a somber breakfast before they set about burying the dead. The huge number of Brog dead they left out for the scavenger animals. Korban went to check on Lila.

She had numerous bandages, but fortunately, none of the injuries were deep or serious. His intervention was just in the nick of time to keep her from deadly gnawing by Brog mouths.

Lila was dozing in and out of consciousness. The healers had given her a potion to rest from the pain of her injuries.

"Korban," she muttered as he took her hand. "Thank you for my life."

"Rest, Lila, and heal from your wounds. We're here to protect you."

"I prayed you would rescue me. I thought I would die."

He leaned over to kiss her forehead.

Sitting back up, he noticed Lanai eyeing him. Her expression seemed a little dark. What it meant; he had no idea.

"Lanai, we must return to the trail. There is no time to stay here. There may be many more Brog in that hole. I'll leave Lila in your care."

"We will keep her safe, sub chief," Lanai replied formally. Korban noted her continuing hard look and wondered what might be in her mind.

Rather than worry about the emotional drag trying to deal with Lanai, he turned to go find his leaders.

The procession resumed the trek riding rapidly away from the site of the battle. On this day, Korban decided to ride forward and join the vanguard. That spearpoint unit had been growing as each group wanted to add members to the whole. It made the group cumbersome, but at the same time they had plenty of men to spread out in many directions.

Marka was the acknowledged head of the vanguard. He made the assignments and created the strategies each day going forward. He also singularly instilled the skills needed to be top-tier scouts in the Vikar sense of the word.

"Sub chief," he said, as Korban rode up beside him.

"Master scout."

Marka laughed. "I can ask, what are you up to, but I probably already know."

"Yes, I'm riding away from that headache. They can stir me up when I need to keep a clear head."

"I won't share any opinions. I doubt you came here for that."

"I would like your thoughts about that Brog attack. Could we stumble into more traps ahead? I worry about riding into an excavation and falling into their holes."

"Although they may be digging up ahead in various places, I can spot hazards. Even if they've dug upward without breaking the surface, I can spot irregular places to avoid. There are other dangers more serious."

"Like what?"

"As we get close and then into the forests of the Greka, predators will be a real threat. The warmer weather there fosters animals. For predators, the horses of Mantu are easy meat as they can race out of the woods in the night to snag prey to drag back into their woods. Once we try to travel into Greka territory, we may find predators are as prevalent as horses in Mantu. It's said the Greka are a protective clan that are highly skilled in avoiding notice. We might never find them. If predators come at us in numbers, it will most surely guarantee losses. Until recently, we've been fortunate about deaths. I think those days are over."

"I can't disagree, Marka. I wish I could say I have a great plan for that problem."

"I don't think any plan is possible, or could save us from risk. Back in Lamali, when we pondered whether to go to Iscali island, there was no plan possible to protect us then. It was a matter we had to adjust to the threat and act according. I know there was harm done to the women, the scope of which we don't fully know, but this mission won't be forgiving. We must still contact the Greka, and whomever lives on the Belshik plateau."

"I worry about both of those tasks."

"Another thought I have is this southern continent we know nothing about. I wonder if our troubles originate there."

"I've thought that same thing. I don't think of the Brog as great thinkers. I believe some force is driving them. It could be a nation in that continent."

"As we travel toward them, perhaps if they have an active hand, we'll see some sign of them to better understand what we face."

"That would be good."

"Do you think about what's happening back in our mountains?"

"With Volta and the others in charge, I feel confident about the tribes. These other lowland countries are more vulnerable. As we just saw, for the Brog, it's much easier here with the lowlands for their digging. As you have suggested, it will only get worse the farther we go."

"I wonder how many Brog swarms are out there. That last swarm may be the tip of the spear."

"We have a large force, but you're right, they may be like swarms of insects, numerous beyond counting."

"I hope we can cope with any peril. It's hard to prepare if we don't know what to prepare for?"

"It's been my worry since the start. They had no qualms about attacking us in the middle of Mantu country. Again, losing nearly all of their attackers didn't bother them."

"If they plan to bleed us, I wonder what changes we could make to counter it. Lila was nearly lost."

"I also worry at how they're able to attack, welling up suddenly in the middle of the camp. It can put terror in the hearts of our forces. We're brave enough, but being snatched away while you sleep is scary. I'll leave you to your scrutiny and return to the main column. Thank you, Marka."

Riding back, he saw Lila riding in the midst of the other maidens. Bandages were visible protruding from different spots. Lanai was riding beside Lila talking continuously to her. Lila looked gaunt.

He sauntered toward them until Lanai noticed him.

She called out, "All is well, Korban. You can take care of your other duties."

He took it as 'unwelcoming' him. Nodding, he continued riding farther back into his forces. Every contingent as he rode past them eyed him firmly, nodding and making gestures of obeisance, many with salutes.

When he got to the rear guard, significant Mantu warriors were riding with them. He decided to ride over joining them. It was refreshing because all of them wanted to talk to him. The Mantu people were fascinated listening as the Vikar warriors recounted again the prior difficulties during the trek. The topic of Lanai came up often as the Mantu were as taken with her as much as the warriors had been, and still were.

When the inevitable questions came about him and her, Korban just shrugged it off and didn't really answer. At last, after hours of questions, he said. "She is the crown princess of Tranta. I have no plans to be a King there. I'll return to the front of the column now. We need to stop soon."

Going back to his normal place, the women rode close together and eyed him strangely. Lila still had her head down. It struck him odd, and to an extent foreboding, but he chose not to inquire. Shifting female moods were his new world these days. He did not relish that difficult issue which always seemed beyond his influence, or his comprehension.

Instead, he talked to some of his nearby trek leaders.

That afternoon as dusk approached, the vanguard force suddenly veered away thundering to the right. Soon they heard battle cries and the sounds of a battle. Korban ordered a significant force of reinforcements into action to support the vanguard, but he stayed back with the column deploying them in a defensive bubble with the women secured in the middle.

It happened there were ample Mantu tribesmen who lived nearby who'd been shadowing the column. When the main attack came, they jumped in to join the defenders.

The Brog attack came in numbers the allies hadn't seen before. Initially, the Brog surge tried to cut them off from the vanguard force. The intervention of Mantu horsemen was an important factor in the escalating battle. The Mantu participation continued to grow as more locals joined them from farther away.

The initial skirmish evolved into a huge confrontation. These Brog were seriously motivated in this attack. They struck without regard to their own safety, rather they tried to do harm to the allies in every way possible. They savaged horses as well as fighters.

This time, Korban surrounded the ladies in concentric invincible rings of steel swords in highly skilled hands.

Even with that, the women eventually had to fight as the Brog were relentless and eventually got to them.

It was a frightening battle. With as much mayhem as the allies could cause, the Brog quickly filled the gaps with more bodies and gnawing mouths. The battle stretched late into the evening well past the time they would have sought a campsite. The battlefield was littered with bodies, a great many of them were Brog. It helped having considerable Mantu horses and horsemen riding into and over Brog attackers trampling them to death.

As exhausting as was the long fight, the ally's skill and strategies with interlocking and overlapping arrays proved too much for the Brog to conquer and with the staggering losses of Brog attackers, the outcome became clear. However, once the fighting ended, the allies were not unscathed. There were many dead, but the greatest numbers were the injuries. Brog teeth could cause serious wounds as they sought to consume living flesh.

The allies could only camp in place in exhaustion and try to eat and drink with their weapons close at hand. There weren't enough healers to rapidly address all of the many wounds. The following morning, they could only take up where they'd left off with applying healing salves and bandaging the wounded.

The command did not continue traveling that day, they couldn't. Physically, serious wounds needed to be treated and begin to heal, but mentally, the unusual threat posed by the dullard Brogs sapped their spirits. It was like fighting endless insatiable giant insects. There were no boundaries or rules of engagement. They fought relentlessly and honored no sense of decency. Devouring innocent women and children as easily as fighting men took a mental toll on the allies. Being outraged didn't change the dynamics of the actual fights. They were still beyond exhausting.

As Korban sat talking with his leaders, Lanai chose to join them.

She asked. "Korban, do you think we have enough warriors with us to complete this mission? I'm worried about how things have gone."

"We're all worried, princess. I can't answer your question. How can anybody know? I don't fear to fight them, but their sheer numbers are the problem."

"Lately, I've had more frightening dreams. I don't know if it means anything. Perhaps it's some weakness in me."

"There's no weakness in you. We all ponder the future and mentally prepare to face it."

She turned her head to Marka. "What do think about this? Do you have these same worries?"

"I have the same concerns about their numbers, but I haven't seen anything yet that they can defeat us. We need to be cautious and never be unprepared, but if it comes to a final battle, if we can gather all of the nations, we will win."

"That's encouraging to hear. I respect your opinion above that of most, just like I respect Volta's ideas."

"Thank you, princess. I hope you know we all respect you also, and hold you in the highest regard."

"Thank you, but as you know, I haven't been at my best recently. I hope to return to a place to merit your high praise."

Suddenly realizing it was obvious to everybody sitting there, Korban's brain trust, that she hadn't included Korban in mentioning the small circle of those she respected and highly regarded, she turned her head. Glancing at him, he was smiling ruefully. He nodded and made a tiny dismissive hand gesture so she wouldn't bring it up. The damage was already done.

"I will go to see about Lila, gentlemen."

Lanai walked away, elegant as always. The entire group watched her go.

They didn't speak for a time. Gradually standing, they started to drift away. Korban walked over to the Mantu villagers to watch them caring for the horses. Usually, the Stakar, also being animal focused as a tribe, they were there too. It was doubly true now as it appeared the entire Stakar contingent was present relishing the moment of watching Mantu skills in action.

Korban exchanged brief greetings and pleasantries before taking up a brush to care for his own horse. It was contentedly munching nutrient rich grasses from the plains. He looked for Lanai's horse, but it wasn't necessary to tend to it. As her horse, it was accorded the same celebrity status as it's rider. There were plenty of Mantu anxious to provide the tender care.

The most serious wounds from the battle led the healers to suggest a longer wait before the allies departed.

Korban saw no reason to rush, so they waited.

Meanwhile, their camp drew many local Mantu villagers to come to see the legendary figures. The saga of Lanai and Korban had taken on epic proportions. Tales of a romance abounded, though the members of the camp could have told a different story. The supposed romance was told in wildly different versions, depending on the teller, again, whether lurid, or tame.

The Mantu decided to perform a sacred horse rite for their new friends. For them, it was a holy ceremony.

Lanai decided to sit beside Korban for the occasion, though mostly because she was strongly urged to do so by her maidens who'd heard a great deal from the camp about troubling undercurrents and prevailing opinions.

Rather than cause a stir by sitting apart, she consented. Korban had no idea about any background rumblings. He merely went to his place of honor and when she came, he nodded to her without comment. The Mantu cheered at the couple sitting together. Lanai waved and smiled amicably at the throng. Korban merely nodded to their reactions.

The Mantu produced drums and instruments to join singers in celebrating the horses and the horse culture. It was a moving experience. When they brought the horses into the circle in dizzying displays of Mantu riding skills and unity, that too was dazzling. What they could do in twists, leans, bending, and such without falling off the horses was amazing. The horses tolerated any of the Mantu actions without flinching. They were well trained and well-practiced in having Mantu riders.

Lanai yelled and clapped loudly in appreciation. Even Korban joined in the applause.

The event wrapped up with the horsemen coming together in tight concentric circles as the musicians performed an inspirational rendition.

The crowd cheered effusively. Lanai stood yelling and hooting along with them. Finally, Korban arose to show his appreciation for both the skills displayed, but also the honor which had been accorded to the allies, the first non-Mantu ever to see this rite.

Numerous Mantu leaders made their way over. They wanted to hear what the celebrities thought. Though they greeted Korban, mostly they crowded around Lanai. She was the perfect royal princess for the occasion. She could make them feel relevant, and she did.

Villager wives glowed at what they perceived as validation from a great royal princess, the highlight of their lives. The princess gave them particular notice and interest.

Lanai was patient throughout the long aftermath stretching into the dark. When she could finally recess to join her ladies, she started walking away only to realize Korban had been short-changed. As almost an afterthought, she glanced back.

"Good night, sub chief."

"Crown princess."

This was a night the women actually placed their bedding apart from Korban, seeking more unexplained separation from all the camp males. However, they were still safe within the circle of the sentry lines. That lesson had been learned.

Korban chose not to think what it meant, if anything. He fell asleep rapidly.

After several more days, the healers finally agreed to resume the trek, though grudgingly. The most seriously injured stayed apart from their units, riding instead with the healers.

The women returned to their usual places in the column. Lanai rode beside Korban, though she made him make first contact.

"I was very impressed with the Mantu ceremony, crown princess. Their riders are the finest I've ever seen."

"Yes, they are. True skills are a sight I always appreciate. How they blended that horsemanship display into their ceremony was stunning to me. The music and musicians were a perfect ending to the rite."

"Yes, that's true."

"You seemed reserved during that time."

"I'm not much of a person for such events. Your royal training and experiences have made you much better suited for proper protocols. I admire that about you."

She turned her head with a surprised smile. "I think that may be the nicest thing you've ever said to me."

"You must know how you're appreciated amongst us. How could you not with how people worship you?"

"Worship, that's a strange way to say it."

She chuckled.

For Korban to see a genuine smile on her face was refreshing.

CHAPTER TEN
The Belshik Plateau

Traveling steadily for weeks, the allied column reached a point to either head westward for the Greka forest, or to turn south and go to the escarpment of Belshik.

Speaking with the Mantu warriors, they could give little advice either way. Nobody had ever ascended onto the plateau, and equally, the Mantu didn't venture into the forests of Greka territory. There were dark stories and rumors about the Greka though nobody could verify whatever was the truth.

After some lengthy discussions, opinions, and considerations, they decided to turn directly south and head for the plateau for no particular reason.

The farther south they went, the warmer the temperatures became. Snowflakes were replaced by rain drops. When the heavy weather garb was shed and packed away, the women were particularly happy at the change. They chatted pleasantly, laughing and joking together. Their good mood spread to the troops around them that perhaps the women had turned a significant corner.

As they traveled too, Korban started to notice predators were more prevalent and seemed unconcerned about staying out of sight.

One group of cats prowled toward the column but were quickly discouraged by Kar arrows. Later a pack of wolves shadowed the column though they didn't come close enough to attack.

When they camped that night, Korban posted enough sentries that, in essence, it was a picket line. The shifts were much shorter. Even at that, the sentries were forced to repel predator attacks on several occasions. Fortunately, those predators were easily deterred and no sentries were injured.

"There were fewer Mantu villages in this area the closer they got to the plateau.

It appeared from a distance this plateau was of a similar height to the escarpment up to the Kar mountains of Vikar territory.

"Do you have concerns about trying to climb that wall?" Lanai looked at him directly.

"I only worry about whoever lives up there, if they attack us while we're vulnerable during the climb."

"Do we have a plan for that?"

"It's one of those risks of this journey."

"That doesn't sound good."

"If you have a better idea, princess, I'm happy to hear it."

"You know I'm not trained in war and strategy. I'm only asking questions to help you prepare. We can't afford to be surprised anymore. Having even the flimsiest of plans is better than no plan at all. Do you agree?"

"How could I not."

She looked at him closely. He took it as a criticizing look. "I will join the ladies." She left him, returning to the company of her maidens. The awkwardness between them was occurring far too frequently. Misreading each other was an ongoing problem.

Again, the thought crossed his mind, *another veiled jab at me for the prior fiasco with falling to Lavia and her priests*. He didn't want to let it bother him, but it did. He could say '*it wasn't my fault*', but that sickly inner guilt feeling plagued him anyway.

He ate with his captains that evening. At night after he'd given instructions to the sentries, he bedded down alone. Korban was being moved in a direction opposite of the person he'd always been before the princess arrival in his life. In spite of his strongest efforts to the contrary, he cared what she thought.

The women appeared together the next morning, chipper and perky, as if the prior night angst had never happened. Even that annoyed Korban, so he ate quickly and left to see about alleged 'camp matters.'

The escarpment of the Belshik plateau loomed as they continued the trek. Similar to when they viewed the Peak of the Moon, it seemed closer than it really was. Instead of days, it took weeks to approach the cliff face.

Nearing it at last, they stopped early to make camp at noon. Due to the height, rather than try to ascend immediately, they opted to postpone that task to the following day.

Lanai came to join the gathering of the allied leaders to discuss the task. She went straight to Korban.

"Am I welcome here?"

"Of course, you already know that."

"Lately, we women get the feeling you would like us to ride away, forever."

"I can't speak for how you feel, or why. There is nothing coming from us intended to give you such a feeling. You've always been welcome in our councils. What you asked me before about having a plan, we're having this council to discuss that very thing."

"Good."

"Feel free to add any of your ideas."

Korban started the discussion. "We know the difficulties of scaling cliffs. We've had that scare in traveling the mountains of Kar. The climb itself is only part of the problem. If the people who live on the plateau prove to be hostile, they may attack us during the climb before we can make our case to them."

Marka spoke, "If we try to climb up there in force, it may seem we're invading them. My idea would be a token group to try to speak as friends and get their permission for a visit."

Lanai added. "Do we need to move significant numbers up there? If our plan is to gain their friendship to join our alliance, that doesn't require large numbers. We have no idea about them any more than what awaited us on Iscali Island. The truth is, they may not be good candidates to join with us."

Korban replied. "That is true. Unfortunately, risk is a part of this mission. I agree with sending a small delegation, but this climb will take particular types. Strong climbers make a certain warlike appearance to strangers. Trying to include our best talkers will be difficult. We don't want to seem threatening."

"I will volunteer to be among the delegation." Lanai announced.

"Princess, this could be worse than that descend down a sheer cliff face. Here, we may be attacked. It's a deadly fall."

"I know that, Korban. That is why you must stay here. You're a Vikar sub chief and our leader. You cannot be lost."

"And you're still crown princess of Tranta who also cannot be lost."

Marka spoke. "You both make excellent points. Perhaps I can safeguard the princess by attaching a safety line where if she slipped, I could secure her?"

"That settles it," Lanai hissed, glaring at Korban. "I'm going."

Korban simmered glaring back at her obstinate expression. It was difficult to keep from verbally lashing out at her.

The gathered leaders eyed him closely. Everybody realized, this could be the most significant decision he'd ever make. It could lead to the death of Lanai. The fact she understood it also but still wanted to go spoke volumes about her innate courage. Korban could only look away. He'd assumed Marka 'had his back.'

"Marka, do you agree with the princess proposal?"

"There are terrible risks, I agree with you. However, if we had her up there to meet these people, it would be very good."

"That doesn't help me. Do you agree with the princess joining your team to make this climb?"

"If she has the courage to offer her life, who am I to deny her?"

She turned her head. "Thank you, Marka. We all must do our part, sub chief. That includes me."

Korban couldn't utter a response. He made a gesture of surrender. The idea the princess could die chilled his blood. It was a fight with him she'd won, again.

Turning his back, he started to walk away.

"Korban," she cried out. "I know this seems reckless and foolish on my part, but what I said is what I believe. I have a part to play too."

He couldn't look at her. "Princess, the choice is yours. I feel the risk is too great, but if Marka thinks he can protect you; I stand aside to him."

"Are you going to further shun me?"

"Shun you? I've never shunned you. I'm not the one who goes apart in camp. Those are your choices."

She huffed, so he continued walking away, increasing his pace.

She came back to sleep near Korban that night, but he wasn't mollified. He turned away from her in his bedroll. Sleep was difficult for both of them that night.

Morning seemed to come too soon.

As difficult as the climb would be, it started to rain adding to the danger.

Marka looked at Korban. Walking over, he asked, "Do you feel I should wait for a dry day?"

"That would seem to be the wise choice. It isn't as if waiting would cause a problem for us."

"I can do either."

Lanai walked over. "I know you want us to delay, Korban. If Marka says we can do it, I want to go. I don't want another night of fright worrying about this. I want to get it over with."

Marka looked at Korban's dour expression. Korban shrugged and turned away.

Later, Marka gathered with his choices of ten warriors, the best climbers. "I will pound spikes into the wall so we can climb to the top. We will have a second climber also pound in spikes beside me to have two paths. The princess will be tethered to me with climbers behind her if she slips."

He started the ascent quickly. Lanai looked terrorized, but she bravely stood her ground and soon was stepping onto Marka's spikes crawling up the cliff face. The ascent was slow as it took time to drive in the spikes.

Each of the climbers carried pouches with food to nibble and water to sip. It would be a long time before they could finish the climb.

Korban couldn't watch, especially when they got high enough that a fall would be fatal.

Moving far back, he and his forces scrutinized the rim of the escarpment. If opposing forces appeared there and proved to be hostile, the allies would try to launch arrows. However, with the great height, it was questionable if they could get shots up that far, or have any accuracy.

The climbers already looked small from this vantage point as they continued to ascend.

The maidens had gone to the base of the cliff watching the progress of the climb nervously. They stayed there together and didn't return to camp for any meals.

Korban left rotating ranks of warriors monitoring the rim for threats. He returned to the middle of the camp to discuss various mundane matters with his leaders. Captains from the Alkar, Kominkar, Stakar, and Drackar, in addition were captains from the Lamali, Strella, and the Mantu gathered. His total force with new additions had grown to nearly twenty-five hundred. Angered at Korban, the Trantan captain stayed at the cliff watching the crown princess making the hazardous climb.

With the increased numbers in camp, still, it didn't feel adequate in light of the recent difficult fights with the Brogs.

The meeting did little more than distract Korban's thoughts momentarily from the climbers.

Everybody was preoccupied with the fate of the brave souls trying to climb another sheer cliff.

It was nearly dusk when the team reached the rim and climbed over the edge. Whatever they found there, the people on the ground could not see. Nobody leaned over the edge to signal them.

Finally, standing on the edge of the plateau, the small force of 'ambassadors' were faced by the angry faces of the locals. They snarled and gestured with their weapons, making grunts and group chants pushing close to the small group of allies.

Lanai feared they intended to push them off the edge down to their deaths. She made a command decision. Stepping toward the man who appeared to be in charge, she let her cloak fall away to expose her face and physique to their scrutiny. Taking out her sword, she jammed it into the dirt and went to her knees as a sign of contrition.

The leader raised his fist and the chanting stopped. Marka came forward and did the same. Jamming his sword into the turf and kneeling beside the princess.

For a time, they stared at the ground and waited.

Finally, the leader spoke. "Who are you, lowlanders, and why have you climbed up to our land?"

"I am Marka, of the Vikar tribe, and this is Lanai, crown princess of Tranta. We've come to speak with you about joining our alliance against the Brog threat."

"Threat? What threat? We, of the Belshik peoples, fear nothing and no one. We have no need of you and your lowland intrigues. Coming to our land is punishable by death."

"Will you hear us out? We had no idea of your rules and we come in peace."

"What is it you think you can say that we would care about? If you think you can save yours lives with some wild tale, I can tell you it won't work. Your lives are forfeit. That is the law."

"That is not a good law. Whatever reason you created it in the past, it shouldn't apply now. What do you fear from merely speaking with us? We didn't come here to make war."

An elderly Belshik man whispered to the captain who got a sly look on his face.

"Perhaps this is a time for a new way. We will take you and her to meet the High Chief. There may be a way you can serve us, especially this light-haired female.

Lanai's blood ran cold. The implications of his words and the frank looks from the Belshik warriors were easy enough to understand.

The allied warriors started forward to join them. "No, your people will stay here. Only you two will go." Lanai glanced at Marka. He had a determined expression. It was difficult to feel optimistic, especially as the Belshik warriors took away their weapons.

They traveled for the balance of the day, camped, and traveled most of the next day to reach their destination. Lanai saw numerous small villages along the way but not any large population centers until they reached the home of the High Chief.

Crowds of people gathered to stare at the first outsiders to ever come to the plateau.

There were many raucous calls from the crowd. With some of their gestures and simulated acts, Lanai clearly saw they weren't being respectful with the derisive shouts.

Marka had noted which one of the Belshik warriors carried their weapons.

They were ushered into a huge circular building that had pie shaped rooms built inside. The center of the building had a large room which served as the High Chief's 'throne room.'

He was a middle aged hard-eyed man. His wife sneered, contemptuous of the 'guests' brought before them.

Both of them stared at Lanai.

"I'm told you are a lowland princess? Is this true?"

"Yes."

"How is it you are here putting your life into our hands? What kind of king would allow his daughter to...?"

"He didn't, I decided to travel on my own. This quest throughout the world is too important to sit aside waiting for disaster to arrive at your door."

The wife looked astonished and then angry again. The chief smirked.

"This is the reason you're here, to warn the Belshik people of disaster?"

"We've made alliances of nearly every other tribe and nation. We did not come here lightly. If you think you're safe sitting on your little hill, you're wrong. The Brog will come for you."

Her response generated great outrage and shouts for punishment.

The chief put up his hand to silence the crowd. "You seem to think a great deal of yourself. Using such affrontery here while standing unarmed and alone doesn't strike me as brave. It's foolish, and you're foolish."

"I'm a royal princess, destined for my father's throne. It isn't something I want, but that is my birthright. With my life experiences, I can recognize arrogance when I see it. You haven't been there to see what the Brog do. We have fought them numerous times. They swarm opponents in overwhelming numbers and attack without thought or fear. They bite, chew, rend flesh and devour any they can catch. If you think you're beyond danger here, you're not leading your people. You're dooming them. The Kar tribes are ferocious and they live up high in their mountains. Yet the Brog managed to get up there and attack all five of the tribes. Nobody saw them passing by. They can do the same here, and they will. Ignore us at your own peril. If you refuse to hear us and wish to stay in your stupor, we will go back down the cliff and leave you to your dire fate."

The High Chief looked angry, but he noted the fire had ebbed out of his people. They were listening closely to this stranger. Her words were frightening, impossible to disprove.

It was his wife who arose. "You call us arrogant? Who are you to lecture us? We don't know you, and don't care to. We've lived here in peace for countless generations without need of any other peoples. Now you expect us to change solely on your strange story? How do we know any of this is true? What else would you want from us? I reject you. Do you think your beauty impresses me? I've been the mate to the High Chief for many snows and given him fine children. He won't fall under your sway so you can replace me."

"What? What are you talking about? I'm not here to take your husband. This is some worry in your mind, but not in reality. My father, the King, expresses who he wishes for me to marry."

She looked at the High Chief who was eyeing her with new interest. "Make your choice now. We have no time for this posturing and these spurious ideas in your minds."

The chief spoke, "I had not thought of taking a second wife. Perhaps you would be a good servant for my wife."

"That will never happen." She put her hand to her empty scabbard as a reflex. Being disarmed struck her at that moment. She was vulnerable.

Thinking quickly, she took a chance. Turning, she shouted to the gathered throng of Belshik citizens.

"Hear me good people. You heard my words of warning. Believe me, we would not have made that harrowing all day climb up your cliff just to be sport for your rulers. He is supposed to be your guardian and protector. Is this a good choice he makes on your behalf? Whatever silly choice he makes about me will come with heavy consequences. You are in danger from the Brog, but if he takes action to soil a virgin princess, he will start a war with all the nations of the world who are now allied against the Brog. Fighting the whole world? Will you tolerate this?"

The crowd was restless and a great deal of murmurs and complaints followed.

The High Chief stood along with his wife.

"Silence, you do not speak to me in such ways."

However, they weren't silenced and grew angrier.

From the crowd, they heard a deep male voice. "We do not shame women, even strangers."

The wife stormed down from her seat straight toward Lanai. The High Chief recognized instantly the reaction of a trained fighter as Lanai turned to her side, bent at the knees, fists up and at the ready. His wife was stocky, although with too many full meals hanging from her mid-riff, filled with rage, but she had no training or fighting skills.

She got up to Lanai, too fast for the High Chief to stop her. Taking a swiping slap at Lanai's face with her hand, the princess easily blocked the slap. With a sweep of her leg, she took out the wife's legs plopping her on the ground on her back. The wife shrieked, but in anger. Jumping on her belly, Lanai grabbed her hair rocking her head back and clapped her other hand on her throat.

The crowd gave an awed shout at feral martial skills displayed by a woman.

"High Chief, stop this foolishness now, before it gets out of hand. I didn't come here to fight, but if this is your will attacking two unarmed emissaries, know that we will not go quietly."

Again, the High Chief was forced to acknowledge the reactions of his people. They weren't angry at Lanai, instead she was developing an adoring following. Lanai was unprecedented in their lifetime of experiences on many levels.

The wife tried to struggle free, but Lanai kept her iron grip locked on her throat.

"High Chief, I hold her life in my hands. You know I can crush her throat, or snap her neck. Put an end to this now. I do not wish to fight you."

He slowly walked down to Lanai. Reaching out he took his wife's hand. Lanai released her hold, got up and stepped back. The wife jumped up, still enraged. Her husband restrained her from attacking again.

"Chief, your threat from the Brog is not limited to direct battle. They also eat animals. Living on this plateau, I'm sure you must take great care how many animals you kill for food. The Brog can easily upset your delicate balance by eating up your food supply. Also, I see no swords or other metal implements among your warriors. If you try to fight the Brog only with arrows and wood spears, you have no chance. To get modern weapons, you need us, the rest of the world. Give us back our weapons and let us demonstrate the use of swords. What danger is there to you with just two of us here?"

This time, the High Chief listened. He recognized Lanai was giving him an out after a series of his foolish taunts and poor choices by his wife. She was still incensed as he held her back, and still eyeing Lanai with hatred.

Lanai felt much better with her sword in hand. Marka smiled at her successful ploys that had basically saved their lives.

Squaring off, they performed a controlled but dazzling fight with their swords. The crowd was predictably dazzled as they oohed and aahed throughout the fight. Lanai was their clear favorite to win the concocted contest.

The only person who wasn't impressed was the wife who wasn't willing to be forgiving. It didn't matter to Lanai who had now achieved the celebrity status in this unlikely place that she achieved everywhere else.

With the crisis passed, Marka was totally in her thrall deeper than ever before.

"Princess, you are truly a marvel to this world. I think perhaps there has never been a greater person in history."

She smiled warmly. "Marka, I think you know I respect you above any others. Your appreciation for my efforts humbles me and I hope you know how dear you are to me."

"I'm unworthy of your high praise, your highness. I'm just a dullard barbarian scout who happens to be standing at your side."

They both laughed. She embraced him.

"If you're a dullard, we need more dullards in the world."

With the total shift in circumstances, the feeling of imminent disaster changed seamlessly to a festive mood, mostly due to the citizens. They crowded around Lanai like she was an angel suddenly among them, descended from heaven.

Mostly, Lanai knelt down to embrace the little children, which endeared her further to the parents. Children always drew her notice, especially the little ones.

An evening festival developed quickly. The High Chief acted conciliatory. Of course, his wife continued to brood and acted dismissive of Lanai. Her people didn't care about her moods. The princess had demonstrated in no uncertain terms who was the better woman.

Lanai went back into her regal mode, the consummate royal princess. She was deluged all around by questions and avid attentions. The best of the unmarried eligible males tried to woo her. They put on displays of their own martial prowess to impress her while she sat between the High Chief and Marka eating the meal.

She clapped daintily and nodded to each contestant.

Consequently, rather than the wife's dire wishes occurring with her being at their mercy, she slept in peace and in safety in a hut along with Marka that night. The following day, they talked for much of the morning. The chief agreed to establishing relations with rest of the world. Soon they were on the road traveling back to rejoin their comrades. Lanai didn't look forward to the climb back down the cliff, but at least this time she had the spikes as an impromptu ladder.

The High Chief assigned a force of his avid warriors to join the quest, so when she climbed down, there were hundreds of Belshik warriors braving the hazard too.

Korban couldn't contain his feelings when she planted her feet safely on the ground. He wrapped her up in a tight embrace.

"Princess, I worried a great deal about this, but I see it was not beyond you. Marka walked over.

"What she was able to do, I think no other of us could have. It could have gone much worse for us. I worried initially they would just push us over the cliff. Scribes will preserve the exploits of her life to stand for all time."

"I think not," she answered coyly, but she eyed Korban for his reaction.

"I don't doubt that. She is a remarkable person."

Lanai walked away from the men to rejoin her happy maidens for their own little 'lady's' celebration.

"The people of that plateau have agreed to join us, but more than that, we agreed to send people up there to help them share in the progress we've made. We need skilled workers to climb up to the plateau to build pulleys and lifts to be able to move goods and numbers of people at a time. They have no metal there, so arming and training them is a first step. Setting up embassies so they have relationships with all the other peoples of the world is another necessary step. These volunteers of theirs are brave young lads, but much of the fighting we do is beyond them. They need our weapons and training in how to use them, as well as learning the tactics of armies in large battles. Lanai and I put on a little demonstration and captured their imaginations. Mostly, it was Lanai capturing their hearts."

Korban smirked. Shaking his head, he replied. "When I first met her, I had a feeling she was special, but I had no idea she would dazzle the entire world."

"Try to remember that, my friend. You must end this enmity between you. Whatever she faces, it doesn't reflect on you. Everybody knows she favors you, but you can be very obstinate. Why? Acknowledge the fact that you're remarkable too. Who does she think about other than you?"

Korban eyed her talking and laughing with her ladies. The love-struck Belshik warriors weren't far away mooning over her. However, she didn't look at them, she turned her head to look at Korban.

He smiled and nodded. She returned the gesture. Her positive reaction warmed his heart, a rare thaw in their recently icy relations.

Korban called together his leaders to discuss the Belshik encounter and what needed to be done. Messengers were sent out to have craftsmen and workers dispatched and also to advise all of the peoples about opening new embassies on the plateau.

Korban chose to wait there while they armed the volunteer Belshiks and started their training, both in weaponry and riding horses. They took to the regimen aggressively, but that didn't equate with quick competence. That would take time.

Not surprising to Korban, those Belshik volunteers asked that Lanai join in training them with their sword fighting practices. She consented as there was little else to do while they waited.

With a month passed, craftsmen streamed into camp and bravely made the climb up to Belshik. A month of training had given the young warriors minimal proficiency with the sword. At least they could now defend themselves, and ride horses.

It was then, those Belshik volunteers got their first taste of the enemy they faced. Suddenly, up out of the ground, another strong Brog surge occurred in the midst of the camp. Just like before, it was an attack in force.

There were more than double the allied forces presence than the last attack. The Mantu mounted up and rode straight into the thickest clumps of Brog fighters trampling them under horse hooves. The Kar warriors from all of the tribes fought mercilessly. Not only had they learned from the prior fights, they remembered those who had been lost. Those who had serious prior injuries were the fiercest of all in taking revenge against the enemy.

Lanai made a point of leading the new Belshik component, trying to keep them from situations beyond their fledgling capabilities.

It mostly worked as the heaviest fighting was handled by the more capable and experienced units of the allies. However, seeing some members of their force slaughtered in a horrible way by the Brogs, it infuriated the Belshik warriors. It was the toughest part of the fight for Lanai trying to keep them relatively safe and controlled from foolish acts. Her courage in facing daunting odds stepping in at risk of her own life to save Belshiks in danger, provoked them. She literally had to push many of them away who were trying to get to her side crowding her in the fights.

As with the prior fights, it was not an easy battle, or a quick ending. The Brog never acted concerned about their huge losses. Whatever injuries they could inflict dominated their actions. Korban led a surprise attack of a huge Mantu contingent riding into the large Brog excavation. It caught the Brog flat footed as suddenly their leaders were under assault. The drones seemed to have little value, but the leaders did. Drones tried to jump in front of Korban's assault, but that didn't stem the tide.

Korban saw what looked to be an elder Brog. The look of intelligence in his eyes caught Korban's attention. It made him think back of his first Brog fight when their leader talked to him, in his language. In this case, the elder stared at him for a time before suddenly his people dragged him back and down into the tunnel out of jeopardy. The battle evaporated quickly afterwards.

Korban rode to find Lanai. Marka was positioned right beside her protectively.

Korban jumped off his horse.

"I must tell you this. When I attacked their hole in the ground, I saw an elder Brog. He looked intelligent and merely looked at me. I had a similar feeling in the first fight in our mountains to rescue our girls, when that captain spoke to me about protecting them. There is much more to this than mindless attacks."

Marka replied. "I remember that other fight. I haven't experienced anything like that since. I've often wondered if they're mindless beasts, why their attacks aren't continuous. They cause great havoc, so why they give us these long respites, I don't understand."

Lanai commented. "That is strange. I hadn't thought about it, but I was so busy trying to survive, I couldn't think about anything else."

"How did it go with your Belshik friends?"

"They are brave enough, but now they understand what we face. They wanted to jump into the fights, but too soon and too recklessly. Clumping around me was foolish. They would have been fodder for the Brog and impeded me dangerously in my fights."

"It's understandable. From what I see, you've added to your legion of suitors, ma'am."

She looked at him sourly, but when she saw his mirthful look and realized he was joking, she smiled. "Perhaps there is a prime candidate among them. I should sit with each of them to spend some time."

"You can do that, crown princess. The Tranta nation would probably love a young Belshik warrior as their next King."

"Who can say what they would accept. As I've always said, I will follow my heart as to who I will make a life with."

For the first time, Korban took a tentative step. "I would say the same thing. Although I haven't dwelt on taking a mate in the past, I can see it is a logical and an enjoyable opportunity."

179

"Wow, sub chief, you've never expressed any interest in a marriage before. What has changed your mind?"

"I've always pondered it, crown princess. I've just been reserved about the matter. I think I was wrong in making assumptions about...well... other people understanding my views and my feelings."

"Are you hearing this, Marka? Is it possible this blockhead of a Vikar is starting to mellow, to use his brain?"

Marka laughed heartily. He slapped Korban on the shoulder. Korban smiled ruefully.

Lanai snickered. "I thought you saw it as some threat, to express your inner feelings, sub chief? Do you think it unmanly to speak of tender things?"

"No, it was that you were always unobservant and unawares. When you took terrible risks, it killed me, but it wasn't for me to dictate to you. It was, and is, your life and your choices."

"That's good to hear, I like that. My father thought to do that very thing telling me how my life would be. I could never have done all of these remarkable things locked back in my bedroom in his palace."

"It will be your palace someday, Lanai."

"I'm still thinking about that. I haven't decided if that is a path I want to follow. I very much like our life in the field, Korban."

She eyed him directly.

Korban thought carefully about what he wanted to say, like he was on the edge of a cliff.

"As always, I leave your decisions to you. If you need for me to say, I feel very strongly about you, I do. I thought you knew that."

"I had hoped, but you left me unclear for all of this time. When we went through that dark time on Iscali, I feared you no longer wanted me. I freely admit, I'm not a perfect person. I've made my share of mistakes. When we deal with our inner demons, it isn't always pretty."

"With that, I didn't do well. I guess I assumed you held it against me that you got taken, that I didn't provide a proper protection over you then."

"Of course not, Korban. No one could have known what that vile priest planned to do. I thought you held it against me and my maidens what was done to us. I guess we were both fools for assuming anything. I realize it's better to speak the truth and trust those close to us."

"I'm glad to hear that. We never knew what they did, but feared you were drugged. If there was something else involved too, I felt if you wanted to tell me, you'd do it in your own time."

"I like this. I feel better about many things that were worrisome. You're a good man, Korban. You know you're a great warrior, an accomplished leader, and the heart of the expedition. You may not understand, but I wondered if I was worthy as a companion?"

"You're worthy, crown princess."

They embraced warmly. He nearly chuckled when he heard the disappointed murmurs from the Belshik men nearby in the background watching them. Their foolish hopes appeared to be thwarted which distressed them greatly. However, reality is a stern teacher that will not be denied.

CHAPTER ELEVEN
The Forests of the Greka

The main camp beside the escarpment up to Belshik became a busy place as once the initial elevating conveyances became operational, they were in use virtually non-stop. The craftsmen continued erecting more elevators and commerce exploded thereafter.

As frightening as it was going up and down the cliff face, more and more people took that journey. When the initial Belshik volunteers went home to see their families and describe the battle with the Brog, most people wondered why they'd waited so long to make ties in the lowlands. The volunteers beamed when they coaxed Lanai to return for a visit, along with Korban. Meeting the chief and his wife again with Korban at her side was a much different experience for Lanai. The wife eyed Korban as avidly as her husband had eyed Lanai.

"High Chief, this is the leader of our united army, Korban, sub chief of the Vikar. He is a warrior of great renown across all the lands, and he has no peers on the battlefield. Your own warriors can explain the battle we had with the Brog and how Korban led a deciding charge into enemy strength to end the fight. It's my honor to know him and to call him my dear friend."

The volunteers shouted loudly and clapped, causing the assembled villagers to follow their lead.

The chief and his wife stood up, walked over and eyed their counterparts appreciatively. Korban towered over the High chief and his powerful physique had done nothing but mature into a prototype fighter. The wife stared at his broad shoulders and large arm muscles.

Her jealousy of Lanai was instantly forgotten. She actually tried to act gracious, which in her case was a stretch.

The High Chief ignored his wife's instant fascination with a barbarian giant. "Sub chief, you honor us with your visit. I'm told our young men did well in fighting off those foul creatures."

"They did. They brought great honor onto your people. We're happy to have them with us."

The High Chief turned his head and spoke. "Princess Lanai, my boys have told me they want to be a permanent part of your army. Is that acceptable to you?"

"Of course. As I've gotten to know them, they've become very dear to me. Your young men learn fast."

They shouted again accompanied by a huge cry from the crowd.

Lanai smiled as she noticed the High Chief and his wife had both donned swords for affect. The fact they didn't know how to use them didn't seem to matter here among the people they ruled.

After the meal and after much pleading, the volunteers put on a display of their new found swordsmanship. The crowning event came next as Lanai and Korban performed a dazzling array of lightning moves so fast it was almost impossible to follow with the naked eye.

Korban was instantly added to the 'legendary' status in the minds of the Belshik peoples. He stayed at Lanai's side as she maneuvered through the crush of adoring villagers after the fight. He said little and mostly nodded.

The volunteers beamed with pride at now being an accepted part of these heroic figures, and battle veterans. Vicariously, they now carried a status as 'legend.' It was a first for any Belshik person.

Riding back down the elevators to the lowland camp, Korban's mind turned to the next leg of the journey, the forests of the Greka.

The Belshik contingent seemed unwilling to leave the crown princess side, like her remarks had elevated them in her esteem to the top position in the allied camp. Korban left it to her to address this, if she felt the need.

Lanai didn't say anything, but merely walked over to join her maidens, ignoring the lovestruck Belshik warriors. Eventually, the Belshiks got the hint and filtered away going back to their assigned place in the camp. They had brought some new recruits to fill the places of those lost to the Brog in the battle.

Everybody was surprised the next day, as Korban rapidly directed preparations for their departure, when a large contingent of Kar warriors rode into camp. There were members from all five tribes. Essentially, they doubled the total number of barbarian warriors riding in this quest seeking for more allies.

Korban was happy to see them. Initially they sought out their fellow tribesmen, but then they jointly approached Korban as the recognized leader of the mission.

He was pleased that they were being led by sub chief Timian.

Korban grinned broadly as Timian got off his horse to walk over.

"It's so good to see you, and I'm glad to see this great force at your back. Did you want to take command of the army?"

"That's not why I came, Korban. You're doing just fine. I'm happy with you remaining the leader here."

"You're my mentor. How could I be over you?"

"That is not an important distinction. You've grown as a man, a leader, and a great fighter. When I heard about that ride down a sheer icy cliff from the Plateau of Heaven, I shuddered. I could not have done it."

"We had no other choice. I certainly was no great leader by bringing us to that place forcing that climb on us."

Lanai had walked over. She smiled warmly. "Sub chief Timian, I'm so happy you're here. I feel safer already."

He laughed heartily. "I'm still just the barbarian leading this mob. Princess, you get more beautiful every time I see you. You make my heart thump."

"Well, you make my heart thump too."

"I doubt that, but thank you for the nice words. Can I ask where we are in this quest? I see a lot of activity."

"Korban answered. "We still have a visit ahead to see the Greka. Hopefully the dark stories about them aren't true."

"Adding in my men to your army will help, I think."

Lanai continued to hug him, and then she kissed his cheek."

"I must return to our packing. I will see all of you later."

While the new forces greeted old friends, they didn't unpack as the departure was planned for the next morning. That night the Kar warriors who'd shared the whole trip talked at length with the new arrivals about all of their trials and tribulations of the epic journey, the good and the bad.

Sleeping in traveling configurations, the new Kar tribesmen seamlessly joined their fellow tribesmen to supplement Korban's growing army. Korban's key leaders slept in his vicinity. On this night with double the numbers, Korban pondered needed changes in procuring food, camp configurations, and traveling assignments. Lanai led Timian to the vicinity of her and her maidens to sleep, which was also near to Korban. She talked to him at length late into the dark before they finally dozed off, sleeping beside each other.

The army of allies left the next day, but they didn't try to leave at dawn. Instead, they attempted to get organized so everybody understood the battle contingencies if there was an attack.

Marka led an enlarged vanguard away at an amble. He paid close attention to their surroundings and what lay in their path. Brog ambushes could be nearly anywhere. They still had some distance to travel to get to the forest.

Korban rode with Timian at the head of the main column. The total of his forces had swelled well over five thousand and closer to six as more Mantu warriors had decided to join them for the trek. The mission had taken on legendary status. Most people wanted to be a part of it.

Lanai rode up to ride beside Timian.

"Good morning, gentlemen. It's nice to have a clear sky today for traveling.

"It is nice, princess." Timian replied. "We can travel as slow or as fast as Marka leads us."

"Marka is another remarkable man. When we went alone to meet the Belshik leaders, I was deathly frightened but his steady even mood calmed me. Even when things got scary, I felt better knowing he was there with me."

"I was told you took terrible risks. Marka said at one point he thought you would be taken down by that whole tribe. I was also told the High Chief's wife tried to attack you, but you throttled her easily, like she was a little schoolgirl."

"I was worried when she sprang at me. I didn't want a big fight, and I certainly didn't want to hurt her. That would have probably led to our deaths. I'm very happy it is behind us now."

"Perhaps you can learn from it. Every outcome is not a good one."

"I'm sure Korban is happy you said that. I often annoy him with my choices."

"We all acknowledge life is chance and risk, but that doesn't mean we should press too far because as Timian says, we can't guarantee good outcomes every time. I just try to urge caution with your choices. You tend to ignore whatever I suggest."

"Korban, I hear everything you say. I don't ignore you, it's just I don't always agree with you. As you know, some of our experiences were beyond our control."

"That's true, but it shows what I'm saying. In my planning, I try to consider what can go wrong, and what unexpected things could be out there. I don't know what we will find in the Greka forests, but whatever is there, we must deal with it quickly. If we got drawn into a battle with the Greka, and the Brog picked that time to attack, it could be a serious blow costing us in many deaths and losses."

"What is it you would have me do, sub chief? I'm not a person to sit back and do nothing. I believe I've made significant contributions. Do you agree?"

"Of course you have, crown princess. No one disputes that. Perhaps we should talk about more pleasant things. Timian, what of my parents?"

"Shosa is gnarly as ever, complaining to everybody, and Menga still makes the best stew in all the Vikar lands."

Korban chuckled. "I miss that stew. I miss her. I even miss my father's gruff ways."

"I like her very much," the princess added. "She's like the mother I never had."

"I'm considering sending a small group riding ahead to test the woods. If there are traps waiting for the unwary, I want to know it."

Lanai turned her head to him. "Sub chief, you just lectured me on undo risk. How is it different for the warriors in that small group? Their lives are as precious as me and my ladies."

"This is a situation where I don't agree with you. I didn't tell you we never take risks. We can't afford to stumble into serious trouble in trying to contact the Greka. I have faith in my men to take proper measures for their safety while still rooting out any hidden hazards."

Timian looked at Lanai with a sly smile. "Princess, I think you have not won this point."

"I will have my say, gentlemen, whether you choose to agree, or not."

Korban remarked. "There is no doubt about that. I'll be back after I talk with Marka."

Korban rode ahead to join the vanguard.

"Marka, I'd like for you to send a small advance team to the forest. If there are hidden hazards, I want to discover them before the main body arrives. They need to use great caution for their safety, and they need to use great stealth so the Greka don't have a call to arms to our approach."

"We can do that. Who did you want to send?"

"I'll leave that to you. I don't know your men as well as you do."

"I'll do it."

"Tell them to be very careful. They'll have a large lead on the column so if they get into trouble, we won't be close by to come quickly to their aid."

"They'll know that, Korban."

"I think being around the princess is affecting me. I'm starting to say unnecessary instructions like she does. You're right, they already know what to do."

Marka chuckled.

Korban returned to the main column.

"Timian, I feel better now. This could be another serious challenge. I have a bad feeling for some reason. I suspect that misery on the Iscali island has put a new worry in my mind."

"It was a prudent move, sub chief."

As Korban had envisioned, with the increased size of his army where more food was necessary, it took more time with virtually every function starting with setting up the camp. Many more women were present as the Mantu females chose to accompany their men. Some brave Belshik women had decided to come along hoping to be trained and become the next 'princess' figure, new darlings of their tribe. They made bee-lines to meet Korban, just like their men mooning over Lanai, where they tried to act alluring. He was pleasant with them, though he noted the dour looks from Lanai watching the exchanges.

Councils included more leaders and therefore more opinions. What was important to a particular individual wasn't necessarily important to the others. It was an aspect of leadership Korban didn't relish.

Another factor for him, Lanai was in such high demand, he had little time alone with her. In his mind, he wasn't sure she even noticed, or cared.

The travel to the forest plodded along steadily, but not rapid enough for Korban's liking. When they finally came to the edge of the tree line, it was disturbing as hung from the branches of trees were dismembered parts, both of animals and of humans. There were strange sounds which they found to be wind chimes. They heard no normal animal sounds. It was eerie, an unnatural stillness.

What they also did not see was any sign of the advance scouts. Marka had stopped the vanguard outside the tree line waiting for the allied column to arrive.

Spreading out a skirmish line far along the border of the forest, Korban and his leaders pondered the dilemma. It would be dark soon. The idea of risking an intrusion seemed unwise.

Lanai asked first. "What should we do about our scouts? What if they need us?"

"They are among the best we have. It's not easy to take down Kar warriors. If they were attacked, they probably went into hiding somewhere."

"Judging by these vile trophies, are these people we want to meet?"

"They mean to frighten away any who approach their realm. They do what they feel they must."

"I don't like it."

"None of us like it, Lanai. Who knows what they faced that brought this about?"

"I still don't like it."

"In this case, perhaps you shouldn't volunteer to represent us as first contact?"

She looked at him dourly, but looked away after seeing Timian's measured look.

"As you wish, sub chief. You can have the honor."

"Thank you, crown princess. Having you here and safe, that pleases me a great deal."

"Your definition of pleasure differs from mine."

Timian interjected, "Perhaps we can discuss an actual plan since your decision is made."

"Yes, Timian, I agree with you." She smiled, batting her eyes irreverently. Both men chuckled.

"You are a rare creature, Lanai," Timian remarked.

"Thank you, I think. Was that a compliment?"

"Yes, your majesty."

"Good, you're a far more discerning man than some people I know." She stared at Korban who shrugged his shoulders.

When they stopped that evening, short of the forest, a very large council gathered.

Korban stepped into the middle to talk. "I've talked with the princess and with sub chief Timian as we rode here about how we should approach contacting the Greka. Their message to outsiders is very clear, stay away, or else. Regardless, we must find a way to reach them. We must persuade them to see things in a different way, and we must help them understand we all need each other. This is a threat like no other, a threat to the whole world. No tribe or clan can depend on their old ways for protection and survival. They can be destroyed just like every other tribe. My worry is the initial attempt. If they chose to act before we can explain why we've come, that can lead to needless bloodshed and animosity. Killing them won't make them allies. I have no doubt they know we're here. With such a large army gathered at their border, they may assume we come to conquer. Trying to creep into the forest is probably foolish and doomed to failure. They probably have warriors amassed just out of our sight inside the trees. They may have climbed up into the trees to shower us with arrows."

Korban paused gauging the reaction of his divergent forces. The expressions varied as much as the diversity. He paid the most attention to those who looked to be the most avid for battle. The Kar tribesmen were among the most warlike, with fighting a normal part of their lives from young ages, but they were the calmest looking. The most recent additions, the Belshik, and the Mantu, generally were excited and anxious for a fight.

"Before we make decisions about this difficult test, I'd like to hear your thoughts and ideas."

It was like opening up pandora's box, a flood of voices started simultaneously.

"Whoa, whoa, whoa, we can't all talk at once. I'll pick each of you to air your views. We have all the time we need for a good discussion."

He selected the Belshik captain first. "Sub chief, we of the Belshik do not fear these Greka scoundrels. Any people who dismember and hang limbs for visitors to see and tremble, they do not deserve our respect."

There was a great shout at his bold statement.

Korban nodded to a Vikar sitting in the front. "Sub chief, I have been with you all of our lives. I know you to be skilled and more than that, measured in your decisions. I don't feel this is a time for posturing and warlike stances. None of us fear facing the Greka, but acting with contempt when we don't know the reasons for their rituals is not wise."

Next, Korban pointed to the leader of the Lamali. "In our land, we've built a self-contained life. If you were at our borders with this army, we would not see you as friends, only as adversaries. That is our problem, to dissuade them from defensive impulses enough to explain why we've come. They may already know about the Brog and may have suffered depredations."

In a surprise, the captain of the small Tranta contingent stood. "We've stayed somewhat to the background during this trek. I guess I'd say we felt our duty was only to protect our crown princess. It's disturbed us a great deal at how often she's been in harm's way, and with her life at serious risk. We request that she not be among those brave souls venturing in first to meet these Greka. For us, we're probably already destined for the most severe punishment from our King for allowing her these choices..."

Lanai jumped up to interrupt. "My choices were mine, freely made, and I regret none of them. Captain, if you think I would leave you defenseless against my father, you apparently don't know me. I think he understands I will not bend to his will, ever. I wasn't born to be the mewling plaything of some weak son of a noble. Let us put an end to such thoughts for him, or any of you. I will continue to do as I see fit. If I stay back, or go forward, it won't be done hastily, or without proper consideration."

"Yes, ma'am."

The assemblage snickered and chuckled at the captain's abashed reply. There was nothing else he could have said to this 'force of nature' woman.

Korban smiled ruefully, and then took command again of the discussions, "I know well the depth and the expanse of our feelings. What I want to hear is how do we approach this without seeming like an attack?"

That question stumped the leaders for a time. Finally, an unlikely person wandered into the circle.

"Lila, what is it? Are you in some distress?"

"No, my lord, may I speak?"

"Certainly."

"I know I have no standing here. I'm merely a servant to the crown princess. I very much enjoyed that horse ceremony when we first came amongst the Mantu. Is it possible we could do that, or some other ceremony to show the Greka a different way? Invaders don't put on endearing ceremonies."

Korban glanced at Lanai who was beaming before replying. "Lila, you are a person who has standing anywhere. I don't know why you don't realize you are treasured. Your idea is a great one. It puts no one at risk, and it will surprise potential adversaries. I think they might at least forestall any attack until they investigate. Can the Mantu organize another horse ritual? I know it's a sacred rite, but it is exactly what we need."

The Mantu leader stood. "The Mantu people are proud to accept your charge, and are grateful you would trust us to such an important task."

This time, when they gathered for the ceremony, the musicians were ten times more numerous, the horses they trotted into position were far more plentiful, and the number of singers were equally increased.

They started at dusk as they ceremony normally took place in the darkness of evening.

The normal sentry line was withdrawn to make an approach more inviting for any nearby Greka.

The sounds of the music swept outward like a magic wave enchanting the surrounding area. The sound of the forest animals ceased as it appeared, they were a part of the audience.

The thundering hooves of horses moving together in precision with riders displaying awesome riding feats and skill led into the choral and instrumental segment. They belted out an anthem with rich chords and contrapuntal answers to the melody that dazzled the listeners and transformed the event into a pseudo-religious rite. When they finished, they looked to the forest to see ranks of Greka warriors emerged, waiting in silence. Korban decided to walk over to them, alone. It was some distance to cover and he felt vulnerable the entire way.

As he got closer, he saw them brandishing weapons. When he got close enough that they could attack, he knelt down plunging his sword into the turf. "I am Korban, sub chief of the Vikar. We've come here to speak to you about the danger of the Brog."

For a short time, nobody moved. Finally, their ranks parted and a woman emerged, heavily covered in body markings, reminiscent of the Iscali priestess.

"I am Jana, leader of my people." She was an attractive fit woman; her weapons were not ceremonial. Her long dark hair was braided and her dark eyes full of spirit and challenge. She was compelling in her confident mien and Korban was duly impressed. Korban got no sense of her being evil, like the priestess.

"Will you speak with us, Jana?"

She didn't hesitate as he stood back up. "Let me explain to you, the Greka have never sought contact with any outsiders. The reason we do so now is, we've had attacks from these Brog you speak of. They are the reason I am recently a new leader. My husband was our leader and was killed in a sudden ambush, welling up out of the ground right in the middle of our camp. There was no chance to go through our normal rituals allowing men to vie, contesting in various tests to prove themselves. The Brog have attacked us again in other of our villages all throughout the forest. If you come in peace, we will have a council."

"Do you prefer we follow you to your home? We can invite you to join our great council of all the factions in our camp. I wanted to show you the horse ceremony the Mantu performed for us. I found it to be spiritual and very moving."

"It was very nice. I will think about your invitation, and talk to our elders."

"I'm sorry for your loss, Jana."

Her face softened as her grief welled up.

"Can I ask you, with those dismembered things you hang in your forest, I understand you intend to frighten away strangers, does it work?"

"Mostly it does, but as you can see there are human parts too. Sometimes evil types think to sneak into our territory whether to rob, or do worse things, like capture women and children to take away. We have no tolerance for them and they pay the ultimate price."

"I can't disagree with you."

For the first time she gave a small smile.

"So, you are a legendary Vikar. Even here, tales of your tribe's great fighting prowess have been heard. We've never seen one of you, though in seeing your great size, I can believe the truth of your exploits"

"I'll return to our camp now. You, or your representatives are welcome to join me, or if you want to meet us tomorrow, that is fine."

"As I said, I'm new to this leadership role. I need to speak to the elders. I can't say what they'll feel. There are some among us who are entrenched in our history and old ways. In spite of the attacks and the losses, they will be difficult to persuade into an alliance."

"We will provide whatever help you need. I look forward to seeing you again."

She eyed him reflectively, as if she didn't quite grasp his full meaning and implications. Her suddenly coy look caught him by surprise.

Nodding, he turned and walked back to camp. Lanai was there to greet him. "Their leader is a woman?"

"Yes, she said her husband was recently killed in a Brog attack. She is speaking to her elders about talking to us. By the way, she said they enjoyed the Mantu ceremony. That was a great idea from Lila."

"Lila is a gift. Now, about this woman, from here, she looked very impressive. You certainly seemed to be taken with her."

"Crown princess, I was representing our forces, I wasn't there to romance a stranger, if that's what you're implying. Yes, she was lovely, but no more lovely than you. I think she is capable with her weapons."

Lanai fought back her smile.

"Well, we'll see about her, sub chief."

"Yes, we shall. It's late, so I'm going to bed down."

"We'll join you shortly. I want to talk with my maidens first."

He was fast asleep when they crawled into their bedding much later.

Korban's sentries didn't go to the tree line, rather they stayed beside the camp. No one needed an incident at this delicate juncture.

The next morning, when they had an early meal, Lanai came to sit with Korban along with all the maidens. They eyed him mischievously.

Lanai spoke, "So, you think I'm lovely now? I believe that is the first time you've said anything nice to me."

The maidens chuckled.

"Lanai, if you're unclear about my thoughts, or my feelings, you have but to ask. You don't need me to tell you you're beautiful. You have an army of men mooning over you."

The maidens laughed and chattered at Lanai. She was taken with the moment and couldn't stop grinning broadly.

"A compliment from the legendary sub chief of the Vikar. What a blessed day."

"Eat your fill, I want to be ready if we hear from Jana. This is an important moment. We aren't yet in an alliance with them. She explained there are some among her elders who are stuck in their past and could be problems."

"Of course, I will be going with you today."

"Of course."

She smiled smugly. "Ladies, perhaps I will wear a dress today?"

That set off a barrage of lively opinions from the ladies. Korban excused himself and left the inane moment.

Later when Jana led a delegation out of the forest into the allied camp, she looked refreshed and of a different mood.

"Greetings, sub chief Korban. I'm happy to say the majority of elders agreed to having a council with you."

She went about introducing ten elderly men.

Korban brought them into the council circle of all the allies, already gathered. Just as they sat down, Lanai made her appearance. She was dazzling in a dress meant to dazzle, and it did. With her blond hair up in a sweep, she looked the monarch she would someday be. Her walk toward them was elegant.

"Jana, I would like to introduce Lanai, the crown princess of Tranta."

She smiled regally at the seated Jana. After a time, Jana arose, eyeing Lanai with a calculating look. Part of that look was eyeing Korban for his reactions.

"You are a princess? I've never met a princess."

"I am. It's my pleasure to make your acquaintance. Do I address you as chief?"

"I'm not sure, we've never had a female leader before."

"I suspect there is a great deal we can learn from one another."

"I think you are right, princess."

"Please call me, Lanai."

"I can do that. That is a beautiful clothing piece. We dress for life in the forest among the Greka. Also, I've never seen light hair like this. Are all of your people like this in hair color?"

"Mostly, but we have hair of all colors. Are all of your people dark-haired?"

"Yes. Does it offend you?"

"Certainly not. You're a very compelling sight as you are. There is no one standard of attractiveness. With your permission, I'll sit with you for the conference?"

Smiling, she replied. "You are welcome to join me, Lanai."

Korban opened the session.

"I welcome the council members of the Greka. I'm happy you've put your trust in us enough we can discuss the issues of mutual concerns. The Brog are not a problem any peoples can ignore. Too many have been lost from tribes all over our continent. We come here to bring you into the alliance of all the other nations, but beyond this, we're unsure about our best future moves. We've heard about the Isle of Doom. Do you have any idea about who or what resides there, if anything? Is it a place we should also visit?"

Jana looked at a wizened scarecrow of a man.

"It is not a place the Greka choose to go. There are people living there, but they are sunken into foul rights and practices. Because their home cannot support a large population, they turn to culling and eating their own to maintain a balance. If you wish to attempt a landing there, it will cost you lives. Plus, I wonder if they are allied with these Brog?"

"Do they land on your shores?"

"There have been some few attempts over time, but with their foul aims looking for victims, those landings do not end well for them."

"What do you say, Jana?"

"My husband never had any incidents to the south he needed to deal with. Our main camp is central in our lands. Those of our people living in the south are sparse. If they go out to fish, they go west into the Cornean Sea. There is an archipelago of islands along the entrance out into that ocean. Our fishermen have built temporary huts for their fishing activities, but there is no permanent residency anywhere in those islands."

"What knowledge do you have about a continent to the south?"

"There is a large land mass, but none of us have ever ventured there."

"Our wisest man, Volta, has implied the root of the Brog problem comes from this mysterious continent. The Brog never appear to be great planners and thinkers. If they're being inspired and led by others who are capable, they could come from that continent."

"That could be true. We have no way to say."

"That is one of the main points for our discussions, should we merely defend against each Brog attack, or should we take the fight to the source and root out any background forces?"

Jana looked at the Greka council members. Many were rapt with inclusion in such a high-level combined meeting, while some others looked intimidated and overwhelmed.

None of them offered her any advice.

Jana spoke. "I wish I could offer all of you a good basis to make these critical choices, but we just don't know enough. We've chosen to be very insular because we could. Now we can see the fallacy of such short-sighted thinking. I apologize. I can only say you must make your best choices and we will support you fully."

Lanai piped in. "Jana, don't misunderstand. None here hold you in a lesser light than any others of us. We've all had challenges of our own. We're in this together and we are with you."

"Thank you, princess. I was afraid we appeared too dull and useless in this esteemed company."

"Hardly, you impress us a great deal. You've been forced to overcome so much with the sudden murder of your husband, and then being the first woman to take leadership, it inspires me greatly. Perhaps we can talk with you later, me and my maidens?"

"I would like that, Lanai."

CHAPTER TWELVE
Points south

Lanai and her maidens were the first people to travel peacefully into Greka without losing their lives and being dismembered for display. In the Greka camp, Jana had the large tent of the chief to herself, so there was plenty of room for them all to stay in a single place.

"It's nice to have you ladies visit me. It does get lonely being without a spouse with my husband gone." Jana smiled warmly.

"We're happy to join you here. In our large army camp, being among the very few women, we always feel eyes on us. Privacy and time to ourselves is difficult to manage. Men seem to have a pathological need to present themselves to any woman who passes by. It does get tiresome."

Jana smirked and chuckled. "Men are simple enough, they want to be fed, and make...babies."

They all laughed at that. Nobody disagreed.

Lanai asked. "Can you tell us about your society and the lives of women here? You make that brutal impression at your border, but what about here in your settlements?"

"You know why we make that dark impression. It saves us fighting wars, although I will say, the Mantu have never been a problem. Their horses are all they care about. There have been travelers from the sea, roving bands of criminals, raiders from various directions. They seem to think there are hidden treasures that we guard. It's not true, but they come nonetheless. Others look to steal women and children. They never leave the forest as we guard our precious ones closely. We don't tolerate it. As far as the lives of women here, I imagine it isn't so different than other places. Women bear and rear the children. That's a critical role that we accept. As I see you ladies armed with weapons, I think you must have more freedom and choices we don't have. You have positions of honor and esteem. We don't have such here."

"After the Brog ambush where Korban saved my life, I made a choice to train to be able to defend myself. My maidens wished for that also. I wasn't given permission by my father. We merely left home to seek our own fates abroad. It has been a wild adventure."

Turning her head, Jana grinned broadly at Lila. "This small pretty woman, do you fight?"

Lila smiled back at her. "Thank you for your nice words. Yes, I have fought in a number of battles. Some of those fights against the Brog caused deaths among our troop. Fear is a great motivator to exceed your capabilities."

"I understand that very well. Some women among the Greka choose to become fighters, but we don't face battles. If a husband is lost, the wife must still feed her children, so we take on hunting and some other tasks done by men."

"Seeing those severed pieces hanging from the trees, strangers get an impression of a craven people living in these woods."

"I think we're no less noble than any others. The choice to butcher thieves and vile intruders occurred long ago, but after much talk. The losses they were taking then were too painful to allow to continue. The ritual is done with an element of regret, believe me, but since we started the practice, we nearly never have incursions and depredations. Our women and children are safe. For us, it's worth the inner price we must pay."

"Perhaps making this alliance will signal a new day and a new way for all peoples. I think women will make their mark from now on."

"Princess, you are royalty. You can see things from a much grander scale than most of us. I'm the first woman to have such authority here and it was only because of the dire circumstances of my husband's unexpected demise. There was plenty of resistance from the warriors to my leadership role, but I've done a decent enough job to cool their complaints. There are many who would see me replaced."

"Women can do anything men can do. If we're given the chance, I think we can reshape the world into a better place."

The women all chuckled and cheered the princess bold assertion.

Lanai smirked at her maidens. "Some things women do much better than men." Her ladies got strange smiles and snickered. Jana eyed them, confused at the exchange only they understood.

Jana shrugged and continued when they gave no explanation. "I do get attention from men, princess. If I took another husband, there would be a man in charge again. I miss my husband and our tender times, but maybe I'm jealous of this new found authority. I don't want to give it up."

"Nor should you. I'm expected to take my father's place on the throne of Tranta in the future. If I marry, I don't know that I would want to accede to him taking power."

Lila added. "I think there are more women who understand and agree about that issue of power than you might imagine. It isn't something I'd face in my life, but for both of you, I agree completely. What you've done, Jana, and what the princess has done, is remarkable."

Lanai commented. "I wasn't born to be some man's thing. I know I say that a great deal."

"What about this titan of a man who leads your army?"

"Korban? He's remarkable in his own right. Our relationship is... complicated. He drives me crazy most of the time, but I admit, I cherish him. How this will end up between us, I honestly don't know. I'm not sure he would want me."

"Princess, are you making a joke? What man wouldn't want you. I've never seen such an impressive woman as you. Even the men here whisper and dream about you."

"They dream about me?" Lanai smirked. "Really."

"You know this. You've lived a charmed life."

"Well...my point is, why must any of us in this tent only have the choice of being somebody's wife and therefore their vassal? I will make my own choice about that."

"I will think about it. My regret in my marriage was we hadn't had children yet. I don't know if growing old alone is something I want. Having power is fine, but I would have no children to cherish and to carry on my legacy."

"I know that issue. I've thought about it too. It may be the deciding factor in my taking a future husband."

She looked at her maidens. "I hope all of you know that you can marry too. We're all young now, but my choice doesn't have to be your choice too. You're nice-looking women and get plenty of notice from men."

She noted the enigmatic smiles from the women. It wasn't difficult to understand what they were thinking.

Mandia spoke, "Thank you, your highness. I think we're somewhat in agreement. The choice to marry would involve the same issues you're talking about. This life on the road with you isn't something we could ever have had. Giving that up to go into some man's home to do his bidding, it's an iffy proposition right now."

"Women after my own heart," Lanai replied. "We're not afraid to try a different path."

"We'd like to see this trek through to the end. Afterwards, we'll assess where we are, and where we want to go."

Shana added, "None of us is in a rush. Our current lives provide for our needs and desires nicely."

Lanai smiled and smirked. "I cannot disagree."

Jana eyed them in curiosity. "Is there more you're not telling me? I'm not sure I understand your full meanings. I sense you have an understanding between you that I'm not grasping."

"It's nothing, just the fun of our little sisterhood. We've been through so much; it has formed an unbreakable bond. We understand each other down to our cores."

"You make me feel envious. We have friendships of our women, but there are no soul testing struggles such as you've had."

"That may change in the future if this Brog matter turns into a vast war."

"I want to say, I'm so glad you trusted me enough to spend the night here in my settlement. This is nice spending time and sharing in your sisterhood, as you call it. What are these other things you wanted to teach me?"

The group talked very late about a variety of topics. The Jana who walked out of her tent the next morning was a changed person. Her night with Lanai and her maidens made an indelible impression and opened her eyes in new areas. She felt at ease, bolstered and self-confident.

When the visitors got ready to return to their camp, Jana hugged each one of them warmly.

"I regret to see you go. This was an experience I won't forget. You are always welcome here and I hope you can return."

"We feel the same. I hope our paths can cross again." The princess kissed her cheek. Jana responded with a long firm embrace.

Heading back to the border, they were accompanied by a patrol of Greka warriors. The ladies chatted pleasantly for most of the ride before it happened. The trail ahead suddenly collapsed and a large swarm of Brog emerged racing out going in every direction. The Greka warriors sprang into action, but it was a deadly situation immediately outnumbered and on the defensive. Lanai began firing arrows along with her ladies. They felled numerous Brog in rapid succession, but there were just too many so close to them. Soon they were assailed and battled with their swords to survive. Their courage heartened the Greka who normally would have retreated under such overwhelming odds.

They were close enough to the border that the guards stationed there raced back to reinforce the beleaguered defenders. The sound of battle, and the sudden departure of the border guards, clued the nearby allied camp something was amiss.

A mass of screaming allied warriors rode out at top speed to join the battle. By that time the princess and her party were in desperate straits. Being battered constantly backwards by the assault, it was being on horses that saved them for the moment, However, the grinding gnawing Brog mouths were getting too close. Brogs were starting to take down Greka fighters. Whether the reinforcements could turn the tide remained in question.

The Brog attack did not relent. Waves of new monsters flowed unabated from their excavation pit. Lanai fought desperately for her life in a panic. Hearing a yelp behind her, she glanced back to see a Brog getting a hold on Wella and starting to pull her off her mount. Lanai spurred her horse rearing up to trample the Brogs from closing on her and then rode over to the Brogs attacking Wella trampling them down too.

The border guard Greka warriors arrived and attacked immediately, but they didn't have the numbers to turn the tide of the battle. They could only stabilize the fight slightly, little more than a delaying action. Joining those remaining members of the patrol, they too fought for their lives. Lanai heard the roars of her brethren coming toward them.

Redoubling her efforts, she rode about to use horse hooves to best effect and to safeguard her maidens. More nearby Greka patrols joined the fight. It was enough to give them the time they needed to survive.

Soon, the crashing sounds of horsemen blasting through the trees changed the dynamics of the battle. The Brog moved to meet the new threat, but the allies had fought them enough times to know how to win.

The Brog surge for easy meat turned into a meatgrinder the other way. The Kar tribesmen especially, fought like banshees. With the princess in mortal peril, their fury had no bounds.

Nonetheless, it was not an easy battle. Other underground holes opened and more Brog attackers poured out to add to a quagmire, a killing field. Korban joined the fight leading a second large wave of warriors from the camp.

There were just too many Brog to end the battle quickly. As always, the Brog didn't surrender.

Jana was unable to lead any forces from her camp to help in the fight because the Brog attacked there too. Her forces were hard pressed immediately and slowly retreated against the relentless onslaught. Trying to conduct a fight to the death while still protecting vulnerable women and children was daunting.

The sounds of the savage fights echoed throughout the forest and prompted others of Jana's people who lived farther away to sprint to the rescue.

Back at the original battle site, the ebb and flow of the battle remained in question for a long time, but eventually, Korban's forces slaughtered enough of the enemy to gain big advantages. Using the edge to press that advantage, the fight went sour quickly for the remaining Brogs as their leader was slain. After they stemmed that tide, Korban looked around at the huge loss of life. This time, his forces had taken too many casualties. However, they could hear a serious battle in progress.

Lanai hurried up to Korban. "Jana is in trouble; we must go to help her."

The allies rode rapidly toward the Greka main camp. When they got there, fighting had moved south out of the settlement into the forest. The allies charged into the rear of the roiling Brog forces. There were numerous Brog chewing on bodies of the Greka, not all of them dead.

The allies wiped them out and joined the desperate fight. Even with barbarian reinforcements, Jana was hard pressed to battle the enemy evenly.

When Korban rode into view and his forces started destroying any Brog they could find, it heartened the Greka who fought with new resolve.

Again, it was not a quick fight and losses mounted. Even dying Brog were a hazard. If they could touch nearby fighters, they could still sink teeth into them.

In one day, any questions the Greka needed the rest of the world were answered in resounding fashion. After it ended, Jana was hollowed eyed at the horror, exhausted and discouraged. Korban rode down to see her along with Lanai.

"This is the nature of leading your people. I look back on our trek and still wonder how we did it. You must remember, we are all with you now. Your people are not alone."

"Without you, I think those Brog would have chewed us all to death."

"They're striking with more numbers. Perhaps it isn't the wisest, but you can collect all of your people from your whole nation and come with us into Mantu. We need to be together more than ever before."

"I would scurry into your arms tonight, but I must think about my people. I can send riders to the southern villages, but it would take time for them to collect their things and come north. They'd be vulnerable the whole time while they're on the move."

"They're vulnerable if they stay where they are."

She looked stricken.

"What is it?"

"I would talk to the elders, but most of them didn't survive the battle."

"Tell them, I ordered everybody to our camp for safety."

Closing her eyes for a moment, Jana leaned her head against Lanai's shoulder before taking a deep breath and going to give instructions to her frightened people.

"Korban sent ample Vikar and allied warriors to accompany the messengers racing south to advise the survivors there of the evacuation plan.

Lanai was surprised at how rapidly the Greka peoples packed up and rushed toward Mantu lands and the safety of the nearby allied camp.

Korban left considerable forces patrolling the forest waiting for the travelers fleeing north.

Over the next week, the total Greka nation crossed out of their lands to join with the foreign forces.

On that first night, it was an emotionally battered Jana staying secluded with Lanai and the ladies surrounded in the allied camp. Badly shaken by the shocking mass attack and loss of life, she was hesitant to venture out, leaving her people in the hands of the other tribes for the night. However, by the morning with the emotional help of her new female friends, she regained her composure and with time resumed her full leadership duties.

Living amongst divergent peoples was eye opening for the Greka peoples. The dire stories they'd been told about the outside world proved to be wrong. The charity and concern of other tribes made a profound impression, especially in the actions of Kar tribesmen. The 'barbarians' didn't act barbaric. On the contrary, their behaviors were as 'civilized' as any of the lowland peoples in the camp.

Having the might of this huge army settlement adding to all the Greka populations gathered together helped to return their feelings of safety and security. The Greka warriors were more than happy to join the joint armed forces of the allies in defense of the entire land. Learning new skills and the tactics of battle deployments and strategies was different than their former lives, but they avidly sought to achieve competence and acceptance from their new friends. Learning to wield swords was a skill requiring time. There was no shortcut to competence there. The Belshik were very helpful in that task. Since they'd recently been forced to learn sword craft, they were ideal for sharing tips with the Greka.

What was left in the Greka forest was an empty land. Incursions continued by the Brog, but they found nothing but elusive animals living there.

In their one attempt to broach the beefed-up allied camp, their element of surprise was gone. In a tentative surge out of the ground, the first of the Brogs emerging from the ground discovered they were right at the sentry skirmish line quickly surrounded. Not only were there no quick and easy victims, the sentries were reinforced by ready reserves leaping into the fray.

This fight was different than any other. The attempted flood of the Brog swarm gained no ground, no foothold, caused no casualties and quickly failed in the assault. It was the shortest battle ever in facing them. Korban had a plan and raced into their midst as they tried to recede back into the ground. His Vikar host savagely hacked and slaughtered Brog until he saw his target. A Brog looked different. He was larger, looking a normal man, but what was significant was the look of intelligence in his eyes. Korban closed on him before he could escape and his warriors hacked down the Brog attackers trying to come to his rescue.

Capturing the man, they dragged him up out of the hole and secured him before dragging him into camp. He was noticeably different in appearance. He wasn't squat and stumpy like the drones. Looking like a regular man, he had normal facial features, not the elongated large mouths of the drones.

He'd stopped fighting them fairly quickly. When they sat him down in the circle of the council, he looked around at their faces, assessing them and his situation. His calculating expression caught Lanai's attention along with Korban.

Jana was incensed and walked straight over to him. "You have shamelessly attacked my people without cause. Now you will answer for your crimes."

She slapped his face before returning to her seat beside Lanai. The Brog individual was unfazed merely continuing to look around.

Instead of the quick death he expected, Lanai got up and went to sit cross legged in front of him. Korban joined her.

She asked him, "Do you understand me, do you speak our language?"

He smiled slyly. "I do."

Korban spoke. "I think I've met another of you back in our mountains. Your people slaughtered older people in our village while we were away and stole some young girls. When we found their hiding hole, there was a leader who spoke and told me he protected our girls. They were alive and we returned them safely to their families. During all that time as captives, they were unharmed. Why are you doing this? There have been too many innocent lives lost already."

"My name is Gralk. I am a chief among my people. There is much you don't understand so it would be difficult to explain."

"Regardless, you must attempt it. These attacks are increasing. Surely you must see we won't tolerate that."

He pondered for a time before continuing. "It isn't the will of the Brog people to do this. I'll try to explain briefly. With our race, our normal life cycle is birthing our offspring, as all of you do, however our roots and ancestry is much different than yours. Our young go through a stage similar to your own where the mother can nourish the child, however later, they go through a phase your young do not. Think of it like insects that go through a chrysalis stage as they evolve. That is the stage you see where they are voracious, eating constantly. Normally it's a phase we can control with a limited duration, but that has been changed. There is another race that has invaded and interfered with us. They have the power to control and overcome us. They've effected our reproductive cycle where now our females are forced into continuous gestation and birthing. The normal transforming cycle is changed to keep the overage of birthing offspring stuck in the transition phase essentially to make them weapons against you. They've thrown us out of balance in our lives, but also out of balance with the world. Watching our youth become fodder for your warriors sickens all of us, but it's not within our control. You capturing me, if you kill me, it won't matter. They will simply put another adult in charge and the attacks will go on. You're right that they've been increasing. That will continue as they build up such numbers that I wonder if any living thing can survive. Without killing your people, they decimate animals."

Lanai asked, "Who are these other people?"

"I don't have much to tell you about them. They call themselves the Immarati. They don't explain things about themselves, they only enforce their will upon us. We have no means to fight them. You don't believe me, but I regret this war and what is being done as much as you."

Lanai looked at Korban. "I don't know what to say."

He replied to the captive, "It is a shocking thing. Would you consider helping us. I don't wish to lose more people to those chewing mouths."

"I'm surprised you'd even consider allowing me to live. I won't fight my own people, but I would certainly consider giving sharing all of my thoughts."

"Was your task in that hole to direct the battle for your side?"

"Not in the sense you mean. There are no tactics I could use. The youth in that stage are driven by instinct and the need to feed. My role here was to try to remove them if the battle went badly. Some other leaders choose not to relent in battle regardless of the deaths."

"Do your adults eat us too?"

"No, we eat animals, as you do."

"Do you live here under our nations?"

"We didn't. We lived in the southern continent. For all of time, we lived there in peace until the Immarati came. One day they were just there. I believe they came from across the oceans. If I could save my people from their control, I would gladly join your cause. Do you understand?"

Korban replied. "We do. This is not what we expected to hear. As terrible as things seemed before, this is much worse. I wonder, what do these Immarati gain if they kill off all life?"

"I don't know. Under their control, we have no opportunity to ponder anything. We only have their terrible will, and our doing what they direct."

"You have not resisted?"

"In the beginning when we saw how things would be, some brave ones tried to resist. They were fed to our own rabid youths who had no thoughts or guidance, only their primal hunger driven to extreme by the Immarati. Our women cannot support any resistance while in the control of Immarati overlords either. They too are caused to crave only one thing. The end of us, and also of you, isn't so hard to imagine. How can any of us change this horror?"

The council members were dumbfounded and equally at a loss hearing this shocking revelation. Shifting gears to imagine the Brog as potential allies had seemed impossible moments earlier. However, nobody denied what Gralk had told them was true.

Lanai muttered, "That the Immarati can control an entire race and alter them, to warp them in obscene ways, it's frightening."

Korban heard very difficult questions quickly being asked by other council members. "Can they even be defeated? With the weapons we have, what could protect us from being controlled too?" He had no answers.

"This may sound strange to ask, Gralk. Can we trust you? If we release your bonds, is our camp safe? Would you escape to the forest to lead more attacks against us?" Korban eyed him darkly.

"I didn't wish to be involved in any of those battles. Adults, don't look to cause battles. It was put upon us by the Immarati. In my life before, I hunted animals for food. Even there, I took no pleasure in killing. All I can offer is if you choose to trust me, I'll let my actions speak for me."

Korban cut away his bonds. Gralk stood.

"Thank you, Korban. I will do what I can. I think you know the real enemy is not the Brog swarm. I can help you to avoid the incursions. There can still be attacks and fights, but not like before where you had vulnerabilities."

"Then I thank you, Gralk. Tell me, do these Immarati come with you onto our continent?"

"No, they haven't, there is no need for them to come. What they do in taking control, it seems to be indelible in the victims, I think. It's a compulsion that blots out all other things. Our young, when they are in their developmental stage, can still recognize parents, respond to instructions and follow guidance. Now, they have no awareness other than to kill and feed, or else they couldn't have killed our own people long ago. Although, strangely I seem to be free of the Immarati control at this moment. I really don't know the whole truth."

"What do they look like, these Immarati?"

"That is another thing. Although they only act to control our young and our women, with the men, they seem to obscure our memories. I know I have met them, but I can't retain my memories. So, whatever they look like, they seem to want that kept secret."

"So…it's possible they could be here among us. I don't understand how a person can hide their appearance? Is this magic, or some other strange thing?"

"I don't know. We are a large community. For them to throttle and bend all of us to their will so quickly is...daunting. Whatever power they have, it seems invincible. You are doing the right thing trying to gather all your peoples in common defense, but will it be enough? What they've done to us, can they also do that to you? I don't know."

Korban glanced at all of the gathered council members, and he looked at Lanai. Uniformly, they had glassy-eyed expressions. The bravado and the martial spirits were gone, drained away by the grim revelations. Trying to fight what seemed an invincible foe was more than frightening. The possibility of the end of their way of life, and their lives, chilled them to the bone.

Korban struggled with what to say. In answer to his dilemma, impulsively his own fighting spirit welled up.

"Whatever these Immarati devils think they can do to us; we will have an answer.

Drawing his sword, he roared his challenge. A wave of deafening shouts swept throughout the entire camp. The warriors, and also the women, leapt to their feet building a battle frenzy shouting at the top of their voices.

It didn't change the serious dynamics of their situation, but it heartened them to resist, no matter the ploys of this mysterious unseen enemy.

Lanai had a look on her face of utter gratefulness. She shouted as loud as all the others.

Gralk smiled as he looked around.

When the din finally died down, he spoke to Korban. "This is inspiring to me. I wish I had the power to stop the attacks of my people. What I can do is if there is another incursion where I'm nearby, I can help in pointing out the leader of that attack. If we capture him, the assault will falter. The young cannot direct themselves. They're not capable in their state of frenzy. It may seem a small thing, but it's better than the needless slaughter on both sides. Once these young are allowed to complete their cycles, they would feel shame at what they were forced to do. I hope this helps you to understand."

"You've given us a different view of you and your people. We welcome your help. If we get more of your leaders, perhaps we can put a stop to enough attacks that they no longer endanger the people."

"That would be very good."

Lanai wandered over. "Korban, you gave us the perfect tonic. It may be that we cannot win in the end, but the people understand your call of fighting them to the end. I will give my life in battle rather than surrender to such fiends."

"There are no beings that are totally invincible. We need to learn about our enemy and discover their weaknesses. If they think they can simply roll over the world, we will teach them otherwise."

"I feel ashamed the Brog nation fell so easily." Gralk frowned.

"Perhaps we can help bring a different result for your people. It brings to my mind a question I had. If the southern continent is your home, how did you get to this continent. Do your people sail in ships?"

"We are not sea farers. How we got here, I think it must have been the Immarati. As I said, we suspected they came from across the oceans. They may have carried us here in their ships in a state of unawareness."

"It's strange they didn't make landings along our coasts."

"They exploited our unique reproductive cycle. Since your people don't share our method, you may not have been vulnerable in that way."

"Let them come," Lanai tried having a fierce look. The men chuckled. On impulse, Korban grabbed her in an embrace.

"You are a treasure, crown princess."

"Thank you, sub chief. I have no words to describe you."

Korban looked at her wryly.

"You're welcome," she added, and then laughed hilariously.

Gralk eyed them curiously.

Korban explained. "Don't try to understand our women. It can't be done."

"I can see that. Although I don't have these exchanges with our females, even with them there are...I can't think of a right way to say it. This is informative. Perhaps there is a different way we should consider our relations with our women. They may be capable of much more than the narrow roles they have in our society."

"Before I met the princess, I never imagined women could do such things as her."

Lanai smiled. "My, my, you have changed, sub chief. Giving me a hug, and now complimenting me. What else can I expect? Have you managed to improve to the point of considering real steps yet?"

"Be careful what you wish for, crown princess."

She laughed again. "I don't fear making cataclysmic changes to the stodgy rules of old men. Do you?"

"You're speaking for you about this, but in your case, you're also trying to speak for all Trantans, your people. Are you sure they would be persuaded to your wishes?"

"I'm willing to find out. Are you speaking for your Vikar peoples with your reticence and undue caution in certain areas? Are you allowing yourself to become the finest Vikar ever to live? You see things on too small a scale."

"Perhaps you see things on too grand a scale?"

"Korban, in all seriousness, this threat we face worries me a great deal. It's not impossible we could be killed, or subjugated by these Immarati. Do we want to pass away from this world without pursuing the fullest measure of life? I've been very clear about my feelings. You've been too afraid to speak of yours, but I believe you feel about me as I feel about you. What are you waiting for?"

"The people of Tranta accepting a barbarian as you're their future leader? I question that they would allow me to..."

"That doesn't stop me. If I'm willing to walk that path, why won't you?"

Before he could answer, there was a sudden stirring at the far end of the camp.

Rushing over to the scene, a Brog surge was welling up from the ground. This time, Gralk was at Korban's side sprinting into the maelstrom searching for the leader. Rather than slaughter any Brog, they held off the attack, merely holding them at bay. Finally, Gralk saw him, the leader of this incursion. Walking forward like a prophet walking on water, he stopped in front of the puzzled Brog adult. After a discussion. Gralk ordered back the assault from the Brog young and walked out with his comrade to talk to Korban.

"This is Soalk. I've explained how things are between us. He's agreed to talk with you. The young ones will stay back until we give them further instructions.

Soalk looked at the powerful and physically intimidating Korban curiously, but he was astonished seeing stunning Lanai boldly walk over.

"Hello, welcome to our camp. As Gralk has told you, we hope to start a new day. Finding a way to free you from those vile Immarati is at the top of the list."

"I had given up hope for our future. If all of our adults could know about this friendship, we wouldn't lead attacks. What the Immarati would do to us in retaliation, I don't know."

"We will deal with it together. What can be done about these youths?"

"We can take them back into the forest to feed on animals, but I suspect the Immarati will notice and take punitive action. They are beyond us."

"I don't have a ready answer, but I feel we must make a start against them. We don't know enough yet, but that can be changed."

"If Gralk accepts this idea of resisting the Immarati, I will join your cause. What he said, dying rather than continuing like this, it makes sense to me."

"This is good news. If both of you can take these children back into the forest and then return here, we can talk about next steps to face this terrible danger. We will not accept this onus put on you from foreign lands. We will all fight them."

CHAPTER THIRTEEN
Choices

With the threat of Brog attacks seemingly alleviated for the moment, Korban was pleased, but as serious as was the murky idea of doing battle with the mysterious Immarati, he couldn't get the ideas out of his head Lanai had brought up. *If this war is possibly going to be my ending, why am I waiting?* Realizing he may never get back to Tranta to face her father...*so?* To an extent, his mind was reeling, as well as his emotions.

When he decided to delay a critical planning meeting in order to walk over to the women, Lanai saw him coming, somber and determined, and realized the portentous possibilities of the moment. She actually looked daunted at the idea she'd been championing for so long.

The maidens eyed him avidly, like they were also being approached...romantically.

He took a deep breath before speaking. "Crown princess, may I speak with you?"

"Certainly, sub chief."

"I've thought about what you said and...I have doubts about the wisdom of such a move in the middle of this coming world war, but if this is your will and your desire, I will ask...would you accept a simple mountain barbarian to be your mate?"

She grinned broadly. "Yes, of course I do. It took you long enough to get around to it."

When she leapt into his arms, the maidens shouted and came racing over. They embraced him too in a group hug. As a result, word spread rapidly and general tumult erupted as happy allies celebrated what had always been seen as the inevitable.

The budding new couple was crushed by a mass of well-wishers and the curious. The calamitous war decisions were put on the back burner for the moment.

Gralk stood, along with Soalk, talking about this new slant at how a society lives.

"This is very strange," Soalk commented.

"Can you deny it's a good thing?" Gralk replied.

"No, it makes me look at our ways differently. This princess is a very appealing female."

"She is unlike any female you'll ever meet."

Meanwhile, Korban waited patiently through the general camp tumult to be able to talk to Lanai privately. That happened during the evening meal.

"Lanai, how do we go about this? I'm sure your Trantan ways would have a massive wedding ceremony at your father's palace. That isn't doable here. The Vikar do have a ceremony, but not like yours. What do you want to do?"

"I never wanted that showy wedding you refer to. A modest rite is just fine for me. I can marry using your Vikar rites."

"You realize they cut us so we blend our bloods together."

"If that's what you're willing to do, I will do so too."

The sub chief of the Vikar, the now legendary Korban, went to see the other sub chief present here, his old friend Timian.

"I may be a fool, but I'm honoring the wishes of the crown princess that we join as mates for life. That life may be a short one with the danger of the Immarati, but we're going to do it for whatever time we have. I'm asking for your blessing since Toma isn't here, nor is the Trantan king."

"You've been like a son to me, Korban. I'm very happy for you. I think this woman will be a test for you all of your life. Perhaps you are the only person capable of taming her."

Korban chuckled. "I don't look to tame her. She won't be tamed by me, or anyone else. She has consented to a Vikar ceremony. There really is no other way. There are no priests of her people here."

"I think her father will not be pleased."

"He will probably dispatch a full army to take revenge on me."

"He has his small detachment with us. I would make a point of having them featured in our blessings. Perhaps that might cool any ire they might have."

"That would be my hope. I'll tell Lanai."

"Has it struck you, this remarkable woman desires to be your mate?"

"Perhaps I'm still in shock. There is so much to do. The war won't wait long."

"Tomorrow, we can have your service. After that, it's in your hands to cope with this wildcat."

Korban grinned and chuckled. "Wildcat, that's a good description of her."

"Understand this, Korban, your old life is over. Regardless of the ideas of any culture, when a couple marries, the woman takes custody of the man." Timian smirked.

Korban smiled ruefully.

It was a difficult night to fall asleep for both of them. Lanai was with her maidens for the last time in their old relationship. Similarly, Korban was nearby in his sleeping covers, but that lure for Lanai being close by was nearly overpowering.

When dawn came, the camp had a sense of a significant portent for the day at hand. A barbarian, even though accomplished and highly renowned, marrying the crown princess of a lowland nation, was unprecedented, but without permission of their king, it was fraught with risk.

The entire throng gathered as a Vikar shaman performed the brief ceremony. When Lanai became his bride, Korban felt elation like never before. With Lanai now his wife, that staggering reality left him dumbfounded. She acted sassy and sexy, even in the middle of all the people. It was immensely provoking for Korban. The planning council about the Immarati threat was postponed, again.

The newlyweds were allowed to recess to a specially erected white tent at the far side of the camp to consummate the marriage. In her white dress, Lanai looked like an angel to Korban. It took his breath away. Their first night of passions, so long delayed, it was a marvel for them both that did not disappoint.

They didn't emerge from the tent all of that next day and didn't come out until the following morning.

Korban had an awestruck expression on his face. Lanai had a satisfied smirk on hers. The maidens accosted her immediately for women's talk, while Korban went to arrange the much-delayed meeting of the council. In truth, he really didn't want to part from his new wife, but his duty called. Love's sweet embrace would have to wait. However, he couldn't fully cope with his burgeoning new feelings. That he could come to cherish her so intensely, it boggled his mind. She was dear to him in a way he'd never experienced before.

Married friends came up, eyeing him knowingly.

Timian mentioned. "Now you understand how it is to have a mate. There is a bond like no other. When I leave my wife behind, it's a dagger in my heart until I return to her."

"I can't get control of these feelings, Timian."

"It will get better."

"Does she feel this way?"

"From what I saw, she's agog. Her and her maidens were like children how silly they were acting."

Korban smiled. I know this will sound terrible, but I want to give her more reasons to smile and act silly."

All of the men standing there laughed heartily.

Timian replied. "Thankfully, that feeling never goes away."

Lanai broke away from her pack of females to join the council meeting. She did not fail to notice being the center of attention of all the men. At first, she looked down to be sure her clothes were not open or some other clothing malfunction. Finally, it dawned on her, as she was arguably the most beautiful woman these men would ever see, the thought of mighty Korban taking her to the marriage bed, that evoked their strong jealous feelings. Tamping down her desire to chastise them loudly, Lanai scowled for most of the morning. That didn't erase the unwanted attention. Their fantasies about her irked her greatly.

When they broke for a noon meal, Korban walked at her side.

"I'm sorry you're upset. Is there anything I can do for you?"

"If you can conjure up thousands of women to be here to distract these ogling men, that would be good. Mooning men should keep their eyes in their heads, and as for their thoughts..."

Korban chuckled. "They mean no harm."

"Well, I don't like it. They act like I've been conquered, surrendered to their male dreams. I tell you, I have not!"

"I know that, Lanai."

"If I take out some frustration against men on you, I would apologize, if I was sorry."

"I will endure the beating dearest. I apologize for all men everywhere, for all time."

She eyed him dourly for a moment judging if he was making sport of her.

"Lanai, I'm the same person I was yesterday...that you married?"

"Well...you can tell your pack of louts I do not take kindly to..."

"Anything?"

"Korban!" She smacked him on the arm.

He snickered. "You must admit, although your ire is understandable, is it possible your rants are a little too much? They got your message. Nobody could miss it. They see our love and...yes, they are jealous."

Korban continued walking with her until she rejoined her maidens. Other women from other tribes had started joining together with them as a daily habit. They eyed Korban admiringly. It wasn't an issue for him. He talked pleasantly with whomever spoke to him.

Lila acted shy with him for the first time, and he noticed. In her case, it wasn't what he expected.

After they finished eating, he leaned over to her.

"Lila, are you unwell? Is something wrong? You're acting strangely."

She glanced at Lanai who was talking to some other women.

"I'm not a royal person, as is your wife. She warrants being with a high person like you. We all know that. In the secrecy of our thoughts, it's easy for us to imagine being the ones to…join with you. It's my being an improper person with such thoughts, but I will cope. I'm sorry to have such unseemly feelings."

"Lila, I cherish you. Please don't fret in this way. It brightens my day when I see you. I feel jealous about you, so that you understand."

Lila got a surprised look.

Lanai turned back. "What are we talking about? Lila, you look upset."

"It's nothing, my lady. I will be fine soon. New circumstances take a little adjustment."

"You're all still with me. Having this big lunk of a man around me doesn't change my affections for all of you."

"Thank you, my lady. We've spent our lives serving you. Now we feel uncertain about how to deal with the marriage situation."

"We will continue living as we always have. Certainly, he will be a part of us going forward, but we will still retain what we had. I cherish all of you."

Lila hugged her warmly.

"My new husband is not a bad thing for us. Think of how you felt about him on this long trek. He was the only type of leader who could take command of us all. We will all look at new ways to live. That includes all of you."

"Are you talking about us taking a mate?"

"I am."

"How could we be with a man and still serve you?"

"The only difference would be you living with a husband but doing your job during the day."

Lila looked uncertain, glancing shyly at Korban.

"Lila, marriage is a wonderful thing. There is no lack of men interested in you, darling. Just think about it."

"Yes, ma'am, I know that. We see how it strongly affects you, in a good way."

Lanai smirked. "It does do that."

Korban listened to the conversation without comment. He felt like an eavesdropper, though he did appreciate his wife's rare complimentary comments. Strangely, the new idea of Lila marrying gave him a strong twinge of jealousy. Having romantic desires suddenly well up for her wasn't a twist he'd anticipated.

Lila glanced at him. "I will return to the other maidens," she stood up. "We will all talk about what you said, my lady."

"My, lord."

She nodded to Korban before she walked away. Now it was he grappling with difficult feelings.

Lanai turned to Korban. "Do you understand, husband?"

"What are you saying?"

"My maidens have been closely attached to me for a long time. They feel their old lives have been sundered. I believe they will understand the new ways when they start down their own marital paths."

"I know. I'm sorry for this distress they feel. My focus was, and is on you, wife."

"It better be focused on me, you great lout." She smirked, smacking his shoulder with the back of her hand.

He returned her smirk and shook his head mirthfully. The thoughts of Lila, he forcefully blotted out of his mind.

The council assembled for the important deliberations.

Korban stood. "Thank you all for coming. I don't expect some surprising answer to emerge about our difficult challenges. I doubt that is possible. What we need to do now is plan for a step-by-step approach to get the information on our enemy we need without compromising the safety of the people. For our new Brog friends, it's important to find a way to stop these battles with your young ones. As we have noted, the danger there is these Immarati will notice the changes we've made. Whatever actions they take, we must be able to cope and overcome. It's disturbing how you describe them taking away your minds and your wills. If this applies to all races, we need to know that. Since they obscure your memories, we have no way to know how many of them may have come and where they are."

He paused a moment looking around at the silent throng. Nobody made any move toward giving any ideas.

Continuing, he spoke, "My thought is to use our numbers to gradually, and carefully move into the Greka forest to reclaim their entire territory, and with our new adult Brog friends to persuade the rabid Brog youngsters to move backwards to cease hostilities. If we can continue to capture more Brog adults, that aids us a great deal. What do you say, Gralk?"

"It's a nice idea, but let me say, not every leader in those attacks will be so easily captured and converted to our cause. In some cases, there is a prejudice against all other peoples for our past treatments in these fights. We can try to reason with them, but in the meantime, there could be other battles. Do you understand? We must approach this phase with great caution. Also, if the Immarati have secretly come with us and are hiding in the vicinity, that is an incredible risk. I don't know if they can retake control of Soalk and I again."

"My idea is we keep you surrounded by friendlies at all times. I'm hoping they can't control all of us, or masses of our people gathered together. There has to be a reason they didn't land on our shores."

"I have that same hope. If we lose our minds, I agree sufficient of our forces need to take quick action whether tying us or knocking us unconscious."

"We won't attack you, but restraints will work as an appropriate response. Does anybody else have any ideas or concerns?"

A Mantu captain stood. "We are fully with you, but our horsemen riding obstructed in the woods isn't the best use of our skills. I worry we would be more vulnerable than other tribes and peoples with slogging through the trees. There are still predators hereabouts."

"I would say, we can try to pick Mantu warriors who can thrive in any environment. You know who among your people could add to our battle prowess, even in forests. That way, the bulk of your horsemen can patrol and protect Mantu lands."

"Thank you, sub chief."

A Belshik captain spoke. "We're in the process of bringing down more of our fighters to add to this army. You know our situation. They need training and new weapons, like swords, we haven't used in our history. I think you can see our original volunteers already here have gained skills rapidly, but time will still be needed for later arrivals."

"I plan to leave our large encampment as a permanent assembly point. I suspect other nations will be sending more troops to increase our forces since it appears there may be great battles ahead. Each tribe or nation will retain sufficient forces in case of attacks in those homelands. Hopefully, if we can solve this problem of the Brog youths, it will greatly strengthen our positions and eliminate serious threats everywhere. I feel comfortable with that camp being positioned in Mantu lands. They are the largest nation; their cavalry forces are mobile and highly skilled so they can move to danger spots faster than any other peoples. With Mantu forces all around our headquarters, if we want to call it that, will be safeguarded. Does anybody disagree?"

Nobody said anything.

"Crown princess, would you like to add anything?"

She smiled and then stood. "Nothing my husband has said gives me pause. There is too much we don't know, but that is no one's fault. Proceeding with caution is our only option at this point. I agree with him, there must be Immarati vulnerabilities or they would have tried to overwhelm us here too instead of sending proxy forces. We must safeguard our two Brog friends as they are critical to taking the teeth out of the attacks of their young. They can direct us with trying to capture more of the Brog adult leaders. Whoever is amenable or whoever is dangerous, they will know. I'd like to thank my husband for giving a woman a chance to speak here. I respect all of you, but I hope you can respect women for more than just birthing your children and feeding you."

The assemblage chuckled. In the background, women who were hanging nearby listening cheered Lanai.

She looked at Korban. He shrugged his shoulders. "I think we can all agree with my wife."

They gave a shout, but not all of it was heartfelt. Some men were stuck in their old ways.

"Is there anything else we need to discuss?"

At that point, many opinions arose about various small issues, camp matters, and minor disagreements, mostly intertribal. Korban let his underlings handle that phase. Taking Lanai by the waist they went to the 'special tent' rather than to their place in the camp for some 'happy time' together.

Lanai always acted coy at those times, like she was being 'put upon' and needed to be coaxed, but in spite of her contrived acts, she wanted the shared intimacy as much as Korban. He quickly learned how to cope with her mystifying behaviors in that area. Whenever they emerged from the tent, she was contented without fail.

When they walked away, she wrapped her arms around his waist.

"Are you proud of yourself that you can evoke these strong feelings in me?"

"Lanai, it isn't a contest. Making you happy should be a good thing, I would think."

"I'm talking about that male brain, like all we could ever hope for is fulfillment in your arms."

"Are you not fulfilled?"

"Of course I'm happy. I'm just commenting about men being smug about it."

"I...eh...is there anything I can ever do that doesn't require your criticism?"

"Probably not." She laughed heartily.

"I don't know what to say to that."

"Just say nothing and accept the truth. Women know better than men."

"How could I fail to understand that, crown princess?"

"You'll get there, sub chief."

"Does it help my cause to tell you, I'm happy beyond my wildest dreams. Life with you is a wonder, although apparently I need to be mindful of more things than any man can ever know."

Again, she laughed heartily. People they passed stared in envy at this 'perfect' couple. Seemingly they were blessed, destined to incredible feats. Korban's, and Lanai's words, took on the mantle of gospel where nobody wanted to disagree with them.

When they got to their place in camp, the maidens were engaged in serious conversation.

"What is it, ladies?" Lanai asked.

Lila replied. "We've talked at length about...you know what. What we should do is unclear. Do servants announce they're now open to being wooed?"

The married couple laughed.

Lanai answered. "I don't think announcements are necessary. It might start a stampede of men trying to snare you. What do you say, Korban?"

"The men need no prodding to seek your hands. I can pass the word quietly among the captains to pass on with the instructions as this can't turn into a stampede. If you get annoyed or if someone causes you grief, let me know and I will resolve the matter."

The following day, Korban spoke to his leaders who then spoke to their troops.

Visits started rapidly after that. Korban had to intercede when some potential suitors already had mates. The maidens were overwhelmed in spite of Korban's best efforts. The princess made a point of being with them during this courtship phase. Invitations to wed came in large numbers and soon they got 'picked off'. Wella was first, followed by Mandia, Lucia, Shana and finally, Lila was the last holdout. Korban was surprised that Marka, the supreme scout, stepped in to express his interest. Even with something of an age difference, it was he that Lila accepted.

A joint marriage occurred soon afterwards with all five brides becoming wives in the same ceremony.

Wedding nights for all five put that same contented look on all their faces. Korban smiled at Marka when they walked over hand in hand the first morning after the wedding.

"All is well with your marriage?"

"You already know that. Lila is a marvel."

She blushed but looked at Lanai who was chuckling. Lanai embraced Lila tightly. They walked away whispering and chuckling. The other new brides joined them.

"I will try to give you more time to enjoy your bride, but you know we can't delay long in hitting that forest. It's critical we strengthen our position and learn about our enemy. They won't wait on our pleasantries."

"I understand. Thank you for your kindness, sub chief. I'll redouble my efforts with my wife tonight so she doesn't forget me."

Korban snickered and punched his shoulder.

He continued. "I'm awed she would take a grizzly old dog like me, but I'm not giving her back."

"Nor should you. Remember, she chose you, my friend."

"I thought I'd live a solitary life. This is so much better. By the way, I'm going to shave off my beard, for her."

"Women change us in many ways."

"I don't mind."

"At any rate, on this initial push back into the forest, I will join you. The Greka will be helpful in leading us since they know the area."

"I will gather my vanguard team. It's much bigger these days, and far more diverse. I see it as a good thing. I worried about if trust and an alliance could work. Now I'm glad we did it."

"I'll join you when you're ready to go. I have a few things to deal with first."

He went to find the two Brog leaders.

"We'll be going into the next phase very soon. Are you ready?"

"Yes. I'm sure you know this will not be easy." Gralk replied.

"I do. Regardless, it is what we must do for the sake of all people."

When Korban went later to the assembled force, Marka was right. It was diverse and it was sizeable. His wife had said nothing that morning, but it didn't surprise him when she showed up with her sword and her armed maidens.

Korban looked at her. "I don't suppose you'd heed me and stay in camp."

"No."

Marka was eyeing his wife, Lila. She spoke before he could ask. "We are here to do our part too, husband."

"Can..."

"No." She cut him off.

When Marka looked at Korban, he shrugged.

As the advance started, Korban went to the front beside Marka along with Gralk, and Soalk.

Gralk spoke. "Let me say, I'm sorry we can't rush through these woods and end the threat quickly. We must proceed slowly and branch out all around. Pockets of youngsters could be hiding anywhere. We can let no one be alone, and sufficient forces must always be at hand nearby. If there are uprisings in multiple places at the same time, remember there are only two of us, so battles might happen whether we want it or not. Their hunger is insatiable. They have no control because their brains aren't able to function normally. Hopefully that will cool your hatred of Brogs. They don't understand what they're doing."

"That's fine, but also as long as you understand our position. Losing our people is not acceptable. We aren't food."

"We do understand. This is a bad situation for both sides."

The column proceeded cautiously. It became clear to Korban very soon that the issue was the size of the forest. In order to cover all of the area, it required spreading his forces to the point they were stretched very thin. A major uprising would be a problem and deaths among allied troops were virtually guaranteed to happen. Although Lanai and her maidens demanded to share the risk, Korban kept them close to him with warriors assigned to personally safeguard them.

He sent word among his advancing forces.

"Be very nimble. At any sign of a Brog attack, immediately retreat until we gather forces to properly deal with the threat. I want no deadly surprises and needless losses."

His directive mostly paid off as there were soon several sudden subterranean emergences to cope with. It took time to get either Soalk or Gralk into position to quell the budding attacks and to capture more leaders. In only one case was there a serious battle. In that case, that particular leader wasn't one to surrender and change sides. There were significant losses on both sides.

Korban arrived on the scene to join the fight out of necessity. It wasn't possible here to capture Brog youngsters in a feeding frenzy, so mostly they fought a delaying tactic until Gralk arrived late. With their leader slain, he took charge of those Brog young and gradually ended the attack. The youngsters recessed back into their hole and moved underground out of the area back the way they had come.

Lanai and her maidens jumped into the fray when Korban did. They fought well, being experienced from numerous prior fights, they were able warriors. Their Kar warrior protectors stayed nearby assuring they would never be in danger of injury or death. Not killing any of the Brog opponents was a difficult task. Mostly they were successful in fighting to keep them at bay.

After the first day of the campaign, they had four additional Brog adults in their ranks. Each successive day they could cover the ground more safely as increasingly a Brog leader could be stationed across much of the front. Successes bred more successes. By the time a week had passed, they had twenty captured adults and the serious Brog incursions were taking a noticeable downturn.

This allowed the allies to further increase the speed of their advance. Casualties were reduced substantially, and the operation became something of a mop-up.

Behind the advance, the Greka were reclaiming homes and settlements and reestablishing their lives. By the time that the armies reached the southernmost region of the forest, Brog attacks ceased completely.

Korban gathered his staff to discuss the situation. There were now thirty Brog adults in attendance at the council.

"Gralk, what are your thoughts?"

"I think there are any number of our young in a dormant state under the ground. Without a leader, they will hibernate. That's not a permanent state, but for them it's a vulnerable time. In order to survive and to emerge into adulthood, they must feed. What we can try to do is find them, put an adult in charge to help them hunt normal animal prey. If they can ascend here to adulthood, it will be good for all of us."

"Has anyone seen signs of the Immarati? Thus far, it doesn't seem they've intervened in any battles."

No one replied.

"It seems to me we have two choices now. We can return to our homes and have a universal pledge to gather an army of the entire continent if a war comes, or we send a great army south to invade your continent, Gralk. If we can find and unseat these Immarati, perhaps we can end the peril for you also. If we simply leave them where they are, I suspect we'd soon be fighting for these same grounds. None of us know if the Brog vulnerability to Immarati influence and control applies to the other races. There would be only one way to find out."

Lanai spoke. "I'm not one to stand by while an enemy recovers their ability to harm us. I would say we plan for a move to the southern continent."

Korban looked again at Gralk. "How would your people react to our army appearing at their shores?"

"It's hard to say under these circumstances. Under normal times with our faculties intact, we would fear an invasion was for conquest. We here can try to allay those fears, if we find people who aren't still under enemy control. If the Immarati there can still cause us to fight against the allied army, and if we here can't retain our freedom from their control, I just don't know. I understand that is a difficult situation for our planning, but it's the true nature of the dilemma."

Marka spoke. "Sub chief, it seems taking a little time to gather information is the only choice. Perhaps we can send a small party, or parties, to enter their continent to assess what we face? We have still never seen any Immarati. I'd like to capture one to bring him here. Perhaps beating it senseless might give us some insight."

The entire council laughed heartily.

Lila edged over smiling warmly to hug her husband.

Lanai piped in. "I agree. It's measured, cautious, and makes perfect sense."

Korban replied, "My only worry is a small force going into the unknown with the nature of the risks being also unknown, we wouldn't be there if they're imperiled, captured, or killed. Certainly, we need information, but those first steps are the most dangerous of the threats we've faced on this long trek. I want to think about this a bit."

The council recessed and went away talking among each other.

Again, no one else ever challenged anything Korban said, or even wanted to. Since they never did, he felt a heavy onus trying to be perfect. For him, being the person in charge seemed as much a liability as a benefit. Korban would get the blame for anything that went wrong, and here it would be on a world-wide scale.

Lanai took him aside to be alone for a brief time.

"Korban, can I tell you how proud I am. I always had a suspicion you were a rare person born for great things. Nothing that's happened has shown me otherwise. You're willing to deal with difficult tests when all others shy away. I trust you completely."

"That makes one of us. My magical answers are nothing more than the competence and abilities of the peoples under me. They are the ones out front facing down the dangers. I just happen to be there too."

She smirked. "That is a silly way to look at it. You and Marka talk the same with this modesty ploy. Your record speaks for itself. Look at the universal respect you get from all tribes. Old rivalries are easily forgotten within your camp. Peoples that would have been fighting each other, sit together and protect each other in deadly fights. This is miraculous."

"Do you think your father will think I'm miraculous for stealing his daughter's virtue and ruining his marriage plans for you? Think of the treaties and allies you could have achieved for your father merely by bedding some noble's son."

"Not funny, Korban. Think of how short your life will be if you continue irking me with more inane aspersions."

He snickered. "Lanai, you know I mean no aspersions. I was reflecting more on where we came from. That Korban and Lanai are gone. We are new people. I'm a happily married man. I think about you constantly. You're always in my mind."

"That's better. At least your brain can still function, even if only on a simple level. I appreciate your comment of thinking about me, but I realize, what you mean is the thought of having your way with me is probably what is in your mind."

"Yes, I'm a simpleton, but I'm your simpleton." He swept her up in a crushing embrace. She did not resist. They took advantage of the free moment and felt much better for it.

For the balance of the day, scouting teams traveled all through the forests trying to help locate hidden Brog nests. The adult Brogs were better at spotting probable sites. When they opened a hole, exerting immediate control, the Brog youths were brought out to feed from forest animals. Their abnormal traits seemed much reduced as well as the abnormal appetite. Having new adult leaders without alien influence, they were able to house them above ground in clear sight of the allies. Thankfully, all battles against them ceased altogether.

In the first group of Brog young captured by the allies, the first conversion occurred as a Brog left the transition phase and became an adult. Seemingly overnight, they radically changed physically shedding the stumpy bodies of the chrysalis phase growing into appealing adult bodies. It was fascinating for the other races to observe the process, and to watch as the adult leaders began teaching them. Afterwards, as more conversions occurred, they picked up in pace. The newly emerged Brog citizens were understandably bewildered, but followed the teachings and guidance of the existing adults. In this new environment, they learned the allies were friends and treated them such. When that entire 'batch' completed the chrysalis phase, another 'batch' started the emergence.

What that accomplished was more time for Korban to consider his next steps. In this important early phase, none of the Brog elders could accompany any expeditions back to their home continent, yet. They were needed with the maturing process and fledgling first intellectual steps for their emergent young.

Lanai paid close attention to the Brog converts. They started showing their sex at that point. The males outgrew the females in size, but the females in no way were inferior. They seemed to learn slightly faster than the males. Lanai was glad for the chance to meet and mentor Brog females. They had separate personalities, aptitudes, and interests. Those females found the company of other females, even from different races, captivating. They were given a much different awareness and perspective than they could have ever had back home.

Lanai mentioned it to Korban one evening. "It's remarkable these Brog females that not so long ago hungered to chew us to bits are now sentient and accomplished allies and companions. I enjoy them as much as any other race we've met. What a strange twist of fate. It's amazing how rapidly they advance in knowledge and competence, and suddenly changing from those grotesque squat forms into attractiveness is amazing."

"It is. However, soon I'll need to get us moving about the proposed invasion to the south."

"I know but we can still have this night to ourselves, if you're of a mood."

"You know I'm always in that mood for you."

She smirked and embraced him avidly. "Good answer."

CHAPTER FOURTEEN
Invasion

Korban greatly enjoyed his time with his wife while he could, but time was not their ally. Increasingly by the day, decisions and actions needed to be taken. It weighed heavily on his mind.

The Brog leaders brought the newly emerged young Brog citizens along rapidly. Those from the first 'batch', most of them were now capable of helping the considerable younger newly emerging 'batches' freeing the leaders for the critical next steps.

As a united camp, turning their attention to the matter at hand, they all gathered in council to make those tough choices. It was not only what steps to take, but who to take them. There were plenty of avid volunteers, but this assignment called for particular skills and particular attributes.

Korban most trusted Marka in the field, but if he was lost, could they recover? Marka was one of those few indispensables. It was a punishing possibility for Korban to consider.

Marka sat with him while they talked about the best men for the mission. All of the maidens decided to join them for that discussion.

Lila spoke. "If you're thinking about sending my husband, I am going too. I'm as qualified and experienced as any man. I will not be apart from him going into such danger."

Marka got a look of distress. "Lila, you are my life now. If you came with me, I would worry about you and not sufficiently concentrate on the task. That could be fatal."

"And I don't worry about you any less? I will not lose you and become a widow at the start of our life together."

Lanai spoke. "I can certainly lead a team. I'm like Lila, the measure of any man. I've proven I can lead, and I can prevail against impossible odds. I've done so before."

Korban eyed her sourly.

"See, Korban. You understand what Lila has said. Why would it be different for us women?"

"Who said Marka is going? We're here just to talk."

"The lives of women are no more important than the men. We all must share in the sacrifices too. Do you think women want to be widows?" She glanced at Jana who eyed her sadly.

"Lanai, and Lila, my decisions must be solely about the person's best suited for this task. The chances of death are very high. I can't send a large force to invade that continent with a chance of losing them all because we weren't prepared. But if I send a small force and they get wiped out, we're worse than before. The enemy is alerted and we don't know what happened to our people. Therefore, I need more than just battle skills. They must be keen to what's around them, seeing and sensing things most others would miss. They must be more than agile, because escape might be their only lifesaver, and of course, they would have to be deadly. If women, or a woman, was there, the men will tend to gather around to protect her in a fight which could put the mission at risk. I'm not talking about prejudice about women and their skills. It's a simple fact of how men would react. It's a part of this consideration."

Lanai and Lila scowled at him.

Lanai spoke. "Korban, every woman is well aware of male vanity, prejudices, and weaknesses. How do you suggest we get past that?"

"Lanai...women have their own types of issues. Debating the merits and flaws of each sex isn't good use of our time. Remember the lesson of that island of Iscali. No one blames you for any of it, but the priestess snared you and took control with long lasting after-effects."

The two women glared at him.

"I'm sorry ladies, but every factor must be considered."

"You seem to have your minds made up. Women can't have the opportunity to prove you wrong? All we have done during this epic trek means nothing?"

"Of course it does; we respect and appreciate everything you've done. Proving yourselves isn't necessary. If our scouts are wiped out and women are among them dead, is that a good goal?"

Korban looked at Marka. "I'm at a loss to help them understand."

"They understand, Korban. They just don't agree, and I would say they won't agree. There is no easy answer to the issues they raise. It's a matter of making the difficult choices. I would never have allowed the princess to do much of what she did, but she's correct that she proved she could succeed against all odds."

"This isn't a matter we can resolve right now. Let's continue talking about potential candidates, and ladies, I will include women in the considerations. The ultimate choices will be made on another day."

Marka mentioned various members of his scout team, leaders from various tribes discussed the best candidates there. Lanai talked about the merits of her females, those who were experienced and sufficiently trained.

Although they managed to come to an end of discussions that day, eventually, after some fractious arguments, the assembled departed with no blows exchanged.

Lanai was riled and would not walk with Korban. Marka had little better luck trying to walk with Lila. Lila actually increased her pace to join Lanai in showing their backs to the men. Marka approached Korban. "Uh-oh, this isn't going to be a restful night."

There were no warm hugs and embraces for either man that evening. Even arising in the morning, the women were quiet, departing quickly.

In the morning, Korban saw Marka as they walked side by side to get food.

"Marriage is not so easy, my friend." Marka muttered.

"Definitely a double-edged sword."

"These women only want to see things as they wish them to be."

"The crown princess taught me that long ago when I first met her."

"I understand. So, what do we do? If we delay, it does not serve anybody's interest. These Immarati could already be enacting dire plans. As we've discussed, the strides we've made reclaiming Brogs from their control will not escape their notice."

"We'll gather the council and we chose the vanguard for the mission. Then, we enact our own plans immediately."

Korban spoke later to start the difficult meeting.

"I wish there was ample time to consider this matter fully, but I suspect not. Therefore, we need to make difficult choices right here and now. Being picked for this first foray will not be an honor, it may be a death sentence, so we all need to think carefully to pick the right mix of people. The only idea I had was with the initial landing on that shore, we take more forces to maintain at least a minimal base camp. As our people filter out to explore the land and discover our enemy, there would be reinforcements at the ready, although admittedly not in great numbers. The second issue is how do we get there. The Brog have no idea how they were brought here. The Greka have no navy. Their boats are fishing vessels. It's limited how many warriors can ride on each boat. We would be more vulnerable in the water than on land. If these Immarati did cross an ocean, they must have great ships. Perhaps there is a great fleet out there waiting for us. Against them in the water, we would have no chance."

Glancing across the faces of the council, he saw only resignation and discouragement.

"Jana, what do you say?"

"You paint a bleak picture, sub chief. There are more Greka fishing boats than you might think, but you're right. Even the largest of them cannot carry large numbers of passengers. Providing enough capacity to transport the vanguard forces can certainly be arranged, but it doesn't solve the problem of vulnerability while sailing. They're not war vessels. Ultimately, if we were to try to invade that continent, it would take a great deal of time to move a large army even if we used every fishing boat we have. There are other peoples that sail, but it would take much time for them to sail here, even if they would agree to join us at all. If the Immarati have superior ships, we would never have an answer for that. From what our Brog friends have said, with what was done to them, they may have strange weapons to render all of us helpless too."

"Our greatest chance against them would be surprise. Catching them off guard may not even be possible, but it would be what we must somehow accomplish. I would add, for whoever took on this suicidal task, evading notice is critical. Somehow, we must creep about in their territory without being seen. If the chance arose to capture one, that would be good. At the very least we need to discover them, their weapons, and their next moves."

Lanai spoke, "Korban, are you only talking about people you choose, or can people volunteer?"

"Considering the needs of the mission, perhaps there can be some small choices given. This is not a task for most."

He turned his head rather than stare at her frosty glance.

"One other thing, Jana. This Isle of Doom, does it pose a problem for boats sailing past?"

"Our fishermen don't really sail there. We've had some people sail along the coastline of the southern continent briefly, but we've never tried a landing."

"Gralk, can you tell us about your homeland. Is it different than what you've seen of the northern continent?"

"I would say not. Mountains, forest, animals, they are all the same. The farther south you go, the colder it gets."

"Are there any other peoples than your kind?"

"I don't believe so. We have not explored all possible corners, so I suppose there could be hermitic tribes. We haven't had contact with other peoples. The western part of the southern continent is mountainous. The rest of the continent is flatter. There are many forested areas, but we aren't explorers to travel about."

"I wonder if a landing on the eastern coasts would be better. Going ashore on the western side to climb mountains doesn't sound like a smart choice."

"On either coast, will our boats draw these enemy ships?"

"We don't know. It's one of the risks. The alternative of sitting back waiting for them to make a move is a worse danger."

Lanai pressed her point. "Korban, who are you selecting?"

He felt great stress at the difficult moment of decision, like he was giving death sentences to dear friends and acquaintances.

"It is with great regret, I ask Marka if you're willing to lead a team?"

"I will, my friend. Don't feel badly about the terrible onus. Someone has to do it."

"Will you help me pick your team?"

Lila piped in immediately. "I have told you both, if he goes, I go." She actually rested her hand on her sword hilt. Her expression was grim.

Marka looked ill. He glanced at Korban, and then Lanai. Lanai looked crossly at him too.

"I...eh..."

Lanai immediately piped in. "That's settled, now who else will travel? If you want other teams, I volunteer to lead one."

Now it was Korban looking ill. He shifted uneasily as he stood.

"Marka, name your team members."

Not surprisingly, he picked members they'd discussed from his vanguard force. Including Lila, there was a total of ten members which was the number the council had picked.

"Now I will pick my team." Lanai didn't wait for approval, she simply started picking. Her choices came from nearly every tribe and nation. The captain of her Tranta escort was her first pick. When she picked one of Marka's vanguard members, he looked at Marka, as if he needed someone to sign off on the matter.

Korban fretted at Lanai having her way on this deadly issue. When he decided to lead a team too, the entire council arose and stopped him forcefully.

The Belshik leader spoke quickly. "You are the leader of all forces. You can't do this. We all understand you wish to safeguard the princess, but we cannot allow it."

He felt like shouting, but restrained his ire, barely.

From that point on, he acted like a robot. Deciding to anoint eight more team leaders which would send a hundred souls total of his people southward, his final instruction after the selections were to the leaders. "Gather the members of your new teams now to discuss your mission. You must be one with them."

He turned and walked away, irate.

From behind, he heard Lanai's voice. "Thank you, husband. I won't fail you."

He didn't acknowledge her, or even look back.

Both the feelings of foreboding and his intense anger led him to childish reactions. He stayed away from all people, instead going into the forest to hunt. When he returned to camp much later, he dropped off the deer for the cooks and then wandered off looking for where Lanai was waiting. It was already dusk. When he approached his wife, she had a wry smile.

Before she could speak, he spoke. "Crown Princess, I will leave you to your maidens and your new team members for your companionship. I feel a great need for solitude. You have won your point, so feel free to enjoy your moment, but leave me to deal with my difficult feelings without glib condescending words.

Her face turned angry. "Do you..."

He turned and walked away before she could unleash her tirade.

His mood lasted beyond just that difficult day as the hundred members of the advance teams were accumulated and sequestered preparing for the departure southward as the fishing boats were gathered. Stubbornly, he didn't participate in any way and didn't attempt to make any camp decisions.

When they were gone south heading for the coast, he felt like a widower. His mood darkened substantially and the entire allied army knew it. There had been a great deal of background chatter and opinions already at Korban allowing Lanai to make such a dubious choice. The irate remainder of the Trantan contingent wouldn't come near him, which he didn't mind.

The Vikar nature in Korban reemerged and he spent much time away, whether hunting or merely riding alone. The only time he allowed any reprieve was on a particular day, far away from the main camp riding in Mantu lands, he came upon a small village and stopped there.

They recognized him and crowded around. It was the small children that melted his heart, so he knelt down to embrace them, as Lanai would have. Tugging at his repressed emotions to the point it briefly short-circuited his anger, he smiled for the first time since that difficult day. Although only temporarily, it gave him a short respite from his abiding anger and his feeling the need to punish his wife. Thinking of her as his late wife had become too easy lately.

Spending time in the village filled his empty heart for a day. He decided to spend the night enjoying being around the little children, the hope of the future, if there would be a future.

It was with regret that he parted from the happy villagers in the morning. Rather than ride back to camp, he rode back to the Greka forest and hunted more meat. Finally riding into the main camp at dusk, he dropped off the kills and went to his usual sleeping place in the camp. All of the remaining maidens were there waiting. All the other women from the various tribes were gathered there too.

"What is it, ladies?"

Lucia walked up. "Why are you acting this way? You left your wife without so much as a goodbye and good luck? She is a great person, but you shamed her with this poor treatment. Our sister, Lila, is courageous enough also to take the terrible risk, but you act like a child at their bravery. We all thought you a different kind of man, someone who could avoid the snares of old rules and old prejudice. We were wrong. You act like every man with your backwards and childish reactions."

Rather than feel ashamed, the chastisement irked him further. He did try to temper a rash reply. Uniformly, every woman was glaring at him. The barbarian impulse to draw a sword at any setback punished him until he could manage to tamp it down.

"Thank you for clarifying your feelings, ladies. It seems I need to sleep elsewhere."

Wella piped in. "You can't run away from this, sub chief."

He turned back to face her. "You're right, Wella, I am still a sub chief of the Vikar. Perhaps it is time for a different way."

Leaving them behind continuing their verbal diatribe, he went to find Timian. "My friend, I must ask for your help with something."

"What is it, Korban?"

"With what has happened, I find I can't continue to lead this army. Can I ask that you step in to fill that void? If the council wishes to choose another leader, I'm fine with it. I may seem a small person with faltering from my inner pain, but I acknowledge that. Many in this camp whisper I should not have allowed the women to leave on this mission. I can't disagree. I have no desire to be here. I just came from being assailed by all the women of the camp. I won't allow that to happen again. I need the solitary life of a Vikar hunter right now."

"I regret hearing that, Korban. Although I understand your feelings, I suspect it is a critical mistake for you, and for us. You don't seem to realize; you were the bond holding all of the factions together. I worry we could fall back into petty rivalries and squabbles. This is still a tenuous alliance. As your friend, I'll honor your request, but I can give no assurances of what I can accomplish in your stead."

"Thank you, old friend. I'm sorry to dump this on you, but there was no one else I could trust with it."

Korban looked away pondering the scope of the troubles and his pain.

"I'll sleep here tonight, if you'll allow it. Tomorrow, I'll start the next chapter of my life."

Timian shrugged and patted him sympathetically on the shoulder.

Far to the south, the brave members of the scout teams reached the coast. The decision had been made to sail to the eastern coast for their landings on the southern continent.

Lanai showed a brave face to her team, but she was frightened and she was rattled. The shocking actions of her husband left her feeling deep foreboding, not only at the dangers of the landings, but at what to expect if she made it back home. She went to speak with Marka.

"I'm sorry to bother you, but I don't understand what happened? I never thought my husband would...cast me aside."

Lila embraced Lanai.

Marka replied. "He didn't cast you aside, princess. The feelings of sending you away without being allowed to come and safeguard you was too much for him to bear. As difficult as it is, you must block that out and concentrate fully on this landing. Your team needs you to lead them. We can have no weak links with this deadly onus."

"You're right. I asked to lead here so I need to do just that. Thank you, Marka."

"Sleep here tonight?" Lila asked.

"I wish I could, but as Marka says, my team needs their leader."

Getting up in the morning, going onto the fishing boats, the implications of the hazards sunk in with everybody. This was truly the most dangerous task ever attempted by the allied forces.

Once they were fully loaded into the boats, they set sail, but uniformly everybody felt queasy. Searching the open seas for any sign of an enemy fleet, luck was with them. It was not a short trip. They had to sail east to skirt around the Isle of Doom before they could turn southward. The Island looked scary though they saw nothing to cause that feeling. It was like something dangerous nearby was setting off inner warnings within them.

Days at sea affected the scout individuals differently. Some dealt better with seasickness than others. A naval battle at that point would have been difficult with over half the people ill and unable to fight.

Even when they reached the northernmost coast of the southern continent, it took some time on land for everyone to regain their full health.

Fortunately, there were no strange adversaries waiting to ambush them. In the teams, there was a one-each Brog leader included. This was their home and therefore it fell on them to be the main guides.

The beach here was wider than the northern continent coasts they'd just left. Beyond the beach were grasslands, although a forest was nearby. The teams made their way into the forest for the cover.

Marka asked Soalk, "Do you live in villages above ground, or do you live below ground?"

"Something of both. When our young are birthed, they spend initial time being weened underground. When they reach the stage of the chrysalis, they're brought up to hunt food. Normally, that isn't a long-term process. It's the Immarati who have frozen them in that state.

"We all have the question if the enemy is watching us now, if we're in imminent danger?"

"I can give no guidance about that. Whatever they did in snaring us, we never knew. If that would work on you also, I also don't know."

"My thought is we keep to the forest at first. If there is contact, stay close enough together to reinforce against any assault. I know that is a problem for trying to cover great amounts of land, but I feel our goal is to discover the enemy, not to explore your entire continent."

"I agree. Although it's home for me, I feel we should spend as little time as possible here. The risk of dealing with the Immarati is a necessary evil, but we shouldn't try facing numbers of them."

"Princess, are you feeling better?"

"I am. The ailments of the sea for me are passed."

He smiled. They both knew he was asking about her fears leading a team into danger.

"Good, tomorrow we will proceed with controlled dispersal. If we trigger ambushes or have any contact with the enemy, we'll be together enough to rush to the fight."

The other team leaders nodded their heads.

"Each of you Brog team members, you must be vigilant beyond your best efforts. If we see you're suddenly snared by this strange Immarati power, and if we're still free of the malady, we will protect you, but we will bind you so you're no danger to us."

Soalk answered. "We agree. We have no desire to serve the enemy."

Marka spoke a solemn prayer. "May we all be protected by providence in this hour of our desperate need."

Sleep was difficult that evening.

Arising in the morning, they had a cold camp. No fires to draw enemy notice. The teams assembled and they started out spreading across the forest heading generally southward. The teams at the edges were gradually farther apart to the point if there was an attack on one of the edges, the entire force couldn't arrive quickly to their aid. Marka was in the middle and worried immediately. He kept Lanai's team next to him, but with each team continuing expanding outward, they were in increasing danger.

The teams were very cautious and not a great deal of ground was covered. The next day they proceeded a little more rapidly, but they didn't expand as far apart.

Moving farther west as a group, they approached the distant mountains.

Soalk motioned them to stop. He moved forward to a point, joined by the other Brog leaders, to dig down uncovering a large nest of Brog youth. The leader of that nest was under Immarati influence and evoked the nest into action. However, it never happened as the ten free leaders squelched the attempt at an assault and the leader was captured and hauled up to face Marka. He smacked the captive until he began to regain his consciousness. Meanwhile the turbulent youngsters were kept in limbo.

When the captive blinked his eyes and the other leaders were able to talk to him, he became another asset for the team.

Marka questioned him. "Do you remember when you were captured and how this spell was put on you?"

"No, I'm sorry I don't."

"You have no memory of this enemy?"

"That is true."

Soalk took over talking to him, at length. The other leaders brought up the youth to hunt and feed before returning them back to the nest back into dormancy.

Soalk reported to Marka. "It's as I thought. The configuration of our peoples hasn't changed. The farther south we go, the greater the population gatherings will be. I can tell you nothing about where the enemy might be."

"Did you live in this area, or elsewhere?"

"I was living farther south. It was cooler where I lived."

"Another worry I have is traveling too far away from our landing area. In an emergency, if we have too far to travel to get back to our boats home, that could be a problem in itself."

"It is a problem."

The following day using the same strategy to stay fairly close to each other, they came upon another nest. Again, it was the Brog adults unearthing a Brog leader who was as easily subdued as the first one. Now they had twelve Brog leaders as a part of the allied team. In this case, for the first time, the results were different when they sat down in camp that evening, suddenly all of the Brog faces went to a blank stare.

Marka shouted his scouts into action surrounding and tying up the Brog adults. They heard the sounds of a large swarm of Brog young unleashed and racing toward them to attack.

"What do we do, Marka?" Lila asked, drawing her sword.

"We're in no position for a pitched battle. We may be about to meet our adversaries. Everybody, form a defensive circle around our Brog leaders and wait to see what the Immarati want to do."

The familiar sound of a large and voracious Brog swarm in their frenzy was frightening to hear as they approached at the sprint. When they broke into view, it appeared they would attack. Once they got to a point near enough to strike, suddenly they halted, snarling and screeching, snapping jaws at the allied defensive circle.

From the forest, figures emerged. They were tall and slender, unarmed, but carrying strange devices. The surrounding knot of the Brog swarm separated and one of the Immarati in a shimmering robe walked up to Marka. After so many battles and confrontations with Brog swarms, this time was markedly different. The Immarati leader ramped up the Brog to a level of insane, manic rage, mindless killers avid to attack. That included all of their converts.

"You are Vikar? Am I correct?"

"I am Vikar. You call yourselves Immarati? Although we don't know this name, we believe you come from across the ocean?"

"You are correct. I'm surprised. You seem to speak with some intelligence. The fact you survived that onslaught on your home continent and have managed to make your way here impresses me. It was a fool's errand with no chance of success, and of course you could never have returned to your homes there, but it was very brave."

Marka glared at him, but felt impotent.

"You will make interesting specimens for analysis and processing. We can study your people and their weaknesses to find better ways to overcome you. Thank you for donating your bodies to us."

Marka thought fearfully, struggling to find a way to save them from this dire moment. The thought of losing Lila terrified him.

"You can drop your weapons now. We won't let you threaten us, as if you could have. You're an inferior species useful only for our research purposes. Welcome to your new lives."

He pressed a button on his device and the Brog frenzy escalated even further to a rabid fever pitch, barely restrained. Even the captive Brog leaders turned feral and started to snarl and bite at the ally's warriors. It was terrifying for the allies, surrounded and at the mercy of a pitiless foe.

"Make your choice, Vikar. Your dream to go down fighting will never happen. We won't allow it."

With ultimate regret, he dropped his weapons. The others followed suit and a file of Immarati came forward and bound them, leading them away. It was an hour walk to their destination, going southward.

The Immarati camp was mystifying for them to see. Technology was something the allies weren't prepared for. The Immarati leader led them into a translucent enclosure.

"Let me reiterate, your old lives are over. Whatever futures you have, we will decide. Some of you may have continuing uses for us and can live on. Others of you may have a short-term use that could lead to your imminent demise. Are there any questions?"

Lila touched Marka's hand. Both were still bound, so it could only be a glancing touch. There were tears in her eyes.

Lanai was stunned. The thought of this ending was beyond her conception. All of her miraculous outcomes seemed long lost and unimportant. She pondered. *Korban, you were right.*

Marka whispered to his wife. "I'm sorry I failed you."

Even in this worst of predicaments, Lanai tried to think. *The Immarati are obviously advanced beyond our understanding, but are there important things we're missing? With our lives at stake, answers are vital. Think Lanai.*

"Process these creatures."

'Processing' was immodest as clothes were removed and taken away, and then they were strapped to tables for examinations. Needles for drawing blood was a first, and also for injecting serum. Those injections caused a variety of reactions. For the first time here, Lanai felt light-headed and out of control of her body. Unlike with the Iscali priestess being unconscious, here Lanai was aware. At one point she lost consciousness during their procedures. Lila was on the table beside her and appeared to be going through the same things being done to Lanai.

It was mortifying, but the helplessness bothered them as much as the indignities.

It was a difficult day for them all. Trying to think ahead was difficult as their prospects were so bleak.

At one point, she saw Soalk brought into the room. He looked the same as when they first captured him. With a blank face, there was no recognition in his eyes. He wouldn't be rescuing them.

After a full day of lab tests, the captives were taken to separate rooms to sleep.

Lanai lay on the cot trying to remember everything. She thought, *at least we're all still alive.*

A painful thought haunted her of precious time spent with her husband, now lost. She couldn't stop her tears, but returning to thinking as quickly as she could, she tried to consider, *what Korban would do?*

The Immarati threats were real. It was beyond terrifying for the helpless captives, not only for them personally, but for the fate of the world.

The thin white pullovers they were given to wear was embarrassingly too short and too shear.

No miracles came to mind before she dozed off to sleep.

Morning came too soon as all of the captives were bleary-eyed and dulled. It was another full day strapped to tables in the lab as they ran different batteries of tests, sometimes using strange machines.

Soalk made another appearance looking still like a zombie. When he came close, she subtly touched his hand. For a moment he paused mid-step, but blinked his eyes before continuing past. It gave her hope, though she had no real reason for it.

They got food in the mornings and food at night with no break during the days. Cleansing themselves had to occur in their rooms as well as bodily functions. The rooms were cleaned while they were out during the day.

Although no one was there, Lanai always felt like she was being watched. Strange devices were always present. What they were, and what they did, she had no idea, but she'd decided to be cautious, betraying nothing to her captors.

Ever present inside this alien enclosure were Brog adults, although without their faculties. They were now the mindless 'servants' doing the bidding of the masters. Soalk was even one of the people sent to retrieve Lanai one morning. Before he bound her, she touched his hand and whispered.

"You know me, Soalk. You can fight this aegis We need you."

This time he turned his face with a confused look. It was only when the other guard started to bind her that he slipped back into the dull subservient state.

It gave her a feeling of renewed hope, like she was finally doing something. Feeling urgency about the Immarati threat to start killing them off, Lanai futilely hungered for revenge.

On this day, Lila looked particularly sedated. It was frightening to see.

"Lila? Lila?" Lanai whispered, trying not to draw the notice of her captors.

Lila managed to blink her eyes, but little else. She tried to utter sounds, but could only make soft noises.

That enraged Lanai. Testing the restraints, she wriggled most of the day and noticed some slight loosening, but by that time the day was over and they were led away. She didn't see Soalk.

The last day of a week in the enclosure worried Lanai. She had a dire feeling that things were about to turn for the worst. She had no more of a plan than she'd had on the first day of captivity, which was nothing at all.

Lanai also worried about Lila's different state. *If I'm in for that same treatment, can I even affect an escape?"*

Again, the thought of Korban was in her head, but he couldn't save her from afar. Only she was here to take any action.

Meanwhile back home, Korban stayed away from camp, hunting food intermittently. He would hunt in the forest and supply meat to nearby Greka villages, and he would also take food to the closest Mantu villages. In the interim staying absent from the camp, he did his best not to think about the mission, or his wife and friends. His feelings of failure mounted and gave him no relief from the emotional onslaught.

During this time, Korban didn't just think there could be bad news, he was sure there would be bad news. As hard as he tried to blank his mind of thoughts, he failed consistently.

If he'd know the truth of what they were going through to the south, he would have gone singlehandedly to attack the Immarati. That was not an option.

Korban never went to the camp to determine what was being done about his departure. It was too painful.

CHAPTER FIFTEEN
Truths

Lanai saw the Immarati leader in attendance when they were taken to the lab the following day. Everybody still seemed to be present of the teams, from what she could see.

He talked to his researchers giving lengthy instructions. Glancing at Lila, she seemed more alert on this day. She returned Lanai's glance.

Soalk was in the lab too. Although passive, when he slyly glanced her way, Lanai saw it, as well as Lila. He quickly looked away to appear passive.

Lila looked at Lanai who blinked twice. Lila changed her expression to placid, but both women felt like Soalk might have made some progress against the crippling noose of these Immarati captor's control.

The leader walked over to speak to Lila and Lanai. Of course, they were bound unclad, as always with every day in their lab.

Staring at them impolitely, he muttered, "I'm acquiring an appreciation for your species. I understand you're both considered very beautiful in your lands." His usual frank perusal annoyed them, but they were helpless to do anything about it, again. Not only were they firmly bound, they didn't have their weapons, even if somehow, they could get free. They continued to resist in spirit, but that was no physical protection.

Neither of them replied, merely glaring at him.

"Ladies, you are allowed to speak to me. Are you considered great beauties?" He smirked at his rhetorical question.

Lanai was provoked. "Among our peoples, there is a saying, "beauty is in the eye of the beholder." It speaks to outside judgments of placing women in boxes of their choosing. There is no single universal standard for beauty." She eyed his smirk before continuing.

"Obviously with people like you, there is no culture or proper decorum about ladies. Forcing bound helpless women exposed naked to be placed on display for your seamy leers and immodest touches is a crime of the highest order. You seem to think there can never be consequences for you. Where would you get such an idea?"

"Are you going to administer these consequences?" He snickered. His comrades chuckled. The allied males reacted tugging against restraints and growling in anger.

Lanai stared at him with a hard glint in her eyes.

He chuckled. "You imagine murdering me. I can see it in your eyes. That isn't even possible, woman. You're just too stupid to understand that."

"Am I? Good to know." Now it was she who smirked. "Give me back my clothes, and my weapons, and we can clarify that theory of yours."

"I like this, you're invigorating. You cause me to rethink our original schedule for the day. Although our tests have proven enlightening, I can think of another avenue for our time together. Yes, let's try another path."

He walked back to his lab technicians revising the plans for the day. They all looked at the bound women like hungry predators.

Coming back to Lanai, he continued. "I think the two of you would make perfect vessels for some new experiments. Perhaps having you birth Brog offspring would give us valuable insights into the cross-breeding of lower species. Or, we can also consider further hybrid births using Immarati fathers. As I think of it, we will do that."

Lanai and Lila got murderous looks tugging futilely at their own restraints.

Marka was livid yanking so hard it appeared he might snap the restraints.

The Immarati leader smiled, looking around at the mass reactions. "I think we have their attention, gentlemen. I knew this would be a fertile ground for our researches. These fools who easily fell into our laps, I like this new direction.

The lab workers laughed.

Lanai looked at Soalk. He was not hiding his anger. Whether others of the Brog captives had also managed to regain some measure of control, she had no way to know.

The Immarati lab techs approached the two women who were then further immobilized on the beds splayed in a more vulnerable position for the heinous assaults. Lanai feared the worst could actually happen. Being helpless to stop them in their newest vile plans drove both women to intense rage. She could barely even wriggle with how tightly they'd secured her body. Lila was in the same helpless predicament, only able to wriggle slightly. Another Immarati approached her with the same lewd intent. He leered at her with a disrespectful comment and then started to crawl onto her bed.

Their leader eyed Lanai salaciously. "Ah yes, I'm going to enjoy this very much, as will you. Welcome to a new life, as my concubine."

The leader moved close, but just as he was climbing onto Lanai's bed, suddenly there was a loud alarm sounded. All of the Immarati froze in place for a moment. She heard the leader whisper, "It can't be."

The two would be rapists leaped off the beds. Hurrying away, the entire Immarati staff vacated the lab at the run leaving the allies alone and bewildered, but still restrained.

"What's happening?" Lila cried out.

All of the allies struggled mightily to escape their bonds. The ominous alarm was still sounding. The captive allied forces had no idea what it was and what it meant, but how the Immarati reacted in a panic, it seemed this was their chance.

The restraints were just too strong, and the women were still held embarrassingly splayed.

The sounds of explosions rocked the facility and other sounds they didn't recognize. Some explosions shook the room they were so powerful.

Lanai cried out. "Marka, what do you think is happening?"

"I think there is a battle. These Immarati villains must have enemies."

Soalk suddenly lurched, like coming out of a trance. He hurried over to release the women and then he started releasing the warriors. Once freed, Marka went to look out the door. He quickly closed it.

"There are strange weapons in use out there in a battle."

Soalk spoke, "Come with me, I know where they have your clothes and weapons."

Hurrying out a back door of the lab and sprinting through the complex to a storage room, they were able to re-cloth and rearm.

They looked at Marka.

"We should not stay here. We'll slip away, if we can."

The allied force moved efficiently trying to affect an escape. Along the way, they gathered the other Brog adults who'd been held captive and enslaved. Those Brogs were newly freed of the mental constraint.

When they left the building, they faced the nearby scene of the ongoing battle. It was mystifying for peoples with no exposure to modern weapons. The two sides clearly were of the same race. The Immarati leader who had so recently taunted them was doing a poor job with his defense. Where his followers tended toward the slender side, their opponents did not. They were tough looking and muscular. These had the look of trained and competent soldiers.

The allies could only stay stationary to observe the progress of the battle as there was no avenue to escape.

As the battle continued to deteriorate for the Immarati, their former captors triggered devices that caused them to disappear from sight.

The commander of the other side spotted the allies. He took off his helmet and casually walked over to them. His weapon, he slung over his shoulder.

The allies could do nothing but wait.

"I'm Colonel Jaife Jorgen, commander of this expeditionary force. You had contact with the Immarati, as they call themselves?"

Lanai stepped up boldly. "Yes, we had contact, to our great sorrow. They've caused great harm here and on the northern continent, which is our home."

"I gather you came here to try to intercede? That was very brave of you with only primitive weapons to use. By the way, my people are called the Mercans. Immarati is a name they created for their little gang. They're criminals back home who fled here to escape capture and to continue their vile experiments and practices. Whatever all of you have experienced, I apologize."

"We're so glad to hear that from you. Once we were brought into this place, we thought we would die here."

"That could have happened. They have no conscience about what they do."

Marka spoke. "Those weapons, they're frightening to see."

"We've been aware of these continents and the societies who live here. Our governments made a decision long ago to leave you to your process of maturing as a people. It was terrible for the Immarati to come here and interfere with your lives. I'm sorry about that."

Lanai explained. "That leader wanted to...violate me and Lila, and nearly did. We had no power to stop him. It was...awful. How can people be so craven?"

"Trust me, they will be dealt with."

He turned to Soalk. "You are native to this land?"

"Yes, they conquered and afflicted us first. With our unique process incubating our young and the chrysalis phase as they grow, the Immarati warped it to make them weapons against our neighbors to the north. Our minds were blanked so we didn't even know what was happening until our friends freed us."

"This does not surprise me. It's exactly the type of thing they would do."

"Are they gone now?"

"They merely fled from the battle they couldn't win. We will pursue them now that we know where they went. I regret they're still hereabouts as a hazard, but they won't be able to subjugate your people like before. I can't promise we can quickly find and apprehend them, but we have the advantage in all areas. I've communicated to our high command about this event. I'll send a further message detailing your dire experiences. I expect we will be making a formal appearance to meet your peoples and your leaders on your continent. Our presence is no longer a secret, and I expect we can help you in a number of ways. The prevailing theory none of you are advanced enough to deal intelligently is certainly debunked. You have requited yourselves well in the most difficult possible circumstances."

"Thank you, Colonel. What should be our next step?"

"We will arrange to transport your force of scouts back to your homes. We have flying craft that will startle you, but they're safe and they can move you quickly over the great distances."

"Flying in the air?"

"Yes, ma'am." He smiled. "I gather you're a person of power and import among your people."

Lila piped in. "She is the daughter of the King of Tranta, the crown princess."

"Lila," Lanai objected, softly, but she smiled, glancing at the Mercan officer for his reaction.

"Very impressive. You've done a remarkable job on many levels, young lady. I'll get my troops moving in the chase to snare the Immarati, and then I'll order aircraft here to pick you up."

"Thank you, Colonel. We're grateful beyond words for your rescue. Our hatred for those vile Immarati will burn in our hearts forever."

"I understand. Believe me, we're irate too. We don't intend mercy when we catch them."

The allies gathered with their new friends from across the ocean back inside the building in the dining room. They were fed unfamiliar food, but it not unpleasant. Lila and Lanai noted the particular attention from the Mercan soldiers. In another surprise, they noted there were women soldiers among the Mercans. Those women were noting Lanai and Lila also.

Lanai, a woman who'd seen adoring looks in the eyes of every male she'd ever met, was surprised to see the same admiring looks from these Mercan soldiers. Thankfully, they weren't disrespectful which was a pleasant change from their Immarati brethren.

She blotted out the distraction from her mind and turned to her dear friend, shifting gears. "I wonder what we will find when we get home, Lila?"

"Terror. Flying things will terrify the people."

"But that will be only momentary until they see us."

"Our world won't be the same."

"Yes. Does that distress you, Lila?"

"I don't know. I will be happy if there is no great war to fight. If these machines change us, I'll wait to see how that plays out."

"I think these Mercan's will be our friends."

Marka had finished talking to some Mercan soldiers and walked over to the women.

"It was interesting talking with them about their land and what they can bring to us."

"Lila has worries about any changes."

"Change is always going to happen. In this case, I think we will have help in reaching greater heights. When I explained our long trek, they were very impressed, especially of you two."

"Little ole me?" Lila replied snidely.

"They meant no harm, wife."

"I've had enough of strangers pawing me to last a lifetime. If I seem vengeful, I am."

Marka chuckled. "I hope you don't kill me off if I try to be your husband again."

Lila eyed him, and then a small smile crossed her face. "I'll make up my mind later."

Lanai asked. "Are you afraid of this flying through the air? I wouldn't have thought it possible."

"I trust our new friends. They said it is not difficult. You just sit on a seat on this 'aircraft' and it transports you through the sky and the clouds."

"Truly, I've often looked at clouds and wondered what they are like."

"You will find out soon enough."

As if on cue, they heard sounds approaching in the distance eastern sky. Glancing up, they saw specks on the horizon, like birds flying far away. These 'birds' approached rapidly and grew in size getting much louder.

The helicopters circled and landed as the allied scouts looked on in awe. Nearby Mercan soldiers motioned them to follow to the aircraft. The noise and the air generated by the rotors startled the allied troops. One by one they boarded and were strapped in to seats on the numerous choppers, enough aircrafts to carry the entire scout force plus Mercan soldiers. Lanai and Lila were seated side by side. They looked at the grim-faced door gunners and the mounted heavy weapons. Though they'd never seen them in use, it was clear they could do some serious damage.

Taking off was disconcerting for people who had no experience with flight. Even up in the air as they pivoted to start flying generally northward, they felt afraid of falling out, even with the seatbelts holding them safe and people seated beside them. Queasy stomachs afflicted them for a short time. With some time, they mostly relaxed. Lanai got her closeup view of clouds as they cruised through some large cumulus formations. It was a pleasant day for flying.

"Look Lila, the clouds are like a mist."

"It is surprising, princess."

Glancing downward it was eye opening as they could see ground movement only as tiny dots. Flying over the Isle of Doom, it was solid trees and vegetation, impossible to spot anything inside that dense forest. It was a new experience flying out of summer in the southern continent back into winter in the north continent. Lush green had turned to brown and snow coverings in various places.

Crossing the southern shoreline of their northern continent, Lanai started to think about Korban and what to expect.

When they reached the escarpment of the Belshik Plateau, a Belshik warrior on her flight looked down in amazement.

"That is my home?"

"It is." Lanai replied. "It gives you a different perspective about our lands."

A little later, they gradually veered eastward beyond the escarpment line to fly to the main camp. It was still a sprawling settlement. As they descended, they could see people rushing around in fright at these 'giant birds' coming at them.

The choppers landed and the allied scout teams climbed off to see a solid line of spears, swords, and wild-eyed terrified warriors.

Marka shouted. "We come in peace."

The defenders were dumbfounded and cautiously approached. The Mercan soldiers waited passively, although they had weapons in hand. When the allied camp finally realized they weren't using their weapons, it helped calm the moment. Once the choppers rotors stopped and silence was returned, introductions started and the people felt relieved.

Going with Lila and Marka at the head of the scouts, she saw Timian waiting.

"Hello, crown princess. Welcome home."

"Thank you, Timian, it's very good to see you. It was a harrowing expedition, but thankfully our new friends from across the ocean saved us."

"These flying birds startle us, but you are unharmed so we accept them."

"Where is my husband? You are leader here now? What has happened?"

He paused before answering.

"It wasn't my choice. I'll try to explain. Your husband feared he made the mistake of a lifetime. It wasn't something he could get past. Korban pled with me to take his job while he went to live alone in the forest. He hunts for meat for nearby Greka villages and for Mantu villages. He has not come back since you left. I think he fears to hear if you were killed."

"If he only knew. We were easily captured by the Immarati and used in their demeaning and vile experiments. These Mercans are of their people. The Immarati are criminals in their homeland and only the intervention of the Mercan army saved us. If Korban was here, I would admit he was right and I was wrong. I didn't think I would ever see home again. Is it possible to get word to him?"

"I can send messengers, but if he doesn't want to be found, it will take time at the very least. He has awesome skills and great wood lore."

"I understand, but I would appreciate whatever help you can give me."

"Now, princess, I think your other maidens wish to greet you."

Lanai grinned warmly as they rushed in to embrace her and Lila. Lila looked at Marka.

"I understand, wife. You can be with your ladies tonight. I'll go out hunting with the scouts and will see you in the morning."

"Thank you for understanding. We're dear friends and this misadventure needs to be shared with them, and chewed on a bit."

Ironically, at that moment, Korban wasn't particularly far away. He'd been drawn to the forest edge by the sound and the appearance of the aircraft flying overhead. He was curious, aroused if they posed some strange new danger, but when he heard no sounds of battle, he decided to camp just out of sight inside the tree line.

The following morning, curiosity tugged at him, so for the first time, he wandered toward the main camp. He was in no hurry; so, it took some time to cover the ground. Mantu horsemen were first to spot him. They lived in a nearby village Korban supplied with meat.

"Ho, sub chief, there are great doings in your camp. Giant birds came down from the sky and brought back the scouts from the south."

"Truly?"

"Yes, they looked for you in camp, but you've been gone."

"My wife is there now?"

"She is. She was disappointed you weren't there to greet her."

"I...will go now."

He felt elated and apprehensive all at the same time. He realized shirking his leadership role would not sit well with Lanai.

When he was spotted riding to the edge to the camp, he nearly turned around, but the helicopters parked nearby drew his attention. He rode slowly toward them, an imposing and foreboding figure. The strange soldiers noticed him and arose, unsure what he intended.

Dismounting, he led his horse as he approached. A camp man took his horse so he could continue.

"Who are you?"

The nearest soldier replied. "We're Mercan soldiers. We're your new allies."

"What are these things. I saw them fly in the air."

"Yes, they are our creations to move us quickly from place to place."

"I didn't know flying was possible."

His arrival set off a huge reaction in the camp. Lanai knew instantly what it meant. She walked along with her maidens, Timian, Marka, and other dignitaries, including the flight officer in charge for the Mercans.

Korban heard them coming but continued talking with the soldiers and only looked back at the last possible moment. Lanai's face wasn't full of the recriminations he feared, rather he saw her abiding love. His mini-rebellion died in an instant. Embracing his wife in a fierce hug, all of his animosity was gone, drained away in an instant.

"I'm sorry," she whispered over and over.

"I thought you would die. I couldn't face it."

"I could have died. We were easily captured by evil men. It was... horrible. I thought I would never see home again. It was so difficult to stay strong against hopelessness. We had no power to escape, or even protect ourselves. If the Mercan soldiers hadn't attacked when they did, dire things would have happened. I was such a fool, Korban. I put us all at risk."

"So...we can trust them?"

"I believe so. They treated me with respect and dignity after those vile men did not. As you can see, they have powers far beyond us. We have no choice but to embrace the alliance they offer. To them, we probably seem like insects on the ground under their feet."

"I surrendered my leadership role to Timian."

Timian had just walked over. "That was a temporary thing. You're still the leader here. The council agrees on that."

"I...I guess I'll talk to these new friends."

"I will be at your side, husband. This is a good thing for all of our people."

"I notice these Mercans wear strange clothes, they are multicolor and of a material I don't know."

Timian answered. "They call them uniforms, better than wearing skins or hides. They blend into the forest to help with concealment. They have offered to teach us much. Like your wife, I feel their coming is a good thing."

Walking back into the heart of the camp, Korban was amazed at the messianic reactions of the people. In light of his missteps, it mystified him, but he couldn't pretend it wasn't true. He nodded often as countless people of all races pressed closed to touch him and express happiness he was back. Lanai was equally adored to the point of worship.

When they arrived at the site of council gatherings, the council was already assembled there, along with a delegation of the Mercan officers.

The flight officer in charge stepped up to greet him.

"It is good to meet you. I've heard a great deal about you and your leadership. Your heroic trek is difficult to comprehend, and of course I had the honor of meeting and knowing your beautiful wife. Hello again, Lanai."

She smiled demurely. "Hello. This is my husband, Korban, sub chief of the Vikar."

He guided them to folding chairs they'd brought. Sitting down, Korban was a little uncertain, but no harm came to him, and the padded chair was comfortable.

"I'd like to discuss several things, if I can?"

"Of course. That is why we're here."

"On our continent across the ocean, we have a mighty nation. We're technologically advanced, as you can see by our various devices and equipment. As I previously said, we decided to leave your two continents in their growth and development stages while you learned and matured as societies. It was unfortunate those criminals came here to cause the death and unrest to serve their diabolical plans. We knew they'd fled, but didn't know they'd come here, or we would have acted sooner. I regret the loss of life you experienced. I hope that now you'll allow us to rectify that matter. It serves no purpose any longer to ignore your lands and your peoples. What we propose to do is bring Mercan delegations to settle here to educate you about us and to expand your knowledge with modern concepts, devices, and practices. Turning you into us isn't our aim, but I suspect that would happen anyway. You will still have a say over what happens here. Do you understand?"

"Can you explain what you intend?"

"First, we would establish travel between the continents. We will bring teachers and technicians here to create buildings and cities, ocean ports, and then establish trade. We will build airports for flights to and from our home as well as flights all over your continents. You will establish embassies across the sea as we will do the same here. We can teach you much about your land, management of your animals, and farming food to feed your peoples. Times of drought and starvation will be eradicated."

"What are cities?"

He chuckled. "I'm sorry, I talk from our perspective. I apologize. Cities are very large settlements where all you need for life on a large scale are provided there. Schools, hospitals, governmental buildings, stores and shops. Korban, you and your wife will be among the first of your people to fly over to our nation. You'll see for yourself what I'm saying. Are you agreeable?"

He looked at Lanai. She smiled and nodded her head in agreement.

"It seems my wife is agreeable. How could I say no."

"Very good. It won't be for a time as we need to pick a site to start building your first national capital city. Your first international airport will be built there. We can then land passenger jets to fly you across the wide ocean."

"National capital city?"

"Think of it like your camp here where you assembled all of the various peoples. Your capital city is like that but taken to a vast scale. It will probably be in Mantu along the coast to also be a port, or possibly in Tranta along the coast there."

"Tranta would be good," Lanai said brightly.

The council members chuckled.

"We can do that, Lanai. There will be other ports built along the coasts. That will include the southern continent. All of your peoples should intermingle and move toward being one people instead of tribes. You're taking a step into the modern world."

Korban looked around and saw no concerning looks on the faces of any of the tribal representatives. Most people looked on passively, or looked confused.

"We agree."

"In the meantime, we are dispatching considerable additional armed forces and law enforcement personnel to apprehend the criminal Immarati. They will not get away. There is nowhere else they can run. They may seem invincible to you because of the devices they used, but we have all of those same devices and much more available. There will be no more attacks against your peoples."

Lanai spoke. "We are very grateful for that. It was the worst experience I've ever had being helpless and at their mercy. They were vile; soulless and evil. It could have gone so much worse, and would have if you hadn't arrived when you did. It's a memory that will haunt me for the rest of my life."

"Our doctors will examine you and the other members of your brave scouting party to assure no lasting after effects from your time in their lab. We know basically what they were doing, and trying to do. You will be fine, folks."

She glanced at Korban abashedly. He scowled at the thought of her demeaning experiences.

"We intend to get to work, my friends. We're going to fly back to the southern continent, but you'll receive contacts quickly from our people. There will be a fleet of naval war ships arriving along your coast. Lanai, you should return to Tranta as the fleet will anchor along that coast. We'll begin naval patrols along the coasts of both continents. You need to advise your father, the King, about all that has happened and all that will happen."

"I will do it. So much has occurred since I left his palace, I hope I can correctly explain it."

"Your husband will be there with you. I'm sure the tales of your exploits are already known to him."

"Yes, whether that is a good thing, I don't know. He saw me as a spoiled little girl."

"That was long ago. Now, you're matured with numerous remarkable experiences, and the most renowned female in your history, married to the most renowned male."

She interlocked arms with Korban and smiled warmly.

"I hope you understand the implications. Where your father is currently your King in Tranta, in your new world the two of you will become the singular leaders of both your continents. He will be subservient to you."

Lanai snickered. "That can't be. How could that be?"

"Trust me, it is already the case. Who else could fill such roles?"

He looked around.

"I have nothing further at this time. We can adjourn to enjoy the rest of the day. The Mercans will fly out tomorrow morning. Lanai, you should leave tomorrow also for your journey home. Take appropriate forces to represent your new station in the world. You should include all of your races in that sizeable force."

Korban replied. "We will, and thank you from all of us."

An impromptu celebration broke out and the Mercan forces joined in the merriment. For Korban to be among all of his old friends, and to hold his wife, it was blissful. That the horrible ending he expected had miraculously been avoided seemed impossible, and yet that was the case.

They embraced as they lay down to sleep together that night. Both were grateful for the favorable turn of events sparing precious lives.

In the morning, an army assembled for the trek north to Tranta. There were far more warriors than Korban would have assigned, but he understood the point of the Mercans. This was the first move to establish he and Lanai in power in the minds of any potential rivals. There were still plenty of folks stuck in the past, seeing women as lesser beings and subservient to men.

Each evening they stopped at Mantu villages to sleep the night. Small celebrations broke out in every case.

It took nearly a month to reach the Trantan border. A column of Trantan royal forces waited there. The officer had a cross look on his face, but he was vastly outnumbered, so a potential needless confrontation didn't happen. It was proof of the wisdom of the Mercan advice.

The Trantan column led them toward the city and the Kings palace. Each night, the soldiers glowered when their crown princess refused to sleep in their midst. Rather, she stayed with her husband. Korban made a point not to take offense to give them any excuse for an incident.

At long last, they entered the city of the King. Royal pennants on the palace were flapping in the stiff breeze rolling down from the mountains.

Korban intended to go alone with Lanai to see her father, but she countermanded him. She gathered a sizeable 'honor guard', well-armed and stacked with many deadly Kar warriors.

The commander of the palace guard tried to object, but the Princess wasn't afraid to face him down.

"I'm here to meet with my father, commander."

"You may not march this rabble into the King's presence."

She glared. "This rabble can make quick work of your pompous collection of fops. I'm still your crown princess. Now get out of my way before you start an incident you can't finish."

Korban worried there would be a fight. When his warriors reached for their swords, their eyes were menacing, ready for battle.

Korban spoke. "Commander, we're not here to disrespect you or your forces, but we're not bound by your rules. Your liege is not ours. Your princess is my wife. We will defend her to the death. Making a foolish stand here for ill-conceived old principles will not end well. You know that. Do you really want to do battle with the very same forces that conquered this entire continent, and the southern continent?"

The commander wavered. His soldiers looked terrified. None of them had battle experience.

"Lanai, we will accompany you to the throne room. If our liege commands us, we will take action."

She replied scornfully. "You do that. Enough of this delay. Lead the way."

The fifty-man palace guard contingent was dwarfed by the thousand allied warriors trailing them marching to the throne room.

The King was seated on his throne and did not look happy.

"What is this? Lanai, you dare bring this horde of barbarians into the royal chambers? How dare you?"

"Hello to you also, father. Sadly, this is exactly the welcome I expected, which is why it was necessary to bring this large warrior force into your midst. I wish it was otherwise as I'm happy to see you. However, the circumstances are as they are. I must tell you; this is not the time for Trantan posturing. Those days are over. I'm not a little girl, or whatever you think these days. I suspect you've been told about my experiences since leaving the palace. I've been through things that would turn your hair white. Coming here doesn't frighten us. I'm going to explain some things that you need to hear. If you choose to remain obstinate, it won't change what is going to happen. Your personal desires and ego can't supersede the needs of your people."

He looked even angrier. Standing up, he seethed and walked down straight up to Korban.

"Yes, I've heard the tales of your unfortunate exploits. So, this man has taken your maidenhood flower? Now he tries to claim you as wife!"

Korban fought to maintain his composure and not react, but it was impossible. His expression grew dark. The king was wearing a sword. Korban expected him to foolishly draw it.

It was Lanai who replied. She was equally provoked. "I didn't come here for you to insult my husband. He is above any man living. What he has accomplished has made him a legend, and I've fought at his side every time. I would have no other man to share my bed. No one else is worthy. Your days of senseless political intrigues trying to match me with some weak son of a noble is gone. That world is gone. I'm respected all over this world. Only here do I receive this disrespect. Sadly, you can't appreciate that I earned my place through my own actions. In spite of that, strangely, I still acknowledge you as my liege here in Tranta, but as our new allies from across the ocean have explained, my husband and I are now the leaders of both continents. In that sense, you're vassals to us. Also, you should know, my husband is the father of my growing child and the father of your grandchild."

Both men looked at her in astonishment.

"Truly, you are with child?" Korban grabbed her in a firm embrace, lifting her and twirling her around. They both laughed in joy. The king could only stand there, unable to think of anything to say.

She continued. "Another thing, and the reason why we're here now is that our friends called the Mercans are coming to give us help in many ways. They are going to build a new city on the Trantan coast as a seaport and the capital city for both continents. Their fleet will be arriving shortly and construction will begin immediately. This is an incredible honor and essentially, it's a nod to me. They would have built the city in Mantu. You can acknowledge the changes which will happen whether you agree or not, or you can 'bow your neck' and live here separated from the wonders of the Mercans, and apart from me and your grandchild. I didn't intend this confrontation, but apparently your pride counts too much in your mind."

His majesty wavered. He knew he had no options, and sight of his outnumbered feeble guards quaking in the midst of the deadly Kar warriors left him no choice.

"It seems your will rules here now, wife of Korban."

"Is this how you want it between us, father?" She asked him sadly.

CHAPTER SIXTEEN
A New Day

Seeing his wife's disappointment at her father's reaction, Korban decided to make a move.

"Though I did not receive your permission to marry your daughter, I want to tell you, I also accept you as my liege here within your borders. I want you to see me as a son for I intend to call you father. I don't know my own history as I was taken in as a baby and raised by a Vikar family. I will honor whatever are your wishes about our relationship. I would wish you won't discard your daughter and our child from your affections. That would be terrible for your people, and for us. If you give us all a chance, I feel we can heal this rift. I've been with Lanai through incredible perils, hardships, fierce battles, impossible situations, and through it all, she's shone through with great courage and resolve and found ways to overcome the impossible time after time. You should be very proud of her. No other woman could have done what she has accomplished. Everywhere we go, every race of people praises and rejoices in her. That was due to her own heroic efforts. Believe me, when she went on the mission to the southern continent, the Immarati was in a position to kill us all. Only the Mercans could rescue us from sure death, and thankfully they did. They are far above us all, but they've proven to be kind enough to offer us equality and fellowship. Building this miraculous city that they propose will be the start of vast changes which will eliminate much of the troubles from the past. There will no longer be a need for militance and bellicose neighbors. Do you see?"

"You've explained I have no choice in that. As far as accepting you as a son, I'm afraid it might take me some time to become accustomed to the idea. However, since you're about to be a father of my grandchild, I wouldn't stand in the way of that."

The king looked at Lanai. "Do you intend to continue this life of yours away from the palace?"

"Father, what I do isn't a reflection on my feelings for you, or Tranta. Korban has spoken rightly. I'm known around the world and they desire for us to be at their head. It's probable we'll be living in the new city, once it's built. I won't be far, nor will your grandchild. He can be raised to abide in both worlds, aware of royalty, but also skilled as a warrior able to be a force in his own right. What I've seen in Korban shows me how I want our son to be, or daughter."

She chuckled, turning her face. "What do you say, husband? Can you abide another strong-willed female in the family?"

"As your father just said, I don't have a choice about it."

Turning her head back she asked him, "Father, can you swallow your pride enough that we can break bread together that you can truly get to know your new son-in-law? The people of Tranta..."

"Granted, Lanai, but can you swallow your pride enough to take off your sword and put on one of your dresses for a day at least?"

"I can."

Korban made a signal and the warriors stood down from their defensive deployment and left the throne room. The King followed the gesture by sending his guards out of the room too.

Once the room was emptied, Lanai's maidens came in. They knelt down to the King.

"My liege," they said in unison.

"Rise. So, you have all had quite an adventure. Seeing women armed and able to fight is a new way for me. They tell me you all have husbands now? None of them are Trantan?"

Lila spoke. "I'm sorry, your majesty. We weren't in a place to consult with you. The men we picked are the finest we could have found. None of us regrets it. I hope this doesn't displease you, but we won't be giving them back."

He chuckled. "This is definitely a new Lila. You were always a favorite and it's what I would expect from you and your other ladies. Be at peace, what is done is done. Seemingly there is nothing I could do about it anyway. My daughter is apparently liege over us all now."

"Father, you know what I was saying. There won't be separate nations now. The Mercan's explained they will be States within a single nation. It will be just fine."

"We shall see."

Lila explained. "Your majesty, it is as she says. We've been with her for all this time and have seen her grow into her life of prominence. It has been truly remarkable. We trust her with our lives. She has earned that trust."

"My daughter birthing a child, I'm at a loss with my feelings."

"She isn't alone. I too have become pregnant."

"Oh, Lila," Lanai exclaimed happily. The other maidens embraced them sharing in their joy.

For the rest of the day, they chatted pleasantly with the King. His poor mood had passed and gradually he started to acknowledge and interact with Korban. What drew him in most was talking through the long trek and the events related to it. He looked at Lanai often at the most harrowing parts, especially the death-defying climb down the ice laden sheer cliff, crossing the valley of fire during a serious lava flow, the disconcerting kidnapping and spiriting to Iscali island and unclear acts of the priestess upon them, and the dangerous initial contact on top of the Belshik plateau with only Marka at her side. Eventually ending with the mortifying capture and abuse in the Immarati lab, it astounded the King it was his daughter they were talking about, now the most accomplished and renowned female in history.

They talked late before retiring for the night. For Korban, going into Lanai's former lavish bedroom, frilly and dainty; looking around it was like culture shock, although he enjoyed the soft bed. Lanai enjoyed seeing his apoplectic reaction as he looked around at the feminine decor, laughing heartily at him.

"Oh, mighty warrior, are you so daunted by my fine things?"

"That would be a no. I can see why you were so soft when I first met you."

"Hah, I didn't have a choice of my parent's, or my birthright. What I chose was to change myself, and my life. Look at me now."

"Lanai, you know I respect and appreciate what you've accomplished. I was jesting, as you were jesting with me."

"I'm sorry, Korban, that is still a sore point for me. I have no reason to harbor those old feelings any longer. You're right, husband. Let's make better use of our time."

She reached out her arms toward him. Snickering, she whispered, "This will be the first time in the palace and in this bedroom for doing this." Smiling, he did not hesitate in embracing her. She didn't try to be quiet with their enjoyable and explosive event, crying out in ecstasy. As a spouse, she could finally enjoy the best of life everywhere without concern.

A new day dawned the following morning, the beginning of a new age. Progress was about to come to the primitive societies of the northern and southern continents.

The king was suddenly plunged into new priorities and new tasks as his days became very busy. Huge numbers of his craftsmen and artisans were conscripted into the army of workers about to start construction of the new capital city and port on the coast. The royal palace was startled on the first day by the arrival of a flight of helicopters. On board were Mercan workers and a foreman in charge of the planning, acquisition, and construction of that port city, but also for modernization elsewhere in Tranta. The brain trust of the Mercans had chosen to initially apply their touch to make all of Tranta the shining gem and showplace for the new and unified country.

Transforming the palace started within a day with installing modern equipment and technologies. The workers, both Trantans, and Mercans performed rapid changes. Where the King had always thought of his home as one of the great feats of Trantan craftsmen, the Mercans showed him what true greatness was. Modernization took a little time to adjust to, as many devices and features were eye opening for unsophisticated folk moving forward. Now, the world was opened to a level of awareness none could have imagined. Visual devices where scenes all over the globe could be seen instantly, devices to talk to people in those distant places, the beginnings of flights to anywhere, building restaurants and different kinds of shops, it boggled their minds. Plumbing and clear fresh underground water available at a touch was a great boon, not only for the elite, but also for the common folk.

Korban and Lanai stayed in the palace in the interim. There really was no reason to go to the coastal constructions in the initial phases. Lila and Lanai incubated babies sharing their feelings and experiences also in the interim.

Helicopters arriving and departing became a daily occurrence. Mercans could be seen everywhere in the King's city, and their work was quickly taking form.

The Mercan man in charge of all the ongoing projects called for Korban and Lanai to join him in meeting the King one day.

"Thank you for coming. I want to share with you, all of the Immarati criminals have been captured and taken back home to face justice. That threat has been eradicated once and for all."

"That is very good news," Lanai replied. "What they did…it still makes me very angry."

"We understand. Believe me, their punishments will be severe, and perhaps execution. As a people, we try to be humane, but some crimes go beyond forgiveness. These aren't people who could be rehabilitated. That was tried in the past and it failed. In our considerations, we won't forget the needless loss of life you suffered. The personal indignities they perpetrated will be given appropriate consideration too."

"I thank you for myself and for all of us that were captive in that lab."

"You're welcome, crown princess."

They chuckled. She noted, "It sounds strange hearing that title coming from you. Royalty must seem such a backwards concept."

"It's a part of our history. We had our own stages while growing as a society. In our case, it happened to be long ago. You should be proud of your status and accomplishments, and we share your joy at the approach of your first child. Children are the future and the lifeblood of any society."

"Thank you."

"For your information also, in our nation, the story of your incredible journey, what you overcame, and the dignity you've shown through it all, it has made you celebrities. You are as famous among the Mercan people as here among your own peoples. I expect that once the airport is completed, you'll be invited to fly to our nation."

Lanai looked at Korban. "Whatever you prefer, wife. We must adjust to new ways."

"I think I would like that. Thank you, sir, for the kind invitation."

"We'll soon be able to transmit live broadcasts from our nation so you will see our cities and peoples. Life there is much different."

"I look forward to that. Father, what do you say?"

"That decision is yours, daughter. I feel I'm able to take more of a background stance in this new society. Perhaps I can try to enjoy my life. It helps if I don't need to worry. Now it's on your husband to deal with you."

Korban got a wry smile. "Thank you, your highness. I think that is a bit of a double-edged sword."

"Absolutely, son." He smirked. Lanai glowered.

The Mercan man chuckled also. "At any rate, I will return to my projects now. If you have need of me for any reason, simply send word. Oh, and one other thing, princess. We're bringing a team of our doctors to be stationed here. They will oversee your pregnancy with modern concepts and understandings. There are dietary measures to take for your growing child. They will explain it when they arrive."

"I look forward to listening to their advice."

She scowled at the skeptical looks on the faces of her father and husband.

"You're not amusing, gentlemen. I do listen to intelligent ideas. I don't listen to people preaching and trying to control me, just to make that clear."

All of the men chuckled.

"Yes, ma'am," Korban muttered.

The team of Mercan doctors arrived a week later. The craftsmen had built a temporary area for them to work in until the first hospital was completed.

For Lanai and Lila, it was a little unnerving to go into a lab again, but that feeling didn't last long. They met their first Mercan females; kind competent nurses and very able in putting patients at ease. Blood draws were explained in detail so the young mothers understood the reason for the tests. Receiving bottles of pre-natal vitamins and other supplements was a first. Swallowing pills was simple enough to do, and painless. When the pills caused no ill effects, the pregnant mothers settled in to accepting the care of the Mercan medical teams. The women also had another surprise, female Mercan doctors. To their happy surprise, they were treated completely by females. The memory and taint of the males in the Immarati lab could be put to rest going forward.

Lanai and Lila chatted one day waiting for check-ups.

Lanai reflected. "What a difference in our lives now, Lila. Not so long ago we were fighting to survive."

"I didn't imagine being anything other than your handmaiden. To become a fighter, to now have an incredible husband, to carry his child, it is a marvel, princess."

"The adventures were exciting and terrifying all at the same time."

"Another thing for me, being raised as a subservient, treating men as superiors, it is amazing the change. My husband is so attentive to me. I know I could control him if I was a different sort."

Lanai chuckled. "Men are simple enough to understand, and what they want. I know I sound like a small person, but butting heads with Korban, or other men doesn't bother me. I especially like when they lose and get frustrated. We will not accept those old roles and they can't seem to cope. Power comes in many forms. I've learned that from our experiences."

"I understand. Even with me, this celebrity they speak of, it has fallen on me also. I'm beloved by total strangers. It's a little unnerving. They say weird things, I'm so dainty, so lovely, appealing, stunning? I'm married! Leave me alone."

"I hear it too. They tell me we're adored in their continent with these daily broadcasts about us, our progress with the babies, stories about our marriages. They love how we contend with our husbands. I've even had some of these people who film us, to use their words, tell me things they want me to say and do, like stoking arguments for them to perpetrate stories is a good thing. I think their new world is something we must approach carefully."

"I've thought that same thing. I'd like them to leave us be to live normal lives."

"I doubt that will happen. They have their plan for us continuing to broadcast to their masses for their entertainment."

"I'll say this. I won't let them plague my child."

"Another of the double-edged swords. Their progress and help, it comes at a price."

The doctor came into the room.

"Good morning, ladies. How are you feeling today?"

With that, the exam began, along with some lab tests.

At the end, the doctor explained, "Your babies are doing well and we see no problems with either of you."

She showed them pictures of the gestating babies inside their bodies.

"You're both going to have daughters."

Lanai looked at Lila. "The men would have liked to have sons."

The doctor spoke, "Ladies, your husbands will be happy with either sex. You may have additional children where you'll have sons. This is not a problem."

Lila uttered. "It will be nice to have a little girl for my first one."

Lanai nodded. "I agree, Lila. Having boisterous boys knocking around and crashing things, I can wait for that to happen."

The doctor chuckled, adding. "I have two boys and what you're saying is so true. They are accidents waiting to happen."

The progress of the many construction projects proceeded rapidly. Beyond the additions and improvements in Tarium, the King's city, the new national capital was starting to take shape. Roads and streets had been laid out covering a huge amount of land. The Mercans were building the city anticipating a great number of residents to move in.

Construction of buildings were already beginning. This was not only buildings for the government and businesses, but the first residential homes were being constructed.

After much discussion between representatives of all the lands, a decision was made to name the city, Glorium.

Another early construction was a global hub airport. It too was a massive site begun just outside the city limits of Glorium. The two couples, Korban and Lanai, and Marka and Lila, flew to the site in a chopper. The foreman on scene tried to explain all of what was being constructed and the purposes. Most of it went over their heads. They simply marveled at the transformations to the country.

The foreman explained, "These long lanes you see are going to be landing runways for passenger aircraft. They can carry large numbers of people. They are how you can fly across the oceans."

"I see," Lanai answered finally, after a pause.

Marka and Korban glanced at each other without comment. Neither were enamored with the 'marvels' the Mercans offered. Each of the men preferred getting back to their old Vikar life, hunting the food in the forest and enjoying simple villager lives.

Marka muttered. "Korban, I heard Toma nearly fainted when this flying machine first landed at his city. Only when Vikar warriors got out of the thing did he put down his weapons."

Korban snickered. "Like Shosa, he is an old grizzly bear set in his ways. I think he won't be taking any flights over the ocean to see the sights."

The women heard them and laughed also.

Lanai reflected. "When I first met him, I thought he would slay me on the spot. I was surprised when he treated me decently and with respect."

Korban replied. "What you don't understand is Loti would not have allowed any bad treatment of a female."

Lanai smiled. "I can believe that. I always liked Loti, and Menga. They made me feel welcomed right from the start."

The foreman interrupted. "If you'd like to go into the city to see the start of your new residence, I can arrange transportation."

"I would," said Lanai.

Shortly, a ground vehicle drove over to take them down a newly leveled road, still under construction. It was a great distance they traveled to reach the hub of the city. The main buildings were centered here and the residence of the rulers would be in the middle of them.

When Korban looked at the huge outline of the foundations, it astounded him at the size.

"Lanai, this will be bigger than many villages and your father's palace combined."

"I think we will have many visitors."

"I have no say in this?"

"You do not."

Lila laughed. Marka gave him a rueful smile and rolled his eyes.

Korban replied, wryly, "Perhaps I will have a need for a great deal of hunting to feed all of your army of visitors."

"They're your visitors too, sub chief."

"Is that right, crown princess?"

"Yes, it is."

Lila piped in. "What do you say, head scout, leader of the vanguard?"

Marka answered, "I worry about getting soft in this lazy new world. How these Mercan's live is not how we live. If Korban can hunt, I will join him. I've seen some of the heavy flabby Mercans on their broadcasts. That won't be me."

"Hopefully we'll still have some amount of freedom." Korban spoke ruefully.

However, wanting something doesn't make it come true. Their worries took new life as time passed. The modern marvels being built in Tranta was gradually expanding across both continents. Many months later both couples were moved into their newly completed palatial home. It was an astounding edifice filled with ample rooms for a very large number of people. Korban invited Vikar leaders to come, but none wanted to take up residence outside of their villages. The King sent considerable additional staff to serve the new national leaders. Lanai's original maidens all moved into rooms along with their husbands, their servant roles eclipsed. In their cases, they too were expecting first babies which would be their new roles, being Moms. They too were celebrities for the Mercan media market.

Once inside the 'home' Mercan crews and representatives absconded with much of their free time. Although Marka and Korban did go off to hunt, it was too infrequent for their liking. The demands of decision making and public appearances were an onus they couldn't avoid. With the completion of the huge airport, the first passenger crafts began regular streams of curious Mercans filling the city. Similarly, even though Lanai and Lila were close to delivery dates, they were loaded onto a private jet for the flight across the ocean. The Mercans had already constructed a building in the Mercan capital city to house an embassy for the new nation.

Although they'd seen some measure of the products of progress, being suddenly immersed into actual modern societies was culture shock. When they landed, the crush of mobs of adoring fans daunted the new visitors. Korban worried about leaving his weapons behind. The Mercan peoples wanted to have actual personal contact. Mercan guards were nearby, but they didn't intercede to keep Mercan citizens from touching them physically. That drew Korban's ire when Mercans tried to paw Lanai. His angry reaction cooled the avid mob only slightly.

Looking at the guard captain, he finally sent troops forward to maintain proper spacing.

Being taken to the Mercan government complex, they talked to untold officials and shook endless hands.

The Mercan President and his wife were gracious, hosting a state dinner that evening. It was more rich food than Korban and Marka could imagine and it led to some small stomach issues trying to sleep that night.

The President spoke, "My friend, you realize you must supply an ambassador and a staff for your new embassy. They will have a direct instantaneous contact with you to inform you about issues and decisions we must jointly make."

"We'll see to that when we go home."

"I realize this is overwhelming for you. I appreciate your patience with my avid populace. You've become folk heroes for them. Your lives seem magical compared to the tame life here with all of our comforts. I also feel amazed at your exploits, and that of your wife."

"It wasn't pleasant. When we left on that first trek, we had no idea what we were getting into. Things could have gone so much worse. We were lucky, and little more than that."

"I understand. What I mean is all of you had the courage to make the attempts. In this country those kinds of opportunities don't exist any longer. People can set personal challenges, but the element of danger really isn't there. I guess from your perspective, that can be seen as a good thing or bad."

"We don't judge you. Our concern is what happens to us from dealing with you. I realize you see our former lives as backwards and unappealing. We don't feel that way. For us, there were many compelling aspects to life in the wilderness. Accepting your changes is inevitable, but retaining what we can of a good life will be a goal. We lived in harmony with our environment. I don't want to reflect on your people, but they seem very inactive. All of these heavy people, can they not see the problem in it?"

"I can't disagree, Korban. We wish it was otherwise. It's a consequence of free choice. People can do as they will. Many do not make the best decisions."

"I see. I'll keep that in mind with changing our own societies."

The women suddenly laughed at some part of their conversation.

"Your wife and her friend are a delight. Our wives really enjoy knowing them. I think all women can relate to pregnancy and children. That's on top of her appealing personality. Her friend is such a dainty petite little thing, it's amazing she is deadly with her weapons."

"I'm still amazed Lanai married me. Marka feels the same about Lila."

"Most men feel overmatched by their women. That's true in any country."

"They are a force in the world, and in my life, I wasn't ready for it. Displeasing Lanai has consequences. I'm forced to consider it constantly in whatever I do. Before, in my ways with a solitary life, I was responsible only to myself."

Even with the difference between our societies, I understand what you're saying completely. In my case, when I married, it was as if my wife took custody of me. I may be the President of the most powerful nation on this planet, but she exerts subtle influences and controls. I admit that. They do make their wills known to us in subtle but significant ways you can't ignore."

The men smiled at the reality of that fact.

"Women also have their subtle ways of revenge if you displease them."

"They certainly do. With your permission. I've arranged for us to take you on a tour of the city tomorrow. You can see the nuts and bolts of this operation and we can show you some ideas we have to help your people."

"Nuts and bolts?"

"I'm sorry, it's one of our expressions."

"I'm sure the women will like that. I do need good information to make good decisions."

Lanai glanced over at Korban.

"Mr. President, I think the women are getting tired. With your permission, we'll leave you now for the night. I'll explain to the ladies your plans for tomorrow. Thank you for the great meal."

Once back into their hotel suite, Korban told the group. "We've been invited to join the Presidential party for a tour tomorrow. Does anyone have an objection?"

"No, it should be fun," Lanai replied.

Marka added. "These events are not my choice to spend my days. I'll be happy when we can go home."

"Lila remarked. "Marka, it's a sign of our new status. We can do this. Although I will be happy to go home too. I don't want to birth my baby here."

Lanai added. "Perhaps we'll tell them a few more days at the most for this visit? I'm sure their wives will understand."

That next morning, they joined the tour which was an all-day affair. More of the abundant rich foods, it was overwhelming as there were so many places they were taken. At the end of the day, the wife of the President said, "This was too much, wasn't it. I should have realized two late term pregnant women shouldn't have been kept out that long. I apologize, ladies."

"We're fine," Lanai replied. "However, we would like to return home. Both of us want to give birth on our home grounds."

"Of course you should. There can be other times for State visits and certainly we can visit you in your home there."

"Thank you for being understanding. We'll leave you now to pack our things and prepare for tomorrow."

"Lanai, this has been the highlight of my life sharing time with you. Everything people believe about you is true. You're better than advertised."

"I don't know what that means, but thank you, I think. Was that a compliment?"

"It was. By the way, you know about our video programs. Their making a new series with each of you as characters having different adventures each week. They expect it to be the greatest hit of all time. The Mercan people are already rabid followers of yours. This will further enhance your reputations and legends. You'll be paid royalties."

"What does that mean?" Korban asked.

"You don't have a monetary system yet, but as your economy transforms and adapts, currency is used to make purchases. You'll understand as time goes on. Your royalties will build up in our banking system until you're ready for them. There is a great deal about modern societies we couldn't get too on this visit. There just wasn't enough time. When your embassy is staffed, we'll work with them as a part of the transitioning."

Korban shrugged his shoulders. He glanced at Lanai, who glanced at the wife of the President.

She chuckled at the confused looks of their 'barbaric' guests. "I know this is just another confusing thing, but it will all become clear soon enough."

The two visiting couples were happy after breakfast to head straight to the airport and board the private plane for the flight home.

Sitting beside her husband, Lanai took his hand. "What do you say about all of this?"

"The same thing I've been saying all along. I regret the loss of our old lives. All of their changes will impact us in ways we can't fully understand yet. I worry as I saw the problem areas they have. There is no arguing they're far advanced over us, but if you ask me if their lives are better, I would dispute that. Sitting around to watch these programs they salivate for; I hope that isn't our fate. It seems too many of them have no real purpose. What do they accomplish?"

"All that I can say is, we continue with our priorities. I still intend to train with my weapons to stay sharp. Who knows when I might need to school my husband?"

He laughed heartily. "That will be the day when you school me, little missy."

Lila piped in. "I'm with you, crown princess."

They heard Marka chuckling. "You're still a feisty little thing, wife. Are you going to school me also?"

"If I need to. You men can get too full of yourselves. It takes the strong hand of women to remind you of that fact, and to set you straight."

"Amen to that, Lila." Lanai smirked.

It wasn't a week after they landed that Lanai gave birth to her daughter, she named her Simona. Later when Lila's daughter was born, she was named Lana. They received visits from virtually all of their old friends. Gralk and Soalk appeared with their wives who were also pregnant.

Lanai welcomed them warmly. "It's so good to see you. I hear your new city is a splendor, but you're also plagued by these tiresome Mercan camera crews."

Gralk replied, "That's true, crown princess."

"Soalk, I'm sure you were as happy as us when those Immarati were captured. They're gone, but I'll never forgot. I really thought we'd die there."

"It is as you say, an ugly thing one cannot forget, like a stain on your soul. Your home is astounding."

"Stay as long as you like."

"We must fly back shortly. There are too many appointments and obligations."

The births were like seismic events worldwide. In the Trantan palace, the King was euphoric, and the Trantan people were ecstatic. Never had there been worldwide renown such as the crown princess garnered. With her in residence, Tranta became an international focal point.

To Korban's chagrin, the broadcasts of the series about them from the Mercan media took hold everywhere and the people quickly were transfixed. He refused to watch any episodes, but was deluged with tales of the fantasy series on a daily basis. It distressed him hearing the Mercan actors displayed no level of propriety as the seamier aspects of their real-life experiences were shown in fantasized vivid detail. Particularly, the Iscali island scenes and the Immarati lab events were portrayed in a way meant to indecently inflame the audience. They took great liberty in expanding on the facts in difficult ways. Predictably for them, they were the most popular of the episodes. Those episodes bothered the allied women a great deal, though they had no ability to sensor the programming. The acceptable state of Mercan sensibilities and morality varied greatly from the standards Korban had been taught. Titillation was not only accepted, but demanded, to an extent.

The two friends decided to make a trip back to the Vikar main camp to get away from the new realities. Flying via chopper, their wives carrying the newborn babies, they landed to a much-developed city from the last time they were there. Tomi and Leti came out to greet them along with along with Shosa and Menga.

Lanai was effusive. "It is so good to see all of you again. Here is our daughter."

"She is beautiful," Menga cooed, taking her tiny body onto her arms. "See Shosa, see what your son has done. This is your granddaughter."

Shosa looked at the baby and then Lanai. "Very pretty, thank you, princess. We worried our son was destined to have a dull life burdened with the brains of a tree stump."

Everybody laughed heartily. Korban smiled wryly at his father.

Lanai replied. "Fortunately, he's somewhat smarter than that."

Settling down a little later to a heaping bowl of his mother's stew was a highlight for Korban. "Mother, no one can match your cooking."

"Thank you. I've had a lot of practice. Your father was like an empty barrel I couldn't fill. This is why I always had to make such large amounts."

Shosa laughed. "And I enjoyed every bit."

"There is much I could say to that, husband."

Enjoying family time away from the glare of attention in Glorium rejuvenated them all. It became a frequent destination for them over the years. When Lanai later birthed two sons and then another daughter, taking trips to see the Vikar side of the family was a favorite spot. Lila also birthed sons, so they both women had young boys crashing around finally. It was all the pandemonium they'd anticipated. Both women looked dourly at their husbands often when the boisterous sons were the most difficult. Mom's saying, "no wrestling in the house" was frequent, just like the boys knocking over end tables and other fragile pieces. Those boys all tended to be very loud.

In both cases, wives thought the men were too lenient. As the father's, they tended to shrug off the boy's behaviors, which did not sit well with the wives. In both cases too, big sisters were as intolerant as their mothers. In spite of that, the boys tended to worship big sisters and followed them around to the girl's great chagrin. It was amazing both households had virtually identical scenes and scenarios.

The Mercan film crews loved the dynamic.

Korban tried to instill the skills of his own youth in woodland lore, understanding the relationship of man and the animals, living life simply and with integrity, these were his goals. Achieving it was challenging. The insertion of Mercan society was too pervasive. His own children became addicted to the series about he and Lanai. Still, Korban refused to watch any of it.

Over time, the world continued to shrink as Korban, in his leadership role, had to concede to the distractions of encroaching progress which consumed so much of his time. The children became accustomed to frequent traveling, often only with Lanai and Lila. Increasingly too, the children were dropped off with grandparents while Lanai and Lila traveled. Having avid Mercans exclaim over them across the sea was a difficult issue for Korban who tried to keep the children grounded and not inflated in their self-concepts. As far as the wives, the excursions lured them. Their family lives evolved as Lila and Lanai's already tight relationship became even tighter to the point, they were inseparable. Leaving husband's behind, for the women, didn't bother them much. The others of Lanai's original servants gradually joined them on those trips.

The society that continued to develop turned away from the old ways and left many of the elders from every tribe scratching their heads. Old lore was being lost at a rapid pace. As elders died off, there were too few willing to learn and retain what had been old knowledge and skills.

Free roaming horse herds posed a hazard to the new roadway systems where vehicles traveled at high speeds. That was only one of myriads of issues brought to Korban for answers. A new national legislature was created mirroring Mercan institutions. It gave Korban an opportunity to shift some responsibility onto them, but it also introduced rivalries and contention.

Years later, as he pondered living this life that he would not have chosen all of those years prior, he talked with Lanai frequently. She'd shouldered more of the burden of child rearing. Korban put his arm around his wife as much as he could, or as much as she would allow it. Their times alone to themselves were at a premium.

"This is the new world? Are you happy with it?" he asked.

"I would say, it has good points and bad points. Neither of us could have known the magnitude of the changes. I think we've done as well as we could have."

"I wish I'd been able to save more of the old ways. As I see things now, I realize that was impossible. I'm not unhappy with our family, or my wife."

"Well, thank you very much." She was a little abrupt, unsure if he was tossing a slam at her.

"Lanai, I meant that as a compliment. Even after all these years married, you still have that edge against me."

"I don't mean to have an edge. It took so long for women to gain proper standing, perhaps I'm still a little sensitive."

"We are here. I hope there will come a time where we can end this heavy onus of leadership and we can have a peaceful life to ourselves again."

"I think your children prefer life just as it is."

"I know that. I think they got independence and obstinance from both of us."

"Perhaps." Lanai smiled warmly. "You must admit, we've had a good life. I'm proud of our children."

She turned to look at him directly. "You must know I love you, Korban. All of that angst of those early years didn't matter. We got here safely. That's what matters."

"Yes, I know you love me. You've culled the barbarian out of me. Are you happy with me, down deep?"

"I am. I'm able to say, I'm not a perfect person, and I make more than my share of mistakes."

"I was never quite sure if you were happy. It's good to hear you say it."

Lanai looked away with a contemplative expression. "We wives have found our ways to cope with stress, and other things. Our experiences marked us, and in some cases, indelibly. So, we cope as there is nothing else that we can do."

She turned her face back and smirked at him, "However, I will always keep you on your toes. That's the job of a woman."

He had no idea what she was saying, or alluding to, but her smile was sufficient at this point in his life. They laughed and hugged warmly.

Korban had managed to corral the most beautiful woman alive, and he'd managed to keep her, an accomplishment in itself. The Vikar boy was now a matured man, ruler of two continents, an inconceivable development from when he lived in the Vikar village and spent his time hunting food. Hunting his food at a grocery store with his wife rather than off in the forest was a change he could never quite cope with. The barbarian itch remained in him, in Marka, and the other former barbarians. Taking his sons hunting wasn't a life choice now. It was a sporting diversion. Forest lore was a sidelight to them. Their interests were in other things. Lanai's daughters grew to be just like her, ravishing beauties highly sought and trained by their mother to cope with the unwanted attention and accolades. They were budding stars in their own right with the Mercan media. Korban left it to Lanai to deal with that issue.

Passing years brought marriages to all their children and eventually grandchildren. By then, the changes brought about by Mercan 'progress' were deeply etched in society. The heavy mantle of leadership was something they tolerated, but they still sought what little privacy they could manage for themselves and precious time with their beloved children and extended family.

The deep bonds of their marriage which had carried them through rough times and good times survived and consequently a great nation prospered. There was nothing else either of them could ask for. The remarkable lives Volta had forecast so long ago had come to pass.

THE END.

9 781778 830037